THE BIRCHBARK HOUSE

THIS MAP SHOWS LAKE SUPERIOR
TO THE RED RIVER WITH
PRESENT DAY MINNESOTA
BETWEEN

LAKE SUPERIOR

6

MONINGWANAYKANING

OLD LA POINTE

RED RIVER

MINNESOTA

HERE THE VALIANT
BUCK ONE HORN
GAVE HIS LIFE

...TS BEARS ON THIS PATH

THE BIRCH BARK
HOUSE

GOOD FISHING
AND
SANDY BEACH

ACROSS THE WATER
TO THE TALL RED CLIFFS
AND THE WILD RICE
BEDS ON THE RIVER

THE
BIRCHBARK
HOUSE

Louise Erdrich

with illustrations by the author

HYPERION BOOKS

FOR CHILDREN

NEW YORK

First Edition

Designed by Christine Kettner

5 7 9 10 8 6 4

Printed in the United States of America.

LIBRARY OF CONGRESS CATALOGING-IN-PUBLICATION DATA

Erdrich, Louise.

The birchbark house/by Louise Erdrich.—1st ed. p. cm.

Summary: Omakayas, a seven-year-old Native American girl of the Ojibwa tribe, lives through
the joys of summer and the perils of winter on an island in Lake Superior in 1847.

1. Ojibwa Indians—Juvenile fiction. [1. Ojiwba Indians—Fiction.

2. Indians of North America—Fiction. 3. Islands—Fiction. 4. Seasons—Fiction.] I. Title.

ISBN 0-7868-0300-2 (trade)—ISBN 0-7868-2241-4 (lib.)

PZ7.E72554Bi 1999   [Fic]-dc21 98-46366

To Persia,

whose song heals

THANKS AND
ACKNOWLEDGMENTS

My mother, Rita Gourneau Erdrich, and my sister Lise Erdrich, researched our family life and found ancestors on both sides who lived on Madeline Island during the time in which this book is set. One of them was Gatay Manomin, or Old Wild Rice. I'd like to thank him and all of his descendants, my extended family.

The name Omakayas appears on a Turtle Mountain census. I am using it in the original translation because I've been told those old names should be given life. The name is pronounced Oh-MAH-kay-ahs. Dear reader, when you speak this name out loud you will be honoring the life of an Ojibwa girl who lived long ago.

This book and those that will follow are an attempt to retrace my own family's history. Special thanks to Steve and Mary Cotherman, and all of the devoted people at the Madeline Island Historical Society. Mom and sister Angie, thanks for your constant encouragement with the illustrations. I would especially like to thank my daughter, Persia, who read this book when it was a manuscript and made important suggestions. Apijigo megwetch Winona LaDuke. You started me thinking. All of my Ojibwa teachers, Naawigiizis (Jim Clark), Jesse Clark, Dennis Jones and Lorraine Jones, Keller Paap, and Lisa LaRonge, apijgo megwitch. All mistakes are mine.

CONTENTS

Contents

THE BIRCHBARK HOUSE

THE GIRL FROM
SPIRIT ISLAND

 HE ONLY PERSON LEFT ALIVE on the island was a baby girl. The tired men who had come there to pick up furs from the Anishinabe people stood uneasily on the rocky shore. The voyageurs watched from a distance as the baby crawled in a circle, whimpering and pitiful. Her tiny dress of good blue wool was embroidered with white beads and ribbons, and her new makazins were carefully sewn. It was clear she had been loved. It was also clear that the family who had loved her was gone. All of the fires in the village were cold. The dead lay sadly in blankets, curled as as though sleeping. Smallpox had killed them all.

The voyageurs trembled at the thought that the disease might already have chosen one of them. Surely, they muttered, the baby had the sickness, too. *She's sick. She looks tired,* said one man when she lay down against one of the blanketed figures. *Let her sleep.* Birds were singing, dozens of tiny white-throated sparrows. The trilling, rippling sweetness of their songs contrasted strangely with the silent horror below. First one then the other of the men turned away. They got back into their canoes.

As they paddled toward the next island, all were silent, thoughtful. Some wore hard expressions. One man had tears in his eyes. His name was Hat; he thought of his wife and decided he would tell her about the baby. If there was anyone in the world who'd go and rescue that little girl, it was his wife. He shivered a little as he thought of her. He couldn't help it. Tallow, she was called, and sometimes she scared him with her temper. Other times, he was amazed at her courage. He grimaced in shame—unlike him, his wife was afraid of nothing.

Neebin

(SUMMER)

CHAPTER ONE

The Birchbark House

 HE WAS NAMED OMAKAYAS, or Little Frog, because her first step was a hop. She grew into a nimble young girl of seven winters, a thoughtful girl with shining brown eyes and a wide grin, only missing her two top front teeth. She touched her upper lip. She still wasn't used to those teeth gone, and was impatient for new, grown-up teeth to complete her smile. Just like her namesake, Omakayas now stared long at the silky patch of bog before she gathered herself and jumped. One hummock. Safety. Omakayas sprang wide again. This time she landed on the very tip-top of a pointed old stump. She balanced there, looking all around. The lagoon water moved in sparkling crescents.

Thick swales of swamp grass rippled. Mud turtles napped in the sun. The world was so calm that Omakayas could hear herself blink. Only the sweet call of a solitary white-throated sparrow pierced the cool of the woods beyond.

All of a sudden Grandma yelled.

"I found it!"

Startled, Omakayas slipped and spun her arms in wheels. She teetered, but somehow kept her balance. Two big, skipping hops, another leap, and she was on dry land. She stepped over spongy leaves and moss, into the woods where the sparrows sang nesting songs in delicate relays.

"Where are you?" Nokomis yelled again. "I found the tree!"

"I'm coming," Omakayas called back to her grandmother.

It was spring, time to cut the birchbark.

—◁○▷—

All winter long Omakayas's family lived in a cabin of sweet-scented cedar at the edge of the village of La-Pointe, on an island in Lake Superior that her people called Moningwanaykaning, Island of the Golden-Breasted Woodpecker. As soon as the earth warmed, the birchbark house always took shape under Nokomis's swift hands. Now the dappled light of tiny new leaves moved on Grandma's beautiful, softly lined face. In one hand she waved her sharp knife, taken from the beaded pouch on her hip. In the other hand she held tobacco. Nokomis was ready to make an offering to the spirits, or manitous. They loved tobacco. Omakayas banged the tree her grandmother had found.

"Yes, here, here it is! This one!"

Omakayas was skinny, wiry, and tough for seven winters. She slammed the trunk of the birch with a big rotten stick. Splinters of soft wood flew.

"Booni!" Nokomis scolded. "Leave it alone!"

She walked up to the tree and put her leathery paw-like hands on the smooth bark, feeling for flaws. "Yes," she decided, her eyes sparkling at her granddaughter. "A good one."

"Is it ready?"

"Geget," said Nokomis. "Surely."

Nokomis's tobacco pouch was decorated with blue and white beads in the shape of a pipe. She had owned this tobacco bag ever since Omakayas could remember. When she talked to the manitous, Nokomis dipped out a pinch of tobacco.

"Old Sister," she said to the birchbark tree, "we need your skin for our shelter."

At the base of the tree, Nokomis left her offering, sweet and fragrant. Then she peered closely, deciding just where to make the first cut. Suddenly, she pressed her razor-sharp knife into the bark. Omakayas stepped back. Light filtered golden and green onto their faces. Tiny white flowers poked out of dead leaves. There were still traces of grainy old snowbanks in the shadiest spots, but in places the sun was actually hot. Pow! As soon as Grandma made the proper cuts, the birchbark, filled with spring water, nearly burst from the tree!

Omakayas helped her grandmother carefully push the bark aside, then the two peeled it away strip by strip. She and Omakayas carried the light papery pink-brown rolls out of the woods, down a trail to a special place near the water.

Here, they set up the birchbark house.

Damp ground made Nokomis's old bones ache, so she spread out her brown cattail mat and sat down there to sew those pieces of bark together. Omakayas helped her, threading the tough basswood strands through holes punched by Grandma's awl. Meanwhile, Mama and Omakayas's older sister tied together a frame of bent willow poles. Finally, as the light faded, they fastened the mats of bark onto the willow frame, a half skeleton of pliable saplings. The bark mats overlapped like shingles, to shed the rain. Each one was secured to the next, so as not to blow off in a storm. When the house was swept out, smoothed, fussily arranged, and admired, they moved in. The children—Omakayas's brother Little Pinch, baby Neewo, Omakayas's older sister, pretty Angeline, and Omakayas herself—spread their blankets around the stone fire pit. Mama and Nokomis hung the smoky woven bags of rice and tools and medicines from the willow poles above.

Omakayas's family were Anishinabeg and this was their island. Her father, her Deydey, was in the fur trade business, which meant that he was often gone, paddling the great canoes for the fur company or sometimes trapping animals himself. Yellow Kettle, her mother, was quick-tempered but always laughing, and her eyes shrewdly took in the world. Yellow Kettle was a strong-looking woman, and beautiful. Her smile was generous, enigmatic, slightly crooked, and kind. She missed nothing when it came to her children—it was impossible to hide a half-done job, ridiculous even to think of sneaking away in the morning before gathering wood for the fire and water for her cooking pot. And if Mama didn't notice the younger children's whereabouts, Omakayas's older sister, Angeline, surely would.

Angeline was smart and so pretty people turned in their tracks to stare at her. Her hair was thick, her hands clever. The beads in her designs were laid down in strict rows. Her stitches never faltered. Her steps, when she walked or danced, were clear and graceful. She was so perfect that Omakayas despaired. Still, she hoped that she herself would turn out like Angeline, and was sometimes embarrassed to find herself following at Angeline's heels like a puppy. Most of the time Angeline was kind to Omakayas, and let her tag along and admire, from a distance. But there were also times her words were sharp as bee stings, and at those times Omakayas shed tears her sister never knew or probably even cared about, for as very beautiful people sometimes are, Angeline could be just a little coldhearted at times.

Omakayas's little brother Pinch was the only really big problem in her life. The sad truth was, and she couldn't tell this to a single person, Omakayas didn't like Little Pinch. She thought there was something wrong with him—so greedy, so loud! But although his ways were mischievous and bold, Pinch loved his mother deeply, and he clung to her side. In fact, he took up all her attention, even more than the baby! He clutched Mama's skirts with fat, tough little fingers. He yelled at Omakayas if she was slow in giving up her willow doll, her little rock people, or anything else for that matter, including food, special pieces of driftwood she found, even her favorite sleeping place, near Grandma. He thought he deserved *everything*.

At least when it came to Neewo there was nothing to complain about. He was so sweet that Omakayas often pretended that he was her very own baby. Of course, she hardly ever got to hold him, for he was still very young. Still, she was sure he preferred her to Angeline, and certainly to Pinch. Sometimes he even held his arms out to her when Mama was holding him, and yelled with delight when Omakayas picked him up.

◄O►

As it grew dark, the family ate makuks of moose stew and fresh greens and berries, licked their fingers and bowls clean, and at last rolled themselves into warm, fluffy rabbit-skin blankets that still smelled of the cedary smoke of their winter cabin. They were glad to be close to fire, sleeping on soft grassy earth, under leafy sky, and best of all, near water. They fell asleep to the peaceful, curious, continual lapping sound of waves. The fresh wind across the big lake blew away the smoke of cooking fires and vanquished the mosquitoes that came out in whining droves and had plagued them in town. It was good to sleep where the village dogs didn't bark all night and where the only sound to disturb their dreams was the pine trees sifting wind in a lulling roar.

Unless, of course, it stormed.

The moon went down to a fingernail's sliver and the corn popped from the ground. The leaves of the birch grew big enough to flutter in the wind. And then, one night, the first storm of the summer struck the island and startled everybody from their dreams.

The fire was down to red winking eyes when Omakayas woke with an uneasy feeling. Something approached. She'd felt a footstep. Omakayas was always the one to sleep near Grandma and now she rolled close. There was a lonely insistance to the sound of the wind, and then everything went still. Far off, she heard one huge footstep. There was a long silence. Then another step fell. The earth shook slightly beneath her, vibrated as though she lay on the head of a vast drum.

A drum! She remembered that Grandma had said the island was the drum of the thunder beings. Closer and closer they came, shaking earth with their footsteps. Omakayas's lonely feeling became fright. She hid her face and tried not to think of balls of witch fire or the hooting of Grandfather Owl. She tried to keep herself from picturing pakuks, the skeletons of little children, flying through the woods, or the icy breath of giant windigos striding over the ground, cracking trees off with every foot crunch. Another step. Another and another fell and then the wind howled to life. Rain slashed against the tightly sewn walls. A breath of air stirred up the slumbering coals and cast shadows leaping and fighting on the inside walls of the little birchbark house.

The willow poles trembled, bouncing with the force of the gusts of wind. The birchbark scraped and flapped but was held on with tight stitches. Omakayas hid her face as thunder rolled, smacking onto the lakeshore, waking everything and everyone with its quick violence. The storm punished the ground and then passed over, dying off in softer mumbles. The dull thuds of thunder falling in the distance now felt comforting, and before the sounds entirely faded, Omakayas was asleep.

—◄o►—

Moningwanaykaning, Island of the Golden-Breasted Woodpecker, sparkled innocently after that night of raw thunder and lightning. Omakayas woke and immediately began wondering. What had the storm done to the trees? What had the waves washed onto the beach? What interesting bits of wood that she could use for pretend dolls? What kind of day would it be? Were the little berries on the edge of the path ripe yet? An unpleasant piece of wondering came to her, too. Had her mother finished scraping and tanning that ugly moose hide or would she have to help her? Oh, she hoped not. How she hoped! There was a saying she hated. Grandma said it all too often. "Each animal," she would say, "has just enough brains to tan its own hide." Mama tanned the moose hide with the very brains of the moose and Omakayas hated the oozy feel of them on her hands, not to mention the boring, endless scraping and rubbing that went into making a hide soft enough for makazins.

From a fire in the center of the bark house a thin curl of smoke rose, then vanished through a crescent of sunlight in the roof. If only she could escape with the smoke! She could already hear Mama and Grandma outside at the cooking fires. They were planning the day's work. In no time at all, that soaking moose hide would be stretched on a branch frame and she would be required to scrape at it with the sharpened deer's shoulder bone that her mother kept in a bundle of useful things near the door. Her arms would tire; they would feel like falling off. Her fingers would go numb. Her back would hurt. The awful smell would get into her skin. And meanwhile, all the little birds would find the luscious patch of berries she alone knew about. By the time she got that stupid old moose hide softened up, they would have eaten every last berry. She must act. Quickly!

The air was fresh, delicious, smelling of new leaves in the woods, just-popped-out mushrooms, the pelts of young deer. The air flowed in, rainwashed, under the strips of birchbark walls she had helped sew together yesterday. Like a small, striped snake, like a salamander, or a squirrel maybe, or a raccoon, something quick, little, harmless, and desperate, she slid, crept, wiggled underneath the sides of the summer house. The seam of bark caught her in the small of the back, stuck tight. If only she hadn't done such a good job of sewing it up! If only, too, Angeline didn't have such quick ears and sure knowledge of her whereabouts at all times. There was a firm pressure suddenly at the small of her back, still caught on the inside. Her sister's foot. Her sister's gloating voice.

"Neshemay! Baby sister! Little Frog, don't go jumping off!"

Then there was her mother, rounding the back of the house, one side of her hair still flowing down, unbraided. She glanced in surprise at Omakayas, trapped, and then unable to hide her amusement, a big grin spread over Mama's face. Her admired big sister, her beloved mother, laughing! There was Omakayas—laughter from the front and laughter from behind—and suddenly, all of last night's thunder in her heart.

◄○►

Omakayas sat near the cooking fire and slowly, with deep inner fury, ate a bowl of cold stew. She dragged out time waiting for her hateful job to start. Mama was wrestling that hide out of the stream now, where it had been soaking for days and nights, gathering up its scummy, woolly slime. Mama had already set up the dreaded frame of branches and there were strings of hide nearby that she would use to tie the skin up tight so that it could be worked. Omakayas knew how important it was to tan the skin, how her mother would cut up the soft smoked hide and sew on the winter's makazins all summer. She pictured her mother finishing them with lovely, soft toe puckers so the girls' feet could twitch and dance. She could imagine Yellow Kettle beading them, lining them inside with the silkiest rabbit fur and pieces of an old wool blanket. Yes, it was an important task, but Omakayas still didn't want it. She finished her stew, cleaned the bowl out with sand at the shore of the lake, and waited with a sigh for her mother to ask her to fetch the deer-bone scraper.

Her mother said something else, though.

"I need my scissors!"

Omakayas sat up, suddenly full of energy.

Omakayas's mother was well known for owning a pair of scissors, and other women were always borrowing them. Omakayas's first job ever since she could walk was to fetch her mother's scissors, kept safe from her small fingers in a beaded woolen case, and bring them home. She had never failed, for it was a job she liked not only because she was sometimes given a handful of manomin, rice, or a little chunk of maple sugar by the borrowing lady, but because there were things to see on the way there and back.

Right now her sister, Angeline, was digging at the ground near spruce trees and cutting lengths of the roots, used to secure the house better and to finish baskets. She was cheerful, humming at her work, glad to have gotten the better of Omakayas. She'd show Angeline! Let her work until her hands fell off! Omakayas had a fun job to do!

"Go fetch me the scissors from Old Tallow," said Omakayas's mother. Without a moment's hesitation, before Mama changed her mind and remembered about the help she needed with the stinky hide, Omakayas ran off.

CHAPTER TWO

Old Tallow

 LTHOUGH SHE LIVED in town, Old Tallow was so isolated by the force and strangeness of her personality that she could have been surrounded by a huge dark forest. She had never had any children, and each of her three husbands had slunk off in turn during the night, never to be seen again. Nobody knew exactly what it was that Tallow, in her younger days, had done to drive them off. It had probably been something terrible. After the last husband left, her face seemed to have gotten old suddenly, though the rest of her hadn't weakened. She was a rangy woman over six feet in height. She was powerful, lean, and lived surrounded by ferocious animals more wolf than dog and fiercely devoted to her. Old Tallow could bring down a bear with her pack of dogs, her gun, or even the razor-sharp spear that she practiced throwing into the splintered base of a tree. The dogs were bull-tough and the yellow one, particularly, showed its wolf origins in the springy length of its legs.

For some reason, Old Tallow seemed to treat her, Omakayas, somewhat differently than other children. She didn't scream at her, or heap distain on her, order her away from her cabin or set her dogs on her. Omakayas thought perhaps it was because Old Tallow respected her mama and grandma. Old Tallow respected almost nobody else, so this was extra-meaningful. The three women often sat together, talking in the dusk. Also, Old Tallow, who loved to hunt and was very skilled, shared her catch with them when Deydey was gone. They would sometimes wake to find a haunch of venison just inside the door, or bear meat, a fish or two. In fact, she now remembered that Old Tallow was responsible for the hide of the moose, which she had shared. Old Tallow liked to make her deliveries at night, which was another thing. Most other people hated to go about in the dark when Grandfather Owl was calling *kokoko, kokoko*, and anything could happen.

But of course, Old Tallow was afraid of nothing.

Omakayas approached Tallow's cabin warily because of the dogs. She stood for a moment at the end of the trail, gathering her confidence before she rounded the corner. One dog in particular seemed to hate her—the big yellow one. Omakayas was careful not to startle him or gaze too long into his mean, clouded eyes. Once, he had snapped at her and worried the sleeve of her dress. There he stood now, to bar her way to Tallow's door. Omakayas screwed up her courage, breathed calmly. She walked forward, shoving him aside as though she had not a care for his dripping teeth. She got ready to deliver a hard kick if he lunged, and walked past him without showing her fear. The dog bristled at her, baring its teeth in an ugly snarl, but let her pass by. The other dogs—the black, the brown with the lopped-off tail, the small whitish one, and the droopy orange runt—merely looked alert and regarded her with neutral interest.

Old Tallow's cabin was small, neat, thickly mudded between logs. There was a log bench beside the door. Sure enough, Old Tallow sat upon it smoking her pipe. A fragrant curl of sweet kinnikinnick smoke stirred from the red stone bowl.

As though she had known Omakayas was coming for the precious scissors, Old Tallow had them on her lap, safe in the bead-decorated pouch of red trade wool that Mama had made specially to hold them.

"Ahneen, little skinny one," she growled.

Old Tallow's legs stuck out like poles, tattered makazins flapped on her wagging feet as she drew impatiently upon her pipe. She tamped the bowl of the pipe with huge hands; her arms were long and sinewy. The old blue dress she wore was trimmed with the teeth of fox at the collar, beaded halfway around the scraggly, ripped hem. Tallow, in her galloping hunts through the woods, was hard on clothes and wore out her makazins one pair right after the next. Even now, a toe stuck out from the ripped front seam. She tucked her braids up underneath a man's hat, a white man's hat with a heavy brim. She was hardly seen without it, even in her own house. In the band of the hat she always wore a little gold-shafted feather. This was the feather of the golden-breasted woodpecker, the bird that gave its name and chattering cry to this island.

"You want the scissors!" Her voice was abrupt, but not unkind.

"Yes," said Omakayas, glad that Old Tallow was outside. The yellow dog knew it was wrong to intimidate Omakayas. Sure enough, Old Tallow scolded him.

"You," she shrieked at the snarling dog, "booni!

Leave her alone. This is your last warning! Touch her and you die!"

The yellow dog turned aside, shrugging and cringing mean-spiritedly, eyeing Omakayas. She imagined she heard the yellow dog say, *I'll get you next time! Wait until there's just the two of us. You'll see!*

Relieved, Omakayas walked past the other dogs straight up to the old woman and stood before her.

"Ahneen, my auntie," she said. "Mino aya sana."

She wished the old woman good health, and called her "Auntie" because it was a sign of affection, though Omakayas was really not sure exactly what she felt. After she'd spoken, she stood politely, waiting. Old Tallow smiled, nodded, and blew a blast of smoke out her nostrils. Then she put her hand into the pouch at her waist. She rummaged around for a bit, then suddenly drew forth a small, grime-covered lump of maple sugar, rock-hard and wonderful.

"You take this," she said, her voice cracked and dry, as though salted. "And this, too." She handed Omakayas the scissors, waved her back onto the trail, and as this was as friendly as Old Tallow ever got, Omakayas went away satisfied.

—<o>—

Before she went back on the trail, Omakayas rinsed off the old candy lump in the lake. It came out beautifully, creamy-golden, translucent and grainy-dark. And sweet. She started walking, her treasure now wrapped in a leaf. As she walked, Omakayas thought. There was no way to share such a tough nut of sweetness. How would she divide it? Omakayas decided she did not want to cause trouble at home. Furthermore, it suddenly made sense to her that at least one person in the family should get the full effect of the maple sugar. She would pop the whole thing into her mouth. All at once! This would save problems. Aaaaah. The lump was delicious, tasting of spring sweetness and the inside of trees. Besides, Omakayas reasoned, as she walked contentedly along, the taste of the sugar would save her from eating every one of the berries she was sure she would find on the path.

Omakayas's feet moved slower and even slower yet. For one thing, the moose hide waited. For another, she was still angry with her older sister, and didn't want to see Angeline. She could still feel that sister foot pressing hateful on her back. If only there were some way to impress Angeline, cause her envy, make her say, "Can I have some of those berries, please, please, please?" You can be sure, Omakayas thought, her face taking on a faraway, haughty expression, she would be slow in answering! Yet the worst of it was this: her sister was usually on her side, helping her plan tricks on the other children in the village or gathering new ferns or snaring rabbits, visiting the grave houses looking for sugar or food left for the spirits, tossing off her clothes to swim with her. And to have her older sister laugh at her hurt Omakayas so much inside that she both wanted Angeline to smile in surprise, to be proud, to envy her, and to feel rotten and be sorry forever. So Omakayas took the slow way back looking for odaemin, little red heartberries, in the sunny margins of the woods near the ground.

She carefully removed the hard lump of sweetness from her mouth, stuck it back in its leaf just inside the pocket of her dress. Just as the taste of maple sugar faded along her tongue, she bent over, pushed back delicate leaves, and found masses of plump red little berries. Ah! One, two, three. She'd eaten a huge handful. Another. She grinned, thinking that she'd allow her sister to return with her to plunder them, but only if Angeline changed her ways.

All of a sudden, a rustle and then a thump in a bush ahead made Omakayas freeze. A long moment passed as she stared through the dark leaves. Suddenly, *crash!* Two bear cubs burst from the bush and rushed pell-mell, tumbling head over heels straight for her. They came on in such a hurry that they didn't see Omakayas until they were nearly in her lap, and then, with comical looks of shock, they tried to stop themselves. One flew flat on its face, bumping its nose and squealing. The other twisted in midair and landed in a heap on the ground, shaking its head in confusion at Omakayas.

The bear boys looked at her. Slowly, she put out

her open hand filled with heartberries. Curious, the
cubs jumped forward, lost their nerve. They scampered
backward, and then crept forward shyly again. The
smaller cub seemed slightly bolder and sniffed at Omakayas's hand.

The bear cub took one berry, then jumped away in
seeming fright at its own bold act. But the taste of the
berry seemed to banish fear. The two now tumbled at
her, growling, mock-ferocious. Their long pink tongues
touched up every berry from her hands, eagerly flicking
them from her fingers as fast as she could pick. They
seemed to like the game. It could have gone on for
hours, that is, until she stood upright. Then they tumbled backward in alarm. Their chubby bottoms rolled

them over like playing balls, and she laughed out loud. She realized they had thought Omakayas was their own size. They were astonished the same way Omakayas had been the first time she saw the trader Cadotte unfold a seeing glass, something he called a telescope, a long, shiny tube that grew in his hands.

She bent down again.

"Ahneen, little brothers," she said to them kindly, and they came forward.

She looked around. No mother bear. Omakayas was well aware that she shouldn't stay so close to these cubs, but after all, they seemed deserted. She looked around again. They were orphans! Perhaps the mother bear's skin was now draped across Old Tallow's bed, although she hadn't heard about a recent kill. But still, no mother bear in sight. And these little ones so hungry. Wouldn't her big sister be thrilled when Omakayas returned with these two new brothers! Eagerly, Omakayas began to plan out her triumphant walk back to the house. She would enter the little clearing with the cubs, one at her heels and one before her. Everyone would make way, impressed. She would lead the bear cubs around the fire four times before she presented one of them to Angeline, who would look at her with new respect.

◄o►

There was no warning. One moment Omakayas was wiggling a leafy stick, making it move on the ground so the cubs would jump on it, biting fiercely. The next moment, she found herself flipped over on her back and pinned underneath a huge, powerful, heavy thing that sent down a horrible stink. It was the sow bear, the mother. Breathing on her a stale breath of decayed old deer-hides and skunk cabbages and dead mushrooms. Owah! The surprising thing was, Omakayas realized later, that although she had no memory of doing so, she had the scissors out of their case and open, the sharp ends pointing at the bear's heart. But she didn't use them as a knife. She knew for certain that *she should not move.* If the bear began to bite and claw, she would have to plunge the tip of the scissors straight in between the bear's strong ribs, use all of her strength, sink the blade all the way in to the rounded hilt and then jump clear, if she could, while the bear went through its death agony. If she couldn't get clear, Omakayas knew she would have to roll up in a ball and endure the bear's fury. She would probably be clawed from head to foot, bitten to pieces, scattered all over the ground.

Until the mother bear made the first move,

Omakayas knew she should stay still, or as still as possible, given the terrified jumping of her heart.

For long moments, the bear tested her with every sense, staring down with her weak eyes, listening, and most of all smelling her. The bear smelled the morning's moose meat stew Omakayas had eaten, the wild onion seasoning and the dusty bit of maple sugar from Old Tallow stuck to the inside of her pocket. How she hoped the bear did not smell the bear-killing dogs or the bear claw that swung on a silver hoop from Old Tallow's earlobe. Perhaps the bear smelled the kind touch of Grandma and Mama's bone-and-sprucewood comb, her baby brother's cuddling body, the skins and mats she had slept in, and Little Pinch, who had whined and sobbed the night before. The bear smelled on Omakayas's skin the smell of its own cousin's bear grease used to ward off mosquitoes. Fish from the night before last night. The berries she was eating. The bear smelled all.

Omakayas couldn't help but smell her back. Bears eat anything and this one had just eaten something ancient and foul. Hiyn! Omakayas took shallow breaths. Perhaps it was to take her mind off the scent of dead things on the bear's breath that she accidentally closed the scissors, shearing off a tiny clip of bear fur, and then to cover her horror at this mistake, started to talk.

"Nokomis," she said to the bear, calling her grand-mother. "I didn't mean any harm. I was only playing with your children. Gaween onjidah. Please forgive me."

The bear cuffed at Omakayas, but in a warning manner, not savagely, to hurt. Then the bear leaned back, nose working, as though she could scent the meaning of the human words. Encouraged, Omakayas continued.

"I fed them some berries. I wanted to bring them home, to adopt them, have them live with me at my house as my little brothers. But now that you're here, Grandmother, I will leave quietly. These scissors in my hands are not for killing, just for sewing. They are nothing compared to your teeth and claws."

And indeed, Omakayas's voice trembled slightly as

the bear made a gurgling sound deep in her throat and bared her long, curved yellowish teeth, so good at ripping and tearing. But having totaled up all of the smells and sifted them for information, the bear seemed to have decided that Omakayas was no threat. She sat back on her haunches like a huge dog. Swinging her head around, she gave a short, quick slap at one of the cubs that sent it reeling away from Omakayas. It was as though she were telling them they had done wrong to approach this human animal, and should now stay away from her. Omakayas's heart squeezed painfully. Even though it was clear her life was to be spared, she felt the loss of her new brothers.

"I wouldn't ever hurt them," she said again.

The little cubs piled against their mother, clung to her. For a long moment the great bear sat calmly with them, deciding where to go. Then, in no hurry, they rose in one piece of dark fur. One bear boy broke away, again tried to get near Oma- kayas. The other looked longingly at her, but the big bear mother abruptly nosed them down the trail.

CHAPTER THREE

The Return

AFTER SHE RETURNED with the scissors, Omakayas quietly took up the deer bone from her mother's skin bag and began working on the moose hide without being asked. Her mother looked at her in some surprise, but said nothing. Angeline said that she had meant to do the work, but Omakayas merely shook her head.

"Go for a swim," she told her sister, "see what the waves brought to the shore last night. Catch some crayfish, ashaageshinh, watch out for their claws. I don't mind helping."

Angeline and Mama looked at Omakayas as though

they couldn't have heard right. But when Omakayas nodded to signal that she meant what she said, and Mama nodded, Angeline started with delight. She had to do grown-up work now every day, and she rarely had free time to play. Angeline looked hopefully at her mother, who waved her out toward the lakeshore. Off she ran, skipping and bounding in her thin summer makazins, her soft old tradecloth dress fluttering.

Baby Neewo was sleeping in his tikinagun. Little brother Pinch was killing his willow doll men over and over with a rock. Omakayas concentrated now on the work beneath her hands. She needed to think about what had just happened to her. Boring work was just what she wanted. Her mind could wander. She sighed, irritated by the smell and buzzing flies. At least there was some breeze that day to blow away the smell. While scraping the hide, she let her thoughts roam.

The longer she thought about her encounter with the mother bear, the more Omakayas was convinced that something she did not understand had passed between the two of them. Not words. Perhaps they had communicated in smells. Or maybe in a language of feelings. Her terror, the bear's pity. Perhaps it was her own grandmother's advice that had saved her life. Nokomis had told her that the bear must be addressed with the greatest respect, as a treasured relative, that the bear had human qualities and nobody quite understood the bear. But that bears understood humans quite well.

When a bear was killed and its skin was off, Omakayas knew it looked fearfully like a person. She'd also heard that bears laugh and cry, just as humans do. Grandma had once seen a bear rocking its young in her arms just as a human mother rocks its young. Nobody on the island ever tossed the bones of a bear aside. Every bear bone was gathered respectfully and buried, all together. At a bear feast, the bear's skull was ribboned and set out on a good red cloth, spoken to, honored.

Yes, there was something about what had happened that made Omakayas very quiet. As she scraped at the hide, nicking bits of meat and gristle from the surface, she began to get all empty and peculiar and faint inside. A thought was coming. A voice approached. This happened to her sometimes. A dizzy feeling would pass over her. If she attended to it closely, once it was gone she would know something a little extra, as though she'd overheard two spirits talking.

She kept scraping, gritting her teeth, and held on to her thoughts, for once again she could feel the presence of the powerful mother bear at her shoulder. Although there were no words and although there was no odor of her presence, no bear sounds, no tracks, Omakayas's heart lightened. Turning from her work, she knew the bear had visited her. She knew the bear had followed her home. She knew that when she needed the bear she would be able to call on the bear. The bear had understood something she had said and she had understood something the bear had thought, and although she couldn't tell exactly what, Omakayas turned back to her task with her head clear and her hands cheerful.

She worked so hard, all through that afternoon, that her grandma, watching her keenly, made a great fuss over the work Omakayas had done on the hide. She said

Omakayas had done as well as a full-grown woman. Her mother promised her a very special pair of winter makazins and Angeline even braided her hair with one of her own red ribbons.

◄o►

Neewo means "fourth" and that was what they called the baby, but soon, Grandma said, the baby would have to have a name. The tiny boy was a spirit, so far, who had come to live here and was deciding whether or not to stay. Grandma told Omakayas to be careful with him, little baby Neewo, because he might decide to go back to the other place if he thought his big sister was mean. So Omakayas was very gentle with the baby. She rocked him in the branch-held tikinagun with great consideration. She gathered spongy moss and old oak punk to stuff into the cradle board and use as a diaper. She twirled and dangled the little web of sinew and the tobacco ties and bitten birchbark pretties that Grandma tied onto the head guard of the tikinagun. She fed Neewo tiny bits of the best food when Mama wasn't looking. She felt, in her heart, streams of love for the baby pouring through and she begged her mother to let her take Neewo out and cart him to the lake on her hip.

But her mother smiled and touched Omakayas's

hair gently and shook her head. Gaween. No. She was too young. Grandma gave her the willow doll instead, told her to let the baby sleep, directed her to play with Little Pinch. But she knew what that would mean! Pinch would jump on her back and yell, "N'dai, get moving!" He would pull her braids. He would use her as a practice bow and arrow target. He would tip over the rock children and rock people she made of specially piled lake pebbles. He would destroy her rock people village down by the beach. No, she didn't want to play with him! Little Pinch? Never!

—◦—

Half the summer went by quickly after the visit from the bear. Omakayas stayed thoughtful. She helped hoe the corn patch almost every day, and never complained. She was kind, hardworking, patient. But she was also lost in her own thoughts. She startled when spoken to, went to sleep early and slept long, dreamed hard but couldn't remember the night's adventures. And she also had those dizzy moments that, her grandma said, meant she was special to the spirits. One day, her mother said to her grandmother, "If she wasn't so young, I'd give her the charcoal."

Grandma's deep and far-seeing eyes took in Omakayas. She seemed to see her granddaughter from the inside out. She watched Omakayas for a long time, then shook her head. No. Not yet. When a mother put charcoal on her child's face, it was a sign that the child was ready to starve for a vision, for power. A child with a blackened face didn't eat for days, and sometimes lived out in the woods alone until the spirits took pity on him or her and helped out with a special vision, a special visit, some information. But Omakayas was too young, according to Grandma, so Mama stirred the fire and worried. She had a lot to think about anyway, including a name for Baby Neewo, who was getting restless, trying to crawl out of the cradle board, acting as though he were anxious to have that name.

There were seven or eight people on the island who possessed the right to give names. Auntie Muskrat was one. Day Thunder, Swan, Old Man Migwans, and an ancient lady named Waubanikway knew how to dream names. Mama had asked, and each of them had tried. But not one of them had yet dreamed about a name for Neewo.

"For some reason," said Auntie Muskrat, "that

dream won't come." She even slept and fasted in the woods for a name, but the spirits were stubborn.

Old Waubanikway, who dreamed many names, had no name for the baby either, but she said that she would give no other name until she found one for the boy. She searched her dreams. Meantime, Baby Neewo grew! Omakayas decided in secret that the naming was up to her. In play, when just the two of them were together, she gave her little brother names. Bird names. Chickadee, she called him. Apitchi. Robin. Little Junco. Sparrow. Grouse Chick. He seemed to like all of his bird names and when he heard them he grinned and waved his chubby arms in delight.

◄o►

Omakayas could hardly resist Neewo, and played with him as often as she was allowed. There was something about the way he looked at her so sadly with big, soft eyes that made her want to cuddle him tight in her arms. There was something about the way he smiled when she made a face, surprised, so grateful, that made her kiss and touch his hair with great passion and indignation in her heart. He should have a name! And clearly, he wanted out of his tikinagun.

Omakayas wanted to help him to freedom.

Her chance came. One morning later on in the summer, Omakayas's mother, sister, grandma, and Little Pinch all wanted to go into the village and see the big canoes that had arrived to unload furs at the trader Cadotte's. Omakayas's father, Mikwam, wasn't with these voyageurs, but Mama hoped that they might have news of him. The thought itself made Mama so anxious that she got ready to go off in haste, though Baby Neewo was still sleeping.

"Why don't you leave Neewo with me," Omakayas asked at the last moment. "I don't want to go. I can take care of him! You'll get there faster!"

She saw Mama's thoughts falter.

"You don't want to go?"

"I don't!"

Angeline and Grandma were already halfway down the path. Little Pinch was tugging on Mama's legging, whining for something to eat.

"All right," Mama decided. "We'll be right back. Now don't do anything. Just rock him, Omakayas, and play with him if he wakes up. Don't *do* anything!"

"Of course not," said Omakayas, trying hard not to show how excited she was to have her baby brother, Neewo, all to herself. She made herself tall and acted as grown-up as possible. Rocked him with one hand, gently, while she waved good-bye to Mama, and kept rocking long after her mother rounded the corner and disappeared into the ferny forest growth. He didn't wake. She quit rocking, just stared at his slumbering face. His lashes were so long and stiff, his little chin so chubby she wanted to stroke it, the skin on his cheeks so fine and delicate and soft she could hardly keep from brushing her lips across them. Tufts of silken hair stood out all over his head and his breath was still sweet with milk.

She touched him, very gently. Baby Neewo. Chickadee. The name popped into her mind. "Today, I'll call you Chickadee," she said.

His eyes opened, as though he understood. His look was bright and filled with secret jokes. He gazed up into her face. For a long time they looked at one another. It was perfect. It was love. And then his face crumpled, one fat tear squeezed from his eye, his lower lip shook. Suddenly, his mouth flew open and he bawled. Omakayas was so close, so dreamy and happy, that the force of it nearly flipped her back head over heels. His squall was like a whirlwind, like a sudden wash of freezing spray, like a harsh wind, weather like a hot wall of sound.

"Shuh, shuh, shuh . . . " Omakayas rocked and muttered, shushed, hummed and sang an old lullaby her mother used. Nothing worked. Baby Neewo screamed louder, with increasing force. Omakayas was alarmed. She'd never heard him scream like this, had she? What was wrong? Was something—a biting fly, spider, tick, bee—something stinging or biting him inside the tight binding of his tikinagun? Only one way to find out— unbind him—and that was forbidden. Still, as Neewo's miserable and now hysterical sobbing continued and even got stronger, she decided to make a grown-up deci- sion and take Neewo from his cradle board. And so she did. She undid the twist of vine that held him inside the beaded velvet wrapping. She carefully untied and spread the embroidered wrapping, then took out his diaper moss and brushed him off like a root pulled from the ground. He was naked, of course, but it was a warm day and so she lifted him immediately into her arms, still weeping, and brought him to a sunny place just beyond the house, behind the trees, out near the water.

Omakayas suddenly realized that Neewo had quieted. Her ears were still ringing with the sounds of his cries. Seagulls wailed, a skinny shorebird ran up and down the sand, busily pecking. Neewo brandished his chubby fists, blithered at the water, blasted spit excitedly at the sparkling waves, and turned his melting and mischief-filled eyes upon his sister to tell her that she was the most wonderful human on earth.

She settled him beside her on a warm stretch of rock. Put a stick in his hand. He looked at the stick, tested it between his gums. He had one pitiful little tooth he was very proud of, and he tried to use it to bite the stick. The stick was too strong for Neewo. He banged it purposefully at little circles of green lichen scattered on the stone's surface. When the stick broke in two, he yelled in sheer joy and continued beating the rock with the short end of it. Omakayas was so happy that she laughed out loud.

"You'll be a drummer, a singer. I'll dance for you,"

she said. Although it was wrong of her to have set Neewo free, it was very obvious that he had always wanted to be banging a stick on a rock and feeling the warm sun on his face. They sat together for a good while longer. Omakayas tossed stones in the water, sending up splashes to surprise her little brother, and he in turn seemed to try and talk to her in serious burps and babbles about what it was like to be a baby packed into a carrier, hanging on a branch all day long, never allowed to throw rocks or stuff leaves in his mouth.

Omakayas thought she heard him tell her this was the best day of his life so far. She thought she heard him tell her that she was his very favorite sister and he liked her much, much better than Angeline. He definitely said to her that he would never forget this, and that when they were very old he would stare at her the way he was doing now, and laugh, and they'd both be toothless then.

"But I have to put you back now, or else I'll get in trouble," Omakayas said. Regretfully, she lifted him into her arms, a delicious baby weight, and carried him jouncing back to the clearing and the house. As she laid him back into his wrappings and began to lace him in, his face crumpled in betrayal and he opened his mouth. Quickly, Omakayas reached into her pocket. The remains of the treat from Old Tallow was still there. She popped the last little bit of the lump of maple sugar onto his tongue. His mouth closed. A look of blissful surprise came over his face. His body relaxed. By the time Omakayas had him laced back into the tikinagun his eyelids were drooping, and by the time her mother came home with no news of her father, but with a bit of brilliant red cloth, four brass buttons, and six thimbles for which she'd traded a load of dried fish, Omakayas was rocking Neewo as though she'd been doing so all along, and her little brother was smiling in his sleep.

⟨o⟩

The month of picking heartberries went by. Little Pinch jumped off a low branch and made a huge gash just over his eye. Blood came pouring down and he seemed both proud of himself and sorry for himself, and he selfishly hogged attention for his injury to the point where Omakayas could hardly bear it. Mama was constantly preoccupied with him. Of course, that left Neewo more and more to Omakayas's hands, and she didn't mind that. After the hours they'd spent in freedom, it always seemed to Omakayas that she and her little brother exchanged a secret knowledge in their smiles.

Grandma began to call Little Pinch by a new name,

Big Pinch, because he grabbed handfuls of food and tried to stuff his face. He was very slow learning manners. It was hard to teach him. He had an eager, greedy, pushing nature. Omakayas liked him less with every day that passed, and wished desperately that someone, Old Tallow or her Auntie Muskrat, perhaps, would ask Mama if they could keep him. When he got on her nerves the worst, she imagined and dreamed. Maybe someone who'd lost a son would ask for Pinch. Or maybe their father, Mikwam, would arrive and say he needed an always-hungry little boy of five winters to accompany him on his next long trip. The missionaries. They might want to use Pinch as an example—but of what? Things *not* to do? He could live underneath the church. Something, anything, just a little relief! He was so annoying to Omakayas that she found herself occasionally wishing a dreadful wish—that an eagle or old Grandfather Owl might snatch him up and carry him to a high nest. She always stopped herself when her heart grew dark, but oh, these wishes were satisfying!

◄○►

It was a cool dark summer night in the first days of blueberry picking time, and Omakayas had just fallen asleep when something made her awaken, a dream or a sound.

She lay quiet with her eyes just a tiny bit open, staring confusedly at the soft flames that occasionally flickered up among the coals that glowed in the fire pit. Omakayas raised her head, drowsy. Grandma was wedged into a thick bearskin beside the door, snoring lightly, and Big Pinch was tumbled at her feet. Angeline was tucked neatly into her blanket on the other side of the door.

Suddenly, a shiver of happiness and excitement ran down through Omakayas so strongly she feared she might cry out and wake everyone. Her heart jumped. She nearly threw off her robes to dance. Deydey, her father, was home! There, at the entrance, just barely lighted, her father's makazins were heaped with Mama's. His were worn through, dirty, beaten up, although not missing a single bead of Mama's tight beadwork. Mama's, on either side, were spruce and neat. They were her fancy ones, trimmed at the ankle with a specially prepared ruff of white rabbit fur.

 Her mother's and father's makazins always had a certain way of turning toward each other, Omakayas thought. Deydey's makazins were carefully made by Mama, and sometimes worn to shreds before he got home. Soft and open, they seemed relieved to flop inside the door and nestle into the safe embrace of Mama's pair. Her makazins protected Deydey's used-up ones, nuzzled them together, and seemed to be watching over and soothing away the many dangers of his footsteps.

Drifting back into sleep, Omakayas knew that by the time she woke her mother would be cutting out a new pair of makazins from the special moose hide she herself had tanned and smoked when the heartberries were first ripening. That thought brought her back to the memory of the bear mother. As she fell back into her dreams, she wondered.

Would she tell her father what had happened? Would she ever tell anyone? Once more, she decided that she would keep the encounter to herself. Not only would she be scolded, maybe even laughed at, for playing with the bear cubs, but she was quite certain that no one else would understand.

Omakayas curled even deeper into her blanket. Smiling in delight, she buried her face in the warm fur, and fell at last into a heavy, dreamless sleep knowing when she woke there would be Father, tall, bold, strong, and joking, to swing her high in the air. Mama would laugh even more than usual. Angeline, too, shy and excited. There would be gifts, new things, special food. Grandma would cook mightily for a feast. Mama would sew on her father's makazins. Uncles would come visiting, cousins, relatives to feast and listen to stories and tease endlessly. Baby Neewo would beg with his eyes for Deydey's songs, and Big Pinch would have to be good.

CHAPTER FOUR

Andeg

THE WORLD CHANGED when Father was home. Everyone had to be more careful and orderly. When Mama and Grandma were in charge, there was a way to do things, of course, and yet there was room to make mistakes. Mistakes were funny, and could be fixed. With Omakayas's father, Mikwam, or Ice, everything had to be done exactly right. He was a commanding person, over six feet tall and with a shrewdness in his expression that impressed other men. Often, he dressed himself quite handsomely—full turban, beaded velvet vest, calico shirt of fine red cloth, a bandolier bag, earrings. He always wore a least one fancy earring, and it glittered and spun at his jaw when he abruptly halted or changed direction in his walking.

Mikwam was very funny, and the camp was always full of laughter. But it was an uneasy laughter. At any moment, Deydey's mood could change to barbed annoyance. Much of the laughter had to do with her father's sly wit and sharp tongue. There was no one he could not imitate, no one who escaped the sharp humor of his gaze, no one about whom he could not make a joke. He even teased Old Tallow, but he loved giving her little gifts, too, and in the evenings he told stories until way after the owls began to call. With Deydey home, things were more exciting, things were more difficult, things were less predictable but somehow more secure.

First thing Deydey noticed was the corn, how tall it had grown, how the rain had plumped up the ears, what a good crop they had this year. Mama and Grandma were pleased and contented with the crop, but Deydey was jealous of the amount of new corn he saw the crows devouring. Early on the morning of the second day he was home, he cut poles and used basswood twine to rope together two platforms, one on either side of the corn-field. When he had tied the legs securely, and when he had positioned them just so, he called Angeline and Omakayas.

Andeg

"I want you to climb up and stay here and drive away the birds!" He gave Omakayas two smooth sticks to clack together to frighten the flocks, and Angeline his tattered old shirt to flap in the air.

He didn't need it anymore, for Mama had made him a new suit of clothes—a calico shirt, skin leggings, a set of blue broadcloth britches trimmed with red wool. Onto the shirt, she had sewn four carefully hoarded brass buttons, gleaming, each marked with the French flower which the voyageurs called fleur de lis.

Now, on a sunny day, with a sweet haze in the air and the promise of rain low and far at the edge of the horizon, Omakayas and Angeline started for the cornfield.

They argued back and forth about everything and nothing. Stubborn and bored with each other, they fell silent. The garden place lay at the end of a short path through the woods, and on the way they walked without a sound, each lost in her thoughts. Perhaps because they had fallen into that angry silence, they walked quietly enough to come upon One Horn, the magnificent buck deer who had lost half of his antler rack defending his island territory. He seemed to have damaged his head in some way so that only one of his antlers grew back properly. It was a beautiful antler, proud and pointed, but the other one was only a stump.

Unafraid of the girls, One Horn stepped out onto the path and stood alert in the early light, basking a little, warming his coat. Omakayas and Angeline stood still, held by his beauty and the strength of his gaze. His graceful, leaf-shaped ears tilted forward as though he could hear their hearts beating. His brown eyes were commanding and kind. He took a step toward them and stopped, another step, stopped, and then suddenly, as though yanked into the air by a giant invisible rope, he leaped. He disappeared.

"He must have heard something we didn't," Angeline said, and sure enough, Deydey was behind them. Right behind them with no warning.

"What's wrong with you girls?" he said, his voice sharp. "The crows are feasting while you stand here and jabber!"

He walked past them, his stride long. They hurried to the field, climbed onto their platforms, and shooed away what few birds had settled in the corn.

At first, it was fun to wave and shout across the field from their perches.

"Boozhooo," called Omakayas.

"Boozhooo," called Angeline.

"Ninoonde wesin," Omakayas yelled.

"I'm hungry, too," was the answer.

"What did you bring to eat?"

Angeline had brought nothing.

"We could roast some cooorrrrn," suggested Omakayas from across the field.

"We could roast some crowwwwwsss," cried Angeline.

"How will we catch them?" shouted Omakayas.

"I'll get Nokomis's fishing net," Angeline answered. "We'll throw it over them when they land!"

So far, not a single bird had eaten so much as a kernel of corn, because the two girls were making so much noise. But as soon as Angeline left her stand to fetch the net from Grandma, a whirling cloud descended. The smart crows and redwing blackbirds knew when their chances of getting a bite of corn had improved! The crows spread over the corn with cries of greed. Ravens, bigger and smarter, waited on the outskirts of the field to see whether it was safe to join the feast. Determined, Omakayas yelled louder and clacked her sticks. She had helped harvest each seed saved in Mama's seed bag. She had watered those seeds with water hauled from the lake, makuk after makuk of water, until they sprouted and grew. Then she had loosened the earth and weeded with Mama's big moose antler hoe and her own smaller hoe carved from a crooked tree branch. She had guided these corn plants and worked hard and she was not, now, going to give up the winter's dried corn soup to a flock of birds, no matter how hungry they were.

Again, the birds fell on the corn with starving cries. Again, Omakayas ran down screaming to drive them off. Deydey was right. The birds eyes glittered greedily as they tore into each plump ear of corn and pecked at the juicy young kernels. Their cries were ferocious. Until her sister returned, Omakayas ran from one end of the field to the other, shouting, flapping her dad's old shirt or clacking the sticks. After a time, she was too tired to run fast and her shout came out a croak as hoarse as the crows'.

Angeline returned with the net, finally, and they tried to cast it over the birds. The net worked much better at catching fish. However wide and gracefully they tried to toss it, the net always flew clumsily. The birds saw it coming, darted off, and even seemed to laugh with taunting cries as they landed, eating noisily, in another part of the field.

"We've got to trick them," Angeline said.

"Trick them how?" Omakayas panted.

"I've got an idea," said Angeline.

They draped one of Grandma's nets carefully over the cornstalks to make a ceiling. Angeline stood behind the cornstalk room with the other net held wide, and Omakayas ran to the other side of the field. When the birds landed before her, she slowly, unhurriedly, with no shouting and no sudden movements, walked toward her sister. The birds hopped before her, or flew a short distance. They were not frightened enough to wheel high in the air. They continued toward the net, and then slipped under the nets to forage, hopped further beneath, toward Angeline, until they finally ran into the wall of twines and flapped high into the ceiling of the net. In alarm, they panicked, tried to fly through the links Nokomis had woven, and caught a foot, a wing, a tiny head. Even though she had hated them just an hour before, Omakayas now felt badly about betraying them, and as she drove the birds into the net she begged them to forgive her, saying the words she had heard her grandmother use, "Forgive us, forgive us, we have need, we have need."

She turned away as Angeline caught each struggling, flapping bird and broke its neck with one quick, strong twist. They harvested birds for the next hour, and the next hour, until the sun sank low and the remaining birds withdrew to their perches for the night. Then, as Omakayas was gathering in and folding Nokomis's net, she noticed one bird was left, struggling hard to free itself. It was a young crow from a late nest. Though it hopped up and down with great energy, it couldn't quite fly. They already had a pile of birds large enough to fill the biggest parching tray, which Angeline had fetched from the camp.

Omakayas decided to set this last bird free and she gently undid the basswood fiber twine from a sharp black-clawed foot, its neck, a ragged baby feathered wing. Holding the bird in her hands, she set it on the ground and waited for it to fly off. It sat still. When she tried to shoo it into the air, it only hopped a few steps, dragged a hurt wing. Omakayas looked around for a heavy stick to club it, to put it out of its pain, and then something stopped her. She looked down at the bird. It gazed up at her with such a calm, trusting curiosity that it almost seemed to speak aloud. Its round eyes were a deep milky blue, and it cocked its head sideways, back and forth, to get a good look at Omakayas. She looked around to see if Angeline was watching. She wasn't. With a swift movement, Omakayas reached down and scooped the bird into the small carrying sack at her waist. It nestled in so silently that she soon forgot all about it.

Omakayas and Angeline spent what seemed like an endless time plucking the birds, cleaning them, scorching the pinfeathers, those just growing in, too tiny to pull off. When the birds were ready to roast, Mama packed them close together along with wild onion bulbs and then pressed rich, streamed muck carefully around them. She set them in a pit in the middle of the fire and heaped live coals around the balled mound of mud. As the birds cooked, bits of steam broke through tiny cracks in the mud and scented the air with a delicious fragrance. A few ears of ripe new corn, blueberries, and a strong tea of wintergreen made the rest of the feast. When the birds were done, Mama used a stick to roll the ball of birds from the fire, and then she cracked open the baked mud. Sitting down together around the fire, they ate roasted ears of corn, sweet blueberries, and picked the delicate meat off the tiny bird bones. Each bird was no more than a few mouthfuls, hot, tasty, spiced with the oniony brown flavor. There was more than enough to fill each person, and they were all satisfied.

"These are my daughters," said Deydey, proudly. "Not only did they save the corn today, but they caught and plucked our dinner! They are hunters!"

He took his pipe from its bag to smoke it in their honor, and each girl felt a warm, proud sensation. They leaned back a little, looking into the fire, and Nokomis also took out her woman's pipe. She filled the bowl with kinnikinnick, tamped her pipe carefully, and lit it with a glowing stick.

Omakayas wanted to ask her for a story, but she knew that her Nokomis always refused, no matter how hard they begged, until the last frog was safely sleeping in the ground. Deydey, with his half-white blood, could often be persuaded because the stories he told were different from Nokomis's. Hers were adisokaan stories, meant only for winter. Deydey usually talked about his travels, the places he'd seen and the people, the close calls and momentous encounters with animals, weather, other Anishinabeg, and best of all, ghosts.

After he'd smoked his pipe, at Angeline's request Deydey spoke.

DEYDEY'S GHOST STORY

◄○►

We were coming out of the rapids about two days from Boweting, in a part of the river I knew all too well, when I tasted a storm. The last thing I wanted right about then was a storm! I wanted to get my men and our canoe past that spit of land—it's shaped like a little hook and juts out into the river. The name of that place is Where the Sisters Eat. I wanted to get past it because we were hoping to catch up with a certain trader and sell to him. Besides, as I'd heard it, nobody liked to camp there at Where the Sisters Eat. Strange things happened at that place.

Still, when the sky opened and rain poured down I decided that my fears were foolish. As much as my men wanted to go on, I decided we had no choice. They grumbled, but we pulled into shore, dragged our canoes up to the drier ground under the pine trees. By then, the rain was driving down, hard. The wind was shaking the trees. There was no question of making a fire. We just had to wait it out in the cold, in the dark. So I heaped pine needles and soft branches in a bed, rolled myself underneath the canoe in my blanket. So far, everything was fine, I thought. Maybe the stories I had heard about the place were lies, things that never happened. I turned over to try and get a little sleep.

I had barely dozed off when a sudden shaft of lightning hit near, struck a tree that crashed down in the woods. All I could do was hope I had chosen a lucky spot where lightning wouldn't strike, where no tree would topple down. I should have taken my tobacco out right then and offered it up to the good spirits. I should have remembered my mother's ways. But I did not, and here is what happened after I fell asleep again, the next time I woke.

I came awake with a jolt, uneasy. Too quiet, that's the first thought I had, too quiet. No wind, no rain. No moonlight either. The clouds hung thick and heavy as a priest's black wool robe. I waved my hand in front of my face, couldn't see even the barest outline. That's how dark it was. That's when I heard them.

I heard the women arguing over bones.

There were, of course, no living women within hundreds of miles, but I was groggy and didn't think of that. All I could think of was how loud these women were talking!

"Hey, you ladies, be quiet! Someone is trying to sleep here," I called. For a little while, they lowered their voices, and then their argument broke out again and they started to shout. They had settled down to quarrel near my canoe and I was now steaming mad.

"Bekayaan!" I yelled at them, loud and harsh, to be quiet. Again, they lowered their voices, but just as soon as I got comfortable again and started to doze they broke into a loud chatter once more.

It wasn't that they sounded ugly. Their voices were high and sweet, though they were having a disagreement. It was just that they were so loud, and right over my head. Sitting on the canoe! I heard their weight creak on the spruce ribs.

"You be careful out there." I was getting even angrier. They took no notice of me. Just continued their excited disagreement. Here's what they said.

"You give me the first meat, Sister, you take the first bone."

"Give me the second meat, you take the first bone."

"I'll have the foot."

"I'll have the head."

"No, you won't! I'll have the head and the leg, too, Sister!"

"How shall we divide the others?"

"Let's gamble for them."

"Let's!"

"It's a good thing we raised that storm," said one of the sisters, laughing. "How else would we catch our food so easily?"

"My stomach hurts," was the answer. "It's been a long time since we caught this many!"

And then, all of a sudden, I understood. I was the first meat, the second bone! We men were the food! The ghostly sisters had come to hold their feast— us. My sweat turned cold. I remembered all too well how bothersome bad spirits were, even dangerous.

These ones had perhaps starved to death, and so were eternally hungry. They themselves had revealed how they struck up storms to force travelers to seek shelter. No wonder my men hadn't wanted to camp out on the spit of land called Where the Sisters Eat.

◄○►

Deydey fell silent, then, and stared into the fire at the center of the wakaigun. Nobody said a word. Even Baby Neewo seemed to listen, horrified, as Deydey thought about his next move, how he would save himself from the cannibal ghosts. Deydey finally went on.

◄○►

Here's what I did. Luckily, I thought of my father's advice. Never let fear take your mind away, he said. Always think. So instead of giving in to fear, I put fear aside and thought. And into my mind, once I let myself hear it, a plan came. Immediately, I put it into action.

Bam! Bam! I began to knock on the inside of my canoe. I huffed like a bear and shouted in a growly voice, "Wasn't he delicious, this man? Best one I ever ate!"

"Did you hear that?" said the sister above me. "A bear has eaten some of our precious food."

"How dare that bear steal from us!"

They were both furious, and to make them more furious yet I stuck the butt of my rifle out and whacked one of their feet, hard!

"Aaaaow! Aaaaow!" she cried. "Why did you hurt me, my older sister?"

"I didn't," said the older.

"Did, too," shrieked the younger. "You and that bear, always lying and greedy!"

"Me and the bear, nothing! Take that!"

"AAAAOOOWWW!"

◄○►

Deydey gave a horrifying shriek that made the skin on Omakayas's neck crawl, heart jolt, scalp tighten with fear. She snuggled deeper into the blankets and robes next to Grandma, who held her tight.

"AAAAAOOOOWWWHHHHH!"

Again, Deydey gave his version of the ghostly shriek. Big Pinch covered his head and crashed into Mama's lap. Deydey let a silence fall and then told the ending in a hushed, spooky tone.

◄○►

The two sisters began to hit at each other, first

*with their fists, then with sticks, then with rocks pulled
from the ground. While they were occupied with trying
to kill each other, I loaded my canoe quick as could be. I
could hear the others doing the same. No doubt, listening to the sisters plan to eat us, the men had been shaking in their blankets. Just as we were pushing off, one of
the sisters noticed us leaving and with a scream she
bounded toward us. I was the last one out, steering from
behind. I shouted to my men, "Paddle, men, paddle
hard!" Still, the evil sister managed to grab my shirt
and rip it almost into shreds. Just see!*

—◄o►—

Deydey solemnly produced the pieces of shirt that his
daughters had used to frighten off the birds that day. Big
Pinch gasped and the girls were silent. "Yes," said Deydey,
"it was lucky I got out of there alive. And do you know,
after I hit the ghost with my gun barrel, the gun split on
me, refused to let me fix it! Fortunately, we did catch up
with that trader who always made such a good price
to us. And luckily, too . . . ."—Deydey drew out the last
word teasingly, which made the girls ears perk with
interest—"luckily, I was able to trade for a few small
things." Deydey drew a little cloth-wrapped package
from inside his shirt.

He opened the package with such care that Omakayas thought he might have brought back a live thing, perhaps a small squirrel, or maybe—she momentarily recalled the tiny bird in her carrying sack, was it even still in the corner? Probably it was quite dead by now. Omakayas felt a pang. She focused again on Deydey's gift. He loved giving gifts, drawing out the suspense, and he always chose wonderful things. This time, he drew from his small sack a long, thick band of indigo ribbon for Angeline. For Mama, a precious dress length of calico cloth, deep red with blue and pink flower sprigs all over it. For Grandma, tobacco, a big twist of it, golden brown. Big Pinch received a small knife and Baby Neewo one tiny piece of velvet to lay against his soft cheek. As for Omakayas, something special was in store, said Deydey. Something he had made himself. She caught her breath.

"Na," he said, "here. This is for you!"

He handed her the sawed-off length of his gun barrel, the one that ruined itself after he struck the ghost sister's feet. The end of the gun barrel was pinched together with tongs and given a rough, sharp edge. It was clearly, Omakayas gulped to see it, a hide scraper.

"When Mama showed me what a good job you'd done on that moose hide for my makazins," said Deydey, "I decided you should have my old gun barrel for your own first scraping tool. The skins you prepared for my makazins are very fine. From now on, I want you to prepare skins often for Mama and for me. Take this," he said.

Omakayas was confused. Pride fought with dismay inside of her, and she took the gun-barrel hide flesher from her father with a conflicted heart. Preparing hides—her most hated work! And now, just because she had done a good job one time, she was picked out, special, for the rest of her life. She would be condemned to soften, tan, work with stinking hides. "No!" she wanted to say, "I won't take it. I want a ribbon like Angeline's, only red maybe, or yellow! Cloth, please, a bit of sweetness. A licorice stub. Anything. Anything else at all!"

But she took Deydey's gift with a tender thanks, knowing how much he delighted in choosing the presents, and how rarely he praised.

Almost resentfully, she looked over at Deydey's new makazins. Surrounded and held by Mama's makazins, they looked fresh, neat, new. Omakayas had to admit—the hide she had tanned was beautiful.

Suddenly, her heart thumped. Her throat shut. Owah! Deydey's makazin. Oh, she was sure she saw it move. It had moved. She was sure of it. Again!

"Neshkey!" Her voice trembled. She pointed. The others looked.

This time, the makazin took a big hop forward and everyone, even Deydey, cried out in surprise. They were all frozen in shock. The makazin sat quiet, still. Nokomis leaned over, poked at it with a stick. The makazin twitched. Then squawked. Omakayas jumped up, for she remembered instantly that she'd left her carrying sack right next to the door with the makazins. Sure enough, her bird popped its head out, bright, and in the sound of everyone's laughter it blinked with interest, cheerful, greedy, hungry, unafraid.

Dagwaging

(F A L L)

CHAPTER FIVE

Fishtail's Pipe

NOW IN THE MORNINGS there was a sharp freshness in the air. Omakayas loved this time of the year and jumped from her blankets eagerly, rolled her sleeping mat and fur blanket, and put them away quickly so that she could help rekindle the outdoor cooking fire. Her crow hopped after her. Though it could fly short distances, its wing hadn't yet healed. Andeg, the Anishinabe or Ojibwa word for crow, was its name. Nokomis was fond of Andeg. The bird often rode on her shoulder and kept her company as she packed dry fish, repaired nets, wove new mats, and, alongside Omakayas, tanned hides they needed now for winter clothing—jackets, makazins, mittens, hoods. Omakayas used the gun-barrel flesher, Deydey's gift. She didn't like the work any better than she ever had, but Andeg's lively company helped. Andeg even frightened off an owl, and once, perched on the head guard of baby Neewo's cradle board, *craackacraccked* loudly and repeatedly until Mama came running to find a curious raccoon trying to steal from the bundles of dried fish and venison she was preparing to cache. Andeg quickly became everybody's favorite. But the crow slept only near Omakayas. He fell asleep just at dusk, perching low on a branch she had tied into the side of the ribs of the birchbark house.

◄◦►

Deydey spent a few warm fall days making repairs on his canoe, and then it was time for him to leave again. He would make one more big trip before the cold rains, and then the harsh snow, slashed down. Once he stopped gathering and selling the furs of other Anishinabeg, he would go out on his own trapline. For the rest of the late fall and winter he would be home and gone, home and gone, and each time he returned, Omakayas thought with a sinking stomach, he would be hauling back skins for her to work on.

One afternoon, his friends and partners came to

visit and make their plans. Albert LaPautre and Fishtail came walking through the woods. When Angeline and Omakayas saw the men coming, they decided to hide and quickly dived into a heavy stand of bush. Peeking between weedy stalks, they had a good view. Albert was round as a kettle and his big teeth stuck out pleasantly when he grinned. He fancied himself quite a medicine man and wore at his throat a circle of bear claws. Next to him walked the tall and handsome Fishtail. He had strikingly long, thick, oiled black hair, and a hawk-thin face with a proud curl to his lips. He carried his pipe in the cradle of his left arm, close to his heart.

It was a fancy pipe, made of a piece of sumac wood marked with a sweet grain. Bands along the stem were carefully beaded in black and yellow. Fishtail took extremely good care of his pipe, cleaned it often, prayed with it every sunrise. To him, it was a living thing. The bowl was red pipestone in the shape of an otter's head, his clan. Dark blue pony beads hung down a swatch of fringe, and Fishtail touched them carefully and lovingly as he stepped quietly along.

Mikwam came out along the path to meet his friends, and the men talked and joked before they made themselves comfortable, sitting on blankets on the ground. Omakayas saw her father open up his leather pouch of sweet kinnikinnick and asema, or tobacco. Fishtail lit the pipe, and the fragrance of burning red-willow tobacco hung peacefully in the air. Each man, as he drew in the smoke, wore a look of concentrated and peaceful attention. The pipe passed around the circle twice before any of the men said a word.

What they said made Omakayas and Angeline creep closer, listen more carefully. Hidden in the grass and underbrush, they breathed quietly and opened their ears to catch the lower tones of the men's voices.

"Chimookoman," said Fishtail, in a growling tone of indignation. The word meant "big knife," and it was

used to describe the non-Indian, or white people, who were traveling in larger numbers than ever to Ojibwa land and setting down their cabins, forts, barns, gardens, pastures, fences, fur-trading posts, churches, and mission schools. LaPointe was becoming more chimookoman every day, and there was talk of sending the Anishinabeg to the west.

"They say we must leave the island," Fishtail went on.

No one commented. Curled against itching nettle leaves, Omakayas eased her hand to her leg to scratch. She scratched silently and kept listening.

"That's right," her father said at last, contempt in his voice, "that's what they are saying. The useless ones."

Albert LaPautre drew on the pipe and frowned, tamping and adjusting the tobacco burning in the bowl. He drew deep and puffed hard. He was part French, like Deydey, but browner than Fishtail. His eyes were greenish-brown. His round, cheerful face beamed. He sighed, and with a faraway look said that he had a vision. Fishtail and Deydey looked blankly and patiently at him when he said this, for LaPautre was known for recounting visions and dreams that had very little meaning, though they seemed to affect him hugely. Now he looked down sternly, gathering his thoughts. Suddenly, he blurted out, "I dreamed I had lice!"

In the brush, Angeline and Omakayas clapped hands over their mouths to stifle their glee. Deydey and Fishtail managed to keep straight faces, but Omakayas was sure she saw the corner of Deydey's mouth twitch.

Albert LaPautre sighed. "The meaning is unclear," he muttered.

"Let us find the meaning," said Deydey. His voice was serious, but the girls both knew that he was having fun with LaPautre. "Was anything else happening in your dream?"

LaPautre frowned, as though overcome with the weight of his vision. "Yes," he said, "we were planning a dance gathering!"

"Ah!" said Father, "the meaning now becomes clear! This was a deep dream, indeed!"

"What?" LaPautre was breathless.

"From now on when you dance," Father said, without allowing the trace of a smile, "you will dance hard enough to shed your lice."

"Yes?" LaPautre's voice was suspicious, but neither Deydey nor Fishtail let on by any sign that Father's interpretation was a joke.

"Perhaps," said LaPautre, "I should tell you my own thoughts." And then, to Angeline and Omakayas's surprise and dismay, he told the other men that he was thinking of taking his family, all ten of his children, his uncles and grandmas and grandpas, to a western post where, he had heard, government payments were made.

Omakayas nudged Angeline. Those children were

their friends. To think that they might have to leave! Omakayas nearly cried out, but Angeline poked her to be quiet.

All of the Ojibwa would be safe on their own land farther west, Albert was saying. No one would bother them. Yes, there were hazards on the way—Dakota war parties, hunger, the threat of winter's dire weather. He'd rather not go. Still, said jolly Albert, he had moved before when the waves of white people lapped his feet.

"West, always west," said Deydey, agreeing slowly. "We hear the chimookoman ax ring in the woods, chopping a tree. We should be gone before the tree falls."

"We have to stop somewhere, someday." Fishtail drew thoughtfully on the pipe and the fragrant smoke clouded his face. "West is where the spirits of the dead walk. If the whites keep chasing us west, we'll end up in the land of the spirits."

"I have dreamed that's where they want us to go, anyway," said Albert. "That will please them."

"They are like greedy children. Nothing will ever please them for long," said Deydey. Although his grandfather had been French, he was raised and considered himself Ojibwa and kept the rules of his mother's dodem or clan, the catfish clan. The Awausesee. Only in some chimookoman things, his cabin for instance, and his ability to play and win the white man's game of chess with the trader, did he take secret pride.

"Not until they have it all," said Fishtail. "All of our lands. Our wild-rice beds, hunting grounds, fishing streams, gardens. Not even when we are gone and they have the bones of our loved ones will they be pleased. I have thought about this."

Fishtail put up his hand and held it there, looked keenly at his friends. "Before they were born, before they came into this world, the chimookoman must have starved as ghosts. They are infinitely hungry."

The men smoked with increased intensity, looking deep into the fire as the breeze came up and dusk lowered. Deydey was thoughtful, his eyes deep and clouded.

Even LaPautre looked serious, the dimples set hard in his cheeks. Watching in the bushes, Omakayas and Angeline waited for them to resume their talking, but that day, mulling over Fishtail's difficult words perhaps, the men kept their silence.

CHAPTER SIX

Pinch

 IG PINCH GOT IN trouble and Omakayas was glad. Here's how it happened.

One day, Mama found a bush of late-bearing chokecherries. They were plump, and so ripe that they had turned a deep blackish-purple color. She picked until her fingers turned red-black at the tips. When she returned, bearing her load of berries, Mama's eye lit on Big Pinch.

"I have a job for you," she said. His eyes got beady and his lip turned out. He pouted at her, but she paid his lowered looks no mind.

"I'm spreading these berries on the bark sheaves so they will dry," she went on, and then she proceeded to spread out the berries on clean birchbark, in the warmest patch of sun she could find. "You watch them carefully now, Big Pinch. Keep the birds away. Listen, my son." Mama narrowed her eyes at Pinch so that he would know he was trusted with an important task. "This is our winter seasoning and food. You'll be glad of them when we are hungry in little spirit moon."

She gave Big Pinch a long, ferny branch to wave and made him sit next to the berries. Then she turned her back on him and went out to the lake with Grandma to check their fish nets. She took Neewo along with her, put him carefully in his tikinagun, petted and kissed him. Angeline and Omakayas were sent to town. They were to sweep out and prepare the family cabin for the winter move. Big Pinch was left alone.

◄◦►

It was hard being Big Pinch, harder than his sisters would ever know. They didn't understand how good it felt to fill a stomach that so rarely got full. They didn't realize how good it felt to shove handfuls of berries into his greedy mouth. Pinch looked at the berries. Bored, he shooed away a few small chickadees. Andeg sat with him, on a low branch. But Andeg knew better than to eat the berries. If only, thought Pinch sadly, those berries didn't look *so delicious!* Mama had found a patch of chokecherries that were much more luscious than most. These were the biggest, fattest berries Pinch had ever seen! It didn't seem as though it would hurt to eat a few. Pinch sneaked one, then a few more, then a handful. Andeg cawed three times, and seemed to disapprove. Pinch made a face at the bird. The berries tasted as good as they looked, better. Richer, blacker, without that mouth-puckering chokecherry taste. He might just have another handful.

Well, he thought not long after he finished that bunch, a handful more would not hurt. And then, just to balance the look of the berries, he took more from one side. The other. He spread the berries out and then the bark looked full again. Pinch waited. The sun blossomed slowly, so slowly, and it took such a long time to dry the berries. Pinch tried to amuse himself, but with nobody there to bother, he was at a loss. Andeg didn't want to play and flew out of reach. There was nobody to annoy except himself!

Another handful. Another and another. Pinch rearranged the berries once again. Now there seemed to be plenty of berries on the bark—they were well spaced, it was true, but the bark sheaves looked full. He kept nibbling, spacing, arranging, and rearranging until sleep overcame him and he curled up tight and nodded away.

◄○►

"Pinnnnnch!" It was Mama's threatening voice. She was standing tall over the berries and she wasn't the least bit fooled by Pinch's berry arrangement. "What happened? Where are the berries I picked, you sleepy boy!"

Pinch woke, jumped up rubbing his eyes, blinking. It was true! There were very few berries on the bark sheaves. Had he eaten so many? How could he? Big Pinch was horrified, embarrassed at himself.

"Pinnnchhhh!" Mama was using her very angry voice now, and Pinch felt so terrible that his brain raced and he seized suddenly upon a blaming lie.

"Andeg ate them. Bad Andeg!"

Pinch pointed up and sure enough, Andeg, sitting out of reach on a high branch, certainly looked guilty as he glared down and preened his new growth of feathers. Mama, furious that her work was all for nothing, shook her fist in the air and called out to Andeg.

"Come on down and eat the rest of them!"

Andeg, not understanding, hopped down to nearly within her reach and cocked his head in a friendly way as though to inquire, "Are you sure?"

"AAAAYyaaaah!"

Mama took Andeg's friendliness as a sign that he really had eaten up the berries. Mama grabbed a stick, shook it hard. Andeg croaked in alarm. With a shout, she threw back her arm, took sudden aim at the bird, and hurled the stick at Andeg.

"CaaaaaH!" Andeg was hit. Although not seriously hurt, he jumped fearfully from branch to branch and fluttered out of reach, then farther, farther away, until he was lost from view.

"See what you made me do?" Mama called, but immediately she sat down, sorry, knowing that the fault lay strictly with herself. "I must get the better of myself. I must. I must." She shook her head. "How could I?" Now her daughter's pet was frightened, and even if he had eaten all of the berries she worked so hard to pick, Mama loved the crow and never meant to scare him. How betrayed by humans the bird must feel, she thought guiltily. And here she had trained him to eat from her hand! Now he was frightened off.

"Come back," she called hopefully into the woods. "Ombay!"

But the bird, still crying out in confusion, only fled deeper into the woods. Mama sat down sadly, ashamed of herself. That was how Omakayas found her mother when she returned from her town errand. Mama told what had happened, how Andeg had eaten the berries Pinch was watching, and how she had gotten angry, frightened Andeg off, how she was now sorry to have done so and would help Omakayas find the bird.

"Surely, he will come to you," said Mama.

Just as she was explaining why it was she had lost her temper and how hard she had worked to find those berries, Big Pinch groaned.

"What's wrong?" Mama asked.

"Oooooh." Big Pinch lay down holding his stomach. "It hurts. Oooooh. It hurts."

"Saaa!"

Mama bent over her boy, inspecting him. "A stomachache, eh?" She was immediately suspicious.

Gently but firmly, she took his hands in hers, uncurled them, saw the tell-tale juice marks of bruised choke-cherries that darkened his fingertips, then the pitiful, berry-stained smile that sealed his guilt!

"Pinch," she said, and this time her voice was worse than angry. It was disappointed. "You lied. The ghost foot carries off liars in the night! As for your stomachache, there is no medicine but enduring the consequences of your greed. You'll have to suffer, Pinch. Maybe this will teach you!"

With that, she and Omakayas left him to Angeline and went off into the woods seeking Andeg.

◄○►

Not far into the woods, they heard Andeg's distinctive croak. "Craawk! Craaawkacraak!"

"There!" said Mama, pointing. "You go to him, Omakayas. He doesn't trust me, and I don't blame him." She gave Omakayas a crust of bannock bread, a treat, and sent her ahead, although she stayed within sight should Omakayas need her. And something happened, sure enough, that made Mama glad she stayed close, though she couldn't have explained it if she tried.

Far ahead, she heard branches cracking, and a sound she knew well, a low chuffing. Bears. High in the oak trees, stuffing themselves with acorns, the tubby young bears moved along the thinnest branches. More crashing. Now a squeal. One of the bears ventured out too far, curious, and tumbled right out of the tree. He picked himself up, and stood on his hind legs. His acorn-chubby belly stuck out like LaPautre's. Then Mama saw both little bears loping and bounding through the woods toward Omakayas.

"Daughter!" she shouted. Bears are shy, and these wouldn't seek Omakayas out to attack, surely. On the other hand, they could be dangerous, especially if wounded or angered. Mama ran toward Omakayas, but then stopped, afraid to disturb what took place. The two young bears bounded curiously toward her daughter. She saw Omakayas turn sharply to the bears, and then, after a moment of surprise, Omakayas greeted the animals. She stood quietly before them, and she was smiling! Mama was further surprised and frightened when without a sound of warning a huge sow bear fattened for winter rambled out of the brush and passed Omakayas without acknowledging her, a human, as the least bit strange or out of place. And the younger bears, was she talking to them? Mama couldn't see. She crept nearer and listened to what her daughter said.

"Ahneen, neshemay," she said to the nearest one. "You've gotten fat!" She smiled at their bumbling, chubby bodies. They were huge! Over the summer, they had grown until they outweighed her by a great deal, though they still were bashful and hung back, just beyond the reach of her fingertips, as she spoke to them.

"So, you're getting ready to sleep," she said, offering the bannock pieces. "Here, my brothers, sleep well!"

The bears stood before her, testing the air, the unfamiliar smell of the bannock, and then each one bent to the bit of bread she held, flicked it up with a muscular tongue, and loped off into the woods behind their mother, who was clearly just a little tired of them following her along, and grumpy because she wanted to sleep.

<o>

Andeg returned that evening to sit just outside the circle of the outdoor cooking fire. He hopped a little closer when Omakayas tempted him with a bit of stew meat. He never did trust Mama again, though, never did perch near and watch her at work, tipping his head side to side as though he were learning her actions. He still warned her of all approaching animals or strangers, but he was wary of her ever after she lost her temper, and kept his distance, which made her sad. Andeg did, however, perform a great service in the winter cabin.

While Omakayas dragged kettle after kettle of mud to the side of the cabin and, along with Angeline, chinked the cracks that had opened during hot weather, Andeg hunted. His vigilance and hatred for mice helped the whole family in their efforts to ready the cabin for winter. He chased mice, tried to pounce on them, swept them away with his wings, even caught a few and pecked them sharply, as though to warn them. And they never did come back. They sought other cabins and wigwams, where there was not a frightful crow to bother them.

—<o>—

Now it was time to harvest the wild rice that grew across from the island in the great sloughs of Kakagon, where Mama's brother and one of her sisters lived. It was a part of the year everyone looked forward to because there would be cousins to play with, games in the rice camps, the pleasures of talk, feasting, more talk, more visiting and feasting. Early in the morning, then, they all set out in the canoe they had worked on a year ago. It was beautifully made, light and strong, carefully water-proofed with pitch by Grandma, who kept it in good repair and in its own house by the side of the lake. They all got in—Mama in back to paddle and steer, Grandma up front taking turns with Angeline, who held Neewo in his cradleboard. They all fit into the canoe with plenty of room to spare. That space, they hoped, they would fill with the wild rice, the manomin, the good seed that would sustain them through the winter.

Omakayas envied her big sister. She wanted to hold and play with her smiling baby brother. Neewo had a second tooth and seemed even prouder of it than the first. Omakayas had saved a bit of hard bannock bread for him to chew on, and she put it in his mouth. Neewo never even bit her. Omakayas put her finger to his cheek, stroked it softly. Why, oh why, did she have to take care of Big Pinch? She sighed, and turned to him. She was in charge of Pinch, or he was in charge of her—she wasn't sure which because it was one of his mischief days when nothing she could do would satisfy him. Andeg, perched on Omakayas's shoulder, was set-tled in for the long ride, and sympathetic to Omakayas. He knew that Pinch had something to do with the bad day Mama had lost her temper.

Before they started out, Grandma gave her tobacco

to the water and asked for a safe, smooth crossing. The sun was mild and the waves low, the wind fresh but still warm, and things would have gone perfectly if Pinch hadn't teased Andeg. But he did. Every time he thought no one was looking, he tried to pull a feather out of Andeg's tail.

"Gaygo, Pinch," said Omakayas.

"Gaygo, Pinch," said Angeline.

"Gaygo, Pinch," said Mama, when he tried again.

"Gaygo, Pinch," said Grandma, wearily.

"Gaygo, Pinch," said Omakayas again.

They must have said it more times as they traveled the lake than there were waves or fish alongside of them! They said it so many times they didn't hear themselves anymore. Stop it, Pinch! Gaygo, Pinch! Stop it! Stop! Same as when they said it onshore, Pinch didn't hear it. He just kept trying to pull a feather. Finally, Pinch got ahold of the black tip of Andeg's pride and joy, his tail.

"Gaygo, Pinch!"

Everyone gasped. This time it was Andeg who spoke!

Terrified at the crow's harsh croak, Pinch nearly threw himself out of the canoe, nearly tipped them all over in his panic to get to Mama, who yelled, of course, "Gaygo, Pinch!" causing Andeg to flap his wings and say again, "Gaygo, Pinch!" which made Pinch cry, an embarrassment he never quite got over. From then on he regarded Andeg with stubborn awe, treated the bird with reserved respect, and in fact behaved just a little better, for just a little while, as Nokomis told him that his rascal ways annoyed even the animals!

"Wait until you hear what Mukwah, the bear, says, or Grandfather Owl! Think of that!" Nokomis scolded.

Pinch didn't want to.

—◀o▶—

When they reached the river's entrance and paddled toward the rice camp, Grandma noted with disappointment the thinness of the rice stalks. Too much standing water in the spring had caused them to grow too quickly. Some of the rice heads drooped right over into the water. She frowned. The season would be a poor one, unless the water in the other rice beds had been lower. They reached the shores of the camp, and there, amid the general happiness at seeing one another, the grown-ups learned the rice was indeed sparse that year. This was not good news, but the children could not have cared less. Nothing ruined their fun! Immediately, Omakayas raced off, her crow flapping alongside her, to find her cousins and introduce them to her friend Andeg.

There under the tree, she saw Wishkob's daughters, Little Bee and Twilight, and her cousins, including Tatah, a thin and quiet boy just a little younger than Omakayas. He was the son of her mother's brother Akewaynzee. As soon as Omakayas saw Tatah, an itchy, joking mood always came upon her and she looked around to see what tricks she could play on her quiet cousin. His older brothers were rough and ran wild, and he had a sister known as a strong, swift runner. Her name was Two Strike Girl, and she was better than most boys at hunting and fighting. She had to be forced to do the things girls normally did, and her mother and grandma had finally given up on her.

"I'm dancing the rice this year!" Two Strike Girl told Omakayas right off. That was most often the boys' job, but she had persuaded the rice chief she could do it.

◄○►

Early the next morning, the rice boss blessed the harvest and Mama set out with Auntie Muskrat, who poled in back while Mama used her rice sticks to bend the stalks toward her and knock the rice grains off into the bottom of the boat. That year, although the harvest was not the best, there was rice for everyone and, as always, work that could not be avoided. Omakayas grumbled when Grandma asked her to go pick reeds.

"Take Two Strike Girl with you," she ordered. "Pick enough for two mats."

So Omakayas and her cousin went to the side of the slough where the flattest reeds grew, and used their knives to slice them off below the waterline, bunch after bunch, until they had great bundles that they carried back to camp on their shoulders.

"Here," said Two Strike Girl, dumping hers off. She gathered herself to spring away, but Grandma caught her.

"Stay," ordered Grandma, "help your cousin weave."

Two Strike Girl looked alarmed, and then horrified at the idea of doing girl's work. Still, because she was ordered to do it by Grandma, she sat down beside Omakayas and began to weave the reeds into strong, simple mats that they would use to smoke the rice. Even now, the great fire Mama had prepared was burning down to its embers, and as the girls' fingers moved unwillingly, Pinch was just as unwillingly gathering up rotten old pieces of maple wood to use in smoking the rice.

When he had gathered several sagging piles of the crumbly maple wood, and when the mats were finished, Omakayas's regular and straight in its weave, and Two Strike Girl's crooked and gaping, Mama took the mats and set them over the smoking maple fire. Then, on top of the mats, she poured the rice, which began, after the mat was properly heated, to give off a most delicate, nutty aroma. Using a rake made from a stick of red willow pulled up by the roots, the two girls took turns turning the rice over and over, smoking and toasting the grains. As the rice cooked, it gathered the taste of the maple.

"I can't take this anymore!" cried Two Strike Girl, throwing down the stick. "If I have to work, at least I'm going to have some fun at it!"

Running over to a bark-lined pit in the ground, she jumped in and began treading rice with a frantic pace that made everyone around her laugh. It was the sight of the impatient Two Strike Girl dancing the rice that Omakayas would remember long after, in the deep winter of the year. Her face was flushed and thrilled with effort. She was tireless. All day, and the next, Two Strike's legs moved up and down, her feet, in clean new makazins, crushed the tough hulls. She never stopped. And all the time her eyes were shining, her white teeth set in a huge grin. Andeg danced up and down with her on a limb above.

"Come help me," she called to Omakayas. Jumping to help her cousin, Omakayas felt as proud and bold. The two held hands and stepped high, day after day, night after night. Although the family did not return with as much rice as they needed, Omakayas and Two Strike Girl became such good friends that, ever after, they called each other sister.

CHAPTER SEVEN

The Move

EYDEY LEFT ON HIS VOYAGE, and the rest of the family worked hard to prepare as much food as possible for the winter. For days, the girls dried and then parched the corn that they had saved from the hungry birds. Around and around they stirred the corn in an iron kettle over a low fire. Nokomis went over to Tallow's place and pounded some of the corn to meal with the hollowed log and great round stick that Tallow kept in her yard. While Nokomis worked on the corn, Tallow gutted fish and dried them on a big scaffold that she set up over a special fire she would feed day and night with cedarwood to give the fish a special flavor. The charcoal from the cedar she would keep to mix with pine pitch. Mixed together, the stuff made caulking for the seams of their canoes.

At the winter cabin, Deydey had built a rough lean-to and attached it alongside the northern wall. Inside the log lean-to, he had dug out a deep, round hole. Angeline and Mama spent one morning lining the earth of the hole with birchbark. They made a tight bark container, like a big makuk, and lined that container with bunches of dried grass. Then they took more curved pieces of birchbark and set them in the interior. This was their food cache. Within the cache, Mama first placed several packs of dried, smoked fish and venison, all tied carefully together in two layers of bark. When those packs were set neatly down on the bottom, she told Omakayas to fetch the parched corn, which she had stored in neat skin bags. There were several makuks of wild rice from the fall's gathering, though the harvest had been so poor. Mama had used the intestines of the moose to store the pounded meat and dried berries they would have on feast days as a treat. She set those very carefully to one side, surrounded by sheaves of bark. Deep, deep in the food cache, unseen to anyone but Omakayas, Mama set eight birchbark cones of maple sugar. These, Omakayas knew, were for the hardest times in winter, when they would need sweetness to survive in spirit, as well as food to keep them strong.

When all was finished, Nokomis came to bless the cache.

In the deep light of the fading afternoon, Grandma raised her arms, the way she did at sunrise near the water. Everything grew very quiet around her. Even Pinch stopped shuffling his feet and rubbing his nose. Outside, the birds hushed. The sky bent to listen. The wind died down. Golden leaves hung balanced in the air. It was as though, Omakayas thought, all of creation was interested in Nokomis's words. Even her own heart beat quieter, and that excited, jumpy feeling in her calmed. Whenever Grandma prayed, she made the world around her feel protected, safe, eternal.

Nokomis bent over and looked very carefully at the cache to make certain that it was properly packed.

"Anishaa," she breathed quietly, standing again, holding in her palm a tiny mound of tobacco. She looked down at the tobacco, touched it lovingly, and asked the spirits for protection against the cold. She spoke to the creator. "We're very small," she said, "just human. Help us to live this winter through. Come to us, especially, during the harshest moon, the Crust On The Snow Moon, when so often meat is scarce, when the ice is too thick to catch many fish, when disease breaks us and the windigo spirit, the Hungry One, comes stalking from house to Anishinabe house. Oh, daga, wedookaow Anishinabeg. Wedookaow Anishinabeg," she asked.

Her voice was soft, but deep and troubled. Stillness swirled about the little cabin when she finished. It was as though everyone's heart were touched a little by the coming cold, as though a shadow of the windigo swept across their minds. Omakayas shivered. Angeline touched her shoulder. Mama stroked Pinch's rough, haylike stack of hair. Baby Neewo was the first to make a sound, and that sound was a sudden cry.

◄○►

They spent that last night in the birchbark house, chilled in their robes and blankets. Already, Omakayas missed summer. When morning came, Mama hardly had the fire going before they all began to pack. Mama stirred the soup in the kettle, heated it through, and brought some to Nokomis in the tin bowl, with the trader's spoon. Nokomis drank it all up, stretched her arms, hopped to her feet with a young girl's agility. She rubbed her hands. She loved moving, packing, changing locations. Before the sun even popped its rays through the lowest brush, she was carefully rolling up the rush mats she had woven. From the inside walls of the house, she lifted down her careful bundles of roots, her bags of berries and dried, crumbled leaves, and long curls of inner bark of certain trees.

For the first time, Omakayas noticed all of these little bundles, how cleverly they were tied. How interesting each one smelled. Their colors, their odd, shriveled shapes. She helped Nokomis take the bundles down, put them carefully in her net to carry.

"I'll take them," she said, her arms full.

"We'll go together," said Nokomis, watching with interest as Omakayas touched a particular root, sniffed a tiny packet and sneezed, rubbed a powder with her finger.

"Are they talking to you?" Nokomis asked, curious, as they walked along the trail soon after. "Do you hear their voices?"

"No," said Omakayas, startled. "I don't hear anything!"

After a while, as they walked the trail, as the medicines grew heavy, she thought to ask:

"Nokomis, do they talk to *you*?"

She nodded. "Yes, sometimes they tell me things, but of course, I have learned how to listen."

"What do they tell you?"

"How to use them when someone is sick, where to find them, how to prepare them just the right strength. I wondered if they had picked you to talk to, my granddaughter. I've been watching how quiet you are sometimes. Your mama told me about the bear cubs in the woods."

"Oh, *they* talk to me," Omakayas said, laughing a little at the memory of their peculiar, sleepy, stubborn looks at their mother, so like Pinch when he didn't want to go to bed.

"Listen to them." Nokomis stopped in the path. Holding her bundles in her arms, she gazed at Omakayas until, understanding the gravity of Nokomis's nature, Omakayas stood still. Holding the medicines and looking curiously at her grandmother, she waited.

"Listen to them," was all Nokomis said, touching Omakayas's face. She spoke so earnestly, with such emotion in her voice, that Omakayas was always to remember that moment, the bend in the path where they stood with the medicines, her grandmother's kind face and the words she spoke.

<o>

By the end of the day, the cabin was once again their home. Neewo slept in his winter bed, a blanket fixed on the ropes so that he could gently rock to sleep. Mama had a fire going in the fire pit, a small hearth that Deydey had made for them of the smoothest, thickest, heaviest stones. Omakayas was always glad to see that hearth once the fire was lighted, for she spent many cold winter nights huddled near, in blankets, listening to Grandma and gazing so long at the patterns in the lake rocks that she saw things—faces, animals—and had come to know them as familiar. That night in their cabin, it was at first too warm to cuddle in a blanket, so she sat on the mat on the earth floor and watched the flames throw shadows leaping across the stones.

There—a long-legged racing dog, a face of an old woman, a raccoon's face, a frog, Omakayas' namesake. She greeted them drowsily, old friends, and fell asleep against her grandma. Halfway through the night, Omakayas woke, freezing. She patted around the floor until she found her blanket, then she snuggled quickly in, for the cold had crept with iron stealthiness into the cabin. Dark air stabbed at them from all along the edges of the sleeping mats. It seized at their shoulders, their feet, even the hair on top of Omakayas's head and the tip of her nose. She buried her face in the fur of her blanket, nestled close against Nokomis's back, and as she fell asleep it seemed to her that there was something odd in the ferocity of the cold that continued to deepen as the night went on. She never quite warmed, kept shifting as cold drafts seized a foot or iced her knees. All night, she woke, slept, woke again, and it took until the darkness lightened before she felt warm enough to drop into a heavy dream.

CHAPTER EIGHT

First Snow

HE AIR IN THE CABIN was brilliant; there was a flash to the light that told her it had snowed while she slept! The first snow!

"Aayah!" Pinch screamed, throwing off his rabbit-skin blanket to run outside.

"Don't slide on the lake yet!" Mama knew what he was up to, and raced to the door after him to stop him from running straight out onto the ice. Although the cold was sudden and the snow had fallen thick and mysterious overnight, the water of the lake was still open just past a skim of delicate ice onshore. Already the air was warming up a little, at least where the sun shone brightest. Mama was worried that Deydey would not manage to make the crossing before the freeze-up. If he didn't, if he couldn't, he would have to wait in camp until the ice was solid and he and his men could pull their toboggans of stretched furs across to sell to the traders.

Down the cleared path now, striding large, feather nodding in time with each long step, came Old Tallow. She held her long rifle loosely under one arm, and growled her Ahneen at Omakayas as she tramped into the brush. Omakayas called back, and Old Tallow's hand went up in an abrupt wave, though she didn't turn to look or certainly to smile. Her dogs followed at her heels, great and wolvish. The slinking yellow dog paused to turn and bare its broken brown teeth at Omakayas, but she crossed her eyes at him and couldn't have cared less. First snow day always lifted her out of her skin, made her feel sharp and alive.

The snow, not deep, softening, gleamed in a white cover over all that she could see. Each branch was neatly outlined, and some still bore their leaves. Omakayas and Angeline admired the intricate way that the snow trimmed the dried reeds of cattails and the brown furry heads were capped with tiny white mounds that made them look ...

"Delicious, minopogwud!" Angeline pretended to bite.

"Take this!" Not only was Pinch annoying, but he had a good aim. Just as Omakayas turned she caught a firm-packed snowball on the side of her face. The snow stung. Pinch had packed a little stone in it! The wet snow licked her neck. Omakayas ran at him without a word and threw herself on him, buried him face first in a mound of snow directly beside the path.

"Gaygo!" Pinch howled and leaped up, mad, packed more snowballs together and set off after his laughing sisters. The more he ran on his short legs, though, the faster they galloped ahead. There was not a chance that he would catch them. He knew it, and finally stopped. He slumped down near the side of the path, muttering to himself and putting more snowballs together until he had a big pile. At the heart of each, he packed a stone. Stones he hoped would sting his sisters until they cried!

◄o►

The girls walked farther into the town, knowing Mama was busy, hoping she wouldn't miss them quite yet. It was exciting to live around other people again, and both of the girls wanted to find out if old friends had stayed to winter. They wanted to see if any new families had come to live near. Angeline was thinking of going to the Catholic mission school, and she wanted to sneak by and see if anyone was there yet, studying the signs and marks that the priest made with a soft white stick on the big black wall. They walked to the edge of the school yard, and then stood outside in the clear air, in the sun, breathing the fragrance of fresh wet snow and new bread, crusty and warm.

The singsong reciting voices floated from inside the log schoolhouse. Omakayas was glad they were outside, but Angeline's face was turned eagerly toward the sound of the priest's instructions. She was curious to know what was happening, but remembered Grandma's advice: "Take their ways if you need them," she said, "but don't forget your own. You are Anishinabe. Your mother and your grandmother are wolf clan people. Don't forget. Also, you sweat-bath yourself clean every day, even jump in the freezing lake, a thing that the chimookomanug do not do. My girl, don't become like them."

Just as the thought of Grandma made Omakayas smile, there was a flurry of stamping feet as children of all ages burst from the back door, leaping wide, flinging themselves forward in a laughing frenzy, thrilled with the prospect of new snow and ready to have their morning break, their fun, and then their small meal of smoked whitefish and bread.

"Ai! Neshkey!" Angeline pointed in amazement.

Stepping with easy care down the stairs of the school-house, solemn, carrying his tobacco pouch, his knife at his belt, was none other than Fishtail! What was he doing at the school? He did not join the children in their wild play, but walked directly from the school toward his camp. Fishtail lived at the very edge of the village, hidden in deep bush. His place was built the old way; it was a birchbark house, but it was quite warm in winter because he knew how to heap the sides with snow and he was an excellent trapper. The interior of his house was always lined with strung skins, hung with lush furs made up into sleeping robes, and red-and-white-point blankets. His wife, Angeline's best friend, Ten Snow, was known as a fine beadworker. People said that she tanned hides so soft that they felt to the skin like the slippery velvet that the traders sold.

"Let's find out what he's doing," whispered Angeline.

"He was visiting the school," said Omakayas, "what's there to find out?"

"I don't think so." Angeline pointed to the book, the sheaf of chimookoman paper, the evidence in Fishtail's hand that he had another motive in attending the school.

"Okay," said Omakayas, now curious. "You go ask him."

"Aaaaay!" Angeline blushed.

"Scared!"

"No, I'm not!"

"You are so."

Challenged, Angeline jumped forward. She walked so swiftly after Fishtail that Omakayas ran to keep up, but when she got to him she walked beside him with no word. Didn't she know what to say? Omakayas trotted behind, just within earshot.

"What were you doing back there?" Angeline finally had the courage to ask.

"I went to the priest's school. To learn to read the chimookoman's tracks. That way they can't cheat us with the treaties."

Surprised and taken aback at this, Angeline and Omakayas could only stand still and watch him as he walked swiftly, gracefully, back to his home.

They turned to go, still thoughtful. The sun was warm as summer, and by the time they returned all the snow had melted in the heat. They took the same path back they had taken before, and as they neared the cabin, all of a sudden, Omakayas felt a wet slap and a sharp, stinging blow on the back of her head. It was Pinch. Dancing with gleeful anger, foot to foot, his snowballs so watery only the pebbles are their centers were left in a pile around his feet, he nevertheless insisted on his revenge.

"I said I'd get you and I got you," he yelled. "I'm the warrior, Big Pinch!"

—◦—

Not long after that first bright snow, another snow fell, grayer and heavier. The ice came in. The water had a transparent skim that broke apart and clicked together, then went solid again, until there formed a tough gray coat of ice. Deydey surely had stopped to camp and to wait until the ice was thick before moving on. It snowed steadily and long, three days. While the snow fell outside, Angeline's friend Ten Snow used the red cloth Deydey had brought last summer as trim for a blue tradecloth dress she and Angeline were making. It was a ribbon-trimmed, graceful dress. Mama had trimmed a matching shawl with thimbles, so that when she walked Angeline jingled softly and enticingly.

Every so often now, she was allowed to visit Auntie Muskrat's house. That was the only place she was allowed to visit alone, for Auntie Muskrat kept a strict eye on her. Any young men who visited would have to stand or sit outside on Auntie's log bench while Angeline stayed, dancing foot to foot, inside the cabin, craning out the window, laughing.

The snow fell deeper yet, and in its grip Old Tallow had the best of luck. On the last day it snowed, she dragged from the farthest end of the island two plump beavers. The furs were thick and would fetch a good trade. She roped the beavers onto a little sled tied to another rope that circled her waist. Happily, she brought the meat to Mama and Grandma to prepare. She stayed in the yard, smoking her little pipe, while they made a fire outside to roast the meat over the coals.

Although snow had fallen, Omakayas thought, it couldn't be truly winter until Old Tallow put on her remarkable coat. Every year, the children watched to see that coat emerge—big and shaggy and always different, sewed with new furs, patched with discarded calicos, even velvets. Old Tallow would wear it until the earliest days of spring. But now, even though the cold already bit in the mornings, she wore only her one earth-colored dress with the raveled hem. She even looked a little too warm as she bent near the fire, pulling a burning stick out to relight the new wad of tobacco in her pipe. She leaned back, adjusting her hat, and stared long at Omakayas.

Omakayas looked into the fire. It was her job to keep smoothing and arranging the coals into an even bed for baking the meat, but Tallow's eyes on her back made her itch. Whenever Old Tallow looked at her like that, she could feel those fierce eyes resting on her skin. There was something peculiar in Old Tallow's look. Something different from the way she looked at every other human. It was something familiar, though, and this time as Omakayas glanced back and caught a corner, just a little shred of that look, she suddenly understood.

Old Tallow was looking at her the same way she looked at her dogs!

This was not a bad thing. In fact, it was good in a way, for in Old Tallow's look there was true affection, something she didn't feel for other humans. It made Omakayas feel both strange and safe inside. She smiled to herself and had the odd, sudden, curious knowledge that, if it ever came to that, Old Tallow would protect her, Omakayas, with her life.

She didn't know why she knew that, but she just knew.

Soon, Nokomis came out and took over, poking the coals this way and that to evenly set them. Soon, she would burn a fine crust onto the skin.

Beaver, or amik, was Deydey's favorite meat. He loved the burnt flavor of its fat, and Mama cooked it in a special way. As soon as the meat singed and slightly burnt, she cleaned the beavers, washed their carcasses with salted water and stuffed them with corn and potatoes. She then sewed them shut and roasted them slowly in the big iron kettle. They sizzled in their own fat and the acorns burned black. When the beavers were tender and completely cooked all through, she removed them, undid the meat from the bones, mixed the stuffing with the fried acorns and cooked it all together, in a soup, once again.

The aroma had Old Tallow pacing back and forth hungrily. She looked eager as her dogs, and when Mama ladled the soup into her bowl she bent to it with a savage will. Eating swiftly, Old Tallow put away one bowl and then another while Mama was dishing up the rest of the meal. It was lucky she ate so quickly, though, and put away so much, for just as Pinch was wiping bread, pikwayzhigun, across the bottom of his bowl and opening his mouth to ask for more, there was a stamping and shouting outside. The dogs barked, then stopped when a familiar voice shouted, "Gaygo! Gaygo!"

It was Deydey, come home.

As if summoned across the new ice by his favorite dish, he arrived in time to eat until he could eat no more. That night, the children went upstairs and slept in the loft, and Nokomis slept there, too, instead of downstairs beside Mama. Nokomis made her bed at the farthest end of the loft, where it was coolest. She put her old rabbit-skin blanket down and slept on top of it.

"I sleep hot," she explained to the children.

They didn't like to tell her, but she also slept noisy. Nokomis snored and often talked in her sleep, calling out to people from long ago. That night, Omakayas woke in the dark and listened to her grandmother's soft regular breathing and then her murmur, half under-standable, sometimes arguing and sometimes pleasant as she dreamed old times and went visiting to places that only she remembered.

Biboon

(W I N T E R)

CHAPTER NINE

The Blue Ferns

 NOW FILLED THE world, falling deeper and deeper, changing the island. The cabin was made in the chimookoman way. Deydey was proud of its snug construction, with thick logs fitted together as closely as possible. The heaviest mud he could find, the stickiest clay, Deydey tamped between the logs to seal the cracks. He'd put cross-beams up top and split logs to make a tiny loft where Omakayas, Angeline, and Pinch slept on their woven reed mats placed over tufts of moss.

Grandma still slept at the coldest end of the loft, only now in her thick rabbit-fur blanket. Cold crept along the floor. Omakayas was glad of the boring time she'd spent over the summer pressing fistfuls of gumbo clay, taken from the center of the island, into those places where the dried mud had crumbled. The warmest places in the house were on the sides she had mended best. Cold air sneaked in just where she'd run out of muck and had to use grass. Sometimes, the wind whistled when it entered. That thin whine sent a shiver down her back.

Now that Deydey was home, the cabin changed, too. Filled with his traps and blankets, his big man's coat and head wrap, his moose-hide mitts and traveling kettles, ice chisels, ax, his makazins old again within Mama's embrace, and his new gun secure on pegs over the door, the cabin seemed smaller, cozier, in a way more interesting, Omakayas thought.

And more difficult, too.

People stopped in at any time of day or even in the deep of night, and these visitors required constant attention. Yellow Kettle and Grandma were known as the keepers of a good store of food and a warm fire, although Omakayas, Angeline, and Pinch were the ones responsible for hauling the water for tea and chopping the wood for the fire that burned in the proud little hearth. The fires needed constant vigilance, as did family needs. Deydey's gun required his concentrated care, and he liked tea at his elbow while he cleaned the workings and barrel.

It seemed to Omakayas that every time the grown-ups began to talk, the discussed travel routes west. They argued whether the pressure of so many newcomers was going to send them the way so many others were sent, into the territory of the Bwaanug, the Dakota. There was now constant talk of government intentions, plans to meet in council, invitations to smoke the pipe. At least there were less serious visitors, including Two Strike Girl, Wishkob and Auntie Muskrat, Twilight and Little Bee. Angeline's favorite friend, young Ten Snow, came by to visit almost every day. Albert LaPautre came early to tell his dreams to Deydey, who tried to take them seriously.

"Last night I dreamed my head got stuck in a kettle," he revealed, his voice low and troubled.

"It must have been a very big kettle," Deydey said, solemnly, for LaPautre had a big round head and a full moon face.

"Geget," said LaPautre. He never understood teasing jokes. "It *was* big. Even so, what does it mean?"

"Some dreams are so powerful they are beyond our humble ability to comprehend," said Deydey.

LaPautre leaned back, satisfied. Only Mama caught Deydey's wink.

Even Old Tallow stopped over to eat whatever she was given, often standing outside the door and bolting soup before she hurried off to hunt.

And, yes, she had now donned her coat!

The coat of Old Tallow was a fantastic thing, woven of various pelts, including one of lynx, one of beaver, a deer hide, and two that belonged to beloved dogs. She had pieced together old blankets, one a faded red, one brown. Discarded shreds of unidentifiable stuffs were sewed patch on patch, including some black beaded velvets and bright calicos. The coat fit across her in a great mound, and flapped when she moved. She wore it well, springing lightly along like a huge, tattered bear.

No cold seemed to bother Old Tallow, but if it was too biting a day to walk outside or slide on the ice, Ten Snow and Angeline sat in the corner of the cabin on bedrolls and piles of skins. There, light from the window of thick oiled paper falling golden on their faces, the two young women sewed and talked. Ten Snow had finished something very impressive, much admired by the other women, including Grandma, who took it in her hands and blessed it one cold day. It was a bag for Fishtail, a fashionable bandolier bag. Instead of the dyed quills Grandma used so skillfully, Ten Snow had sewn the bag with trade beads bought in precious pack-

ets at the company store. The bag was covered with four beaver-skins' worth of white beads—they were expensive! Fishtail's square bag was beaded all over in swirls of green vines, leaves, and glowing crimson flowers that popped out vividly against the white beads of the backround. The shoulder strap, too, was entirely beaded. The strap's design was simple, unusual, and consisted of blue curls that Ten Snow bashfully explained were the uncoiled heads of new spring ferns, her husband's favorite food. Looking at it, Omakayas had to blink her eyes, for the beads were so perfect and the repeated pattern so compelling that the ferns seemed to move like little waves.

"Will you teach me how to bead that pattern?" Angeline asked her friend.

"Ayah!" Ten Snow removed from her little sewing kit a needle, and Angeline took out her own work, her own beads, bought with dried whitefish. They began.

"Gayay neen," said Omakayas, "me, too!" Ten Snow smiled gently, and Angeline looked at her little sister in surprise.

"You?" She grinned. "Little Frog, little jumper, can you sit still that long?"

Stung by her sister's amused tone of voice, Omakayas dropped her head to her chest, eyes squinting narrow. A huge space opened up in her head, black and rushing as a freezing winter stream. She was old enough to tan the stinking old hides, wasn't she? Her work was valued there, wasn't it? Why shouldn't she be trusted to use the precious beads? She was eight winters now! She wasn't that little! She could chop wood, haul the water from the hole Nokomis kept open in the ice with an ax and a long, sharp pole. Why couldn't she bead like the older girls?

Angeline laughed out loud. Omakayas turned away. Her heart shrunk cold in her chest, tiny but heavy as a lake rock. How her sister's words could stab her sometimes! But now, as though she hadn't noticed Angeline's remark at all, Ten Snow's hand was stroking Omakayas's arm and she was speaking.

"Sssshhhh, ishte, Little Sister, I made something for you."

Into Omakayas's hands she placed a small leather packet. Omakayas looked up at Ten Snow, uncertain.

"Yes, for you." Ten Snow gestured for her to open it and slowly, with unbelieving delight, Omakayas did. The leather packet was lined with broadcloth and into the cloth two needles were stuck. Two! Around a peeled twig Ten Snow had wound a long length of the finest sinew thread to use in beading. At the end of the cloth, a small pocket held a lump of fragrant, summery yellow bees-wax to use in strengthening the sinew thread. And best of all, she saw, as Ten Snow lifted up the dark blue strip of cloth, there was a tiny sack of all colors of beads, seed beads, the little grown-up kind of beads, shining and gleaming against the cloth.

Manidominenz, they were called. Little spirit seeds.

"Megwetch, megwetch, megwetch!" Omakayas thanked Ten Snow over and over again until the older girl couldn't help smiling. The youngest of her family, Ten Snow had no little sisters and, as yet, no children. So she was extra-kind to Omakayas. As the older girls returned to their work and their talk, Omakayas curled near the fire to look at her beads and to imagine what she would make with them. At first, she thought that she might bead some tiny makazins for her dolls. Then she thought Angeline might make fun of her project. Mama, something for Mama? She had so many quilled things, and preferred them. Besides, Grandma was always making a box or an ornament for her. How about for Grandma, for Deydey, for Angeline? Certainly not for Pinch, who would spoil anything he got. Or Neewo, who might chew off the beads.

Neewo. Suddenly she knew, as though the beads told her themselves, that they were meant for her little brother. Omakayas would make something very special for him—she saw what she would make coming clear. Makazins! Warm makazins, trimmed with rabbit fur. In her mind, she planned them out, sewn from scraps of moosehide that were left over from the summer. She saw them with white flowers beaded on the ankles, woolen balls of blanket thread to decorate the cuffs. Admiring her idea, gloating, planning, Omakayas turned the leather sewing kit and bead packet over and over in her hands.

Mama and Grandma set their work out on blankets before them. Grandma was completing the edge of a great round box of birchbark, one that she would use to store her red willow kinnikinnick. She was binding the edges with strips of basswood bark and sinew. She had cut fancy shapes of stars out to sew on the sides. Mama had set aside Deydey's fancy moose-hide coat jacket in order to finish Angeline's fine clothing to wear at the gathering dance that would be held as soon as a few more families had set up their winter households.

Grandma, meanwhile, had finished a beautiful dance fan made of a partridge tail. Its handle was birch-bark, bound tightly, quilled with sweet flowers.

The thimbles that Mama was sewing onto Ange-line's shawl caught orange sparks of fire as Mama worked each one onto the wide strip of ribbon. First she punched a little hole in the tip of the thimble with her awl, then she threaded a bit of red cord through, knotted the end well inside the thimble, and sewed the end of the cord underneath the ribbon so it didn't show. As soon as she took the last stitch, Angeline clapped her hands.

"Let me try it on!" cried Angeline, impatiently.

Laughing, Mama handed it to her, and beautiful Angeline wrapped herself in its fine swirl. Grandma handed her the dance fan. Everyone admired.

"Mama," said Omakayas, "can you help me now?"

"Ayah, geget," Mama said.

They left off looking at Angeline, and started work on Neewo's makazins. From the moose hide left over from Deydey's makazins, Mama helped Omakayas cut out a pair of makazins for Neewo, winter makazins with cuffs well up his legs for warmth. Omakayas planned out a flower and began immediately, imitating Mama, to sew the beads into the design. It was harder, more exacting work than she thought. The sinew tangled and knotted. Beads bounced off the needle's tip. Even when she fastened the beads on, sometimes they looked odd or crooked, and she had to take them off. She put her needle down. Tears of frustration stung.

"Don't give up." It was Angeline, her voice gentle, kind. "You are doing very well, neshemay, little sister."

Omakayas looked at her big sister in surprise, then gratitude. Nothing felt as good as this unexpected kindness from Angeline. She wiped her tears away, and took up her beadwork again.

Neewo was napping in his little blanket hammock just above them. Deydey had tied two ropes into holes in the wooden beams, and between the two he'd fastened a warm blanket into a hammock. Mama could rock Neewo by moving her foot, tied to one of the ropes, or Omakayas could swing him by moving the other end of a rope.

The sky darkened. Pinch was sent out to bring wood. He made a face at Omakayas, for with her bead-work she was set apart, another of the women, and Pinch was left to fetch wood all by himself. Deydey and Fishtail sat in the corner, talking low and thoughtfully, drinking Grandma's tea. Soon they got up and left, for they had decided to try their luck with the fishing nets let down through big holes chopped in the ice. They went out the door, talking louder the minute they were outside. There was a little space of quiet around the women, all together. The time seemed just right to ask Nokomis for a story.

"Weendamawashin, daga, Nokomis," Omakayas asked. "Tell me a story."

"What story do you want to hear?"

"Windigo!" said Pinch, returning, his arms stacked with wood.

"Are you sure you want to hear it?" Nokomis growled deep in her chest, showed her sharp teeth.

"Owah!" Pinch's eyes rounded, but his grin was full

of excitement. He inched closer to Nokomis and tried to shush baby Neewo, who had awakened. Neewo could wiggle out of his cradleboard now, at last, and was learning to walk. He pulled himself along by grasping shoulders, clothes, hair, anything to keep upright. When eventually he plumped down, he showed his pleasure by trying to bang his stick doll to pieces against the side of the hearth.

"Gaygo," Omakayas said, but her voice was gentle as she showed Neewo how to dance the doll instead of break it.

"Pinch!"

From outside, the men were calling him. The big men! He clattered down the wood, jumped to his feet, and ran out the door. Being called by the men was better than a story, even a windigo story, any old day.

Once again, the women and Neewo were left alone.

"Now," Nokomis said, "I can tell you an old story about my grandmother." She looked tellingly at Mama. "You know the one."

"Geget," said Mama, only half-teasingly. "Do you think they're old enough to hear it?"

"I was eight winters old when it happened," said Grandma. "Same as Omakayas now."

"Then tell it," Omakayas begged.

"Yes, tell it," said Angeline.

Ten Snow put down her work for a moment to beg, laughingly, along with everyone else.

GRANDMA'S STORY

◄○►

Fishing the Dark Side
of the Lake

When I was just a little girl, said Nokomis, her voice lilting high, and dropping low, her voice far away, I was told by my grandfather, who I lived with, who raised me, never to fish the dark side of the lake.

Why, you wonder? I never knew that either. Never found out until, of course, being a young girl and very curious, I took my grandfather's canoe out one day while he was sleeping. I put my fishing spear and nets in the canoe. I would fish where the water was deepest, strangest, bluest on clear days and blackest on the cloudy days. That's where I paddled. I had a stick and line. I let that down, baited, and I waited to see what sort of fish I would catch.

The wait was long, my grandchildren, and as I fished there I grew uneasy. I remembered my grandfa-

ther's warnings, the way he insisted that I was never to approach this deep water. I'd seen him looking out there, sometimes at sunset, his eyes sad and clear. Sometimes he mentioned my grandmother. She had gone away young, I knew that. Not much more. Her favorite food, he said, was fresh plums. She could stand beneath a plum tree and eat all day, he said. When he said that, he smiled.

Fresh wild plums. I had taken dark red plums with me. As I sat in the boat waiting for the fish to bite, I put them slowly, one by one, into my mouth. What was wrong with this side of the lake? I had to wonder. Except for the depth and darkness, it wasn't much different. I would find out what was different, I decided. I kept my line in the water.

My bait must have been wrong, though. My bait must have been no good. I didn't get a bite, even a little nibble. Maybe, I thought, Grandfather told me not to fish this dark side of the lake because no fish lived here! That would be a joke on me! Just then, I looked over the side of the boat and I spilled all the rest of my plums into the water. Saaa! I was disgusted. Down they went, to the bottom. Not long after they sank from sight, though, I had a strong tug on my line. Then not just a tug, a real pull. Soon I was struggling to keep from being dragged overboard. I had caught something. Something very huge!

A hand reached out of the water! Pulled itself up my fishing line, finger over finger, fist over fist, until suddenly the beautiful face of a woman appeared. She looked up at me and kept climbing.

"Do you have more plums?" she asked.

I said no, but I helped her into the boat anyway. Her hair was black and endlessly long, covering her, and underneath it she was naked. Her smile was gentle. Her skin was purple, gray, cold, the color of those plums. There was something familiar about her, something awful and yet familiar. I was very much afraid and began to paddle quickly back to Grandfather. Still, I was a curious child.

"Who are you?" I asked as we traveled along.

"I am your grandmother," she said, "here's what happened. Long ago, I married your grandfather. We could not be parted. We were like one person, he and I. He was stingy with me. After I bore our first child and lay her in his arms, after she grew for a year, I became my daring self again. I became again the wild girl he'd loved from the beginning. One night, I dared him to swim with me in the lake. We went out in our canoe to the deepest part of the lake, the darkest and the coldest side, where you have found me. We threw off our clothing. I dived in deep as I could, pulled my way down, down, until I reached the bottom.

"My dear grandchild, that's when I got lost. It was so dark down at the bottom that I got turned around. I could not find my way back up again, and so, tired, I curled up in the cold weeds and I went to sleep. Until now."

My grandmother looked toward the shore. Her face glowed in the twilight. I saw, as we approached, that she was watching my grandfather as he came down the path from the camp to the edge of the lake. He walked closer, closer. Something strange happened. I rubbed my eyes. I passed my hand across my face.

I could not believe what I was seeing.

As he approached, my grandfather's step seemed to pick up life. His hair got darker and darker until it turned the pure black of his youth. Lines disappeared from his face. He straightened his bowed back. Just as our canoe touched the shore, he smiled. And oh, my grandchildren, suddenly he had all of his teeth!

I got out of the canoe. He looked upon me kindly,

said good-bye to me, and then he took my place in the canoe with his young wife. The two gazed into each other's faces with great happiness. I watched the two paddle away together, into the darkness, into the night. Two shooting stars passed over through the sky. The lake was silent. I never again saw my grandfather, but eventually his clothing was found on the shore, washed up on the dark side of the lake.

—◄o►—

When Nokomis finished, no word was spoken. Omakayas could say nothing because stiff hairs prickled at the back of her neck. She couldn't get the sight of that hand, reaching out of the water, from her mind! Ten Snow and Angeline were wiping tears from their eyes. Mama sighed and continued her work, slowly, carefully, on Angeline's shawl. Perhaps she was thinking of the big gathering, where Angeline might meet someone and go away with him, far from her mother's gaze. Although she didn't want that to happen, it was inevitable, and Yellow Kettle's fond look said all that was in her heart. How deeply she loved her children. How dear they were to her, the center of her life. Being naturally cheerful and bold, though, she soon grinned and joked. Yellow Kettle could not help turning the mood her way and soon everyone was laughing over Neewo's tumbling and Andeg's playful squawks as Neewo followed him, grabbed for him. Andeg knew how to stay just out of reach of those chubby, curious fingers!

The Visitor

 FIRE WAS KINDLED in the center of the dance lodge, and its fragrant smoke rose through the central opening in the roof. The fire was hardly needed though, in spite of the cold, for the crowd of dancers, the drummers, the children, the old men in the farthest corner gambling, seated on soft skins, the old ladies at their games and gossip, the young women in the center and the young men surrounding them, the people of all ages talking, laughing, and dancing, kept the great lodge warm.

Omakayas loved the drum. The beat throbbed through her, drumming her entirely alive and eager. The soles of her feet tingled. Her hands moved in time to the song. Angeline danced, too, wearing her new shawl and holding Grandma's partridge-tail fan. Standing at the center with Ten Snow, she gracefully bounced to the beat. Thimbles ringing, her body moved in exact time. Mama, when she was only known as that swift girl Yellow Kettle and had no children, had always loved to dance. She bobbed in the corner, contented and proud of her daughters, Neewo alongside her. Even Nokomis couldn't help dancing. Omakayas stopped to watch her grandmother step along with such care and dignity she seemed to be crossing a rushing stream on small stones. Her steps were small and light as a deer's, Omakayas thought, watching her proudly.

Heat radiated from the fire, and the faces of the girls and young women turned rosy-red and warm. Trade silver tokens, bracelets, armbands, crosses flashed and ribbons swirled as the dancers moved in joy and excitement, crying out for another song as soon as each was done. The drum intensified, the laughter turned ever more hilarious. The old men won and lost in their makazin gambling game, and the children wove in and out of the movement, hiding from one another, tagging around the side of a parent, teasing and sometimes dancing, too. Around the middle of the night, everybody stopped to partake of the feast—a big kettle of venison and corn soup was brought in by the fire and children were sent back to houses and lodges for birchbark makuks and tin bowls.

While they were eating, teasing, commenting on the soup, flavored with low-growing juniper berries and parched hot summer corn, something happened that disturbed everyone and changed the course of the winter. Indeed, what happened changed the way Omakayas and her family lived from then on. A visitor entered. He and his voyageur crew had just dragged their sled of furs across from the mainland, and were staying for the night. Thinking back, Omakayas could even remember him, sitting by the fire as close as he could without scorching, a tired-looking man, thin and scraggly braids, coughing and feeble. A bit confused-looking. A flushed, fevered face. It was hearing of his death in hushed tones, though, the next day, that she would always recall. The report of it. For the horror flooded swiftly from house to house, lodge to lodge.

He died of smallpox.

Although the visitor's body was taken to the farthest end of the island, although everything he'd touched was burned, including the lodge he'd stayed in and the blankets he wore, although the generous family who let him in purified themselves in the sweat lodge, burned all of their belongings, and threw themselves upon the mercy of the mission, fear abounded in the settlement. Had the visitor left another, more horrible visitor behind? Sickness? Death?

Angeline's face was taut with worry. She knew that her kind Ten Snow, noticing the stranger's discomfort, had put her own bowl, filled with soup, into his hands. She then brought that bowl back to the lodge she shared with Fishtail, and although that bark onagun was thrown far away and buried now in snow, there was no knowing whether it would bring down the disease and its evils.

During the next few days everyone watched carefully for any signs of the sickness. And signs soon came. Ten Snow was the first to fall into a fever, and then those in the lodge where the sick man had stayed fell ill, one after the next. The entire family down to the oldest grandfather and the tiniest baby suffered in the helpless hands of missionaries, who closed the school and kept them fed and warm on the floors of the building, just below the blackboard where Fishtail had finally learned to write his chimookoman name.

Six days later, just when Mama and Nokomis were hoping that the scratching sickness had passed them over, Angeline did not rise from her blankets. Overnight, the fever had seized her and she lay hot and stifled, face red, eyes wild with fear when Mama came up to check on her. Omakayas came, too, behind Mama, but with a stern look Mama sent her back down the ladder.

"Take care of Pinch and Neewo. Keep them downstairs," she ordered. Her voice, as she called Deydey and looked over the edge of the loft, was calm with despair.

"Build a bark lodge outside, good and warm," she instructed. "Nokomis will take care of the children. You stay out there, too."

And so, by the end of the day, the little family was divided. Inside the house, supplied with firewood and water, Mama and Angeline battled the invisible enemy. Outside, the others slept heavily and fearfully in the lodge made from rolls of bark saved in the lean-to. Neewo curled with Omakayas around the tiny lodge fire. Pinch huddled next to Nokomis. Deydey slept alone.

On the third day, the evil day, Mama did not appear at the door to bring in the water Deydey fetched. Nokomis went in and did not return for a long time. When she did show her face, she called from the doorway to Deydey.

"My daughter has the sickness along with Angeline. Keep the children warm. Feed them good."

She then disappeared into the cabin, and Deydey

spent the day chopping wood, hauling water, hunting, and talking to Old Tallow, who had come near in grim worry. The two sat hunched over the fire for a long while, drinking cups of strong swamp tea. Finally, Tallow lifted her gun, looped her rabbit snares around her wrists and set out to hunt, now with more urgency than ever. On the eighth day, Pinch fell sick and was moved into the cabin where Nokomis took care of them all. Outside, Deydey worked continually, emptying pots from inside and chopping holes in ice, fishing to keep them strong, making sure the water in their kettle was always fresh and clear, their wood piled high.

Higher. Higher.

"Why are you continuing to pile up the wood?" Omakayas asked him, fearful, watching how he sweated and labored at the woodpile. "Rest, Deydey," she begged, in fear at his fixed and set face, his deep eyes. He gave her a look of annoyance, as though from far away, and then, seeing that she offered him a cup of rabbit soup, seeing that her face was chilled with terror for him, he softened.

"Gaween, my little frog," he said, pausing, his voice unusually gentle. "I cannot stop. I want to get a lot of wood ahead so I can take a little rest, eh?"

He smiled at her, but his smile was weary. The

gentle exhaustion in his voice terrified her more than anything that had happened so far. That night she lay sleepless, gazing at the flickering of the flames on the ceiling, wondering what was happening inside the cabin, listening to her father's even breathing and Neewo's tiny, rumbling snore. It was as though the sickness was sucking first one, then the next, and the next, into the cabin—where they disappeared and did not emerge. How could Nokomis care for them all? What if Deydey got sick, too? Somehow, it never occurred to her that she or Neewo could sicken. Deydey was the one she watched carefully. Not Neewo. It was as though her little brother were part of her, she kept him so near. She didn't understand at all when Neewo fell ill.

Or maybe she couldn't let the fact in, because she just loved her little brother so much. Maybe that.

It happened in the night, as she held him close. Omakayas felt his small body turn heated and molten, soft and fiery with the fever's rage. He was red, quiet, and limp in her arms when Deydey woke, and Omakayas held him close, gently bathed his face with a bit of snow, hoping that he would grin at her, hoping that again he would be healthy and sweet. She didn't want the house, the sickness, to suck him in, too. It couldn't! She wouldn't let it! But as soon as she dozed off, Deydey lifted little Neewo away. She woke immediately, crawled to the door of the lodge, and then, as Deydey walked toward the silent cabin with the tiniest thread of smoke coming from the chimney, Omakayas saw him stagger. He didn't fall, but she knew from that misstep that Deydey was ill, that he'd hidden his sickness, and that he was going into the cabin with Neewo, never to return.

Omakayas acted without hesitation. She put out the little fire in the birchbark house.

If they were all to die together, then let it be so. She would not stay outside alone and away from those she loved, no, not even if it meant her life. She followed Neewo inside.

◄○►

The air in the cabin was thick with the stink of disease, but the hearth was warm. Nokomis had the sick ones arranged in their bedding, blankets pulled neatly up to their chins, mats clean on the floor all around the fire. Although Nokomis sat next to Mama in a stupor of exhaustion and did not at first speak to Omakayas, she nodded encouragingly at Angeline, who slept easily now, her fever broken, her hands limp on her blanket. Omakayas crouched beside her. That's when she saw that the beautiful face of her sister was covered with ugly sores and vivid lumps, and her mouth, when she opened it to breathe, showed that her gums bled painfully and stained her teeth red. Her hair was caught in a thick mat, but she was alive. Her breath moved steadily, in and out.

Mama slept, also covered with sores, unconscious and still in the depth of her danger. Pinch kept tossing off his covers or dragging at Mama's. With a weary, loving, unthinking movement that showed she had done this thousands of times before, Nokomis replaced the blankets. Held a tin cup of water to Pinch's lips. Trickled a little water between Mama's lips, then Angeline's. Deydey, slumped over by the fire, she did not disturb except to lower him to the earth. Motioning to Omakayas, she indicated Neewo, who was trembling now, his tiny arms and legs moving jerkily as the heat in his body increased, and increased, until he had not the strength to even cry.

"Keep holding him," said Nokomis tenderly, giving Neewo to Omakayas, seating them by the fire. She placed her dry, old, cool hand on the back of Omakayas's head. "Just keep holding him," she said again.

And so Omakayas did. She held Neewo through the night, dozing with him, waking when he thrashed, cleaning him, bathing with cool water his forehead and his tiny, straining, bony chest. His clenched hands and his beautiful feet. She held him when he melted into a troubled sleep. When his breath rasped. When his cough deepened. When he cried and cried until his voice was gone. She held him when he grew still and quiet, too quiet. When his fever came back.

One day passed, another blurred, and still she held her little brother. Held him close in her arms. She held him as he looked mysteriously into her face, his eyes huge. She held him when he spat up blood. When he whimpered for Andeg, who sat high up in the roof beams, head underneath his wing. She held him through another night, held him when his chest went drum-tight and he struggled for breath. Held him when he drew that breath, deep from the heart.

She held him when he died.

She held him close. She didn't know exactly when his life went except that Andeg croaked three times, longingly, as though for his playmate. Then, Omakayas knew that something had changed. Her little brother's body no longer warmed her with its heat, they were the same temperature and then he was colder. Still, she did not let him go. Nokomis had to take him from her arms, and when she did Omakayas fell down on the blanket, arms still held in the cradle shape of her brother, and knew nothing all that day.

It was night when she woke.

Opening her eyes, she knew at once what had happened and the bleak knowledge made her shut her eyes again. Maybe, almost, she wished that she were sick, too, that she could join him. For Nokomis had said that the Ojibwa must walk a path that leads out of this life into the next, and since Neewo couldn't walk very well yet, who would carry him when he got tired, when he fell? Who would make sure he was fed in the other world? Who would make him toy man dolls to dance? Who would care for him when he was lost?

The answer, once she had risen, once she began working with Nokomis to care for her family, was a sad answer. Old Tallow brought the news later that day. She set four snared rabbits down near the door, then waited to speak.

"Ten Snow is gone," she said.

On the road to the next world, surely, she and Neewo would meet, thought Omakayas, tears blinding her as she tipped water to her father's lips. Surely Ten Snow would take hold of Neewo's hand, swing him up in her arms, carry him along past the rough spots and danger, to the place where they would be safe.

Old Tallow took the horn spoon from Omakayas and ordered her to lie down, to sleep. She made Nokomis lie down as well in the corner, with her grandchild.

"You two rest now! Go on or I'll take a stick to you!" Her voice was fierce, rasping, angry, and strong. Nokomis obeyed her, sank into the skins, slept before her head touched the back of her blanket.

Omakayas was glad to do the same.

Old Tallow then proceeded to work. She built up the fire, high, to a greater heat than Nokomis had dared, for she knew she could chop more wood as needed. She brought a new kettle of water in, skinned her rabbits by the light of the fire and boiled them for a nourishing soup. She cleaned every corner, the way she never cleaned her own house. She left her dogs to run wild and tended every need, cared for the humans she loved and, although she never would admit it, loved even more than she loved her dogs.

Old Tallow's work helped them, but the next day she left once more to hunt. Nokomis weakened, though she wasn't ill. Omakayas alone was left to tend to the sick ones. She had to keep the fire going, haul the water, cover them, bathe them down, comfort them when they were restless. She hardly slept an hour at a time. First one needed her, then the other. Then a third, the first again. There was no stopping. Their cries were pitiful.

When the terrible itching that gave the disease its

name started, Omakayas wrapped their hands with cloth, bit down their fingernails, anything to keep them from scarring themselves. The itching nearly drove them from their minds. Pinch was worst, and he'd weakened so badly that Nokomis was afraid for him. Night and day, one or the other sat with him and did not let go of his hand for fear he would run to the land of the spirits. Even Andeg seemed to sense how close Pinch was to death. Andeg perched near Pinch, as though keeping guard. Every time Pinch slipped too far away the bird croaked, "Gaygo, Pinch!" One stubborn eye flared open and Pinch fixed his annoyed little boy glare upon the bird. He was mad, but he got well. "Gaygo Pinch! Gaygo! Gaygo!" called Andeg. What he really meant was *Don't go! Stay here!*

One night, Omakayas woke to see Deydey trying to rise to his feet. In the dim light of a low fire, she saw him throw off his blankets. He tried to stagger outside. She knew that was certain death. Many died of this sickness when they became so fevered that they lost their minds, threw off blankets, and walked outside to freeze.

"Please, Deydey," she said, to draw him back.

He sank onto all fours, but kept crawling determinedly toward the door, groaning, hair wild. His eyes did not know her and his face was frightful. He clawed

at the door, fell to his knees. Got up on his knees. This
time, he was so determined that Omakayas knew there
was no way she could save him from going outside. He
was too strong for her, even in his sickness.

"Gaween onjidah," she said, "I'm sorry."

Raising a block of wood high, she brought it down
on his head with all of her strength. He crumpled to the
ground. Omakayas sobbed as she dragged his blankets to
him and covered him. He was too heavy to drag near the
fire. For a long time she kneeled next to him, praying for
him to live. She loved him, her Deydey. What would they
do without him? Back in her own blankets, she immediately sank into a fierce oblivion. When she woke, it was
morning. Instantly, she remembered the night before.

Was her father dead? Had her blow killed him? Fear gripped her as she crept to his side, put her hand to his lips. His breath came evenly. He seemed a little better, even, than the day before. As the morning went on he sipped broth for the first time. Opened his eyes.

"My little frog." He smiled, closing his eyes again, this time to sleep comfortably. "You could bring down a bear with the strength in your club." His fever was broken at last.

Omakayas's constant attention brought the little family through the first part of the illness's danger. One by one, they improved, all because of her careful nursing. Later, it was the vaccine of the Reverend Hall, fetched from the mainland, that guarded the rest of the Ojibwa who had been exposed and who survived the smallpox of 1847. Eighteen Ojibwa died of the disease, and one tried to kill himself by other means.

That man was Fishtail. No one had understood it of him, but his wife was everything. When Ten Snow left him, Fishtail would not leave her body. He slashed his arms and was found in the blanket beside her, half alive. He survived. But once he had the strength, he cut off his long, thick, splendid hair. He buried it with the sweet woman who was called Ten Snow not because her own skin was white, nor because she had much of anything to do with snow at all, but because the kind assurance of her nature had reminded her namers of the way the deep snow covers and forgives all it touches when it falls.

◄○►

In the deep of winter, Neewo and Ten Snow were buried side by side. A great bonfire was lighted in order to thaw the ground. Neewo and Ten Snow were wrapped in red blankets, then birchbark, and at last laid gently into their good mother, Akeeng, the earth. As soon as Deydey was better, he and Fishtail worked side by side constructing the grave houses for their loved ones. At the western end of each little house, they carefully framed a small windowlike opening, and built beneath it a shelf for spirit offerings. Although food was scarce, Mama often brought Neewo a little something saved from her own bowl and placed it on the shelf with tobacco.

She stayed long in the cold, wrapped in her blanket, praying for her little boy. At the burying ground, there were many new graves. The winter was hard. As she sat talking to her child's spirit, someone else almost always came near, added their tobacco, said a few words of comfort, and passed on to their own grieving.

Omakayas got sick, too, but not with the smallpox.

A wholly different fever followed upon her family's recovery, an illness of weakness and grief. Even as her mother strengthened and her father got better and became more and more himself, Omakayas retreated from the world. She ate less and less, thought long into the night. Often, in her mind's eye, she saw Neewo's tiny makazins, forlorn in the firelight, as they sagged, tipped over when in his fever he kicked them off. He never wore them again in his short life.

Her brother Pinch, however, more than recovered. From the loft, she could hear him downstairs, ruder and louder than ever. She heard her bird, Andeg, scratching on the floor. She heard Old Tallow come and go. She heard her grandmother, singing an old song as she stirred something fragrant in the kettle. Gently Mama called her from the base of the ladder. She heard this, but Omakayas kept her eyes closed.

Food did not interest her. All she did was think of Neewo. She considered what she could have done to arrest the illness. Fed him more soup? Forced him to keep his makazins warm on his feet? Taken him out, away, into the woods? There lived alone with him until the smallpox had run its course? And Mama, Omakayas worried about her, too. She was so quiet and thin, so restrained. When she sat, she didn't just sit still, it was like she turned to stone. In her eyes there was such a deep and penetrating look of loss that Omakayas could not bear to see her at all. Angeline was some comfort, though still weak. She kept badgering Old Tallow to bring her a mirror, but the old woman refused until one day Angeline screamed at her, shockingly, that she wanted to see herself. "Am I so bad-looking?" she yelled in rage. "Am I so ugly now?"

"Gaween," said Old Tallow, very slowly, the lines in her face shadowing, "you are still beautiful."

Omakayas, lying next to her sister, closed her eyes in pain. The smallpox had left Angeline's cheeks pitted with scars and slightly twisted Angeline's perfect hunting bow of a dark mouth. The smallpox had thinned her face until her teeth stuck out. The smallpox, worst of all, had killed Angeline's tiny brother and the friend of her heart, Ten Snow. Pain and loss showed in deep furrows around her sister's mouth.

The mirror came, a scrap of it anyway, and Angeline stared into it. Slowly, her eyes filled. When she had seen enough, she put the mirror down gently, turned away, and refused for a long time to speak.

—◄O►—

It was difficult for Omakayas to understand all that had happened. Why Neewo was gone, though at night she still imagined that she heard his cries. Why her sister's face would never again be smooth. Why she herself was still too weak to run and crept back to her sleeping blanket whenever she could. She slept and slept as though she would never wake. She didn't want to think about the things that had happened, but there were times that questions came to her, occurring in the deep of night, sometimes even in dreams.

The spirits, the manitous who lived in all things, why had they ignored her prayers, her mother's prayers, and the powerful prayers of Nokomis? Why had Deydey's strength not helped? And her grandmother's medicine, so useful at other times, why hadn't it worked for Neewo? Nokomis said, sorrowfully, that she had no medicines for this white man's disease. But Omakayas did not have smallpox. Omakayas had something else. Why didn't the strong tea made of bitter bark, the tea that Nokomis brewed for Omakayas, send her jumping up lively as she used to be?

Sometimes she thought that if only her mother would laugh, she also would begin to feel better. But

Yellow Kettle was dull and angry with sorrow, and couldn't help her own daughter. Day after day passed, and Nokomis's teas grew more bitter. She made a stronger concoction, burned sweetgrass braids, fanned Omakayas, too, but the deep cold seemed to have seized her heart. She was ashamed of the way she thought sometimes, up in her blanket. Listening to Pinch, her annoying brother, who didn't seem sad at all, she wondered why Neewo was taken and Pinch left behind. Why was Neewo taken to the next world and *she* left behind? There was no explanation that satisfied her. Nothing that gave her the hope she needed to rise and take up the rest of her life. Not even when Angeline bravely smashed the little piece of mirror one day and left the cabin, walking out the door, determined to go to the missionary school and learn the meaning of the white man's writing, like Fishtail, not even then was Omakayas inspired to come downstairs.

Nokomis sat with her, quilling, through the whole day sometimes. She told her old stories, adventures of Nanabozho, the tricky and generous teacher of the Anishinabeg, who cleverly outwitted dangerous foes and taught the Anishinabeg to survive. Omakayas listened, but did not find in the stories the will to go forward. Could Nanabozho have outwitted smallpox? Could

Nanabozho push back the dreadful day, send home the awful visitor who had taken Neewo and Ten Snow? Could Nanabozho at least say a word or two in his own defense, or encourage Omakayas to go on with her life? Nothing happened. No voices explained things. Her dreams were blank.

One day, however, Old Tallow unexpectedly appeared at the top of the ladder. In her rough, steady hand she held a bark container of rabbit soup boiled up with potatoes from the storage cache. "Eat this," she urged Omakayas. "Or else!" she threatened when Omakayas was reluctant. After Omakayas had taken the first taste, Tallow insisted that she drink until she couldn't fit in another drop.

"Ah, there," said Tallow, approvingly. "You need to get your strength back."

Omakayas nodded and closed her eyes.

"Don't sleep now," said Tallow gruffly, "the sky is clear. Your brother is sliding on the lake. Go out. Be childish."

Omakayas kept her eyes closed and lengthened her breath, hoping that Old Tallow would believe that she had fallen asleep. After a while, the old woman fell silent, though she continued to sit near Omakayas, pondering what she should do next. Of course, she was suspicious.

Omakayas felt Tallow's gaze locked on her. After all, she was a hunter used to waiting at the dens of animals. If anyone could find a way to surprise Omakayas back to life, it would be her. Omakayas determined to outwait her, to crawl deeper and deeper into her dark burrow of sleep. Eventually, as though from far away, Omakayas felt the tentative brush of Tallow's tough, creased palm, and heard the rustle of her clothes as she got up and quietly left.

At first, Omakayas tried to think she had won, that she had outwitted Old Tallow and made her impatient, as even the wariest animals often failed to do. But then the time stretched long. Omakayas couldn't sleep. Her feet tingled to run. Energy from the rabbit soup flowed through her and she drummed her fingers against the floor. She was stubborn, shut her eyes. Who was fooling whom? she wondered. The sun was shining brilliantly outside. Had she really bested Old Tallow, and at whose expense? None other than her own. With a sigh, Omakayas got up. She went out. For the first time since the illness, she felt the sun on her face, but even its promise of warmth did not make her smile.

Hunger

 EATH, THE VISITOR, had stayed long that year and taken many Anishinabeg to the next world. Those left behind had the task of going on with life even as the harshest snow fell, the bitter cold deepened, the game hid, and the fish sank deeper into the lake. Now, as Omakayas began to gain a little strength, she wished heartily to eat and craved any sort of food at all. But there was only enough cornmeal in the morning for a few mouthfuls of mush, only enough wild rice for a handful each during the day. The family scrounged a potato, sometimes a bit of bannock. No meat once the fish and dried venison from the meat cache were gone.

Omakayas was strong enough to bring in wood, though she trembled as she walked. Mama improved slowly, too; at least she got stronger physically. Her face remained unchanging and sad, and her eyes remained haunted by the sorrow of Neewo's loss.

◄o►

Deydey was recovering so slowly that he didn't have the strength to hunt. Though he tried to fish, he hadn't much luck and could not stand the cold for long. He had to borrow against next year's furs. The family ran up a bill at the traders, bought expensive salt pork.

One day, he notched his counting stick and spoke to Omakayas.

"Cadotte will have all of next year's furs by the time this winter is finished," he said, "unless some game throws itself at us! Or unless I get Cadotte another way."

His eyes flashed and the shadow of a grin twisted on his face, the intrigue of the old Deydey who'd never been sick.

"Bring me the chess game," he said to Omakayas.

She knew just where it was, that precious set that had belonged to Deydey's grandfather, the man who had taught him this chimookoman game. The chess set was always reverently kept in its own blanket, hidden in a corner of the room with the medicine bags and Deydey's ceremonial clothes. Wrapped in red cloth, it was considered something very special. Every few days, Deydey took it out to play solitary games and try to teach the strategies to others. Carefully, now, she bore it in her arms to Deydey.

He took the chess set, and there before the fire he arranged the pieces in their special order. The pieces were hand-carved of maple, finely grained. The queen, or ogema, wore a small pointed hat. Omakayas liked the horse, its neck curved and strong. The pawns were little round-headed people. The bishop looked just like Father Baraga, the priest who walked miles in his snowshoes to baptize, stealing souls from the other mission and also from the manitous. The little towers at the ends, those that moved so honestly and directly, were Omakayas's favorite pieces.

The two began to play. Deydey usually beat her in short time, but today she managed through desperate measures to think ahead far enough to draw the game out to a phenomenal length.

"Geget chi wohningeyz," said Deydey, approvingly. "Good job! My girl, maybe you should be the one to play Cadotte."

Deydey's compliments were so rare that when he

gave them Omakayas at first didn't absorb what she'd heard. It took until later, lying curled in her blanket, for the warmth that his approval gave her to sink into place around her heart, warming her as she fell into a good sleep.

The next day, Deydey took the chess board and headed to the trader's to play for supplies. He did not allow his family to come and watch him, for those who gathered were often rough: layarounds, drinkers, wintering voyageurs who idled their time with gambling and trader's rum. Fishtail and LaPautre were there, however, and it was from LaPautre's daughter Twilight that the girls heard the details of the game.

As Twilight told it, Deydey had walked in humbly, played poorly at first, causing the trader to raise the stakes. Then Deydey dragged the game out awkwardly until Cadotte thought he was unbeatable. Cadotte was sure that he was going to win, and felt confident enough to agree, laughingly, to cancel part of Deydey's debt. That was when Deydey pounced! In six swift moves Deydey finished him off. Deydey's triumph resulted in a small square of salt pork, a bit of flour, some dried apples, and a bladder of fish oil. That last item, none of the children were happy to see.

Dosed every morning with the awful stuff, they

were sure to stay healthy now. But the price was high. Drinking the oil down gagged Omakayas. Tears came to her eyes and more than once she wished her father was not quite so good at the game of chess.

◄o►

Old Tallow was sitting by the fire, cleaning and oiling each part of her ancient, frail gun. She usually had more luck with her sharp lance, but claimed that out of hunger her arms were weakening and her aim with the razor-keen instrument was off. Even her snares, set so cleverly just where a rabbit usually wanted to and needed to hop, yielded almost none at all. Rabbits were suddenly dying from a rabbit disease that seemed to eat up their insides.

"Neshkey!" Old Tallow split a poor waboose, rabbit, and opened its skinny body to show that the creature was mush inside, a bloody pudding as the result of disease.

"Probably a sickness brought by the chimookoman, too!" she growled. Since the death of Neewo, she refused to attempt to speak to anyone who was not Anishinabe. The traders got her cold eye, the missionaries her hard glare, the few other white visitors who chanced onto the island received from Old Tallow no welcome. She blamed them for the disease. She blamed them for the poor quality of game and the scarcity of food—naturally, when so many animals were hunted for sale to white traders for fur, there would be fewer left to eat for survival. The only thing wrong with their lives that she could not blame on the chimookoman was the weather, though she tried.

"Their loud voices scare off the sun! The sun is afraid of their hairy faces!"

"If the sun is not afraid of your face," said Deydey, "I'm sure no chimookoman could make it hide."

"You are mixed blood," jeered Old Tallow, pleased to be in a mock exchange of insults, "wisikodewinini, half-burnt wood. Am I speaking to the white half or the Anishinabe?"

"Go ahead, cut my arm," offered Deydey, "see if you can divide the white blood from the red blood."

"Saaa." Old Tallow looked toward Nokomis for help, but she just raised her eyebrows. "Mikwam! If you're so strong, melt away this ice."

"You're the hotheaded one," said Deydey. "You melt it."

Nobody could, for after a few weeks of kind weather the earth had frozen with a vengeance, and spring seemed far away. Omakayas was tired of all the different kinds of ice around her. There was the just plain ice, the kind you couldn't see through, that covered the lake and hid the water and the fish below. That was the ice she had to help Nokomis chop every day from the deep hole they fished through. The fish were biting only rarely. They could fish all day and not even come up with a skinny lake trout. The nets they lowered through the ice hole came up frozen solid the moment they reached the surface, of course. Empty ice nets! There was the ice on the oiled paper window, ice on the inside of the cabin walls on cold mornings, ice on the frozen paths and ice in the water bucket. Transparent ice, white ice, ice so black and solid you couldn't see through it.

"If only we could eat ice. If only ice was food!" said Pinch. As he said this, into his mind's eye came the picture of the berries he'd stuffed into his mouth last summer. Mama was right. If only he had them now!

All Omakayas was interested in, she thought one evening as she fell asleep, was thin ice. Then no ice. Melting ice. She thought that until she had her dream.

Nokomis put charcoal on her face one night, sent her to bed with no food, told her to remember her dreams, if she should have any. Omakayas knew that Nokomis wanted her to search for and find a spirit helper, someone great in the spirit world who would help her to recover her will to live. Omakayas tried to make herself better, to stop dwelling on worthless sadnesses. Omakayas couldn't help it. She didn't care about the world. Still, she did as she was told and went to sleep determined to remember any dream she might have.

No dream. As before, in the dead of winter, her dreams were blank. The moon shifted one quarter, then Nokomis tried again. Nothing. At last, when Omakayas had a particularly slow day, Nokomis made sure that she tried to dream yet again. She smoothed the dry powdery black charcoal onto Omakayas' face and sang to her as she fell asleep.

That night, Omakayas dreamed.

Everything was ice in her dream, and she was sliding on it. Faster, slipperier, she was sliding through the woods and then down to the lakeshore. Something drew her onto the icy lake shore and although she knew the ice covered the rocks she kept walking, exploring. Before her, there was a cave. She entered.

"Ahneen," said a soft voice from deep in the darkness.

"Ahneen," said Omakayas, "where are you?"

In a glimmer of light, a motherly woman showed herself. She was dressed in the most beautiful furs and her face was very kind, her eyes deep, thrilling, wild.

Black fur rippled against her dark skin. She opened her mouth. Her teeth were long and sharp, but there was nothing to fear.

"I'm going to help you," said the woman. "I feel sorry for you, and I love you. Just remember to give me tobacco. I'm the bear spirit woman. I knew your great-grandma and great-grandpa. They live with me now."

Omakayas woke slowly. It was like floating to the surface of a warm depth of feeling. She wanted to stay in the dream, but in just the same way that she always bobbed to the water's surface in the summer, no matter how hard she tried to sit on the lake bottom, she lost her struggle and knew after a time that she was fully awake. The dream was gone.

Later that day, Omakayas told Nokomis about the dream.

Immediately, Nokomis took her aside and brought her to the corner of the house near the window of oiled paper. There, sitting across from her, Nokomis smoothed Omakayas's hair to each side with her worn hands and smiled lovingly into her granddaughter's eyes.

"These bear people want to help you. You must not forget to give your helper tobacco whenever you think of her. She's with you, your lady. She's going to help you. She will be looking out for you in this world."

◄○►

The only thing good about this time of winter was the stories. While the snow and ice still held fast, Nokomis told them tales about the world of manitous and windigos, tales of Nanabozho, the comical teacher. Those last were favorites of the girls. Maybe because she so often felt small and helpless, Omakayas thought long about one particular tale Nokomis told. She loved to hear it when the flames jumped and the frozen world outside the small cabin was dark. One night she asked her grandmother to tell it once again.

"Nokomis, very soon, the ice will break and the lake will start moving. The animals will stir and the frogs will wake up! I know there will be no more stories until next winter. So please, the diving muskrat one now?"

Nokomis nodded, pleased that Omakayas asked, for this story was an important teaching story, or adisokaan. While her fingers swiftly flew at her quillwork, she told the story of how the earth began.

NANABOZHO AND MUSKRAT MAKE AN EARTH

—◄◦►—

Maywizah, Maywizah, long time ago. Rain started. More rain, as though it would never quit. The water rose so fast that our Nanabozho ran to the top of a hill. The water followed him. At the top of the hill there was a pine tree. Nanabozho climbed the tree. Still the water kept rising. He said to the tree, "Brother, stretch yourself." The tree stretched twice as long. He climbed some more, then asked the tree to stretch again. The tree stretched four times. That's how tall it was.

Finally, the tree told Nanabozho that he couldn't do any more for him. That was as high as the tree could go. But then the water stopped. Nanabozho was standing at the top of the tree. He had his head back and the water was up to his mouth.

After a while, Nanabozho noticed that there were animals playing in the water, Beaver, Muskrat, and Otter. Nanabozho spoke first to Otter, asking, "Brother, could you go down and get some earth? If you do that, I will make an earth for you and me to live on."

Otter said to Nanabozho, "I will try."

Away he went, down to the bottom of the water. But Otter didn't get halfway to the bottom. He drowned, then floated up to the top. Nanabozho caught hold of the otter and looked into the otter's paws and mouth, but didn't find any dirt. Then Nanabozho blew on Otter and brought him back to life.

"Did you see anything?" he asked.

"No," said Otter.

The next animal Nanabozho spoke to was Beaver. He asked him to go after some earth down below and said, "If you do, I'll make an earth for us to live on."

Beaver said, "I'll try," and went down. Beaver was gone a long time. Pretty soon he floated to the top of the water. He had also drowned. Nanabozho caught hold of the beaver and blew on him. When Beaver came to, Nanabozho examined his paws and mouth to see if there was any dirt, but he couldn't find anything.

"Did you see any earth at the bottom?" Nanabozho asked Beaver.

"Yes, I did," said the beaver. "I saw it, but I couldn't get any of it."

These animals had tried and failed.

Muskrat was also playing around in the water. Nanabozho didn't think much about the muskrat, because he was so small, just a little animal, too weak. But after a while he said to him, "Why don't you try and go after some of that dirt, too?"

Muskrat said, "I'll try," and he dived down.

Nanabozho waited and waited a long time for Muskrat to come up to the top of the water. When he floated up to the top, he was dead from his exertion. Nanabozho caught hold of Muskrat and looked him over. Muskrat had his paws closed up tight. His mouth was shut, too. Nanabozho opened Muskrat's front paw and found a grain of earth in it. He took it. In his other front paw Nanabozho found another little grain, and one grain of dirt in each of his hind paws. There was another grain in his mouth.

When he'd found these five grains, Nanabozho blew on Muskrat until he came back to life. Then Nanabozho took the grains of earth in the palm of his hand. He held them up to the sun to dry them out. When they were all dry, he threw them around onto the water. A little island rose. The four went onto the island—Nanabozho, Otter, Beaver, and Muskrat. Nanabozho got more earth on the island, and threw it all around. The island got bigger. It got larger every time Nanabozho threw out another handful of dirt. The animals at the bottom of the water, whoever was there, all came up to the top of the water and went to the island, this earth we are on today.

◄◦►

Omakayas knew that her Nokomis told her this story for a larger reason than just because she asked for it. She thought many times of the muskrat diving down, down, down for that little bit of dirt that made the world. She imagined Muskrat finally pulling to the very bottom and grasping that bit of earth in its tiny paws.

"If such a small animal could do so much," Nokomis always said, after she'd finished the story, "your efforts are important, too."

As if he had understood Grandma's story, Andeg made his own effort. Her crow hunted mice these lean days with more savage intentions than when merely keeping them away from his family of humans. He hunted for survival. The bird eagerly awaited any mouse who dared enter the house. Hungrily, Andeg dropped and struck, hard, killing the little animal and quickly eating it. Andeg also hunted in the woods for seeds and nuts cached by squirrels. That winter, Andeg found a little hollow in a tree next to the cabin. Some squirrel had filled the hollow with acorns, seeds, hazelnuts. Enough to feed the family for a day or two!

"Neshkey," said Mama, her hands full one morning. "Look what that good bird found for us!"

Andeg was looking at the food cache as though he wasn't quite sure he'd meant to share, but Mama was pleased. She scattered a big load of acorns on the hearth stones and looked at them with satisfaction before she began to break the little shells with her smoothest pounding rock. She shelled the acorns, ground them fine, roasted them with a bit of cornmeal and that night the family had sweet acorn cakes. From the last cone of maple sugar, she made a taste of syrup for them all, and that night, at least, they went to sleep with a comfortable warmth in their stomachs. All of them, before sleeping, thanked Andeg, who, though he usually slept outside, was invited in that night. He sat above the fire on a thick twig perch Deydey had fastened between the mortared stones. Andeg preened his feathers, very glad to be so warm, bobbed his sleek head, and blinked his brilliant eyes.

Tomorrow, resolved Omakayas now that she had a bit of strength, she would make her small, important effort like the muskrat. She would go out with Andeg and find more squirrel caches in the woods. She didn't reckon on her own weakness, however, nor could she ever have imagined the swiftness of Old Tallow's justice.

⟞⟨∘⟩⟝

The day dawned pure and cold. Nokomis and Mama mixed up some water with the thin paste of acorn flour left from the night before. Deydey came in with a fish so tiny and poor-looking that, in spite of their hunger, everyone laughed out loud when he lifted it proudly into the air. Everyone, that is, except Mama. She just rested her eyes a little more softly on her husband than usual, and went on with her beadwork. Omakayas, ready to do her part, dressed in her warmest clothes, wrapped lengths of rabbit-skin around her feet, put makazins over them and then, Andeg on her shoulder, went to look for the squirrel caches.

Although she had fished with Nokomis, this was the first time Omakayas had ventured into the woods since the day she had entered the cabin. On that day, she had followed the sickness inside and determined to do battle with the evil spirit of the disease. She had lost her beloved Neewo. Now she decided that she would not lose any of her family to the weakness of hunger. She would find food. Somewhere. Dizziness overcame her. Her knees felt watery and her blood ran thin. She paused, holding onto a tree, and made her way toward the woods beyond. First, she had to pass Old Tallow's place, and she narrowed her eyes at the path and stepped forward with determined quickness, prepared not to stop until Andeg told her where to find more nuts and acorns. She didn't reckon on the yellow dog.

He was there in her path as she neared Old Tallow's cabin. She wouldn't look at him, she decided, but she couldn't help remembering the words his look had given her last summer. *Wait until next time! I'll get you then! I'll get you when no one is around.* What could he do to her? Even in her weakness, she would be mentally stronger, she would show him no fear. But as though he sensed the truth of her condition, and not the determined pluck of her heart, the yellow dog stepped forward. As always, he snarled and then retreated when Omakayas grabbed a stick. When she brandished the stick, however, a spinning haze of brilliant dots flooded up before her eyes. Suddenly it was as though she stepped over the

edge of a black cliff. She stumbled, fainted to the ground. The
yellow dog lunged forward.
Andeg screamed and tore with
his beak at the dog's eyes, but
the dog was eager, at last,
to get the better of a
human. As the clum-
siest hunting dog of Old
Tallow's pack, he needed
to stand tall over some-
thing, even if only a sick little girl.

Omakayas groped for her stick, but suddenly the
yellow dog had it in his teeth. He growled, worried the
stick as though he'd caught a gopher, then dropped it
and with an eager bite tore into the blanket that fell
from her arm. With a vicious lunge, he bit Omakayas
above the wrist and jumped back, eyes blazing with cowardly triumph. Omakayas tried to yell, but her voice
stuck in her throat, a squeak. She felt a rushing blackness overwhelm her again, tried to throw herself
upward, tried to growl back and challenge the dog. With
excitement, though, the dog realized he had her at his
mercy at last. He jumped forward again. This time, he

fell upon her leg and bit deep. Omakayas heard a loud scream, her own scream, and pain blotted her sight then as she swirled into the dark.

She woke a moment later, in Old Tallow's arms.

"What happened?"

Nearby, the yellow dog cringed and tried to slink away from Old Tallow's glare. Seeing that Omakayas was all right, Old Tallow carefully put the girl down. With a swift, bearlike swipe, she grabbed the dog and held him by the scruff of the neck with one hand. He whimpered, and snarled at Omakayas as though to say, *She made me do it!* Old Tallow shook her head, sadly, and lifted her ax. Ignoring Omakayas, who panted weakly on the snowy ground, Old Tallow spoke to her dog as she would to a human. Sadly and firmly, holding him by the neck, she told the dog what he had done.

"Didn't I warn you, didn't I say to you, didn't I tell you many times that you must never hurt this one? Yes, n'dai, you look at me now with pleading eyes, but I spared you many times before. Each time I spared your life, I always told you what would happen if you were so foolish again. Now, my foolish friend, you must die."

With that, Old Tallow brought the blunt end of her ax down on the yellow dog's head. He crumpled to the ground.

"Ai! My auntie!"

The yellow dog had hated her, perhaps even meant to kill her, but Omakayas hadn't counted on such a cruel and sudden end to the dog's cowardly life. Old Tallow's justice was harsh. Her sentence was carried out in an instant, but that didn't mean that her heart was hard or that she didn't mourn for her friend. It just meant that Omakayas was more important. The last that Omakayas saw of the yellow dog, he was bundled in Old Tallow's arms. The strong old woman was walking away, and in her step there was the sadness of parting with an old but dangerously foolish friend.

Omakayas got slowly to her feet, wobbled forward, and knew that she would have to return to the cabin. She still wasn't strong enough to hunt for food. With Andeg's encouragement, she made it back to the door and fell through, her vision darkening. Her stomach creaked, so empty it stuck to the back of her body. She needed Grandma's help to dress the bites that throbbed and stung. They must have food, they must have food. Soon they must eat, she knew, or they would all lie in the ground with the two who had gone before.

◄◦►

It was the great buck One Horn who saved them, who

gave them his life. Grandma woke two mornings later and called Deydey to her side to talk, for she was so weak from hunger she could only sit wrapped in her blanket by the fire.

"I dreamed last night," she told him. "And now you must do everything just as I say."

Deydey listened intently.

"Take the small path to the north, that leads past the fish camp," said Grandma, gesturing slowly. She squinted. Looked deeper into her dream. Nodded slowly. "When you come to the tallest of the trees, go toward the lake, then around the rocks and back into the trees. There, the buck will wait for you."

Deydey knew when Grandma dreamed, especially in this extremity, it was a true dream and must be followed. First, however, he prepared himself carefully to meet the animal's spirit. He washed, put on his best clothing, new makazins, and had Mama comb and braid his hair. He cleaned and oiled his new gun and prepared it with extra care. Then he went immediately out and followed Grandma's directions exactly. Just as she had said, in the clearing past the rocks and back in the trees, One Horn was waiting. The great buck stood still in the calm light. Deydey lifted his gun, breathed his hopes. Then thanks. One shot. The shot went true. One Horn died easily, right then.

Deydey gave tobacco to the deer's spirit and thanked him, brought back as much as he could carry, then buried the rest of the deer in snow. Returning, he gave the venison to his starving family and to Tallow, who shared it out to Auntie Muskrat, to LaPautre's hungry children, and to Fishtail.

That night, as Omakayas ate the stew of venison that Mama cooked, she felt herself grow stronger with each bite. She remembered the day she and Angeline stood before the beauty of One Horn. They had looked on him, amazed, and he did not run away. Had he known, at that time, that they would need his very existence? Again, Omakayas remembered the proud,

soft radiance of his brown eyes. She closed her eyes and saw One Horn feasted, honored, and decorated with her grandmother's finest beadwork. Opening her eyes again, she thanked the animal for saving her life, and then, just as she finished thinking this solemn thought, Pinch, whose belly was full, backed up too close to the hearth and set the seat of his pants on fire.

"Mama!" He jumped away, a little flame shooting from his rear. In sudden inspiration, he sat down directly in the water bucket. Everybody looked at him, at first in shock, and then once he was seen to have suffered no harm it was Mama, first of all, who started to laugh. And Pinch laughed, too. Laughed so hard that he wedged his behind farther into the bucket, and could not get out. Laughed and laughed. Harder and harder! Ever after that terrible winter, as though he understood from then on how important it was to be funny, Pinch gave laughter to them all. He became a joker, a trick player, and joked on himself as well as others. Perhaps it was that first saving laugh, the best thing any of them had heard since before the death of Neewo, that made him proud. He had saved his family, in a way, every bit as much as One Horn.

The great deer had saved their bodies, and Pinch's absurd jump had saved their souls, for Nokomis said shortly after that her own grandmother had believed that the soul of the Anishinabeg is made of laughter. If there is no laughter, the soul dies. Pinch brought laughter back to life. He brought their souls back into their bodies. The harder they laughed the more they knew, now, they would survive.

Zeegwun

(S P R I N G)

CHAPTER TWELVE

Maple Sugar Time

 EVERYONE IN THE CABIN heard it—the far-off creaking and groaning, the boom of the lake ice. The lake had started to move again. The ice was breaking up. Once the waves began, huge sheets of ice shoved against each other, pushing towers into the air. Nokomis, Mama, Deydey, Pinch, Angeline, and Omakayas all ran outside, gazed on the horizon, and saw the crackling and snapping waves of the ice. They felt the surge of lake water in their blood. They knew, at last, that the back of winter was entirely broken.

Omakayas grinned. Her smile was now whole—new teeth had grown in over the winter. She was older. Soon, spring plants would poke up through dead leaves.

The curled heads of ferns. Buds, roots, fresh new leaves. Fat lake trout would sleepily rise from the bottom, hungry to be caught. Siskowet and whitefish would fill their nets. They would be able to think of something other than the next bite of food. They would live again, truly live.

—◄○►—

Angeline went to the mission school every day now. She was learning to write her name in Zhaganashimowin, the white man's language, and she taught Omakayas the things she learned. Using a pointed stick to write in wet mud, Angeline showed Omakayas and Nokomis the meaningful signs, which looked like odd tracks.

"What animal would leave these?" Omakayas teased.

"Be patient," Nokomis counseled. "Let's find out what your sister has learned."

"They're letters," Angeline said, eager to share her knowledge. "One follows the next. You look at them, just like tracks. You read them. They have a meaning and a sound."

"Howah! That's a good idea! Like our picture writing," Nokomis said.

The girls knew people like Fishtail's father, Day

Thunder, who kept the records for the religious gatherings, the Midewiwin, and etched stories and songs on scrolls made of birchbark. They had seen some birchbark writing, and they knew that Nokomis could etch pictures into bark, too. She also knew where certain marks had been placed upon lake rocks long ago. Some of the marks were made by the spirits, some were made by humans; others were drawn by a giant race of people who had lived on earth in the old days and had disappeared. Angeline's description of the white man's tracks interested Omakayas, in spite of herself.

The system sounded incredible—sounds, meanings—but the idea made sense. Thereafter, to learn the Zhaganashimowin letters and sounds became a source of amusement, for the evenings were still long.

"Aaaaay," said Angeline, tracing the letter on the rough stone of the hearth.

"Aaaaay," said Omakayas. "Beee. Seee. Deee." She learned to make the pictures, and she learned to make the sounds, slowly, all of them. Words would follow, Angeline said, but Omakayas could not believe that would happen. She remembered that last winter, before the sickness began, she had seen Fishtail walking from the mission school. Had he learned to make the white man's tracks? Had he learned to write his name? Had he learned to read the words of the treaties so that his people could not be cheated of land?

"Boozhoo, nindinaweymaganidok," called Fishtail one day.

He was at the door of the cabin, calling hello to his relatives. Grandma greeted him kindly, for he was ashamed of his thinness and weakness. She brought him inside. His hair was short and wild as porcupine quills, his face starved and sallow with grief. No longer did he wear the proud, somewhat disdainful look he'd worn when walking seriously along through the woods, his pipe cradled in his arms. He was still hawk-keen, with a strong and handsome face, but his eyes were more human, humble, gentle. He gazed pityingly down at Omakayas and touched her hair.

"Little Frog," he said, and there was a hint of smile in his voice, as though to see her brought him comfort, "my good wife loved you as her little sister. You made her laugh with your quick ways. She told me you were much loved by the bear people. She told me, also, that you had a bird named Andeg."

"Andeg!" called Omakayas, and like a dark arrow her crow swooped down and landed on her shoulder. Andeg looked curiously at Fishtail, wondering whether he possibly had something to feed him. The bird danced from foot to foot, took a strand of Omakayas's hair in his beak but did not pull. Andeg tucked the hair behind Omakayas's ear just like a grandfather soothing a child to sleep!

"Owah," said Fishtail, in wonder, "you *are* much beloved by the creatures."

Over his shoulder Fishtail carried a blanket, meaning that he had much to say and planned to spend the night. Deydey greeted him, holding him by the arms, and Nokomis stirred up the fire, adding a stick there, a bit of wood in exactly the right spot to make it blaze up cheerfully. Mama had made a good stew, filled with flaky chunks of fish, and the kettle bubbled hot, hung above the hearth fire.

Fishtail took off his big moose-hide mitts and Angeline dished up a wooden bowl of the soup, eager for him to sit and warm himself. Because he was related as a cross-cousin, and also because he had been the husband of her friend, she was familiar around him and not shy at all. She tried to cheer him up, to bring a smile to his face by teasing him gently.

"Deydey needs snowshoes all winter, but you," Angeline pointed with her lips at Fishtail, "already have yours on, eh?"

Fishtail gave a little smile, but there was still too much sadness in him to laugh. He waggled his feet—they were big, it was true, almost as big as snowshoes, as big as Old Tallow's huge long ones.

"Ayah! They come in handy!" Fishtail acknowledged. "If I lose a paddle I've always got one attached."

He took great gulps of the fish broth, and slowly, feeling better, he warmed to the talk with Deydey. They were planning this year's sugaring, a time everyone looked forward to with joy and excitement, as much as ricing, maybe even more. For when the maple sap began to run it meant that warmer days, pleasant sun, all the beauties of spring were close at hand.

"This sweetness just at the raggedy end of winter!" Nokomis was excited as a girl, and her enthusiasm made everyone smile with affection. "But the creator expects us to be ready. While you talk, you men work!"

She herself was smoothing out a paddle to use in stirring the syrup, and just the day before Deydey had started hollowing a peeled, smooth piece of basswood for a trough. Now Deydey asked for the use of Omakayas's gun-barrel flesher. She brought it quickly from its place in the corner. She was glad to find another use for Deydey's gift besides the usual unpleasant one of scraping hides. Taking the hide flesher in his hands, Deydey sharpened the end well on his sharpening stone. Holding the barrel in his strong fingers like a chisel, he hit the other end with his mallet, tapping long slices of wood away from the inside of the log. Every strip of wood he tapped from the inside, Pinch grabbed and threw into the fire. The trough grew smoother, deeper. Fishtail, meanwhile, smoked peacefully and looked into the leaping flames.

"You get to work, too!" Angeline said, smiling. She tossed him a bit of venison jerky, though, for him to chew on when he finished smoking his kinnikinnick.

◄○►

The family sugaring place was at the other end of the island. When they traveled to the sugar bush, the family packed as lightly as possible. Once they arrived, they would use the frames set up last year for their big sugaring house. There was a smaller wigwam where the tools were stored. There usually was a food cache buried last fall, filled with good things that had lain far beneath the snow. But this year, Deydey had already made a trip to the end of the island and raided the cache. To keep from starving, they had already eaten their store during the lean moon.

When they arrived, the first thing Mama did was unroll the reed mats for the roof of the shelter, then the blankets, then take out new paddles and the cooking pot. Deydey dragged a big kettle and more wooden troughs and paddles from the small storage house. Anything that wasn't at the sugaring place, or anything that broke or wore out, they could make for themselves. Nokomis and Omakayas arranged the food they'd brought. There were packets of split, dried fish, a makuk of special powdered fish, moose meat, a little manomin traded for with deer meat, smoked fish, and a bag of dried pumpkin flowers to thicken soups.

"Neshkey," said Nokomis, happy they had so much. "We'll have a good feast."

Once a soup was in the making, Nokomis left Angeline to stir and called Omakayas to come along and help chop taps to open the maples.

The two wandered a bit until Nokomis found a good ironwood tree. She took out her sharp hatchet and expertly chopped into the tree at regular angles. She made a series of perfect cuts down the side of the tree, and then chopped sideways and split from the tree ten perfect wedges of the hard ironwood. She did this until she had a huge sackful of wedges, which Omakayas lugged back to the camp.

For two days they prepared, knowing that the sap was just about to start running. There was a feeling to that time before the sap began, a quietness that had the going-out taste of winter. All that happened in the snow and cold, the storytelling and the sadness, too, was left behind. Omakayas opened herself to the warming wind. Before them, the sweetness of the maple waited, the warmth of the sun.

◄o►

Omakayas, Twilight, and Little Bee carted heavy rocks from the lakeshore to weigh down the makuks, and then hauled wood for the fire. Omakayas's arms were tired, and her cousins', too. They complained impatiently to each other as they hunted for the right-sized stones or hauled load after load of wood in their arms, dumping it near the big kettle, which was boiling and steaming away. As yet, not one taste of the maple syrup! Just the cold, sweet sap. It was always this way before the first taste. The boiling down seemed to take so endlessly long! Pinch watched jealously. Jumped on a log to observe Grandma's paddle when it came up and dipped back down again. Still not ready. Still not. Still not.

Then ready.

Onto the surface of a big makuk filled with clean snow, Grandma dribbled a thin dark-gold stream of syrup. Pinch could hardly wait for it to cool—gum sugar! He grabbed while it was still a soft rope, swung the strand into his mouth, and ran, for once quiet instead of yelling, only because his mouth was stuffed. Andeg was caught up in the excitement and he jumped from foot to foot, nearly tumbling from Omakayas's shoulder as Angeline poured out more syrup and then helped Grandma ladle the rest into a sugaring trough. He pecked at a bit of the syrup, but didn't seem to like the sticky feel of it on his beak, and shook his head comically. He put his head in the snow, wiped his beak back and forth, but couldn't remove the hardening syrup. He flew up to a low branch and glared down at them, betrayed, preening his feathers, making his feathers sticky with the syrup too.

"Minopogwud," said Omakayas, licking up a dollop of thick syrup.

The first taste usually made her smile. Not this time. Sadness overwhelmed her when she tasted the sweetness. She instantly recalled the special day she spent with Neewo on the shore of the lake. On that day, long ago last summer, she had freed him from the tight bonds of his tikinagun, let him tumble and play. When it came time for her to put him back, she'd sweetened his confinement by placing her last bit of sugar on his tongue.

"Chickadee, my brother," she cried to Neewo under her breath.

She looked around. Pinch was running and jumping, striking out with a stick and pretending to hunt doves. Nokomis was stirring the syrup using a dancing kind of smooth movement with her arms. Mama was putting together a stew and Deydey was off somewhere with Fishtail, planning ceremonies that would be held during the sugaring, not far from their camp. Angeline looked at her and said, "Neshemay, go get some more wood!"

She, Omakayas, was the only one thinking of Neewo. The knowledge made her lonely. If only she could talk to him, look into his cheerful, upslanted eyes, share with him her feelings that he never laughed at, play with him in her arms. She missed him terribly, so much so that her heart seemed to drop right through her stomach with a thud. Muffling her cries, she ran from camp straight out into the woods.

Angeline was surprised. Usually her sister did not fetch wood with such enthusiasm.

"Howah!" she called after her little sister. "Meg-wetch!"

Omakayas knew that she would not come back, however, and Angeline could fetch her own wood. She ran with an angry heart. Breathing hard, skimming away as fast as she could, she got away from everyone before she sat down on a little patch of dry, sunny ground. At last, it was all right to sob and sob, to let herself cry as much as she wanted to. But the strange thing was, as soon as she sat down she didn't feel like crying anymore. She heard the song of the white throated sparrow, and was soothed by the piercing refrain. She smiled. Neewo's spirit was comforting her. Her eyelids got heavy, the sun warmed her, and she was just about lost in a dream when she was startled by the crackle of sticks and twigs, the shuffle of feet, the interested snuffling, and most of all the commanding and unmistakeable odor of bear.

They were with her.

Standing quiet at the edge of the little spot of sun, the two young bears gazed curiously, knowingly, at Omakayas. Andeg flew down suddenly, as though he, the little crow, had to protect her from her brothers! The two bears startled a bit at the crow's angry charge, but then shrugged and ignored him.

"It's okay," said Omakayas, and Andeg returned to her shoulder.

The bears continued to look closely at Omakayas, peering with their dim bear eyes, taking in every dot of her scent, remembering it all, knowing. Omakayas wished that she had something to give them—she had run away from camp with nothing more than a handful of spirit tobacco in her pocket. They kept looking at her, waiting and watching. The only thing she could think of to give them, in the end, was some human advice. She decided to warn them about other humans and the dangers they posed.

"There's a woman," Omakayas said, softly, "her name is Old Tallow. She's my aunt, but *you* must stay away from her."

The young bears' ears twitched a little. They seemed to listen closely. "Be careful, too," Omakayas went on, "when you see something better to eat than usual, out in the woods. If it's hanging up out of reach, there might be a pit underneath. That's a trap. You'll fall in and die. And guns. My brothers, run fast from men carrying big sticks on their shoulders. Stay away from them. Don't go near the humans, either the Anishinabeg or the chimookomanug. Stay deep in the woods. Hide if you hear Old Tallow's dogs."

Omakayas reached into her pocket and took out the little handful of tobacco. She put the tobacco on the ground. When she did, she knew she was asking for something, but she wasn't sure what it was. Words she had not expected came from her lips.

"Will you give me your medicine?"

She asked this, but her voice was uncertain. She really didn't know what she meant. She felt embarrassed at herself. "I'm pitiful," she said, just as her grandmother did sometimes when praying. "I don't know anything. I want to know your medicine. I want to be like Nokomis. I want strong medicines to save my family."

Tears came into Omakayas's eyes and she could hardly see, hardly noticed when the bears wheeled and silently disappeared. "Help me," she whispered to the ground, "help me."

Once she'd finished talking, she lifted her face and looked around. Her bear brothers had vanished, and she felt better. She set to work gathering a huge load of dry sticks, dead branches torn off during the winter by heavy snow and ice. As she was piling the branches higher and higher, she saw, on the side of a dry piece of birch wood, the gray hoof of a mushroom. A tiny voice whispered in her head, a low voice, muttering. When she picked up the branch, the voice grew louder but she still couldn't make out individual words. She added the branch to her pile, bound the pile with a thong, carried it back to the camp on her shoulders.

From time to time, as she walked back to camp through the woods, she heard a small sound, a word or two, muffled under the snow and leaves. By the time she reached the sugaring camp she felt a little bit afraid. What were these voices? What did the whispering mean? Standing in the clearing, safe, she peered into the maze of branches and undergrowth. Shining scraps of snow lighted the ground as far as she could see. The sounds of voices, small and whispery, still floated from the depth of the woods.

"What took you so long?" Angeline said, a bit annoyed. She'd burned her finger in the process of pouring some hot syrup, and she was hurting badly. "What's wrong with you?"

Omakayas put down her load and told her sister that she had something important to do.

"So do I!" Angeline yelled back. Omakayas walked over to Nokomis. She was fashioning small cones of birchbark for the sugar. She had saved a string of duck bills, too, that she'd fill with hard sugar for a special treat. Omakayas sat down beside her.

"Nokomis," said Omakayas, her voice soft and troubled, "I talked to my bear brothers. I listened to them like you told me."

Immediately, Nokomis set down her work, wiped her hands on her skirt, and brought her granddaughter over to a wide fallen log to sit with her. She smoothed Omakayas's hair down to either side, and looked keenly into her eyes and face.

"Wait." Intent and serious, Nokomis filled her red stone pipe with tobacco. It was a sign that she was going to hear something important, and she took a long time perfectly tamping her pipe, which was good, because during that time Omakayas had the chance to think about just what she would tell her grandmother. When Nokomis lit the pipe and drew on it, the coals burning, the sweetness of the smoke filled the air around them and made a small, holy room in which they sat, their minds close together.

"I talked to them," Omakayas repeated.

"What did you say?"

"I told them how to be careful of humans."

"That's good," said Nokomis, reflecting, "unless we need meat. What did you say next?"

"I asked my bear brothers for help," said Omakayas carefully.

"What did they do?"

"I don't know."

"What do you mean?" A wreath of smoke swirled around Nokomis's face.

"I asked them for medicine," said Omakayas, "and when I looked up, they were gone. But as I walked back here, I heard voices." Omakayas looked quickly at her grandmother to see if she understood, and as she only nodded, Omakayas went on talking. "They were odd voices, all different types of voices."

"Did they come from the woods?"

"Yes."

"Did you understand what they were saying to you?"

"No."

"Neither did I," said Nokomis, her voice pleased, "not at first."

Omakayas looked at her grandmother, remembering the time she had asked whether the plant medicines had ever spoken to her. Nokomis took the pipe from her lips and gave Omakayas a long and searching look of regard. Her eyes beamed out a quiet message of love. Nokomis understood the meaning of what had happened, understood why the voices had spoken, understood what it meant for Omakayas's future, and was proud and glad to have a granddaughter who was chosen to be a healer.

"Even now, today, I sometimes don't know what they are saying. But then, I'm old and getting weak," said Nokomis. "You are young and strong, Omakayas, and as I teach you about my medicines you'll hear them more clearly."

"Do they talk to you every day?"

"Oh, no, but often enough."

"Why were they talking all at once?" Omakayas wondered.

Nokomis thought for a while. "I think they talk to each other all the time," she said, "but our minds are not always peaceful enough to hear them."

—◦—

Nokomis told Omakayas that bears dig for medicine. They are a different kind of people from us. They don't use fire, but they laugh. They hold their children. They eat the same things we do and treat themselves with medicine from certain plants. They are known as healers. Those in the bear clan are often good at healing others. Nokomis said all of these things while stirring syrup, sugaring, constantly checking and rechecking the fires, making extra makuks and cones of birchbark to hold the sugar they would have that year.

It turned out to be a good year. The sap went down into the roots during the cold nights, came up strong when the sun warmed the trunks during the day. The winter had started out bare, frosted the trees deeply, and then the deep snows had fallen. That was known as the best kind of year for maple sap. No thunderstorms marred the flavor of the sugar. No prayers for good weather went unanswered.

—◄o►—

Omakayas's family sugared close to Auntie Muskrat's, and her cousins flooded into their camp, a wave of flying limbs and eager faces, ready for the vast games the children played all though the trees and brush. Omakayas forgot the bears, forgot the whispering of the plants, became a cousin within a pack of cousins, roaming the camps, stealing bits of sugar, laughing at each other. The girl cousins and her friends Two Strike, Twilight, and Little Bee played together in such a lively way. They were a tangle of girl! She even went to sleep each night with a tiny sense of anticipation in her heart. Still, she thought of Neewo. Even her cousins could not take away that sadness. The work came first, but then lengthening light in the afternoons kept the children at play outside and kept the aunts talking, the men gossiping, the grandmas reminiscing about their own playing days as small children when they roamed the sugar camps.

Always, in the near distance, sacred drums were sounding. The sound of the drums called people to the good life, a way of kindness, love, and deep respect for all

that lived. Deydey sometimes sang to help Fishtail. Often, there was a healing ceremony, a doctoring to cure the winter's illnesses. The old people talked to the young people, teaching them about the way to live as an Anishinabe in this world. Nokomis taught, but someone had to tend the sugarhouse fires, so many days she stayed instead of going to the ceremonies. Mama came and went, Angeline, too, and sometimes they brought Omakayas to the big lodge with the endlessly burning sacred fire.

Always, on entering, Omakayas walked around the fire the same way the sun travels and then she sat down in the calm of the lodge and listened to the crackle of the scented flames, waited for the throb of the drum. Pinch came, too, but he never sat still, not for an instant. He dived in and out of the lodge, snagged food wherever he could get it, fell asleep on the blankets Deydey kept spread in the corner near Fishtail and Day Thunder's drum. Pinch woke, jumped up, bolted from the lodge. He was on the move all day and night. Pinch was the quickest, the boldest, the most irritating of the boys in all of the camps.

One day, while Omakayas was busy helping Deydey, and the others were at the big lodge, Pinch made himself a small bow, strung with a bit of sewing sinew, and a couple of arrows made from sharpened plant stalks. He sneaked through the woods longing to make his big kill—if only a deer just his size would pass by, or a moose, maybe. If not that, a fish. He could surely spear a fish with one of his arrows. Pinch tramped the edge of the lake and many times edged out as far as he could go on the rocky shore. There was a small margin of water now, before the ice began, and the fish were hungry. Pinch got in plenty of shots, but none of them went true. He kept having to wade into the foot or so of freezing water to retrieve his arrows, so eventually Pinch's attention turned back to the camp. Making his way home, he resolved that he would hunt and shoot something, anything, to impress his family, especially his sisters, who thought he was a nuisance, beneath notice, as irritating as a fly.

Halfway back, Pinch nearly stumbled over the carcass of a dead deer. It had died not long ago, and lay cold and still right in his path.

"Howah!" Pinch yelled fiercely. He had an immediate thought. Drawing his arrows out of the quiver he'd constructed for himself, he managed, though with great difficulty, to stick them into the carcass of the deer. He lodged one at the heart and one at the throat. Then he gave four loud ferocious shouts. He'd made his first kill! Now there would have to be a feast for him!

"I made my first kill!" he yelled as he approached the camp.

Everyone turned to look at him. Thrilled with himself, he bounded forward in such intense excitement that he bumped straight into Deydey at the side of a kettle, just as he was pouring boiling-hot syrup into a sugaring trough!

Pinch screamed as the syrup spilled over his feet. Even through they were protected by makazins, much of the sap flooded in through the open top flap and burned poor Pinch—badly, much worse than Angeline's finger. Pinch was no silent sufferer, and yelled so loud that Omakayas thought the whole camp would came running to his side to see what was the matter. The drums were too penetrating, though, and blocked the sounds even of Pinch's pain.

Gently, Deydey removed Pinch's makazins. The burns were deep, the skin was already bubbling and dangerous looking. Pinch needed quick treatment, and most of Nokomis's medicines were back at the cabin. Deydey set out at once to fetch Nokomis, leaving Omakayas alone with Pinch, who howled miserably. Omakayas blocked out his cries in order to think, clearly, what she should do. Nokomis had left her small pouch in the sugarhouse, the one that she always carried for emergencies. That pouch contained remedies for all sorts of common problems, including burns. Omakayas remembered it, took it from its corner, and sat down near Pinch to look at his foot.

"Don't howl," she said to him, kindly and soothingly, "you'll bring all your blood to the top of your skin and make it worse."

Whether or not that was true, it seemed to scare Pinch into making some effort to control the noises he made. For the first time, he looked up at his big sister with trusting eyes.

"Help me," he whimpered, "it hurts."

That was all she needed to hear.

"I'm going to make it better," said Omakayas, and once she said this she was determined to do exactly that.

Omakayas examined him carefully. She had seen her Nokomis treat burns. Omakayas looked at and smelled the leaves and dried flowers in the birchbark packets that belonged to Nokomis. Horsemint. Omakayas removed the packet, and tried to remember what to do next. Pinch whimpered and gasped. Omakayas took out the stone Nokomis used to prepare her medicines. In the center of that stone there was a hollow, and into that natural small bowl Omakayas put the leaves that smelled summery and sharp, fresh and potent. With the other long stone Nokomis often used, Omakayas crushed them to a paste. From a bag of deer tallow, she added a yellow smear of grease and then, forcing Pinch to lie still, she spread the paste on his burns and propped him against a tree. She brought him lots of maple-flavored water, stroked his forehead carefully, soothingly. And as she did this, surprisingly enough, he stopped howling. He looked up at his big sister with a gaze of intense trust.

By the time Nokomis, Deydey, and the others returned, Pinch was quiet and looked alertly around, bright-eyed as Andeg, wondering what trick he could play next. Nokomis bent to her grandson's feet, looked carefully at what Omakayas had done.

"*Ho!* I couldn't have done a better job," she said, pleased. Nokomis gazed proudly at her granddaughter for several long moments. "My girl, you're strong in healing."

"And now," said Deydey kindly, touching his son's prickly hair, "what was that I heard you yell before the syrup spilled onto your feet? What about your first kill?"

Pinch looked at his father. He opened his mouth. He tried to tell about the deer, but somehow he just couldn't. He was amazed at himself for not lying.

"It was just a mistake," he mumbled at last, looking at his sister. "Megwetch," he said, embarrassed to be caught thanking her. It was just that his feet had hurt so badly, and then felt so much better! How had she done that?

So that was the very first time Omakayas made someone better with her medicine. Through the years, she would think back to that moment proudly, for her treatment worked. Pinch's feet were better in very little time. His pain was soon gone, and he had no puckered scars. It felt very good to her to heal another human, even if that human was Pinch.

CHAPTER THIRTEEN

One Horn's Protection

"THIS WAS SUCH A good sugaring year," said Deydey, "we'll be able to pay off most of our bill at the trader."

"I want to come, I want to come," yelled Pinch. Deydey was loading his big pack frame with bound makuks of sugar. There was much, much more than they would use all year. Old Tallow had her fill of sugar, too, and Nokomis said that in all of her memory there had never been a sugar year like this one.

At the trader's, Deydey paid off the winter's debt and bought a length of blue broadcloth for Mama to sew into a dress. He bought Pinch some calico trim for a pair of makazins, and a piece of velvet cloth for Angeline to use as she wished. For Nokomis, sewing needles and a cup of shining copper. For Omakayas, he bought a small cross stamped out of German trade silver. The night Deydey gave her the cross, she sewed it onto the front of her dress. Andeg loved the look of it and tried constantly to pluck it from her dress—he landed on her shoulder over and over and nearly hung upside down to try and peck at it with his beak.

In the morning, Andeg greeted Omakayas with fluttering wings, ducking his head to accept a little scratch, cooing with a sweet and gurgling sound. Omakayas had never heard a crow make such a sound before, and she knew it was a special sign of affection. She was certain of it one day when Andeg hopped toward her with a twig in his beak. She carefully took it, thanked her crow, and laid the twig aside. All that day, wherever she turned, there was Andeg, hopeful, carrying a piece of bark for her. At last, Omakayas scratched Andeg's neck and sat down to feed him and talk to him. He listened, his lids closed, blue, his head tucked down in quiet bliss.

"You want to make a nest with me, don't you?" said Omakayas. "I can't. I love you, but I'm not a bird." She was surprised to find that, as she said this, tears formed in her eyes. Andeg loved her so much!

"You will have to find another crow," she said, very gently. Andeg didn't seem to hear. Still, after that he would leave for hours at a time. Now Omakayas was afraid that he would be taken for a wild bird and shot or killed. She attached a bit of red wool to his leg. Andeg managed to pull it off with his clever beak. He could untie almost anything if he worked hard enough.

One day, while Omakayas was working just outside the cabin in the cool air, watching a fire Nokomis had made to smoke some of the fish Deydey caught just at ice breakup, there was a sudden harsh cawing of crows. A group of wheeling, excited black birds passed overhead. Just like that, without a good-bye, Andeg jumped off her shoulder. He flew, zinging upward into the midst of the flock. In a second, he was indistinguishable from the others.

Omakayas felt her heart squeeze shut painfully as the birds passed out of sight. He was gone. Maybe she should have cut away essential feathers from his wings, but she couldn't stand to think of him a captive. No, she decided, though her heart hurt, it was better that he join with his own kind. He wasn't human, no matter how often he said "Gaygo, Pinch," or greeted her at the door, croaking out, "Ahneen, Ahneen!" Andeg stole and hoarded bits of bright cloth and shiny metal shards, he wasn't a human, he was still a crow, and she couldn't change that.

She couldn't change that any more than she could change being who she was, Omakayas, who heard the voices of plants and went dizzy. Omakayas, who talked to bear boys and received their medicine. Omakayas, who missed her one brother and resented the other, who envied her sister. Omakayas, the Little Frog, whose first step was a hop. Omakayas who'd lost her friend.

She thought she had cried all the tears she had

to cry, but still found there were some left for Andeg. Omakayas put her hands to her face and sobbed until she felt just enough better. After all, she thought, Andeg was wild and she had always known it, always expected this moment to come. The thought comforted her. There in the yard, looking into the heart of the fire, Omakayas suddenly experienced a strange awareness. Like Andeg, she couldn't help being just who she was. Omakayas, in this skin, in this place, in this time. Nobody else. No matter what, she wouldn't ever be another person or really know the thoughts of anyone but her own self. She closed her eyes. For a moment, she felt as though she were falling from a great height, plunging through air and blackness, tumbling down with nothing to catch at. With a start of fear, she opened her eyes and felt herself gently touch down right where she was, in her own body, here.

CHAPTER FOURTEEN

Full Circle

 NCE AGAIN, THE FAMILY was building the birchbark house, moving out into the woods, dragging pots and other provisions out to the fishing camp where they would live. While she sewed mats together and reset the willow poles, Omakayas often experienced the haunting sense of things missing. She thought she'd forgotten something, or someone, then of course she remembered. Neewo and Ten Snow had left huge holes in her life, and Andeg a tiny one black as pitch and hoarse with laughter. Although spring, with all the force of its poised new growth, called to her, although the tender new buds, opening magically, touched her heart, there would always be a shadow to her laughter, a corner of sadness in her smile.

All day, Omakayas and her grandmother worked hard retying the intersections on last year's willow frame. Nokomis cut new bark, made fancy overlaps and rain diversion flaps. As soon as the house was finished, when there was no way left for him to help any way at all, Albert LaPautre came by for a visit. His round stomach had flattened out a trifle from the starvation winter, but he was by no means thin. He was excited. As usual, he'd had a vision, only this time he seemed to think that it was something very, very special. It was so amazing that he couldn't contain himself from blurting it all out at the fire, in everyone's presence.

"I have a new spirit helper," he declared, his voice portentous.

"Owah!" Father made an exaggerated sound of surprise and sat back, filling his pipe. Fishtail smiled in good humor, and made a gesture toward LaPautre that meant, "please, continue."

Puffing out his chest, raising his voice to an important pitch, Albert commenced his story.

"I admit to you that this occurred because of evil in my heart!"

"Oh, really," said Nokomis, her voice amused. "And *you* a man of such true virtue . . ."

"Yes, I know." LaPautre waved his hands modestly, as if to sweep away his incredible perfections.

Everyone then waited, expectant, for LaPautre to continue. Of course, having caught their interest, he puffed long in concentration to draw out the suspense.

"I was thinking about taking, well, actually *stealing*, one of Old Tallow's traps," said LaPautre. He put his hands up at the sounds of Mama's outrage. "Wait," he said to Mama, "hear me out."

She glared, but gave him the courtesy of her silence.

"She owes me a good trap!" protested LaPautre. "I gave her two skins once!"

"Two skinny muskrat skins," muttered Nokomis, but she hushed herself.

"So I went to her house when she was gone," said LaPautre, "to remove a trap from the lean-to where she keeps them. That's when it happened."

"What?" Pinch was breathless.

"Please be silent while I tell my story," LaPautre admonished. "It is powerful, I know, but you must respect my relationship with the winged ones and listen closely."

"Well, get on with it, we're listening," said Deydey, straining to keep the laughter from bursting out of his voice.

"Here is what happened!"

LaPautre made a final puff and drew himself up to his most solemn height. Unfortunately, whenever he pulled up his shoulders, his round belly popped out in a comical arc. Nevertheless, he went on. "I was approaching the house, I was putting out my hand, I was choosing the trap I would take . . ."

"Go on," said Nokomis, grim with protective fury for her friend Old Tallow.

"Anyway," said LaPautre, "I was about to close my fingers on the trap when I heard a voice."

Nobody really wanted to encourage LaPautre, but at last Angeline could not contain her curiosity.

"What did it say?"

"It said"—LaPautre leaned forward and fixed them all with his keenest, slightly cross-eyed stare—"'Gaygo'. In other words, the voice said *not to do what* I *was doing.* I opened my eyes. My friends, a crow was sitting there, its eyes black and shiny as lake stones. My friends, it spoke to me. 'Ahneen,' it said. 'Ahneen,' I answered. 'Gaygo,' it warned me again. Then flew off."

LaPautre sat back and folded his arms across his

chest. He waited for the sounds of amazement and the hushed tones of respect. He waited for the nods from Deydey and the serious expressions of wonder from Mama and Nokomis. Instead, after a moment of amazed delight, his entire audience burst into howls of laughter. Deydey was overcome with hilarity, and every time he tried to explain to LaPautre, he sank into helpless sobs and guffaws. Nokomis and Mama were holding each other and laughing so hard tears came down their cheeks. Angeline had turned away and was pounding the dirt. Pinch jumped up and down, yelling. Omakayas was laughing for another reason besides the coincidence, for Andeg was near, had survived, might come back someday!

LaPautre, slowly picking up his things, turned to the laughing family in a state of bewilderment. He put out his hands as though to ask, but then, when Deydey tried to blubber an explanation, only to collapse in fresh laughter, LaPautre swiped his hand through the air and scratched his head. This was definitely not the reaction he'd expected! As he walked away, he wondered whether the entire family had eaten some sort of strange medicine, taken leave of their senses perhaps? He stroked his chin. Yes, he'd sleep on it. Maybe his guardian bird, the crow, would return and speak to him again. Maybe he would have another vision, and somehow obtain an answer.

◄o►

Again it was time for the family to plant; Yellow Kettle chopped at the tough winter-packed earth of their family garden. While the others broke dirt clods and struggled with roots, picked stones and smoothed out rough rows to plant, Pinch pretended to help. He kicked at tiny weeds and smoothed circles in the dirt with his hands. He threw mud balls until Yellow Kettle gave her hoe to him and told him that if he stopped working just once she would take away all of his play warrior weapons. His lower lip stuck out. He grumped. As he dug into the earth he wished he was a grown man already with nothing of this sort to bother him. Still, he found himself occasionally dragging makuks of water over to splash on Omakaya's planted seeds. His sister even thanked him once, which made him so warm and shivery inside, that he had to run and shout, louder than ever, at nothing.

The pumpkin seeds wore little silver patches, like French medals, and Nokomis blessed them gently as she pushed them into the soft new earth. The corn seeds were chubby and yellow in Omakayas's fingers. Angeline had acquired, from Fishtail, some corn with red flecks in it and Mama put these seeds into the ground with a special blessing, curious to see what their growth would bring. The ground harbored the sunshine and spread warm beneath their feet. As she planted one hill after another Omakayas felt the calm and sweetness of the earth and tears burned. Where was Neewo? She missed him. When they had finished planting, as though summoned, rain sprinkled down in a mist. The shower deepened the calm of the woods, ticked through the new leaves, lightly wetted the seeds sheltered in the earth.

Suddenly, just as they were leaving the field, Andeg appeared, wheeling through the air, dive-bombing the family with his familiar *"crawwk, crawwk."* Andeg swooped near but refused to land with his usual sweep on Omakayas's shoulder.

"Come, come, ombay!" called Omakayas with a thrill of happiness.

Pinch, who never was still, never kept himself from excitement, acted differently. He stood motionless and waited right next to his sister. He seemed to know something that Omakayas, in her eagerness to hold her pet, couldn't grasp. Andeg had become half wild, afraid of humans. Omakayas's waves and anxious calls were frightening to him. Pinch, on the other hand, actually understood that the quieter he stood the more likely their old friend was to trust him. And sure enough, Andeg did land. Right on Pinch's head. Pinch's eyes rolled up. He tried to see Andeg. The bird hopped up and down uttering his greeting. *Craakacraakacraak!* Omakayas was hurt, but instantly, and this was the gesture that forever changed the nature of the friendship between her and her little brother; Pinch gently edged next to his sister, and with a short hop her Andeg jumped onto Omakayas' shoulder.

In the old days, Pinch would have teased her and made her feel bad because her bird preferred him. Something had changed.

"Megwetch, little brother," said Omakayas, surprised to say the word.

Pinch didn't seem to hear, he ran off immediately, shouting his head off. Tears burned in Omakayas's eyes, for as soon as Andeg was on her shoulder he trusted her once more. He pecked at her silver cross, hopped onto her head, gazed at her with the old, curious, questing expression of bird intelligence. As they started back from the field, he rode on her shoulder. Tenderly, as they walked along, the bird plucked up a strand of hair that had fallen loose from Omakayas's braid, and then he tucked it behind her ear.

◄○►

Not long after, Old Tallow brought deer bones to share with Grandma. For a time, the two woman sat by the outdoor fire. The air was cool and the fire burned high, stacked with dry wood. Nokomis baked the deer bones, cracked them and used a special long carved spoon to scoop out the hot rich marrow. After a while, Nokomis went out to look for Pinch, and Tallow called Omakayas over to sit near the fire with her.

"Have some tea," she said, "I made it fresh."

Omakayas shook her head, suspicious. Tallow was behaving in too serious and friendly a manner. Since when did Old Tallow make tea? Since when did she act as though she had something important to say? Omakayas tried to slip back into the lodge. But the tough woman seized her hand and bent her fingers around the handle of the cup. She had something in mind in this visit, it was clear, but Omakayas decided that whatever it was, she didn't want to confront it. Ever since she'd had a taste of Old Tallow's justice, she'd been wary of the fierce woman, and now, stubborn, Omakayas waited. She felt something flare in her heart. She didn't like to be bossed around.

Unwillingly, Omakayas accepted a cup and took a sip.

"Good. While you're drinking this," said Old Tallow, her strong, ropey arms arranged on her knees, her big feet breaking from her makazins as usual, her hat pulled low and her fierce eyes flashing, "I'll tell you the story of Omakayas. Maybe that will help you get over your little brother."

Omakayas put the cup down, picked it up again at Tallow's abrupt gesture.

"All right! I'll drink it! What do you mean?"

Omakayas frowned. What was this, a plan to get her to forget all about Neewo? She wasn't interested. She was still sad and loyal to her tiny brother. What did Tallow understand? Bitterly, she spoke. "I know the story of Omakayas. It all happened in the winter. She has a beautiful friend, a favorite baby brother. They die. She is left to cry for them."

"Not that story."

"What other story do you know about me?"

She wanted to tell the old woman to let her be, to go off and hunt, her favorite occupation. But because Old Tallow was, after all, an elder, and because Mama had always insisted that Omakayas be polite as possible to her elders, Omakayas pretended to listen to the story.

"When you were very tiny," Old Tallow began.

"What do you mean, when I was very tiny?" Omakayas tried to be good, but irritation burst out of her. "Mama had me, not you, and she held me, fed me, dressed me, all of those things. What do you know? What more is there to say?"

Old Tallow drew a deep breath, her eyes almost crossed with fury, but she kept her temper,

"You don't have any excuse to be rude, no matter how sad you are. You can't treat me in this disrespectful way."

Omakayas felt her throat shut with shock and embarrassment. She wanted to cry. Why was she acting like this?

"Eyah, okay then, I'm sorry," she said, more softly. "What are you going to tell me?"

"Haven't you wondered," said Old Tallow, a bit testy with the difficult girl Omakayas had become, "hasn't it occurred to you to ask why you didn't get the chimookoman's sickness?"

"*You* didn't get sick," said Omakayas, stubborn.

"I *never* get sick," said Tallow.

"Nokomis stayed well."

"Your grandma already had the smallpox."

Omakayas remembered the tiny whited pit in the skin of her grandmother's cheek, but was still surprised to hear that Nokomis, too, had suffered the disease. She pondered for a moment, and then could not hide her curiosity.

"What about me?" she demanded, abrupt as Old Tallow herself.

"You, too."

"Me, too, what?"

"Had the scratching disease."

A panicky feeling bubbled up inside Omakayas, and she wanted to laugh to drive the feeling off.

"I couldn't have!"

"You wouldn't remember exactly what happened. You were a baby."

"Then why didn't Mama have it? Why did Mama get sick, too, this time?"

"Because," said Old Tallow, "you weren't with your mama, then."

Omakayas wanted to stop talking now. She could feel it. There was something else, something coming toward her, something deeper and huger that she didn't want to know. She tried to stop herself from asking the next question, but her curiosity was too great. She felt her voice rise.

"Where was I?"

"A different island," said Old Tallow. Her voice was stern, but there was an ache in her look that Omakayas had never before seen. "An island called Spirit Island where everyone but you died of the itching sickness— you were the toughest one, the littlest one, and you survived them all."

Tallow smiled mirthlessly, grim. "Starvation nearly got you next, but I managed to cheat the old hungry skull. Fed you broth of rabbits. Brought you back with me. This was before you were two winters old, my girl, before you said words yet, before you can remember anything."

Omakayas's mind tried to grasp what she was hearing, her heart tumbled into darkness and she could not speak. Now the line was crossed. She had to know everything.

"Mama, Deydey, Nokomis?"

"They took you as their daughter, loved you as their daughter, you are a daughter to them, and a sister to your brother, and to Angeline."

"You? Why did you give me away?" blurted Omakayas.

Old Tallow glared away, into the distance.

"Count yourself lucky! What kind of life with an

old bear hunter like Tallow? Nobody has ever stayed with Old Tallow. She drives them off. Eyah!"

The two sat together for a long, long time, there at the fire with the darkness gathering above them and to all sides. Old Tallow made a move to leave, but Omakayas said, her voice strange and hollow and small, "Daga, please, don't go."

Inside, she knew that there was something still to ask. Something about the story, which seemed both unbelieveable and perfectly understandable, all at once. But she couldn't put it into words. Tallow went on speaking.

"I know now the reason you were sent to Yellow Kettle, to the old woman, to your Deydey, your brothers," said Tallow. She rustled in the tatters of her dress, groped for her smoking pipe, then remembered she was out of tobacco and let her hands splay restlessly in her lap.

"You were sent here so you could save the others," she said. "Because you'd had the sickness, you were strong enough to nurse them through it. They did a good thing when they took you in, and you saved them for their good act. Now the circle that began when I found you is complete."

Omakayas knew the question she needed to ask. She took a deep breath, and asked it forthrightly.

"Found me? How did you find me? How did you

know I was there unless you were on that island? Unless you, too, survived the sickness?"

Now Old Tallow fell silent, and in her mulling Omakayas could tell there was some unwillingness, something she did not want to say. But she shrugged, eventually, and told it right out.

"There was a canoe of men, my husband, Hat, among them. They passed by Spirit Island. Saw the dead. Saw you."

"So it was they who brought me back?"

"No," said Tallow, simply.

"They saw me," said Omakayas, making sure, "but they didn't save me."

Old Tallow shook her head in the dusk. Then she shook herself all over, just like one of her dogs.

"Hiyn! My husband, Hat, was a fearful fool. I was going to put his things out the door, anyway. When he told me that he and the other men had seen you, and gone on! Leaving you!" Old Tallow's voice took fury. "I made him leave. 'Don't show me your face, ever!' I said to him. And then I took my canoe over to that island."

The wintery trees clacked their branches, ticking and moaning. The wind picked up often, at dusk, on the island. Omakayas could feel in her heart what it was like for that baby, for herself, all alone with the dead, with her mother, walking from those she loved as though walking stone to stone. Somehow, deep inside, she remembered.

"It was spring," she said softly. "Zeegwun."

"Owah!" said Old Tallow in surprise, peering closely at her. "You remember!"

"The birds," said Omakayas, "I remember the birds, the songs of the birds."

"Owah!" Tallow was excited. "I had forgotten, myself. There were birds on that island, singing so prettily, so loudly! Too small to eat. The little birds with white throats, those sweet spring cries. Eyah! My girl, you remember them."

"They kept me alive," said Omakayas, to herself, not quite understanding her own words. "I remember their song because their song was my comfort, my lullaby. They kept me alive."

◄○►

Omakayas woke to a piercing spring music. Morning, it was morning, and it was the very same song she remembered from that other island, so long ago. This morning, in a tree near the birchbark house, she heard the white-throated sparrows calling out to one another.

"Where are you going?" Angeline asked sleepily.

"Out," said Omakayas.

"Errhg," said Pinch as she stepped over him and out into the fresh dawn world.

The sun was just peeping over the water, its light winking and growing. All around her there sounded voices of hundreds of white-throated sparrows. In the mild air of spring they were singing cheerfully, sweetly, as though to keep her company on the first morning of her life that she, Omakayas, knew the truth of her past. She was the girl from Spirit Island. She lived in a birch-bark house. This was the first day of the journey on which she would find out the truth of her future, who she was. Singing, singing, the little birds told her something more. Their delicate song surrounded her, running in waves though the leafless trees.

Omakayas walked toward the strongest center of their music, and then, on a patch of thawed grassy ground, she lay back in the sun, her head against the bark of a fallen log. The birds, the whole earth, the expectant woods seemed to wait for her to understand something. She didn't know what. It didn't matter. Drowsily, she whistled along with the tiny sparrows. *Ingah beebeebee. Ingahbeebeebee.* Those sweet, tiny, far-reaching notes were so brave. The little birds called out repeatedly in the cold dawn air, and all of a sudden

Omakayas heard something new in their voices.

She heard Neewo.

She heard her little brother as though he still existed in the world. She heard him tell her to cheer up and live. *I'm all right*, his voice was saying, *I'm in a peaceful place. You can depend on me. I'm always here to help you, my sister.* Omakayas tucked her hands behind her head, lay back, closed her eyes, and smiled as the song of the white-throated sparrow sank again and again through the air like a shining needle, and sewed up her broken heart.

AUTHOR'S NOTE ON THE OJIBWA LANGUAGE

Ojibwa was originally a spoken, not written, language, and for that reason spellings are often idiosyncratic. There are also many, many dialects of Ojibwa in use. I apologize to the reader of Ojibwa for any mistakes and refer those who would like to encounter the language in depth to A *Concise Dictionary of Minnesota Ojibwa*, edited by John D. Nichols and Earl Nyholm, to the *Oshkaabewis Native Journal*, ed. Anton Treuer, and to the curriculum developed by Dennis Jones at the University of Minnesota.

GLOSSARY AND PRONUNCIATION
GUIDE OF OJIBWA TERMS

adisokaan (ahd-zoh-kahn): a traditional story that often helps explain how to live as an Ojibwa

ahneen (ah-NEEN): a greeting, sometimes in the form of a question

Akeeng (ah-KEEN): the earth

amik (ah-MIK): beaver

anishaa (ah-NISH-ah): a complex word used to begin an Ojibwa prayer, connoting humility in the mysterious greatness of creation

Anishinabe (AH-nish-in-AH-bay): the original name for the Ojibwa or Chippewa people, a Native American group who originated in and live mainly in the northern North American woodlands. There are currently Ojibwa reservations in Michigan, Wisconsin, Minnesota, North Dakota, Ontario, Manitoba, Montana, and Saskatchewan.

Anishinabeg (AH-nish-in-AH-bayg): the plural form of Anishinabe

apitchi (ah-PITCH-ee): robin

asema (ah-SAY-mah): tobacco of the sort normally used for smoking; one of the four most sacred plants of the Ojibwa

ashaageshinh (ah-SHAH-geh-sheen): crayfish

Awausesee (ah-WUHS-suh-see): the catfish dodem, or clan, a group within the Ojibwa tribe. Other dodems include migizi (eagle), mahingan (wolf), mahng (loon), and mukwah (bear)

ayah (ah-YAH): yes

bekayaan (beh-KAH-yahn): be quiet

biboon (bih-BOON): winter

booni (BOO-nee): leave it alone

boozhoo (boo-SHOE): an Ojibwa greeting invoking the great teacher of the Ojibwa, Nanabozho

Bwaanug (BWAHN-ug): the Dakota and Lakota people, another Native tribe, whose reservations spread across the Great Plains

chimookoman (chi-MOOK-oh-man): word meaning "big knife," used to describe white people or non-Indians

chimookomanug (chi-MOOK-oh-man-ug): the plural form of chimookoman

daga (dah-gah): please

dagwaging (dah-GWAG-ing): fall

Deydey (DAY-day): Daddy

gaween (gah-WEEN): no

gaween onjidah (gah-WEEN ohn-jee-dah): I don't mean to do this

gayay neen (guy-AY neen): me too

gaygo (GAY-go): exclamation meaning "stop that"

geget (GEH-geht): surely, or for emphasis, truly or really

geget chiwohningeyz (gay-GET chi-who-ning-ehz): phrase meaning "good job" or "you did well"

hiyn (high-n): exclamation of sympathy or chagrin, meaning "that's too bad"

howah (HOW-ah): a sound of approval

ishte (ISH-tay): exclamation meaning how good, nice, pleasant

kinnikinnick (KIHN-ih-kihn-ihk): type of smoking mixture made of the inner bark of dogwood or red willow, sometimes mixed with regular tobacco

makazins (MAH-kah-zinz): footwear usually made of tanned moosehide or deerskin, often trimmed with beads and/or fur

makuk (mah-KUK): a container of birchbark folded and often stitched together with basswood fiber. Ojibwa people use these containers today, especially for traditional feasts.

manidominenz (mah-nih-DOH-min-eynz): tiny beads; the word means "little spirit seeds"

manitous (MAN-i-toos): spirits; beings who inhabit the Ojibwa world and often communicate in dreams

manomin (mah-NOH-min): wild rice; the word means "the good seed"

maywizah (may-wih-zah): long time ago

megwetch (mee-gwetch): thank you

Midewiwin (mih-DAY-wih-win): religious gatherings

mino aya sana (mih-noh ah-YAH sah-nah): I wish you good health

minopogwud (mih-noh-POH-gwud): delicious!

Moningwanaykaning (moh-ning-wah-NAY-kan-ing): Island of the Golden-Breasted Woodpecker, also known as Madeline Island, largest of the Apostle Islands in Southern Lake Superior, spiritual home of the Ahnishinabeg

mukwah (muh-kwah): bear

n'dai (en-die): my dog, my animal (often used also with a horse or car)

Nanabozho (nan-ah-boh-ZHO): the great teacher of the Ojibwas, who used his comical human side to teach lessons, often through hilarious mistakes

neebin (nee-bin): summer

neshemay (neh-she-may): little sister or little brother

neshkey (nesh-kay): look

nindinaweymaganidok (nin-din-a-WEY-mah-gah-ni-dohk): my relatives

ninoonde wesin (noh-noon-day WEE-sin): I'm hungry

nokomis (no-KOH-mis): grandmother

odaemin (oh-DAY-min): strawberries

ogema (oh-geh-ma): queen

ombay (OM-bay): come here; let's go

onagun (oh-NAH-gun): birchbark bowl

owah (oh-WAH): exclamation of alarm or surprise, like "oh!"

pakuks (pah-KUKZ): skeletons of children that fly through the air

pikwayzhigun (pih-kway-zhi-gun): bread; literally "that which is cut"

tikinagun (tick-ih-NAH-gun): a cradle board made of lightweight wood, with a footrest on one end and a bow-shaped frame at the other. A baby is wrapped snugly into the tikinagun with cloth, blankets, and skins. The tikinagun can be carried on the mother's back, leaned against a tree or a wall, or safely hung from a tree branch. Small toys such as shells, dream-catchers, or pieces of birchbark with bitten designs are often hung from the bow-shaped frame near the baby's head to amuse him or her.

waboose (WAH-booz): rabbit

wakaigun (wah-KAH-ig-gun): house

weedookaow (wee-doh-KOW): help

weendamawashin (ween-dah-MAHW-ih-shin): tell me

wigwam (WIHG-wahm): a birchbark house

windigo (WIN-di-go): a giant monster of Ojibwa teachings, often made of ice and associated with the starvation and danger of deep winter

wisikodewinini (wiss-ih-koh-DAY-wih-ninni): "half-burnt wood;" a descriptive word for mixed-blood (part white) Anishinabeg

zeegwun (ZEEG-wun): spring

Zhaganashimowin (zha-gah-NAHSH-ih-moh-win): white man's language; Omakayas refers to English as taught by Protestant and Catholic missionaries

ANDEG POINTS WITH HIS BEAK TO THE GENERAL REGION OF THE ISLAND ◦ MONINGWANAYKANING ◦ WITH HIS FOOT HE SHOWS ◦ OLD LAPOINTE ◦ WHERE LIVED OMAKAYAS AND HER FAMILY c. 1847

TO THE GREAT STANDS OF MAPLE THAT WERE TAPPED EACH SPRING FOR SYRUP AND SUGA

HERE THE LOVELY TEN SNOW LIVED WITH FISHTAIL

THE DOCK WHERE DEYDEY ARRIVED AND THE TRADING POST WHERE HE TRIUMPHED AT CHESS

THE CABIN OF OLD TALLOW

AUNTIE MUSKRAT'S CABIN

OMAKAY

THE MISSION WHERE FISHTAIL LEARNS TO READ AND WRITE

THE WINTER CABIN

DATE			

GENESIS OF SHANNARA

THE ELVES
OF CINTRA

GENESIS OF SHANNARA

THE ELVES
OF CINTRA

TERRY BROOKS

BALLANTINE BOOKS
NEW YORK

Copyright © 2007 by Terry Brooks

Published in the United States by Del Rey Books, an imprint of The Random House Publishing Group, a division of Random House, Inc., New York.

DEL REY is a registered trademark and the Del Rey colophon is a trademark of Random House, Inc.

Interior map by Russ Charpentier

LIBRARY OF CONGRESS CATALOGING-IN-PUBLICATION DATA

Brooks, Terry.
The Elves of Cintra / Terry Brooks.
p.   cm.—(Genesis of Shannara)
ISBN 978-0-345-48411-6 (alk. paper)
1. Shannara (Imaginary place)—Fiction.
2. Elves—Fiction. I. Title.
PS3552.R6596E48 2007 ·
813'.54—dc22   2007015127

Printed in the United States of America on acid-free paper

www.delreybooks.com

2 4 6 8 9 7 5 3

FOR LAURIE

My sister, with admiration and love always

ONE

LOGAN TOM HAD climbed out of the lower levels of the compound and was starting up the steps to the walls when he heard the cries. They were sudden and sharp and signaled shock and excitement. He was still inside and could not tell what was happening, but he redoubled his efforts instantly, charging ahead, abandoning stealth, throwing caution to the winds.

If he was too late . . .

If they had already thrown Hawk and Tessa from the walls . . .

If, if, if!

The words burned in his mind like live coals. He couldn't be too late. Not after coming so far and getting so close. He should never have left Hawk in the compound. He should have found a way to take him out when he had the chance. Relying on breaking him free now was a fool's game, and anyone with an ounce of common sense would have known it!

He was running hard, his black staff held ready in front of him, his concentration complete. He passed dozens of the compound's inhabitants on the way up, but while a few turned to look, no one tried to stop him. Maybe they could see in his eyes that getting in his way for any reason was a bad idea. If what he was thinking was reflected there, mirrored in eyes that were hard-edged and enraged, they couldn't miss it.

He was up the steps all the way now and outside, the sports field spread away below him. The spectator seats in this section had been ripped out long ago to provide space for makeshift housing, and he found himself in a cluster of small one-level cottages built out of bricks and wood that were cobbled together to form rooms and stacked from one level to the next. They registered in his mind as he tore through them, following the lanes purposely left clear for passage, charging upward toward the top.

But something unexpected was happening. Those gathered on the walls to watch the death sentence on Hawk and Tessa being carried out were rushing back down almost as fast as he was rushing up. He stopped where he was, bracing himself against the swarm, trying to pick out something that made sense from the babble of words being exchanged.

". . . nothing ever like it before this, a demon's work if ever there was one—did you see that light . . ."

". . . bright as a flare or maybe a . . ."

". . . wasn't a trace of them on the ground, and then it got dark again and you could see down . . ."

Logan moved into the shelter of a narrow aisle made over into a walkway between huts, waiting for the way to clear. Whatever had happened, it was all over now. But *what* had happened?

He grabbed a young man who got close enough and pulled him out of the swarm of bodies. He put his face close. "Tell me what's going on. Why is everyone running?"

The young man stared at him a moment, seeing something that might have scared him even more than what he had witnessed on the wall. He tried to speak and couldn't, then yanked his arm free from Logan's grip and threw himself back into the surging mass of the crowd.

Logan shifted his approach from the common lanes and began making his way upward between the huts in a less direct fashion. He went as quickly as passage would allow, dodging or knocking obstacles aside. Buckets, brooms, pots, and other cooking implements went flying, and shouts of anger from their owners followed after him. In another time and under different circumstances, he would have drawn more attention. But the majority of the compound population was either coming down off the walls or fighting to get to the front gates, anxious to see whatever was out there.

Not the boy, he prayed. Not the girl.

He reached the upper levels where the housing grew sparse and scattered, a concession to the winds and the chill that made living higher up less desirable. The smells of the population gave way to the odors of fish and seaweed floating off the water, and the darkness deepened as the fires and generator lights were left below. Up here, what few lights there were pointed outward toward the gates and the approach to the walls. He passed out of the tangle of huts and walkways, the bulk of the crowd gone past now, and moved along the high wall toward an opening that led out onto what was once the concession area.

He found more buildings here, the same makeshift huts, these mostly for storage, not living. A scattering of the compound's residents still remained on the wall, looking down over the rim. He chose a young girl standing with her back to him, her attention on whatever lay outside below the walls.

"Where are the boy and girl?" he asked, walking up to her.

She turned and stared at him. She was no more than fourteen or fifteen, her freckled face squinched up as if she had swallowed something unpleasant. "What?"

"The boy and girl?" he repeated. "What happened to them?"

She hesitated. "Didn't you see?"

"I wasn't here. Tell me."

"Well, wow, what *didn't* happen! It was so *amazing*! They threw them—the guards threw them off, together, you know. They flew right out into space like—like scarecrows or sacks of sand. Then a light appeared all at once, a brilliant light. It came right out of nowhere and swallowed them up. When the light disappeared, they were gone, too."

She glanced over her shoulder and looked down at the rubble-strewn pavement as if to make certain. "I've never seen anything like it.

No one knows what happened." She turned back. "I heard one man say it was demon magic! Do you think?"

Logan didn't know what he thought. "No," he said. "Did the light seem to come from one of them—from the boy, maybe?"

She shook her head. Her long, sandy hair rippled in the dim light, and she brushed strands of it from her eyes. "No, it didn't come from anywhere. It just flared up out of thin air and surrounded them. You couldn't see them at all after that. Everyone just went crazy! It was wonderful!"

He took a moment to consider what this meant. The most logical explanation was that Hawk's magic—the wild magic of the gypsy morph—had surfaced in an unexpected way. But if the girl was right, if it wasn't Hawk's own magic manifesting itself in some unknown way, then it had to have been an intervening magic. Yet where would such magic have come from? Had Hawk and Tessa been saved or tossed from the frying pan into the fire? He knew he wouldn't find the answer here.

"Hey, mister, do I know you?" the girl asked him suddenly.

He shook his head. "No."

"You look familiar."

He peered down over the walls to the rubble below. Nothing, not even the feeders, was there now. Whatever had happened, it had disrupted their plans to absorb the combination of magic and life force expended by Hawk's death. All those feeders, he thought, gone in the blink of an eye.

The girl was leaning on the railing next to him, studying his face. She must have seen him when he'd come to the compound earlier in the day. She would remember soon enough. It was time to go.

Suddenly her gaze shifted. "Look at that. See all the lights out on the water? Like a million little fires or something."

He looked to where she was pointing, but what he saw that she couldn't were the feeders massed along the waterfront, a surging horde of smooth dark bodies writhing and twisting in an effort to get closer to whatever was approaching on the water. He looked beyond to the lights, hundreds of them, couldn't make any sense of it at first, and then heard the drums and went cold.

At almost the same moment a horn blew from somewhere farther down the walls of the compound, high up in a watchtower, a mournful wail that signaled danger in any language. Someone else had spotted the lights and, like Logan, knew what they meant.

He turned away from the girl. "I have to go. Thanks for helping me."

"Sure. Weren't you here . . . ?"

He wheeled back, cutting short the rest of what she was going to say. It was an impulsive act, one born of frustration and despair. He was tired of people dying. "Go find your parents and your brothers and sisters and anyone else you care about and get everyone out of here. Tell anyone you meet. Those lights come from boats carrying an army that will besiege this compound and eventually destroy it."

She started to speak, but he grabbed her shoulders and held her. "No, just listen to me. I know what I am talking about. I know about this army. I have seen what it can do. Get out of here, right away, even if no one else will go with you. I know you don't want to, but do it. Remember what I said. If you stay, you will die."

He left her staring after him, her eyes wide, her face rigid with shock and disbelief. He had no further time for her, nothing more he could do for her. She would believe him or not. Probably not. They seldom did, any of them. They thought it was as safe as it could get inside the compounds. They thought it was so much more dangerous out in the open. None of them understood. Not until it was too late. It was why they were being wiped out. It was the reason the human race was being annihilated.

To his surprise, she came after him, grabbed his arm, and pulled him around. "You're not serious, are you? About what will happen? None of that's true, is it?"

He studied her a moment. "What's your name?"

"Meike," she answered uncertainly.

"Well, listen closely to me, Meike. Everything I said is true. There are madmen on those boats. They were human once, men and women like those in this compound. But they've shed their humanity to serve demons that intend to destroy us all. They kill humans or put them in slave camps. They've done it everywhere, all across the country. They will do it here, too. The compound leaders think they can stand against them, think they are safe enough here behind their walls. But other compounds thought the same, and they all fell in the end. This one will fall, too."

"I don't have any parents or brothers or sisters," she said. She brushed at her long hair, her eyes filled with fear. "I don't have anyone. I don't know what to do. Where should I go?"

He wished suddenly he hadn't told her. All he had done was scare her half to death. Besides, it was one life. What difference did saving one life make to what was going to happen here? Even if telling her got her out of here, what did it matter? She would end up dying in the countryside instead of in the city, nothing more. He was suddenly furious with himself. That was his problem, trying to save people like her. He was wasting his time when what he needed to do was what he had come to do in the first place—find the gypsy morph.

He gave her a quick glance and shook his head. "Go anywhere away from the city. Go into the country. Look for others who might want to go with you. There's safety in numbers."

He turned away abruptly and started down the walkway for the stairs, intent on getting out of there before anyone realized who he was. Once he was identified, things would become considerably more complicated.

"Mister!" she called after him.

He ignored her, moving faster now, hurrying deliberately to get away, reaching the stairs and descending them two at a time. The crowds had dissipated. He could hear them at the gates below, milling about in confusion as the watchtower horn continued to sound its warning. Already, squads of defenders were forming up in the parade grounds at one end of the field, soldiers carrying weapons, buckling on light armor and belts of ammunition. Well trained and organized, they would go out to meet the threat. They would try to stop the invaders at the docks, to prevent them from landing. They would fail, and then retreat through the streets to the compound, where they would feel safe. They would not be safe; they would be doomed. But it had nothing to do with him. The fighting at the docks and in the streets would last through the night. By tomorrow, he would be far away.

He glanced ahead at the clusters of compound inhabitants, choosing his path. He would go back down to the lower levels and out through the underground passageway. Panther would be waiting, and together they would find the other Ghosts and decide where to go to get away from what was about to happen.

But how in the world, he wondered, was he going to find out what had become of Hawk?

He turned down out of the arena and into the building interior and ran right up against a squad of compound defenders coming out.

"Hold it right there," one said, and he pointed his weapon at Logan.

PANTHER HUNKERED DOWN in the rubble at the edge of Pioneer Square, waiting impatiently. An awful lot had happened since Logan Tom had gone into the compound, and most of it was a mystery to him. He had carried out his assignment, going to the front gates and providing the diversion that Logan needed. He had done a good job of it, yelling up at the guards, demanding that Hawk be freed, that he be allowed to talk to him, that they give him food. He had made it look like he was a half-crazed street kid, and he must have succeeded because the guards on the walls laughed at him. After he'd shouted at them for what he thought was twice as long as necessary for Logan to sneak past them to where the old transportation shelter would give him access to the compound, he had backed off and returned to the spot where he'd been told to wait, finding a place to hide and settling in.

For a long time, nothing had happened. Then he had seen the flash of light at the gates and heard the cries of those gathered on the walls, but he didn't know what it meant. He thought about moving to a better position, one closer to the gates, in an effort to find out. But he was worried that if Logan Tom returned with Hawk and couldn't find him, he might leave him behind. So he stayed where he was, frustrated and edgy. Night deepened until only a pale gray light remained in the western sky and the lights of the compound began to switch on. More time passed, and he found himself increasingly unsettled.

Then, through gaps in the city buildings, he caught sight of lights out on the water. He stared at them, unable to tell how many there were or the nature of their source. They appeared to be moving, coming closer. Boats, maybe, he decided. But what would boats be doing out on the bay at night, and who would be manning them?

When the horn sounded from atop the compound walls, he was even more confused. He had heard the horn sound before, so he knew that it always signaled trouble, a threat to the compound and its inhabitants. But had the horn blown because of a sighting of the lights or because Logan Tom had been discovered? Was it a call to arms to respond to the Knight of the Word's rescue of Hawk?

"Frickin' hell!" he muttered.

He slumped back in the shadows, watching the approaches to the square from the compound, searching for movement in the rubble. Nothing appeared. He thought again about moving closer in an effort to find out what was happening. Panther was not good at waiting; waiting always made him feel vulnerable.

There was movement in the streets behind him, dark figures appearing from one of the ruined buildings. Panther saw them out of the corner of his eye and froze. Whether they were responding to all the noise and activity at the compound, he couldn't tell. But something had brought them into the open. He counted almost a dozen, far too many of anything to suit him.

Then, as he watched them move out from the shadow of the building, he realized what they were.

Croaks.

Even though he couldn't make out their features in the darkness, there was no mistaking the odd, jerky movements they made as they walked. Flesh eaters, monsters, they were off on a hunt for food. He held himself very still and willed them to go another way.

But as they separated into smaller groups, a pair of them started to come directly toward him.

"WHAT ARE YOU DOING?" the compound soldier asked Logan boldly, keeping his weapon pointed. "You know the rules. All able-bodied men are supposed to be with their units. You look pretty able-bodied to me."

Logan had two choices. He could lie about his connection with the compound and hope the men confronting him believed him, or he could tell them the truth and hope they let him pass anyway. They were all looking at him by now, most of them with their weapons raised. It was a dangerous moment; everyone was on edge with the wailing horn and a heightened sense of something bad about to happen.

"I don't have a unit," he said. "I don't live here. I'm only visiting. I was invited to watch the execution of the boy and the girl."

"Invited to watch?" The speaker studied him. "By whom?"

Logan could not remember the name of the compound leader. He shrugged. "By the leadership."

"Hey, weren't you at the gates earlier, asking to see the boy?" one of the others asked.

Logan gritted his teeth. "I knew him a long time ago. I knew his family. I brought a message from them."

No one was saying anything, but he could tell from the looks on their faces that they didn't believe him. If anything, he was making things worse. But he didn't have much choice. He couldn't let them take him prisoner.

"I am a Knight of the Word," he told them. "I came for the reasons I told you whether you believe me or not. In either case, I don't belong in here; I belong out on the streets. Your compound is in danger. There's an invasion force in the harbor. Instead of standing around, we should be down on the docks trying to stop it."

"Don't be trying to tell us our job!" the first speaker snapped at him angrily. "We don't answer to you!"

"Lower your weapon, please," Logan told him calmly.

People were slowing down as they saw the confrontation that was taking place, sensing that something was wrong. In a moment, the passageways would be so clogged with people stopping to watch that there would be no place for Logan to run. And he already knew he was going to have to run if he was to escape.

"If you know something about the boy, you might know something about what happened up on the walls," the speaker declared, his weapon still leveled at Logan's midsection. "I think you'd better tell all this to our commander, and he can decide what to do with you."

The black staff was hot in Logan's clenched fist, held upright before him, a shield that nothing could penetrate. Already, its magic was coursing through him, as hot and fluid as his blood. The runes carved into the staff's hard wooden surface were beginning to glow softly.

"I don't have time for this," he told the speaker. "Let me pass."

The weapons stayed pointed at him, and he heard the click and snap of released safeties and cocked hammers. *Stupid*, he thought, thinking of both these men and himself.

His arm came up in a quick sweep, the magic already deflecting the bullets that were being fired at him, at the same time sending his attackers flying backward in sprawling heaps, the wind knocked out of them. He turned and ran through a crowd that scattered at his approach, abandoning any idea of trying to leave through the front gates, heading instead for the tunnels that had brought him in. A few others tried to stop him, but he brushed them aside easily, barely slowing, gaining the shelter of the stairwell and scrambling down.

In seconds he had reached the lower levels and was charging along the corridors that led to the tunnels. He could hear shouts and cries behind him, the sounds of a pursuit being mounted. He could hear the pounding of feet coming down the stairs after him. He didn't slow. He wished he could have had a chance to look around the front gates, to see if there was any trace of Hawk and Tessa. But that wouldn't be possible now. Besides, he knew in his heart that whatever had happened to them wasn't the sort of occurrence that left clues. Magic like that—and he was convinced by now that it was magic—made a clean sweep of everything it touched.

He gained the entry to the underground tunnels and passed through, slowing now as a concession to the darkness, using the glow of the runes off the staff to guide him. The gloom was thick, but not complete, and his eyes adjusted quickly. He moved through the tunnels as swiftly as he could, but he had to take enough time to make certain he did not turn down the wrong branch. He became aware that no one was following him. Given up, he mused, to pursue more important matters. Like finding a way to stay alive.

At the end of the tunnel and the door leading out into the bus shelter, he stopped to listen, to reassure himself that no one lay in wait. Then he slipped outside, climbing the steps to where he could look around and see what was happening.

The open spaces surrounding the compound were filled with men pouring through the gates and moving down the streets toward the waterfront, all heavily armored and armed. A pair of ancient mobile Scorpion attack vehicles were chugging along behind them, their huge cannons pointing the way. He hadn't seen one of those since his days with Michael, had thought them all extinct. They fired armor-piercing shells and starburst canister alike. They could sink any of the approaching boats with a single shot, but it would take an awful lot of single shots to make a difference.

Out on the open waters of the bay, the booming of the drums continued, a steady throbbing in the night.

He watched the activity for a moment, all of it heading away from him, and then slipped from the shelter and moved back across the rubble-strewn ground to where he had told Panther to wait for him. The black staff throbbed softly in his hand, and the heat of the magic still roiled within him. He felt hot and cold at the same time, a response to the mix of emotions warring within him. At least he hadn't been forced to hurt anyone. He wished just once the people in the compounds would listen to his warnings about the demons and once-men. It wasn't his problem, but he wished it anyway. It was hard enough tracking down and destroying the slave camps without knowing that those he set free could easily be replaced by the men and women and children of the compounds, fresh fodder for the Void's extermination machine.

He hated even thinking about it. A world turned mad and its people turned victims. But maybe the boy Hawk, a gypsy morph born of wild magic, could make the difference.

He reached the edge of Pioneer Square, expecting to find Panther, but there was no sign of him. He called his name softly, knowing that the compound inhabitants probably couldn't hear him if he screamed it, but cautious nevertheless. No answer. He looked around. Nothing moved.

He stood alone in the empty street, wondering what to do next.

TWO

SPARROW CROSSED THE ROOF of their building in a rush, intent on reaching the stairs and getting down to the street as quickly as she could manage it. The moment she realized what the lights on the water were, she realized as well the danger they were all in. It would take the invaders awhile to get ashore, but as soon as they did they would go hunting for strays like her. She had heard the stories from her mother and seen the results. The hunters of humans were mad things, beasts with claws and teeth and hair, predators. Street kids were a favorite prey. The other Ghosts had to be warned.

But just as she reached the stairwell and was preparing to start down, she heard footsteps coming up. They were heavy and rough, and no attempt was being made to hide their approach. She stopped where she was, listening. The footsteps did not belong to the Ghosts or even to the Knight of the Word. Or to anything human, she added quickly.

She backed away from the opening, both hands tightening around the slim metal length of her prod. Then she heard deep, guttural voices from the darkness below, voices harsh enough to override even the heavy tread, and she froze.

Croaks.

Her mind raced as she tried to think what to do. She did not want to have to fight her way past Croaks. They were slow and not particularly smart, but they were enormously strong. If they got their hands on her, she was finished. She stared into the black of the stairwell and took another few steps back. She did not know whether she should chance trying to get down to a lower level where there might be somewhere better to hide, or stay where she was. If she was lucky, they might lose interest and go away. If not, if they came all the way up, she was in trouble. She glanced around quickly. The roof was open and mostly flat save for a handful of small mechanical housings and the debris from their catchment system. There was almost nowhere to hide. She turned back to the stairs helplessly. There was no other way off the roof.

Or was there?

She raced to the side of the building that fronted the alleyway and looked down. A fire escape ladder was attached to the concrete by heavy bolts, a narrow metal ribbon almost invisible in the gloom. She stared at it a moment, then glanced out at the water where the lights from the invading boats were drawing closer. The drums continued to sound, beating out a steady rhythm, announcing what lay ahead to those in the threatened city. Already the gates of the compound had swung open and squads of defenders were making their way down to the docks. A battle would be fought there soon. When that happened, the Ghosts would be well advised to be far away.

She brushed at her thatch of straw-colored hair and took a deep breath. She hated heights, but anything was preferable to an encounter with Croaks. She looped the prod's carry strap over her shoulder and across her back, stepped up onto the narrow, flat surface of the building cap, grasped the curved railing where it arched up from below, and started climbing down backward.

She wanted to close her eyes, but she settled for keeping her gaze fixed on the wall and her attention focused on finding secure footing upon each rung as she descended. Her efforts were made easier by the deepness of the night, which the narrow canyon of the alleyway made almost complete. Even the torchlight from the compound and the water didn't penetrate here. She steadied herself by thinking of her warrior mother, of how she had orchestrated escapes of this sort so

many times when Sparrow was little. Her mother had told her about
some of them, and Sparrow had been present at a few near the end.
She had marveled at her mother's calmness in the face of such excru-
ciating pressure. It had taught her something about the necessity of
composure, of knowing that the worst danger you faced would often
be your own uncertainty.

She kept that foremost in her thoughts as she made her way down
the side of the building, a fly against the wall in the gloom, trying not
to think about how it would feel to fall.

The descent went much more quickly than she had expected, and
her feet touched the ground before she realized it was there. She
stepped away from the ladder, unslung the prod, and looked around
guardedly. She could not see or hear anything. The alley was empty.
Moving quickly down its length, she gained the street and peered out
into the night. She was at the side of the building now, the street running down from Pioneer Square to the waterfront. Everywhere, the
shadows seemed to move in response to the fires and the drums.

A quick glance up at the roof revealed nothing.

She started up the street for the square, intent on going after the
other Ghosts and warning them of the danger. She wasn't sure what they
could do about it until the Knight of the Word returned with Hawk, but
at least they would be prepared for what she knew was coming. She
swore in her best thirteen-year-old street language at the Croaks that had
forced her to climb down that ladder, furious at the delay. What were
Croaks doing in her building anyway? They knew the rules. They had
never entered before, never even dared. They must have seen the Ghosts
leaving, must have realized that they were abandoning the building. It
was a desirable dwelling, easily defended and safe. They just decided to
move in once it appeared that the Ghosts had moved out.

But they could have waited a day or two, couldn't they?

She reached the head of the street where it intersected the square,
moving cautiously, eyes sweeping the darkness, knowing that if there
were Croaks inside the building there were probably Croaks outside, as
well. But the square seemed deserted, and so she started to turn north
up First in the direction the others had gone when she heard her name
called.

"Sparrow! Wait up!"

She wheeled around at the sound of Panther's voice, watching as he came up the empty street at a trot, dodging among the piles of debris, his prod cradled in the crook of his arm, his breathing audible even from where she stood. He must have run all the way from the compound. Something must have happened for him to come back like this. Something bad.

She started to ask what it was, and then saw the dark forms shambling along behind him, still a way back, but clearly in pursuit. More Croaks.

"Frickin' Croaks!" he spit out angrily. "Chased me all the way from the edge of—"

She hissed at him in warning. "Keep it down, Panther Puss! There are more inside!"

Too late. Heavy bodies appeared from the doorway of their building, eyes turning their way. Ragged forms with gimlet eyes, fingernails long since grown to claws, and teeth sharpened like those of wild animals.

Sparrow shoved Panther in frustration. "Now you've done it, big mouth. Get moving!"

They hurried across the square, Croaks at both ends of the street and closing. The fires and the drums didn't seem to have any effect on them. They had their own concerns to occupy their attention, and Sparrow knew that most of those concerns revolved around food.

"Where's Hawk?" she asked as they ran toward the buildings across the way. "Why are you back here alone?"

"Don't know about Hawk. Don't know about that Knight of whatever, either. He left me at the edge of the square, told me to wait until he came back. He never came, but these Croaks did and I had to make a break for it. They're all over. Did you see the fires on the water?"

She glanced over at his dark face. "I saw them from the roof. Boats filled with invaders. If they're the ones I think, we're in big trouble. Mama used to tell me about them. Once-men, she called them. They destroy everything, kill everyone except the ones they put in the slave camps. Worse than the militias. We have to warn the others and get out of here."

"You won't get no argument from me." He slowed suddenly, grabbing her arm. "Uh-oh."

A pair of Croaks had appeared out of the buildings in front of them, blocking their escape. "What is it with these things?" Panther snapped furiously. "We don't see any for weeks, then all of a sudden they're everywhere! Where'd they all come from?"

Sparrow took a quick look around at the ones following. Another few minutes and they would be right on top of them. "We have to get past these two," she said. "You take the one on the left. Try not to do anything stupid."

Without waiting for his response, she launched herself at the one on the right, her finger on the prod's trigger and the staff's electric charge at full strength. She jabbed the prod's end into the Croak's leg, and the Croak grunted and began to shake and jerk uncontrollably. Sparrow didn't back away, keeping the prod jammed into its leg, knowing that if she gave ground it would be on her in a second. To her left, she caught a glimpse of Panther moving in close, his prod lancing into the other Croak's throat with such force that it broke the heavy skin. The Croak gasped and tried to extract the killing tip, but Panther used his strength to force it backward and down to its knees.

In seconds both Croaks lay twitching on the concrete. Sparrow grabbed Panther's arm and pulled him toward the building's alleyway. "Stop staring at them! Run!"

Prods held at the ready, they disappeared into the dark corridor of the alley.

          ■   ●   ■

LOGAN TOM took a few minutes more to look around the rubble where he had told Panther to wait, and then gave up. He didn't know what had happened to the boy, but he couldn't take the time to find out. He had to get back to the other street kids and hope that Panther would find his own way. Maybe something had scared him. That didn't seem like Panther, but you never knew. Whatever the case, he wasn't here now.

Unless he was, but couldn't answer.

Logan didn't want to dwell on that possibility, but he couldn't quite put it aside, either. He hated the thought that he might have somehow failed the boy, that he might have brought him along only to get him killed. He had lived for years with the guilt of never being able to do quite enough for the children in the slave camps. He didn't need another name added to that list. Funny. He had known Panther for less than twenty-four hours, but it felt a lot longer. He liked the dark-humored, moody boy—liked his aggressiveness and readiness to take on anything. Maybe it was because he admired the toughness in street kids that he liked Panther so much.

Or maybe it was because he reminded him of himself.

He started back up the street into Pioneer Square, chased by the sounds of the drums on the bay and the marching of the compound defenders to the docks. He hated the thought of taking on this new responsibility, looking after the Ghosts, shepherding them to wherever it was he was supposed to go. Losing the gypsy morph was a major breach of his duty to protect it. Pretty hard to protect something that had been swallowed up by a ball of light and was now who-knew-where. But being left with the morph's family . . .

He stopped himself, rethinking his choice of language.

Being left with *Hawk's* family, with a pack of street kids to look after, was galling. It limited his freedom of movement. What was he supposed to do with these kids and the old man and that wolf dog while he was trying to figure out how to find Hawk?

He realized that until he had come face-to-face with the morph, he had never thought of it as a child. Even though it had started out as one in the time of John Ross and Nest Freemark, even though it had never been seen as anything else after those first few weeks, he had never thought of it that way. He hadn't really given it any thought at all. When Two Bears had asked him to find the morph, he had seen it as an escape from what he had been doing for so many years: attacking the camps, killing the defenders, setting free the prisoners, and—he hesitated before finishing the thought—destroying the experiments that someday would become demons. The children. He had thought he would be leaving all that behind. He had thought himself free of it.

He had never imagined that he would find himself tied up with a bunch of street kids.

But as with so many things in his life, it appeared he had been wrong about this, too.

He moved ahead into the shadow of the buildings and the dark canyon of Pioneer Square and tried not to look back.

⬛ ⬛ ⬛

OWL HEARD THE DRUMMING first and looked back over her shoulder past River, who was manning the wheelchair, toward the dark stain of the bay waters. Hundreds of lights dotted their smooth surface for as far as the eye could see.

"Turn me around," she ordered the dark-haired girl.

River wheeled her about obediently. The other Ghosts saw what was happening and stopped to look with her. Bear slowed the heavy cart that was filled with their possessions, and Candle, who was leading the way, walked back. Fixit and Chalk, carrying the Weatherman on his makeshift litter, set him down, stretching aching backs and rubbing weary arms.

"For an old man, he weighs an awful lot," Chalk muttered.

Owl didn't hear him, her attention focused on the lights. Torches, she decided. More than she could count. They would be burning from the decks of boats, which meant a huge fleet had come to the city. But not for anything good.

In her lap, Squirrel stirred and lifted his sleepy face from her shoulder. "Are we there, Mama?"

"Not yet," she whispered.

He snuffled and rubbed his eyes. "What's that noise?"

"Nothing to worry about." She stroked his fine hair. "Go back to sleep."

She was worried about him. He should have been better by now, the sickness defeated. But he couldn't seem to shake it, and he was growing weaker despite the medications and care. He had only been able to walk three blocks from their home when they left for the freeway before tiring and climbing into her lap. She didn't mind holding him; he didn't weigh hardly anything.

She glanced down at his wan face. She wished Tessa were there to offer advice. Tessa knew more about medications and sicknesses than anyone.

Candle was standing at her shoulder, young face intense and worried. "We have to run away," she said.

"It's an attack," Bear declared. His big frame blocked the heavy cart so that it could not roll. "Those are war drums. That many boats means an invading force, probably come up from the south."

"It is the thing that comes to kill us," Candle said quickly. She was shivering, hugging herself as she stared out at the lights. "It is the thing from my vision."

Owl reached out for her and turned her around so that she was no longer looking at the lights. "Just look at me, Candle," she said softly. She waited until the little girl stopped shaking. "Can you do that?"

Candle nodded. "I won't look anymore."

"Good." Owl glanced around at the others. "Whatever it is, Candle is right. We need to get as far away from it as we can. Has anyone seen any sign of Sparrow or Panther?"

No one had. Chalk and Fixit were arguing about who should take the front end of the Weatherman's litter. River stalked over angrily, pushed Chalk aside, and picked it up herself.

"Owl says we have to go. Fixit, pick up your end." She glared at Chalk. "You can push the wheelchair for a while since you're so tired."

They started off once more, still climbing inland from the waterfront, having followed First Avenue to within sight of the Hammering Man before turning uphill toward the freeway entrance. It was there that the Knight of the Word had told them they would find his vehicle and should wait for him to join them. Owl hoped he would hurry. She was growing steadily more worried about being separated from Sparrow and Panther. It was bad enough to lose Hawk and maybe Tessa, but unbearable to think of losing the other two, as well. The Ghosts were a family, and as mother of this family she didn't feel right when the group wasn't together.

"Chalk, are you really too tired for this?" she asked quietly so that the others could not hear. She looked back at him. "Do you need a rest? Maybe Candle can fill in for a few minutes if you need to take a break."

"I'm not tired," the boy said, refusing to admit anything, glancing over at River for just a minute before looking away again. "I can do anything that anyone else can and do it better. Especially her."

Even in flight and in danger, they squabbled like the children they were, Owl thought. But they loved and would do anything for one another. Wasn't that true of all families, whatever their nature and circumstances? Wasn't that a large part of what defined them as families?

They continued their climb toward the top of the hill and the freeway entrance, following the sidewalk, angling between piles of debris and derelict vehicles. The darkened, mostly empty buildings formed huge walls to either side, leaving them layered in shadows and silence. A cold wind blew up the concrete-and-stone canyons, coming off the water in damp gusts, carrying the smell of pitch from the torches. The drums throbbed in steady rhythm, the sound deep and ominous.

"I'm not scared," Squirrel murmured into Owl's shoulder.

She gave him a quick hug. "Of course you aren't."

They reached the freeway entrance, a long curving concrete ramp littered with rusted-out cars and trucks, some still whole, some in pieces. Owl looked expectantly for Logan Tom's Lightning S-150 AV, having no idea what it was she was seeking, but knowing it wouldn't be like anything else. Her efforts were in vain. Everything appeared the same to her. Nothing but junk and trash.

"It's over there," Fixit announced.

Because he was carrying one end of the Weatherman's litter, he couldn't point, only nod, so none of them was sure what he was indicating. Owl looked in the general direction of his nod, but didn't see anything.

"It's behind that semi-trailer, over there by the pileup," Fixit continued. "See the big tires? That's a Lightning AV."

Owl was willing to take his word for it, even though she still didn't see anything. Fixit knew a lot about the vehicles his elders had ridden in before almost everything on wheels stopped working. The source of his knowledge was something of a mystery given that he read so little and was content looking at pictures in old magazines, but she supposed it had to do with his mechanical nature.

She looked doubtfully at the abandoned vehicles, clusters of them stretching away down the ramp and onto the freeway for as far as the eye could see. It made her wonder what that last day had been like when the owners had simply abandoned them. It made her wonder what had happened to those people, all those years ago, when the city began to change.

Mostly it made her nervous about what might be down there that they couldn't see. Lots of things made their homes in old vehicles, and you didn't want to disturb them.

Still, they had no choice. They couldn't afford to wait where they were, so far from where Logan Tom had told them to be. Not unless they were threatened, and as yet, the only threat came from the waterfront behind them.

"Lead us down, Fixit," she told him, trying to keep the reluctance from her voice. "But everyone stay together and keep a close eye out for anything that might be hiding in those wrecks. Candle? Warn us if you sense anything."

They started down the ramp, a strange little procession, Fixit and River at the forefront carrying the litter with the Weatherman, Candle right behind, Bear following with the heavy cart, and Chalk, pushing Owl and Squirrel in the wheelchair, bringing up the rear. There was a pale wash of light from the distant compound, the walls of which they could just begin to see, and from the torches beginning to close on the docks of the bay. The drums still beat, and now there were shouts and cries, the sounds of a battle being fought. She heard weapons fire, as well.

Her thoughts drifted to those still missing. She hoped that Sparrow was well away by now. She shouldn't have given her permission to go up on the roof for that final check; she should have made her come with the rest of them. She wondered about Panther and Logan Tom and about Hawk and Tessa. Too many people missing, too many ways for them to get hurt in what was happening down there.

Everything is changing, she thought without knowing exactly why she felt it was so. But the thought persisted. *Nothing will ever be the same again after this night.*

She thought suddenly of their home, of how cozy it had been. She remembered cooking for the others in her tiny, makeshift kitchen.

She remembered telling them her stories of the boy and his children. She could picture them sitting around the room, listening intently, their faces rapt. She could hear their voices and their laughter. She could see herself tucking Squirrel and Candle in for the night, their faces sleepy and peaceful as she wrapped their blankets around them. She remembered the quiet moments she had shared with Hawk, neither of them speaking, both of them knowing without having to say so what the other was thinking.

No, nothing would ever be the same. She glanced around, looking at each of them in turn. The best she could hope for was that they would be able to stay together and stay safe . . .

She stopped herself suddenly, aware that something was wrong. She counted heads quickly, certain that she must be mistaken, that she had simply missed him.

But there was no mistake. Cheney was missing. The big wolf dog, there only a moment earlier it seemed, was nowhere in sight.

Where was he?

She started to ask the others, and then stopped. In the shadows of the broken-down vehicles ahead, dark shapes were emerging into the light, crawling out of the wrecks.

Not just a few, but dozens.

THREE

TIME STOPPED, an intransigent presence.

But at the same time, it seemed that it fled in the wake of their pounding footsteps on the city concrete, another frightened child.

Panther was ahead when they reached the T-intersection at the end of the alleyway Sparrow had sent them down, and he drew up short, uncertain which way to go.

"Go left," she ordered as she came up behind him, her breathing quick and uneven.

He did what he was told, unwilling to argue the matter. He could tell she was beginning to fail, her strength depleted from their struggle with the Croaks and her own physical limitations. She was younger than him, and her endurance was limited. She would never admit it, not to him and probably not to anyone else. Sparrow, with her dead warrior mother and her legacy of self-expectations, he sneered to himself. Frickin' bull.

But he held back anyway, just enough to let her keep pace. He didn't look around, didn't do anything to indicate he knew she was tiring, just slowed so that she could stay close. Say what you wanted to about that girl, she was a tough little bird. She gave him a hard time, but she was a Ghost and no Ghost ever abandoned another. Didn't matter how much she bugged him; he would never leave her behind.

They reached the end of the alley and emerged onto a street filled with swarming forms that had come up from the docks and the waterfront and maybe the square, as well. Spiders and Lizards and Croaks and some others Panther had never seen before in his short life—things dark and misshapen—all of them massed together as they ascended the hill to get away from the battle being fought below.

"Must be bad down there for this to happen!" he declared, catching Sparrow by the arm as she almost raced past him into the surging throng.

He had never seen anything like it. Normally these creatures, their strange neighbors, kept carefully apart from one another. Some, like the Lizards and the Croaks, were natural enemies, fighting each other for food and territory. Not today. Today the only thought, it seemed, was to escape a common enemy.

"What now?" he demanded.

Wordlessly, Sparrow turned back into the alleyway, and they retreated down the darkened corridor to a pair of metal-clad doors. Panther didn't ask what she was doing. Sparrow never did anything unknowingly. He watched as she climbed a short set of steps to the doors and wrenched on the handles. The doors opened with a groan, but only several inches. Sparrow pulled harder, but the doors held.

From deeper inside the alleyway, a handful of shadowy figures lumbered into view, coming out of the T-intersection and turning toward them.

Panther went up the steps in a rush. "Let me try," he said, all but elbowing her aside. He heaved against the recalcitrant doors, and they moved another few inches. Rust had done its work. "What's in here, anyway?"

"Hotel," she answered, shoving him back to let him know she didn't appreciate his aggressive attitude. "Connects to buildings farther up through underground tunnels. We can avoid all the Freaks if we can get inside."

"Big *if*, looks like," he said, hauling back again, straining against the handle. "Isn't there some other way?"

She surprised him by laughing. "What's the matter, mighty Panther Puss?" she taunted. "Cat's on the wrong side of the door and can't get in?"

He tightened his lips, grunted as he heaved against the door, and wrenched it all the way open. "Ain't nowhere I can't get in!"

They slipped inside ahead of their pursuers and followed a short corridor to a down stairway. Sparrow, leading now, switched on her solar-powered torch to give them light in the blackness, and they descended the stairwell to the long, broad corridor below. The corridor ran straight ahead before branching. Sparrow didn't hesitate in choosing their path, turning left for a short distance to a second fork, then turning right. Panther followed without comment, his finger on the trigger of his prod, his eyes sweeping the dark corners of the spaces they passed through.

From somewhere farther back, he could hear the Croaks again, shuffling their way after them. *Stupid Freaks*, he thought angrily. *Ain't got the sense to know when to quit!*

He looked down at the power level readout on his prod. Less than half a charge remained. They needed to get out of there.

They hurried on, reached a wide set of stairs, and began to climb. At the top of the stairs was an open space, a common area serving a series of ruined shops. An escalator rose ahead of them, frozen in place, metal treads dulled by time and a lack of care, a black scaly snake. It was so long that its top could not be seen.

"We have to go up that?" Panther growled.

"The street's up there, and right across from that, the freeway." Sparrow took his arm. "C'mon, let's get to where we're going and be done with it."

She practically raced up the steps, leaving Panther to either watch or follow. He chose the latter, hurrying to catch up, taking the stairs two at a time. Their shoes padded against the metal, and once or twice Panther's prod clanged against the sides of the escalator. *Too much noise*, he chided himself. But he didn't hear the Croaks anymore, so maybe it didn't matter. He watched the steps recede beneath his feet and found himself wondering how escalators worked, back when they did work.

How did those steps fold up and flatten out and return to shape like that? Fixit would know. He shook his head. Must have been something to watch.

They crested the stairs and moved across an open space to a set of wide double doors that opened into the lobby of another hotel. The lobby stretched away through gloom and shadows to a wall of broken-out glass windows and a pair of ornate doors that were closed against the world. Old furniture filled the lobby, most of it torn apart and tipped over. Fake plants lay fallen on their sides, still in their pots, dusty and gray, strange corpses with spindly limbs. Bits and pieces of metal glittered on railings and handles, but the rust was winning the battle here, too.

He was starting across the lobby toward the doors when Sparrow grabbed his arm. "Panther," she whispered.

He glanced over quickly, the way she spoke his name an unmistakable warning. She was looking up at the balcony that encircled the lobby.

Dozens of Croaks were looking down.

"I don't believe this!" Panther muttered.

The Croaks began shuffling along the railing, their strange, twisted faces barely visible in the gloom, their bodies hunched over. There didn't seem to be any of them on the lobby level, but by now Panther was looking everywhere at once, his prod held ready for the inevitable attack.

"We have to get to the doors," Sparrow hissed at him. "We have to get outside again."

She had that much right, even if she'd gotten everything else wrong. Panther started toward the doors, turning this way and that as he did, searching the darkness, watching for movement. Overhead, the Croaks had reached the stairs and were coming down, the sounds of grunting and growling clearly audible. Too many of them to be stopped if they attacked, Panther knew. If they trapped Sparrow and him in that lobby . . .

He didn't bother finishing the thought. He gave it another two seconds, measuring their chances, then yelled, "Run!"

They broke for the doors and almost instantly a Croak appeared right in front of them, seemingly out of nowhere. Panther jammed his prod into the creature's midsection and gave it a charge that knocked it backward, twitching and writhing. Others were surfacing all around them, come out of the shadows in which they had been hiding, so many of them that Panther felt his courage fail completely. He hated Croaks. He had seen what they could do. He didn't want to die this way.

He howled in challenge, a way to hold himself together, and with Sparrow next to him leapt for the double doors that led to the street. The Croaks were too slow to stop them. They gained the doors, and Panther shoved down hard on the handles.

Locked.

Without hesitating, he grabbed Sparrow's arm and pulled her toward the largest of the broken-out windows. Sweeping his prod around the frame to clear out the fragments of glass, he shoved her through to the street, then dove after her without turning to look back at what was breathing down his neck. Claws ripped at his clothing, slowing but not stopping him. Twisting, he broke away and tumbled out onto the concrete.

He was back on his feet instantly, turning to run. But more Croaks had appeared in front of them, come from inside the hotel or from across the street or maybe from the sky—who knew? He screamed at them, rushing to the attack. What else could he do? Sparrow was next to him, her pale face intense, her prod swinging like a club, electricity leaping off the tip as it raked the Croaks.

They fought like wild things, but both of them already knew that it wouldn't be enough.

■ ■ ■

SPIDERS!

It was Owl's first thought. An entire community of them, living in those rusted-out vehicle shells. It was an odd choice of habitat. Spiders preferred basements or underground tunnels with a dozen entrances and exits. Shy and reclusive, they mostly kept away from the other denizens of the city. They were not normally a threat to anyone. But she shivered anyway, despite herself. There was something creepy about Spiders—about the way they moved, crouched down on all fours, arms and legs indistinguishable; about their hairy bodies and elongated limbs, disproportionate and crooked; and about their flat faces, which were almost featureless. They were Freaks like the others, mutants born of the world's destruction, humans made over into something new and unnatural. Rationally, she understood this. Viscerally, she had difficulty accepting it.

As she watched this bunch creep into view, still nothing more than a featureless cluster of dark shapes in the gloom, she tried to think what the Ghosts should do. They could turn back and seek sanctuary in the buildings at the top of the freeway ramp and wait there for Logan Tom. Or they could continue ahead and try to make their way past the Spiders to where the Knight of the Word's vehicle was parked. If they kept to the far side of the ramp and managed not to act hostile, perhaps it would be all right. Maybe they could even explain what they—

She froze. The first of the dark shapes had emerged into the faint glow cast by the distant lights of the compound and the ambient brightness of stars peeking through cloud-concealed sky. As their faces lifted out of the shadows, she saw that these weren't Spiders, after all.

They were street kids.

But they were something else, too.

While they were still recognizable as human, it was clear that the poisons that had permeated everything had damaged them. Their faces were deformed, their skin burned and riddled with lesions. Some of them were missing eyes and noses and ears. Some carried themselves in ways that suggested they could not move as normal humans did. Some had no hair; some had so much hair they could almost be mistaken for Spiders. They were dressed in ragged clothes that barely covered their mutilated bodies. She had never seen street kids like these, all twisted and broken. She wondered how they could have been living so close without the Ghosts knowing.

Then it occurred to her that these kids were not from here at all, but had come from someplace else. They were nomads. That was why they were living on the freeway in abandoned vehicles rather than in a building where they could be better protected.

"What are they, Owl?" Chalk asked from behind the wheelchair, his voice uncertain.

"Children," she answered him, "like you. Only they have had a much harder time of it." She glanced at the other Ghosts. "Don't do anything to threaten them. Stay close to me. Do what I tell you."

Despite her orders, Bear was already taking out the heavy cudgel he favored for close-quarters combat, an old, gnarled staff that could crack a skull with a single blow. The others looked uncertain, glancing at one another and back at the approaching shapes. In her lap, Squirrel stirred slightly, restless in his sleep. She considered handing him to one of the others, but decided against it. He was safest where he was.

"Candle?" Owl called out. "Can you sense anything?"

The little girl with the preternatural instincts turned. "I'm not sure. I can't tell if they mean to hurt us or not."

Owl hesitated, then said, "Move me to the front, Chalk."

The boy wheeled her forward, but she could sense his reluctance. He eased her wheelchair past Bear with his cart and Fixit and River with their litter and stopped. Ahead, the strange collection of street kids continued to advance. She held Squirrel tighter in her lap and stroked his fine hair.

"Who are you?" she called out.

The advance halted immediately. For a moment, no one said anything. Then a strong voice answered, "Who are you?"

"We are the Ghosts," she said, speaking the litany of greeting. "We haunt the ruins of the world our parents destroyed. This city is our home; we live down by the water. But an invasion force has landed to attack one of the compounds, and we are leaving." She paused. "You should leave, too."

"Everyone says that to us," the voice answered, laced with unmistakable bitterness. She could tell now who was doing the speaking, a tall figure near the front of the advance. "Maybe you're just like all the others, telling us lies to make us go away."

"I don't know about anyone else, but I'm telling you the truth. We're all in danger here. You should get away. If you want to stay, though, at least let us pass. We need to go farther down the ramp and wait for our guide to come for us."

The speaker for the newcomers came forward and stood directly in front of her, a thin, ragged boy with scars everywhere, the right side of his face so badly mutilated that it looked like melted candle wax. His hand was resting on the butt of a strange black weapon, a handgun of some sort, that he had stuck into his belt.

"I don't believe you," he said. "Maybe you should turn around and go back."

Those with him began to advance again. Owl glanced at them. There were an awful lot of them if it came to a fight, even if they did seem half crippled. Already the other Ghosts were tensing. Bear had stepped away from the cart. River and Fixit had put down the litter with the Weatherman and brought out their prods. Even Chalk had stepped up beside her protectively. If she didn't find a way to calm them all down, things were going to get out of hand quickly.

It was at times like this that she wished she weren't confined to the wheelchair, that she could walk around like everyone else.

"We didn't come here looking for trouble," she said to the speaker. "Maybe you should think about where this is leading."

"Maybe you should give us what you've got in the cart," the other replied. "Then we might let you go."

And he drew the weapon from his belt and pointed it at her.

* * *

"PANTHER!" Sparrow cried out, her voice sharp with desperation.

He risked a quick glance over from where he was fighting his own battle. One of the Croaks had caught her from behind and pinned her against a pole. She was trying to bring the tip of her prod around to jolt it, but it was holding her off with one arm while it strangled her with the other.

He was at her side in seconds, fighting through the two that had been trying to trap him, his prod shedding electrical charges as the tip raked the metal surfaces of a series of trash containers. He slammed its heavy length into the Croak's head, and it staggered back, releasing its grip. Panther grabbed Sparrow's arm and pulled her after him, trying to find a clear space in which to run as other Croaks appeared from the shadows. The battle careened down the length of the cross street and into the path of those coming uphill from the waterfront. All at once they were in the thick of the exodus, and there were Lizards and Spiders and more Croaks and street kids, too, all about them. There was yelling and screaming and growling, and Panther couldn't tell whom he was supposed to be fighting. Sparrow latched on to him as if he were a lifeline, her prod gone and her face spattered with blood and as pale as Chalk's. He had never seen her look afraid, but she looked afraid now.

"Hold on!" he shouted over the sounds of the crowd.

He used his strength and weight to bull his way toward the far side of the climb, seeking a small measure of space in which to catch his breath. He could no longer tell if anyone—or anything—was chasing them. A clutch of Lizards was tearing at a handful of Croaks that had crossed its path and foolishly decided to attack, and the Croaks quickly disappeared from view. To his astonishment, Panther thought he saw Logan Tom off amid a scattering of street kids, but the other disappeared from sight almost immediately. Unable to look further, Panther continued to fight his way through the rush, Sparrow pinned tightly against him, until they broke through and were able to take refuge in a doorway.

"Frickin' brainless stump heads!" he shouted angrily. "Hey, I think I saw that guy, the Knight of whatever back there!"

"Doesn't matter. The Croaks are still coming!" Sparrow cried.

He looked to where she was pointing, brushing dirt and sweat from his dark face. A handful of Croaks was pushing through the crowd, eyes fixed on them. "Damn!" he muttered.

Sparrow grabbed his arm and pulled him up the sidewalk and into another alleyway. Free of the surge of the crowd, they ran down its dark length, found an opening into one of the buildings, and began making their way through a tangle of corridors, dodging piles of broken crates and garbage of all sorts. Sparrow set the pace, running as if she had caught fire, heedless of the strain.

"Not so fast!" Panther gasped as the pace began to tell on him. He was the one who was tiring now. "Ease off, Sparrow!"

"Just another block or two until we reach the freeway!" she called over her shoulder. "Come on!"

They burst out of the building and found themselves back on a cross street not a hundred yards from where the crowd continued its uphill climb. Panther exhaled sharply in relief, and then an instant later caught his breath. The Croaks had reappeared, come out of the crowd like rats out of the shadows, eyes gleaming, claws and teeth sharp and ready.

Panther glanced down at the readout on his prod. Almost empty. He looked at Sparrow. They could run, but only by going in the wrong direction. If they wanted to reach the others, they would have to find a way past the Croaks.

He looked into Sparrow's eyes.

"I'm through being chased," she declared, as if she had read his mind, as if she knew what he wanted to hear.

Wordlessly, they turned to face the onslaught.

Then abruptly a stream of white fire surged out of the darkness behind them, lancing into the Croaks and exploding across the entire width of the street ahead.

Panther had not been mistaken. Logan Tom had found them.

OWL STARED down the short black barrel of the handgun and fought to stay calm. She saw that wires attached to its handle ran to a solar pack strapped to the boy's waist. Some sort of stun gun, a variation on a prod. It would shock its victim if fired. Maybe it would kill. In any case, she didn't want to find out the hard way.

Around her, the other Ghosts had frozen in their tracks, no one wanting to do anything that would cause the kid with the weapon to hurt her. But they wouldn't stay still forever.

She took a deep breath and said, "What's your name?"

He scowled. "What does it matter?"

"Just tell me, I want to know."

"You don't need to know my name." He looked uncomfortable, his ruined face tightening further. "Are you going to give us the cart or not?"

"My name is Owl," she said, ignoring him. "I am mother to the Ghosts. It is my job to protect them. Like it is your job to protect those who travel with you. Sometimes people make that very hard. Sometimes they make us feel foolish and weak and even helpless. They do this by threatening to hurt us because they don't like us. That's happened to you, hasn't it? That's what you were talking about when you said everyone always tells you to go away."

She waited for him to say something, but he just stared at her, the gun steady in his hand.

"Tell him to quit pointing that at you," Chalk said at her elbow.

"The thing is," she continued, keeping her eyes fixed on the boy's face, "you are doing to us what others have done to you. You are acting just like them, telling us we have to do something we don't want to. You are stealing from us and telling us to just turn around and leave. Why are you doing that?"

Again, no answer, but she could see the confusion and anger mirrored in the boy's one good eye.

"Don't you see that you are no better than those people you don't like if you do this?"

"Stop talking!" he shouted suddenly.

Everyone tensed. Bear came forward a few steps until he had moved between the cart with their goods and the street kids who wanted it. He didn't say anything, but she could see the determination in his eyes. A few of the street kids glanced his way uneasily.

"What do you expect us to do?" she asked the boy with the gun. "Do you expect us to just stand here and let you take everything we have?"

"Everyone takes everything we have," he snapped angrily. "Everyone calls us Freaks! We're not Freaks!"

"Then don't act—"

"Don't tell me what to do!"

There was sudden movement to her left, and he shifted his weapon in response. Owl raised her hand to stay his, saying, "No!" The boy flinched, turning back to her as quickly as he had turned away. Seeing her raised arm and mistaking her intent, alarm flooded his face.

Then he shot her.

FOUR

I T WAS THE WAY that everything changed so suddenly that shocked Hawk the most.

One moment he was falling from the compound walls, the hands of his captors releasing him for the long drop, his stomach lurching as he struggled in vain to find something to hold on to, his fate a dark rush of gut-wrenching certainty flooding through him. He glimpsed the rubble waiting below, the sharp outline of the bricks and cement chunks clearly visible even in the fading light of the sunset. He caught sight of Tessa tumbling away next to him, her arms windmilling and her legs kicking, her slender body just out of his reach. He wanted to close his eyes to shut the images away, to escape what was happening, but he could not make himself do so.

A moment later he was surrounded by the light, gathered up by its white brilliance as if cradled in a soft blanket. He was neither standing nor sitting but sprawled out, his muscles becoming lethargic and leaden, his mind drifting to faraway places that had no identity. He was no longer falling, no longer doing anything. Tessa had disappeared. The compound and his captors, the city and the sunset, the entire world had vanished.

He didn't know how long this cocooning lasted because he lost all sense of time. His thoughts were as soft and image-free as the light that bound him, and he could not seem to make himself think. All he could do was revel in the feeling of the light and the welcome hope that somehow he had escaped dying. He waited for something to happen, for the light to clear and reveal his fate, for the world to return—for anything—but finally gave in to his lethargy and closed his eyes and slept.

When he woke, the light was gone.

He was lying on a patch of grass so bright with color that it hurt his eyes to look at it. Sunshine flooded down out of clear skies that seemed to stretch away forever. Gardens surrounded him with a profusion of colors and forms and scents. He blinked in disbelief and pushed himself up on one elbow to look around. Wherever he was, he clearly wasn't anywhere in Seattle or even anywhere he had ever been in his life. He had seen pictures of gardens in Owl's books and listened to her read descriptions of them to the Ghosts. He had imagined them in his mind, spreading away from the edges of the pages that framed them in the picture books.

But he had never imagined anything like this.

And yet . . .

He stared off into the distance, off to where the gardens disappeared from view, going on and on in a rough carpet of plants and bushes, of petals and stalks, their colors so vibrant that they shimmered against the horizon in a soft haze.

Yet it was all somehow very familiar.

He frowned in confusion, sitting up for a better look, trying to understand what he was feeling. His mind was clear now, his limbs and body fresh and rested. The lethargy was gone, dissipated with the light. He felt that he might have slept a long time, but could not account for how that might be. Everything had changed so completely that there was no way he could make sense of it. It was magic, he thought suddenly, but he had no way of knowing where such magic might have come from.

Not from himself, he knew.

Not from Logan Tom, the Knight of the Word.

His confusion exploded into questions. *Why am I alive? What saved me from the fall off the compound wall? How did I get here?*

Then he remembered Tessa, and he looked around for her in a welter of sudden fear and desperation.

"She is sleeping still," a voice said from right behind him.

The speaker was so close and had come up on him so quietly that Hawk jumped despite himself, wheeling into a defensive crouch without even thinking about what he was doing. Breathing hard, arms cocked protectively in front of him, he stared up into the face of the old man who stood there.

The old man never moved. "You needn't be afraid of me," he said.

He was ancient by any standards, rail-thin and bent by time, his body swathed in white robes that hid everything but the outline of his nearly fleshless bones. His beard was full and white, but his hair was thinning to the point of wispiness, and his scalp showed through in mottled patches. His features were gaunt, his cheeks sunken, and his brow lined. But all of this was of no importance to Hawk when he looked into the old man's eyes, which were clear and blue and filled with kindness and compassion. Looking into those eyes made the boy want to weep. It was like seeing a reflection of everything that was good and right in the world, all gathered in a perfect vision, bright and true.

"Who are you?" he asked.

"Someone who knows you from before you were born," the other answered, smiling as if having Hawk standing before him was the most welcome of sights. "Someone who remembers how important that event was." His eyes never left Hawk's face. "What matters is not who I am, but who you are. Here and now, in this time and place, in the world of the present. Do you know the answer?"

Hawk nodded slowly. "I think so. The Knight of the Word told me when I was locked away in the compound. He said I was a gypsy morph and that I had magic. I saw something of what he was talking about in a vision when I touched my . . . my mother's finger bones." He hesitated. "But I still don't know if I believe it."

The old man nodded. "What he told you is the truth. Or at least, the part of it he knows. It is given to me to tell you the rest. Walk with me."

He started away, and Hawk followed without thinking. Together they moved down the pathways and grassy strips that crisscrossed the gardens, passing through rows of flower beds and flowering bushes and trellises of flowering vines. They moved without purpose and without any seeming destination, simply walking, first in one direction and then in another, the boundaries of the gardens—if there were any—never drawing any nearer, never even coming into sight. They continued for a long time, the old man moving slowly but purposefully, with Hawk matching his pace as he tried to gather his thoughts, to give voice to the questions swimming in his head. Spoor and tiny seedlings drifted in the air around him, shimmering with a peculiar brightness. Hawk could hear insects buzzing and chirping. He could see flashes of bright color from birds and butterflies. He could not stop looking.

"Did you bring me here?" he asked the old man finally.

The old man nodded. "I did."

"Tessa, too? She's all right? She's not hurt?"

"She sleeps until we are done."

Hawk scuffed his tennis shoes on a patch of gravel, looking down at the skid marks, still trying to make what was happening feel real. "I don't understand any of this," he said finally.

The old man had been studying the landscape ahead, but now he looked over. "No, I don't suppose you do. It must all seem very strange to you. A lot has happened in the past few weeks. A lot more will happen in the weeks ahead. You are different from who you were, but not as different as you will be."

He made a sweeping gesture at the gardens. "This is where you were conceived, young one. Here, in these gardens. A small, unexpected gathering in the evening air of magic from earth and water brought you into existence, a wild magic that only happens now and then with the passing of the centuries. I have seen it before, but not like this. The brightness of the gathering was unusual, the joining quick and sure, the suddenness and the frantic need so apparent that it caught me by surprise. That takes something special. I have been alive a long time."

Hawk believed it. The old man had the look of something about to crumble and be scattered by the winds. "How old are you?"

"I was here at the beginning."

Hawk shuddered despite himself. *At the beginning?* He knew instinctively what the old man was talking about, and at the same time he did not believe such a thing was possible. "How do you know what you saw happening with the magic was me?" he asked sharply. "I mean, it wasn't me then. It was just . . . just something happening in the air, wasn't it?"

"Oh, it was you. Such things cannot be mistaken. You weren't a boy then, just a possibility of becoming something wonderful. I saw the potential of the magic that would form you and dispatched it into the world at a time and place where you might find help in making the necessary transformation. I could not tell what that transformation would be; only that it would be special and powerful and mean something to the world. You were found and caught up by another Knight of the Word, then taken to your mother. You found your purpose with her, merging with her, becoming her unborn child. She took you inside her, gave birth to you, raised you, then gave you back to me."

Hawk stared, and then said the first thing that came to mind. "I don't remember any of this. I don't think it ever happened."

The old man nodded. "I took away your memories."

"You took away . . ." Hawk couldn't finish. "Why would you do that?"

"You didn't need them then. It wasn't time for you to have them." The old man kept walking, not slowing or quickening his pace, just ambling through the flowers and the sunlight, his time and Hawk's of no importance. "Let me start again," he said, "so that you will understand."

Hawk folded his arms over his chest, already prepared to dismiss everything he was about to hear. He didn't know who the old man was or how he had brought him to these gardens, but when you started believing that someone could take away your memories or make you become a boy out of a seed, it was time to back up a few steps.

He waited for the old man to begin, but they continued walking in silence. Hawk was impatient but knew the value of not rushing things when you were at a disadvantage, which he clearly was, so he waited. Finally, they reached a small pool and stone fountain surrounded by ancient wooden benches, and they seated themselves next to each other facing down long rows of small purple flowers that hung from vines off lengths of trellis, climbing and tumbling away like a waterfall.

"Wisteria," the old man said quietly, gesturing toward the flowers.

Hawk nodded, saying nothing, still waiting. He wanted to get this over with. He was anxious to see Tessa, to make certain she was all right. He was eager to return to the Ghosts, assuming the old man would let him do so. He couldn't be sure of that. He couldn't be sure of anything just at the moment.

"You asked before who I was," the old man said, looking not at him, but off into the distance. "I have no real name, but the Elves in Faerie time called me the King of the Silver River and the name has stayed with me. Like you, though you doubt your origins still, I am a Faerie creature born of the Word's magic. We sit in the Gardens of Life, which have been given into my care. All life begins here. Once conceived, it goes out into the larger world to play its part. This is what happened to you. You were wild magic conceived first within these gardens, then within the world of humans. A Knight of the Word named John Ross caught you up before you were fully formed, and when you took the shape of a small boy he took you to Nest Freemark, who became your mother. She did not know your purpose, but she possessed magic as well, a legacy of her unusual family. She kept you for as long as was necessary after giving birth to you, but eventually it was necessary to take you away from her and bring you here."

Hawk shook his head. "I remember the Oregon coast, swimming in the ocean, lying on the beach, being with my family there. I don't remember anything of what you are telling me."

"Because you weren't meant to until now. I gave you those other memories so that you wouldn't know who you were until it was time." The old man smiled. "I know this is hard to accept. But your memories will begin to return now, and they will help you to understand. You must be patient with them and with yourself until they do."

He studied Hawk a moment, then shook his head. "I should be better at this, but I don't get much practice. Mostly, I tend these gardens and let the affairs of humans and others take whatever course fate decrees. But the old world is ending, and the new one requires my help. So I must do the best I can with this. Logan Tom has begun this task, but it is up to me to try to finish it.

"Here is what you must know. You have powerful enemies, one in particular. They hunt you relentlessly. They have done so since the time of your conception in the world of men. For many years, they thought you dead. Nest Freemark saved you and took you away from them, her unborn child, a life they could not detect while it grew inside her. But after you were born, the danger became greater. You did not yet know what or who you were. You did not yet understand that you possessed magic. The magic had not yet manifested itself. But I knew that sooner or later it would, and when that happened your enemies would come for you."

He folded his hands in his lap, skeletal digits as white and brittle as bleached bones. "There was a second, perhaps more important, consideration. The fate of the human race in its war with the demons had not yet been decided. The balance between the Word and Void had not yet been tipped, and until that happened—or even if it happened, because at that point no one could be sure—you couldn't be left exposed when your time and the need for your peculiar magic was not yet at hand.

"For these reasons, I took you from Nest Freemark and brought you here to live until the balance was not just tipped, but toppled and the end assured. Then I sent you back into the human world to fulfill your destiny. You have a purpose, and that purpose is to save the human race."

Hawk almost laughed, but the look on the old man's face kept him from doing so. He tried to say something, but he couldn't find the right words.

"You are the boy who will lead his children to the Promised Land," the King of the Silver River said to him. "Your dream is your destiny. I gave you that dream when you left my care and went back out into the world. But the dream is real, a foretelling of what you are meant to do. Your small family in the ruins of the city, those you left behind when you came here, are the beginning of a much larger family. You will lead them to a haven that will shelter them until the madness is finished. The destruction is not over, nor the devastation complete. That will take time. It will take more time still for the world to heal. While that happens, some will need to be kept safe and well so that the people of the Word will not all die."

Hawk nodded, then shook his head no. "I don't think any of this is right. I don't think I can do any of what you seem to think I can do. I believe the dream, but the dream is a small one. It is only for me and for the Ghosts. My family. Not . . . how many are we talking about?"

"Several thousand, perhaps. Humans, Elves, and others. An amalgam of those who struggle to survive the demons and the once-men and all the others who serve the Void."

Hawk stared. *Elves?* "How am I supposed to do this? You say I have magic, and maybe I do. I think I may have helped heal Cheney when he was injured by a giant centipede. But that's not going to mean much with what you say I have to do. Healing is one thing. Fighting off demons or whatever to get several thousand people to a safe place is something else again. I mean, look at me! I'm not anything special. I can't do anything to save all these people! I can barely help the family I've got now, and that's only nine kids, a dog, and an old man!"

The more he talked, the more adamant he became. The more adamant he became, the more frightened he grew. The enormity of what the old man was asking of him—no, telling him he must do—was overwhelming. He tried to say something more and gave it up, getting to his feet in disgust and staring off into the distance in a mix of rage and frustration.

"I just don't think I can do this," he said finally. "I don't even know how to begin."

He waited for the old man to say something, and then when he didn't turned around again.

The old man was gone.

HE SEARCHED FOR the old man then, hunting through gardens he knew nothing about, not even where they began or ended. When that proved fruitless, he searched for Tessa. He walked aimlessly because moving was better than sitting; doing something was better than doing nothing. The effort began to tire him, and he slowed and finally stopped altogether. He looked about in bewilderment. Everything looked the same as it had when he had started out. The fountain and the pool were off to one side. The wisteria hung from the trellis in a shower of purple. It was as if nothing had changed—as if he had not moved at all.

Maybe that's the message, he thought. *Maybe no matter what I do, nothing will change and I will get nowhere.*

He was very thirsty, and after thinking it over he tried the water in the fountain. It tasted sweet and clean, so he drank. He reassured himself that the old man wouldn't bring him all this way only to let him drink poisoned water.

When his thirst was satisfied, he took a long moment to reflect on what he had been told and decided that maybe he believed it was all true after all. Well, mostly true. All but the part about how he was supposed to save all these people by taking them somewhere—to a safe place, a Promised Land, a haven from the ravages of the world's destruction. He didn't really believe he could do something like that. But he maybe believed the rest, although he couldn't say exactly why. It was in part because he knew there was something different about him, in part because of his dreams of a place he was meant to go with the Ghosts, and in part because of what he felt about the old man. The King of the Silver River. He spoke the name to himself in the silence of his mind. Despite his doubts, he could not make himself believe that the old man was lying. Not about any of it. Even the most wild, improbable parts of it felt true.

He sat down on the wooden bench again, wondering what he should do. He tried to think about something besides his situation, to give himself a chance to let everything go for a few moments, but it was impossible. He told himself that he should be grateful he was still alive when by all that was reasonable he should be dead. The old man had saved him and brought him here deliberately, not on a whim and not without reason to believe he was needed. Hawk couldn't dismiss this out of hand, even doubting it as he did. Not even the part about leading all these people to a place where the world's destruction would not affect them.

As if there were such a place, and the old man shared Hawk's dream.

It occurred to him that he hadn't gotten around to asking where this place might be, let alone how he was supposed to get there. If he really was supposed to lead someone, even a handful like the Ghosts, then—

"The dream was only of the Ghosts in the beginning, because that was all that was needed," the old man said, sitting next to him on the bench. "But it was always intended to include others, as well. A world starting over needs more than a few children."

He had materialized out of nowhere and without making a sound. Hawk jumped inwardly but kept his composure. "I don't know what a world starting over needs. Where were you?"

"Here and there. I thought you might need a little time alone to think things over. Sometimes it helps. As for what you know, young one, you know more than you think because you are imbued with the wild magic. Your intuition and your innate understanding are stronger because of it. How you were formed and of what pieces is what makes you so unexpected. That is why you are here—why you were formed here, why you left, and why you have returned. It is why your enemies are so afraid of you."

Hawk shook his head. "Afraid of me? No one is afraid of me." He met the old man's gaze and held it. "You keep talking about how I am formed of wild magic. What does that mean? Am I real? Am I even human?"

"You are as human as any other boy your age. You are as human as this girl you love." The old man smiled. "But you are something more, of course. The wild magic sets you apart. What that means is that while you are human, you are also a creature of Faerie. You transcend the present world and its peoples. Your origins are very old and go back to the beginning of the world. You are flesh and blood and bones, and you can and will die someday like other humans. But your life is set on a different track, and it is given to you to be able to do things no one else ever will."

"Things. What sort of things?"

"No one knows. Not even me, and I watched you being born. What you will do and how you will do it is knowledge you must discover for yourself. Your dreams tell you of your destiny, but only by taking the road to that destiny will you discover how you are meant to fulfill it."

"By going to this place where the people I lead will be safe? By seeing what will happen when I do?"

"Just so, young one."

"I have to just do this and hope for the best?"

"You have to trust in who and what you are. You have to trust in the dream you have been given. You have believed in it until now, haven't you?"

"For myself and my family. Not for thousands of people I don't even know!"

The old man studied him. "Why is it any more difficult to believe in the one as opposed to the other? Is it really so odd to think that you will guide thousands as opposed to a handful? The dangers are the same, the journey the same, the destination the same. It is said that there is safety in numbers. Perhaps that will serve to ease your efforts. You will not be so alone."

"But I will have responsibility for so many!"

"Ask yourself this: what would their chances be without you? If you believe what you have been told, you know what is going to happen. The old world is ending and must start anew. Most will not live to see that happen. But there will be survivors, and some of those will go with you."

Hawk shook his head and closed his eyes against what he was feeling. "Go with me where?"

"To where I will be waiting."

The boy's eyes snapped open. "What? Here, in these gardens? I'm to bring them all here?"

The ancient face did not change expression, nor the eyes leave Hawk's. "You are to come in search of me, and you are to find me. You will know how to do this. You will bring those you lead with you."

Hawk stared at him. "Well, why don't you just do all this yourself? Why do you need me?"

"I wish it were that easy. But my powers are finite. It is not so difficult to bring one or two, as I did with you and the young girl. It is immeasurably harder to bring hundreds, impossible to bring thousands. They must journey on foot. They must be led. It is given to you to lead them."

"Why didn't you start all this sooner? Before everything was destroyed! You could have saved so many more! Look how many are already dead!"

The King of the Silver River watched him carefully, and then shook his head. "You already know the answer to that question. Don't you?"

Hawk hesitated. "Because you couldn't bring them until it was certain that the world was going to end. You had to know for sure. When you knew, was that when you sent me back into the world?"

The other nodded. "That was when your destiny was determined. I placed you back in the world with the new memories I had given you and let you build your life while I waited for the time when it would become necessary to bring you here once more and tell you everything. Had your life not been in such danger, I would have left you there longer before speaking with you as I am now. But that wasn't possible."

Hawk put his hands on his knees, his back straight and his head lifted as he looked out into the gardens and thought about what lay ahead. But it was what was hidden in his past that troubled him most, the memories that had been taken from him. He wanted those memories back. He wanted to know the truth about himself.

"How long before I go back again?" he asked.

"Soon. A few weeks will have passed in your world, but time has little meaning here. It will seem to you as if no time at all has passed."

A few weeks. Hawk thought of the Ghosts, wondered how they were managing without him. "How will I know what to do?"

"You will know."

"How will I find my way back here? Where are we, anyway?"

"Nowhere you can find on a map. But you will find the way nevertheless. Your heart will tell you where to go."

It sounded so absurd that Hawk almost laughed, but the old man's tone of voice did not suggest that he had any doubts in the matter. Hawk glanced at him but held his tongue.

"You have doubts?"

"Your faith in me is stronger than my own," Hawk answered.

The King of the Silver River shook his head. "It might seem so, but perhaps your faith in yourself is stronger than you think."

Hawk didn't care to argue the matter. "Can I see Tessa now?"

The old man rose, his arm extending. "Down that path a short distance. She is sleeping. You might want to join her."

Hawk started away, then stopped and turned. "If I do this, whoever I bring is welcome?"

The old man nodded.

"The Knight of the Word, Logan Tom, will protect me?"

"To the death."

The words hung in the air, hard and certain. Hawk understood. Logan Tom would die first, but that might not be enough to save him. He hesitated a moment, then started away again. This time, he did not look back.

THE KING OF THE SILVER RIVER watched him go. The boy would find the girl less than a hundred yards away, so deeply asleep that he could not wake her, even though he would try. Eventually, weary himself, he would lie down beside her and fall asleep. The dog who had chosen to be the boy's companion would be next to him when he woke, and the three would be back in their own world. Their journey would begin.

It would be a journey of more complicated and far-reaching consequences than the boy realized.

The King of the Silver River watched him until he was almost out of sight. There was much he had not told him, much he kept secret. To tell the boy everything would have placed too great a burden on him, and he was already carrying weight enough. There was an element of chance, of fate, to everything. It was no different here. But the boy would know this instinctively and without needing to hear the details.

The boy was beyond his line of sight now, and he turned away.

"You are as much my child as you are anyone's," he said quietly. "My last, best hope."

In the golden light of the gardens, it seemed possible to believe that this would be enough.

FIVE

THE HANDGUN FIRED BY the boy with the ruined face made a soft popping sound as it discharged a pair of filament-thin wires. Owl could barely make out the wires in the darkness, could only just see the gleam of metal threads as they connected with their target. It happened so fast that it was over almost before she knew it was happening. Her hand was still raised to stay the boy's precipitous action. She was still saying, "No!"

Then the wires found their target, the charge exploded out of the solar pack, and it was too late.

But not for Owl. Although the charge was meant for her, fired directly at her midsection, it was Squirrel who took the hit. Curled up in her lap, he provided an unintended shield against the strike. Perhaps the boy with the ruined face hadn't even seen him, his vision limited by his injuries. Perhaps he really didn't care. That he acted carelessly and out of fear and confusion was a given. That he actually understood what he was doing was less certain.

Whatever the case, the wires from the handgun struck Squirrel, and

the electrical charge surged into him. Owl heard the little boy gasp
sharply and felt his small body jerk. In the next instant the wires re-
tracted into the barrel of the handgun, and Squirrel went limp and still.

Bear was already charging for the boy with the ruined face, roaring
with rage, his heavy cudgel lifted. It was a terrible sight, for Bear was
big and powerful, and when he was angry, as he was now, he looked as
if he could go right through a stone wall. The boy with the stun gun
wheeled toward him, trying to defend himself. He had gotten close to
Owl before firing his weapon because he knew it wasn't accurate beyond twelve to fifteen feet. But getting close to Owl meant getting
close to the other Ghosts, as well, and Bear was on top of him in seconds. The boy had just enough time to aim and fire his weapon once
more. But the gun jammed, and then there was no time at all. Bear's
cudgel came down with an audible *whack* on the boy's head, and the
boy dropped like a stone, his weapon spinning away into the dark.

Bear was still roaring, looking for fresh targets, and he would have
had plenty to choose from if the boy's companions had chosen to stay
and fight. But when they saw their leader fall, they turned and ran as
fast as they could manage, vanishing back into the tangle of abandoned
vehicles, spilling down the ramp, and fleeing into the darkness until the
last of them were out of sight.

Owl sat in the wheelchair watching, unable to move. While Squirrel
had received the brunt of the attack, she had been its secondary victim,
the recipient of the residue of the electrical charge. It hadn't been enough
to knock her out, but it had shocked her nevertheless, ripping through
her body and leaving her temporarily paralyzed. The jolt had been powerful enough that it had even knocked Chalk backward because he had
been holding on to the metal arm of the wheelchair with one hand.

River and Candle rushed to Owl's side, panic mirrored on their
young faces. Both began talking to her at once, asking if she was all right,
begging her to say something. They touched her cheeks and rubbed her
hands. They didn't realize that the seemingly sleeping Squirrel was the
one who was most seriously injured, and Owl couldn't tell them. She
tried, but the words came out as odd sounds.

"Not me!" she managed finally, gasping from the effort. "He shot
Squirrel!"

Immediately they turned their attention to the little boy, lifting him out of Owl's arms and laying him on the ground. River bent close, putting her head to his chest, her ear to his mouth, checking his pulse, her hands moving everywhere, her face stricken. "He isn't breathing!"

She began CPR on him, pumping his chest, breathing into his mouth, working to revive him. It was a skill Owl had taught her, one that she had learned from one of her scavenged books. Fixit hurried over with a blanket, but River motioned him away. Chalk was on one knee next to her, urging her on, telling her that she could do it, she could save him. Bear stalked out of the darkness, the heavy cudgel gripped in one hand, his face twisted with anger. The boy with the ruined face lay where he had fallen, and Owl could not tell if he was dead or alive.

"Breathe, Squirrel, breathe!" Chalk was saying, over and over.

Candle stood beside Owl, and one small hand reached out to hers. Owl could feel the pressure, and she squeezed back. The effects of the stun gun were wearing off now, and the feeling was returning to her body. "It was an accident," she whispered to Candle. When the little girl's eyes met her own, filled with doubt and horror, she nodded for emphasis. "He didn't mean it."

She watched River continue her efforts, listening at the same time to the din of the battle being fought on the waterfront. The sounds were louder and more frantic now—the automatic weapons fire, the discharge of heavy artillery, the shrill whine of flechettes, and the shouts and screams of the combatants. The skyline was lit with the glow of fires burning from stricken ships and from old warehouses on the docks. She could smell the smoke, could see its shifting haze against the backdrop of the fires and the starlight.

Fixit walked over and put the blanket across Owl's knees, staring down at Squirrel as he did so. "It isn't working," he said softly. "He isn't breathing."

If anyone heard him, no one was saying so. They stood grouped together in silence, watching River work, praying silently for a miracle. The minutes passed. River continued her efforts—breathe mouth-to-mouth, a dozen quick pumps with her crossed palms against Squirrel's chest, breathe mouth-to-mouth again, a dozen more pumps, over and

over. There was determination mirrored on her face and an almost fa-
natical insistence to her movements. She would bring Squirrel back to
life; she would find a way to make him breathe.

Finally, Owl said, "That's enough, River." When River ignored her,
she said it again, more sharply. When River looked up at her in disbelief, she said, "He's gone, sweetie. Let him go."

The words hung in the night air against the backdrop of the waterfront battle and the freeway ramp of ruined cars and scattered bones.
The words whispered of other times and other losses, conjuring memories of Mouse and Heron when their lives had ended. The Ghosts
stood together in the near dark and remembered, and their memories
made them feel empty and helpless. Tears filled their eyes. Several cried
openly.

They were still standing there, frozen by shock and dismay and in-
comprehension, staring down at Squirrel's silent form, when a ragged
Panther and Sparrow appeared at the head of the ramp shadowed by
the dark, spectral figure of the Knight of the Word.

* * *

LOGAN TOM knew something of CPR and combat injuries, and he
tried his luck with Squirrel, even knowing how unlikely it was that he
could do anything. But his luck proved no better than River's. The
shock of the stun gun's electrical charge had been enough to stop the
boy's heart, an organ already weakened by sickness and maybe even by
genetics. There was probably nothing anyone could have done, he assured the others, knowing even as he said it that no one was listening
to him.

Sparrow was devastated. She had been Squirrel's primary caregiver,
his nurse and companion for the weeks of his illness, and she could not
accept that he was gone. Disdaining the help offered for her own injuries and ignoring her bone-aching weariness, she knelt next to the little boy, wrapped him in the blanket that Owl offered, and held him
while the others listened to Panther and Logan Tom explain what had
happened at the compound.

"You're saying that he just disappeared into thin air?" Owl demanded when she heard the Knight's explanation of why Hawk wasn't with them. "Tessa, too? They just vanished?"

"So those who saw it claim." Logan Tom could hear the disbelief in her voice and shrugged. "You never know. But it does seem clear that something supernatural intervened to spirit them away from the compound and those who wanted to hurt them. That means they were saved one way or the other."

"Or taken prisoner by those demon things you keep talking about," Panther declared. "You can't know."

"No, but I can take a reasonable guess. The demons don't have the power to lift humans out of thin air. They can find them and kill them by physical means, but they cannot extract them with magic. No, this is something else."

"What sort of something else?" Panther persisted.

Logan Tom shook his head.

"Well, how are we supposed to find them again?" Chalk wanted to know. He was almost as impatient and angry as Panther. "What are we supposed to do now?"

"Get away from here, first of all," Owl declared. "It's not safe to stay even another minute."

"Tell me about it," muttered Panther, walking over to Sparrow. He reached down and stroked her hair gently. "You be strong, little bird," he said. "You be tough."

Logan Tom glanced down at the city and the fires and fighting on the docks. The invading boats had secured a landing and were disgorging their occupants onto the waterfront in droves. Thousands of feeders, drawn by the bloodletting, swarmed invisibly as the once-men engaged in hand-to-hand combat with the compound defenders. The defenders were brave and fought hard to hold their ground. The battle would rage the rest of the night, would last until the defenders were driven back behind their walls. When that happened, the once-men would begin to search the city for strays. It would be a good idea to be as far away as possible by then.

"We should leave," he said, agreeing with Owl. He glanced behind at the overpasses, which were flooded with refugees from the city—the

Freaks and street kids and others that had come up from the water-front. They had disdained the freeway ramps, intending not to abandon the city but to look for shelter farther inland, thinking to come back when the attackers moved on. As yet, none of them had chosen to come down the ramp the Ghosts occupied.

But that could change at any moment.

"Pick up everything you want to keep," he instructed. "Carry it down to the Lightning. Tie the cart to the rear hitch. Strap the old man into the carrier on the AV's roof. He'll be all right for now." And safer for all of them if he stayed out in the open air with his plague sickness, he thought, but did not say. He glanced down at Sparrow, who was still cradling Squirrel's body. "We'll put the little boy inside where he will be safe until we can find a place to bury him," he said. "You can stay in there with him."

The Ghosts began to gather up their possessions, a sad and desul-tory group, none of them saying anything. Bear walked over and lifted Squirrel's body out of Sparrow's arms, hushing her sobs as he did so, telling her to come with him. Fixit and Chalk picked up the Weather-man, and River took the handles of Owl's wheelchair and turned her about.

It was Panther who said, "What about him?"

He pointed at the boy with the ruined face, who still lay sprawled in the street where Bear had flattened him with the cudgel. When no one else moved, Logan Tom walked over and bent down, checking the boy's pulse and breathing. "He's unconscious, not dead."

"Leave him," Bear growled, stopping long enough to look back, still holding Squirrel in his arms.

Logan glanced at the others. "Can you wake him?" Owl asked. "Can you get him on his feet?"

Logan examined the damage done by the blow that Bear had ad-ministered, a deep, purplish bruise on the left temple. "I think he'll get past this and wake on his own."

"But if we leave him?" she pressed.

Logan glanced at the throng on the overpass, and then at the fight-ing on the docks. He shook his head. "He probably won't make it."

"Leave him!" Bear repeated, shouting it this time.

"Leave him," Panther agreed.

The others repeated the words, all except for Candle. "Squirrel wouldn't want that," she said quietly to no one in particular.

Owl's dark eyes fixed on the little girl's, and she nodded. "No, he wouldn't. We'll take the boy with us."

"Frickin' spit!" Panther snapped at her. Bear muttered something under his breath as he turned away. The others gave Owl dark glances of disapproval, but no one said anything more. Logan waited a moment, then picked up the disfigured boy and trudged downhill after Bear. He thought it was a mistake to take him, but it wasn't his place to say anything. Not yet, anyway. Later, perhaps. He knew how it worked. Sometimes you did what you had to, not what you wanted to. Sometimes you did what you knew was right even when you knew you would regret doing it. He had learned that particular lesson from his time with Michael. As a result, he had accumulated enough regret to last him a lifetime, but he had done what he had done because it was what was needed.

Now he was looking after a pack of street kids because he had failed to rescue their leader. Not necessarily because they needed it or because it was given to him to do so, but because it seemed like the right thing.

Still he found himself wondering, as he glanced at his ragged young charges, if doing what he thought was the right thing made any sense at all.

* * *

THEY TRAVELED through the remainder of the night with Logan driving the Lightning S-150, the Weatherman and the boy with the ruined face strapped to the roof, Squirrel and Sparrow riding in the back, Owl riding in the passenger's seat, and the cart with the assorted possessions salvaged by the Ghosts attached behind. The others either walked or rode on the wide, flat fenders, taking turns when one or more needed to rest. Panther and Bear walked almost the entire way, riding only when Owl ordered them to do so, unwilling to acknowledge any hint of weakness. Logan kept the car's pace slow enough so that even Candle did not have trouble keeping up. Speed wasn't crucial just yet. A destination wasn't immediately important, either, which was a good thing since none of them—including Logan Tom, or maybe especially Logan Tom—knew where they were supposed to be going. At some point soon, they would need to have some sort of destination in mind. But for tonight it was enough to maintain a steady pace that would take them out of the city and into the surrounding countryside, far away from the once-men and their madness.

They traveled south, the direction in which the freeway took them after coming down off the entry ramp and the one with which Logan felt most comfortable. He had come into the city from the north and east, and he was not anxious to go back through those mountain passes. Perhaps it was the possibility of another encounter with the ghosts of the dead or perhaps it was his aversion to retracing his steps when his enemies were always looking for him to do so. He did not know yet where they would have to travel to find the missing Hawk and Tessa, but he knew he would be happier searching for them somewhere other than where he had already been.

He also knew that in order to make any sort of journey, they would require a trailer large enough to haul both themselves and their possessions. It was all right to poke along the freeway at a snail's pace for tonight, but after that they would need a means by which they could move more quickly, if the need arose, and the Lightning couldn't hold them all.

These considerations and others flitted through his mind as he eased the AV down the long ribbon of concrete into the darkness, weaving through a tangle of abandoned vehicles and trash heaps and the bones of the dead. Distant now, but still visible, the fires of the ships and the compound lit the night sky in a yellowish haze. He found himself thinking of the people who lived in the compound and likely would die there before this was finished. In particular, he found himself thinking of Meike, with her freckles and anxious eyes. He wondered if she would do as he had told her or make the easy choice and stay put. He decided that maybe he didn't want to know.

When they got far enough down the highway, all the way to the far end of a huge airfield, he turned off the road and drove them to a piece of high ground that overlooked the airfield and, farther back the way they had come, the city. He drove the Lightning into a small copse of trees where it wouldn't be immediately noticed, parked, and climbed out. He had a pair of tents and blankets in the back, enough so that with the interior of the vehicle to use, as well, they could all get a little sleep. That they needed to rest was a given. Everyone was exhausted.

Using the boys to help set up the tents and Owl to provide encouragement, Logan put them all to bed. Owl went last, taking time to clean the wounds of the boy with the ruined face before insisting that Logan put him inside with the Weatherman. Logan agreed, but handcuffed one wrist to a ring at the rear of the vehicle.

Alone again, he set up watch in the driver's seat, facing the AV out toward the roadway they had just traveled down. He didn't expect any pursuit, but he had learned never to take anything for granted, even the reliability of the Lightning's warning systems. With the uneven breathing of the Weatherman drifting out of the rear of the vehicle, he stared out into the darkness and fell into a light doze.

He was drifting somewhere between dreams and reality when the Lady came to him.

＊　＊　＊

HE SENSES HER PRESENCE *before he hears her voice, and it is enough to cause him to rise and move out onto the grassy knoll on which the Lightning S-150 AV sits. He sleeps poorly this night, his mind restless, his thoughts dark and rife with foreboding. Memories of missed chances haunt him, come like ghosts to plague his rest. He dozes for a few minutes here and there, but he fights a losing battle with his personal demons; they give him no peace. Mostly he tries to pretend that he is equal to their challenge and to the wounding accusations they whisper.*

"Logan Tom," she says, speaking his name.

I am here, *he wishes to answer, but his throat tightens and he cannot give voice to the words.*

He crosses through grasses grown long and shaggy, breathing in the cool night air and the smell of damp bark and dried leaves. A few of the Ghosts snore, Bear more loudly than the others, wrapped in their blankets and hunched close together for warmth. He glances back to where the boy who killed Squirrel hunkers down inside the Lightning, awake now, though still chained and shackled. The boy does not look in his direction. It doesn't matter, of course. Even if he turned, he would not see her. She is never seen unless she wishes it. This night, he believes, she does not.

He crosses the grasses in the direction of her voice, not yet seeing her, but knowing she is there. His staff reclines against the seat inside the Lightning, next to where he sleeps. He never goes anywhere without it, but on this night he has given it no thought; her voice is that compelling. Remembering his oath to keep it with him always, he feels a twinge of regret at his failing. But there is nothing to fear. When she calls to him, he knows he will be safe in coming.

"I am here," she says.

She is standing right in front of him, an ephemeral presence, an exquis-ite radiance. Her gown flows from her like a thin sheet of water down a bridal falls, gathering in a pool that stirs restlessly beneath her feet, even though she herself does not move. She hovers in the air, slightly elevated from the grasses through which she comes, ghostly white save for the dark pools of her eyes. The long sweep of her hair falls beyond shoulder length and ripples like silk tossed in the wind.

It is the first time she has appeared to him since sending him to Hopewell and his meeting with Two Bears. As always, he is stunned by the simple fact of her, and without thinking he drops to his knees.

"Brave Knight," she whispers, "you have done well."

He cannot imagine why she thinks so given the mess he has made of things. It seems to him he has failed on every front. But her praise gives him fresh hope that somehow he has misjudged the success of his efforts.

Again he tries to speak, and this time he manages to do so, although his words are weak and halting. "If you think so—"

"Why would you doubt me, Logan Tom?" she asks, cutting short the rest of his protestation. "I would not say it if it were not so. You have done well at the task you were given. You have found the child of wild magic, you have given him the bones of his mother, and you have helped him discover the truth about himself."

Her voice soothes his doubts and eases his discomfort. It makes him want to believe.

"The boy?" *he whispers through the sudden dryness in his throat.* "Is he safe?"

She moves slightly to one side, gliding on the air as if sliding on ice. The city glows faintly behind her, its fires still burning in the night. He can see bits and pieces of their hazy light through the pale shimmer of her body, as if she were as transparent as clear water.

"He rests in the arms of another servant of the Word, Logan. He gathers his strength for the journey ahead. When he wakes, he will come north to find you and the rest of those he will lead. You must go to meet him."

"Meet him where?" *he asks, confused.*

"On the banks of the Columbia. He will come there to begin his journey. He will have many with him. All will need your protection. You must give it, brave Knight, no matter the cost to yourself."

No matter the cost. He supposes he has always known what that means, what it might eventually require. "I will do my best."

"Another Knight of the Word comes to stand with you. She will bring the Elves. They will bring the magic of their Faerie past, which shall be the magic of humankind's future."

Elves? He doesn't think he has heard her right. He can't have heard her right. There are no such things as Elves. She has said something else and he has misunderstood.

He starts to ask for an explanation, but her hand lifts and stays his voice. "Be careful how you go, Logan," *she tells him then, her voice soft and cautious, as if someone might hear.* "There are dangers waiting for you. The demons are coming. They hunt the boy. They will destroy him if they can, even without understanding the nature of the danger he poses to them. It is enough that they fear him for reasons they cannot put a voice to. He is a gypsy morph who has embraced the Word, and that is enough to convince them that he must die. You must prevent that."

Her hand lowers slightly as she pauses. "You must not fail me in this. You must not fail the Word. You must do what is needed to keep the boy safe and to help him reach his destination. Beware. There are known dangers, but unknown dangers will threaten you more. Some reside in the outside world; some reside in your own heart. Watch carefully for these. Keep them at bay."

She begins to fade, to disappear back into the night. He tries to stay her going, calling out to her. But his voice once again has no sound. He tries then to hold her back by sheer force of will, but it is like trying to hold back mist with your hands. Nothing he does can touch her. She watches him without expression, without any hint that she understands his need. Perhaps she doesn't, or perhaps it simply doesn't matter. He has been given a task; he is expected to fulfill it.

"I will come to you another time, brave Knight," she promises. "You may rest now. You will be safe this night and until you wake."

Then she is gone and he is alone. He has a moment of recognition, realizing that it is a dream and he has not left the AV and his bed and that her presence and her words come from inside his own head.

Then he sleeps.

SIX

"WHAT DO YOU THINK you are doing?" the voice repeated.

In the deep sub-basement of the Belloruus home, surrounded by the histories of the Elves amid layers of gloom and shadows, the disembodied voice was a wraith without a presence. Neither Kirisin nor Erisha could see anything of the speaker, and neither could decide what to say or do in response to the question.

"Cat got your tongue?" the speaker chided.

"Culph!" Erisha said finally, just as Kirisin had decided they might really be in danger. "You don't have to scare us like that!"

The elderly keeper of the histories moved into the edge of the light that sat on the plank flooring between the Elven girl and boy, hands on his skinny hips, body bent like the trunk of a gnarled old tree. He was short and withered looking, an elder of indeterminate age. His wrinkled face was shaded by what appeared to be a halfhearted effort at growing a beard and was dominated by a pair of huge ears.

"You haven't permission to be down here, missy," he declared, extending a bony finger at the girl. "King's daughter or not. And you," he added, moving the finger over to Kirisin, "don't even have permission to be inside this house!"

"I invited him!" Erisha snapped back, no longer afraid, starting to bristle at being spoken to like this by anyone who wasn't family.

"Did you?" Culph gave her a sharp look. "Asked him over to do a little late-night reading, is that it?"

Even in the pale wash of the torch's poor light, Kirisin could see that Erisha was losing her temper. "I asked for her help," he said quickly, drawing the other's attention. "I wanted to see what the histories had to say about the Ellcrys."

The old man crouched down next to them, his sharp eyes flitting from face to face. "Oh, is it more of that business about the tree asking the Chosen to use the Loden Elfstone to keep it safe?" He nodded soberly, and Kirisin, who had been trying not to reveal too much, was reminded that it was pointless to be circumspect with Culph since the King had already set him to work on researching the matter. "I know all about it, you know," the old man declared.

Kirisin decided to take a chance. "Well, the King doesn't believe that the Ellcrys spoke to me. But Erisha does because the tree spoke to her, as well. So we decided to see what we could find out."

"Not accepting that what I did was sufficient, is that it?" Culph said almost teasingly. "What could an old man like me know about such things, you might have asked yourselves. Probably couldn't even find the right book, you might have said."

"That is not what we thought," Erisha snapped, jumping back into the conversation. "We just wanted to see for ourselves." She hesitated. "The truth is, we didn't know what you might have found. My father doesn't want me involved in this business for reasons he won't reveal. He was very insistent that I not do what the tree asked of me. He was adamant. So I can't be certain that what he told me is the truth. Or even that he told me everything he knows. Maybe there's more." She gave him a hard look. "Is there?"

Culph shrugged. "How would I know? I don't know what he told you. I do know what I told him. But why should I tell you? Why shouldn't I just wake your father and turn you over to him. That way it isn't my problem anymore."

Erisha glared. "You'd better not."

Culph grinned mirthlessly. "Or I might be very sorry I did, is that it? What I might be sorry about is if I don't and get found out. Your father is hardly the forgiving kind these days."

"What about the Ellcrys?" Kirisin pressed. "If we don't try to help her, she'll simply ask one of the other Chosen. She's already made it clear that she feels threatened. Don't you think we have an obligation to do something?"

The sharp old eyes fixed on him. "What I think is that you might be hallucinating about all this, the both of you. How do you know for certain what you've heard? Move the Ellcrys by using an Elfstone that no one has seen or heard of in centuries? Move our most precious talisman because the end of the world is coming? Am I supposed to accept your word on this without stopping to question it?"

Kirisin hesitated. The old man had a point. "It means something that both Erisha and I heard the Ellcrys say the same thing at separate times. The humans have been working at the destruction of the world for years; that isn't something we didn't already know. There are signs of wilt and decay all through the Cintra. If you've been outside this building, you must have seen them. To just dismiss everything as the King has done is both dangerous and wrong. As Chosen, we have an obligation to find out the truth. We came here tonight to try to do that."

"By reading the histories to see if there is any mention of the Loden or the blue Elfstones, yes, I understand all that." Culph seemed unpersuaded. "But even if you were to find these artifacts, what would you do then? Would you actually try to move the tree?"

Kirisin took a deep breath. "I don't know. At least we would have a choice in the matter."

"Maybe my father will have changed his mind by then," Erisha said. "Maybe other things will have changed, too."

"Like the end of the world coming, that sort of thing." Culph sniffed and worked at rubbing away the stubble of his failed beard with one gnarled hand. "Well, you both seem pretty certain about this."

"We wouldn't be here otherwise," Erisha said.

"No, probably not, considering how your father would react if he found out what you were doing. He won't even discuss the subject with me, even though he might learn something if he did." The wizened face tightened. "Does he seem different to you these days? Less reasonable, less patient with matters in general?"

Erisha nodded, looking unhappy.

"Well, it isn't just me, then." Culph sighed. "I suppose turning you over to him wouldn't accomplish much. Even if you don't belong down here and are being disobedient." He thought for a moment, studying them. "Have you found anything yet?"

Erisha shook her head. "Have you?" Kirisin asked at once.

"Maybe." The old man considered the matter. "Maybe you'd like to hear what it was."

Kirisin felt his heart jump. "We would. We would like that very much."

Culph rocked back on his heels. "Then I'll tell you. But only if we all agree that anything said down here in this room goes no farther. Because if I tell you what I know and it gets back to the King, I am out of a job and maybe exiled, as well. I don't care much for either result. I'll be taking a chance on you if I tell you anything. So everything stays right here. Do we have a bargain?"

Kirisin glanced at Erisha. She nodded doubtfully. "We have a bargain."

They settled themselves more comfortably on the plank flooring, leaning into the light and closer to each other, conspirators against the night. Kirisin could hardly contain his eagerness; this was the sort of help they desperately needed and could hardly have expected to find. He was a little surprised that Culph was willing to share what he knew with them, but maybe the old man's sense of responsibility for the Ellcrys was stronger than his sense of loyalty to the King.

"We begin at the beginning," Culph declared, clasping his hands in front of him as a teacher might to command the attention of his students. "The Elfstones are an old magic, going all the way back to the time of Faerie. They were mined by Trolls and given to Elves to be made over into talismans. Because it was the Elves who infused them with their magic, only the Elves could use them. They were of different colors and designed to do different things. They were formed and shaped in sets of three. The mix of minerals and magic made each set individual. It took years to make even a single set. There is no surviving record of exactly what it was they could do, at least not in the pages of the histories we have. Except for one kind. The blue Elfstones were seeking-Stones and could be used to find what was hidden from or lost to the seeker."

"The ones the Ellcrys said must be used to find the Loden," Erisha interjected.

Culph gave her a look suggesting that interruptions and unsolicited comments were not welcome. "All the Elfstones had defensive capabilities. They were infused with power to protect the user. Their power was dependent on the individual, a reflection of the combined strengths of heart, mind, and body. The Stones were the most powerful of the Elven magic, and all of them were lost when the world of Faerie disappeared."

He gave Erisha another look, cutting off what he knew she was about to say. "Let me tell it, missy." He tightened his lips. "Again, except for the blue Elfstones. But they haven't been seen in centuries, their whereabouts a mystery."

The way he said it told Kirisin at once that he knew something of that mystery, something that might lead them to the Stones. But he held his tongue, knowing it was better to let the old man tell them what he knew in his own way.

"We know even less about the Loden Elfstone. The Loden was a single Stone designed for a particular purpose, one that was very special. Of all the Elfstones, only the Loden and the Black Elfstone were regarded as more important than the others. But we don't know why. Maybe, as the Ellcrys has told you, the Loden is meant to act as her protector. Maybe it can form a shield for her as she forms a shield against the demons within the Forbidding. Whatever the case, we know almost nothing about it. There is no description of it in the histories and no explanation of how it is to be used. And no mention of where it might be found."

He paused again, regarding them in turn, a bright expectancy in his sharp old eyes. "But there is something."

He actually smiled then, and it was a frightening sight. Smiling did not seem to come naturally to Culph, and it must have cost him something to do so now. But at least he was showing some interest in their efforts, thought Kirisin.

"Everything I just told you is contained in the histories, and I am certain you would have found it all by yourself." The old man frowned. "It would have taken you more than one night, perhaps. It took me two days just to reread it all after the King asked me to look into the matter, and I had already read all the histories at least several times before!"

He paused again. "The thing of it is, knowing all of it doesn't help you at all. The histories are only part of our lore, only a small piece of our recorded knowledge. There are other sources, too. Books that are not a part of the histories. Books that give us little-known information and unexpected insights. These books are also housed in this library, but they are not well read and not paid attention to. Most are rarely even opened."

He paused. "Some have never been opened by anyone living. Except for me."

"What did you find?" Erisha asked eagerly.

"Not so fast, missy," the old man snapped, patting the air in front of him with the palms of his hands. "Haven't you learned anything about the value of patience?"

But Erisha wasn't the least bit interested in learning about the value of patience. Nor was Kirisin feeling particularly patient either, at this point. They were eager to hear what the old man knew that he hadn't told them. And waiting for him to reveal it was torture. "So there *was* something in one of these books?" he pressed.

Culph gave him another of those dreadful smiles. "Something, indeed. A very important reference to the blue Elfstones you seek. Let's have a look."

He rose, disappeared into the gloom for a few minutes, and then returned with a slim, worn book bound in leather that was cracked and faded. "A diary," he said. "One of any number kept by various scribes over the centuries. They are stored in bins at the very back of the room. This one is an unofficial recording of a royal family's life and death, written thousands of years ago by a man who served as their personal assistant. I call it a diary because it is this man's private recollections, not recorded for official use, but as a personal undertaking. I found it some time ago when I was reorganizing the library, but didn't pay much attention to it. When the matter of the Elfstones was raised by your father, I remembered it. After quite a search, I unearthed what I am about to read to you."

He sat down between them and opened the book carefully, turning to the very last page. "It is written in an ancient language, an old dialect of Elfish, so my translation is a bit rough. But this is the gist of what it says:

"I helped bury Pancea Rolt Cruer on this day, Queen to her people and mother of a family that has served the Elves long and well. With her passing, I resign my post and retire to the Hibbling Auer to live out the rest of my life. Then something, something, I can't be sure. This entry shall be my last. She rests in the depths of Ashenell with the Stones sewn in her clothing, the decision her own, made years ago at the start of her reign. It was accepted thinking by then that the old magic had outlived its usefulness, that the time of Faerie was of the past and the time of Man was of the present and quite possibly the future. Magic gives way to science, and that path is different from our own. It was the Queen's firm belief that use of magic now only places our people in danger. She would not be a part of that. But the decision was arrived at without consultation and in secret, and a record should be set out for those who come after. Something, something more. The world changes, and no one knows what the future holds. I leave it thus."

The old man looked up, his wizened face expectant. "It ends there. Nothing more. But it tells us where the Elfstones are. Sewn into the clothing of a dead Queen, who lies buried somewhere in Ashenell."

"The burial ground for our dead!" exclaimed Erisha excitedly. "All we need to do is to go there and find her tomb!"

"Yes, simple enough, it would seem," Culph replied with a grimace. "I thought as you did. I even went to Ashenell to have a look. Secretly, of course, so that your father would not know what I was trying to do. I found the family plot for the Cruer Kings and Queens, but there was no marker bearing her name."

Erisha stared at him, then glanced at Kirisin. "How can that be?"

Kirisin frowned and shook his head, his mind on something much more troubling. "You haven't mentioned the Loden. But the King made it very clear to Erisha that he knew something about it, something that troubled him enough that he didn't want his daughter using it to help the Ellcrys. What did you tell him that made him react like that? What did you find?"

Culph hesitated, an uncertain look in his sharp eyes. "We had an agreement when we started this conversation. Do we still have it? Whatever we say or hear stays within this room?"

Kirisin and Erisha exchanged a quick glance. "That was the agreement," Kirisin affirmed.

"Then I will tell you that the King either knows something I don't or is assuming the worst." Culph's aged face tightened. "I found nothing more about the Loden than what I have told you—vague mention and general comment given in the context of the larger reference to Elfstones in general. I found nothing anywhere that explained what it was that the Loden was supposed to do. I found nothing that said using the Loden was dangerous to the user. Not in the histories and not in the diaries and personal journals. Not anywhere."

There was a long silence as the boy and the girl digested this unexpected piece of information. "Then why would he forbid Erisha from even thinking about using it?" Kirisin asked.

Culph shook his head and shrugged. "You would have to ask him. That particular piece of advice did not come from me or from anything that I might have said to him. It is a conclusion of his own making, and I wonder myself about the nature of its origin."

"I don't understand," Erisha said softly.

Neither did Kirisin, and it was a troubling mystery. It was one thing for Arissen Belloruus to want to protect his daughter from a danger discovered through a reading of the histories or from personal experience. But it was something else again to fabricate a threat out of nothing more than unfounded fears and doubts. Still, what else could explain his strange behavior in this business? Without any apparent knowledge of the way in which the Loden functioned, without any history to support his thinking, he had determined that the Elfstone posed a danger to his daughter and therefore had forbidden her to use it. It was a reaction that would have been bad enough coming from a father, but was immeasurably worse coming from a King. As King, his first responsibility was to his people, to the maintenance of their health and safety. And the welfare of the Elves depended before all else on the health of the Ellcrys.

"Well, it doesn't matter what he thinks," Kirisin ventured. "We know what we need to do, and we are going to do it. Aren't we, Erisha?"

He looked directly at her as he said this so that he could take the measure of her reaction. He needed to be certain that she would not change her mind about choosing to help.

"You don't have to ask me that," she snapped, her response fierce. Her eyes held his for a moment in challenge, then shifted to Culph. "I think Kirisin and I need to visit Ashenell and have a look for ourselves. I don't know if it will do any good, but it can't hurt. Maybe fresh eyes will spy out something you missed. It's possible, isn't it?"

The old man shrugged. "Of course, it's possible. In fact, I will go with you. Later today, if the two of you can manage to stay awake that long. Sunrise is only three hours away, and you haven't been to bed. But I don't guess you need sleep the way I do. Suppose we meet at noon. I don't have anything to keep me here after that. The King won't notice."

"You don't have to become involved in this," Kirisin offered. "You've given us more than enough help already."

Culph laughed. "A little late for me to decide not to become involved, don't you think? How much farther out do I have to stick my neck before it matters?" He shook his head, his aged face turned suddenly serious. "I made my choice in this business. I could have reported you to the King. I could have kept what I knew about the Elfstones to myself. But I happen to think you know what you are talking about. You wouldn't have gone through all this if you'd only imagined that she spoke to you. I don't want to think back about what I could have done to help when it's too late."

Erisha smiled. "Thanks, Culph. For taking a chance on us."

His sharp eyes fixed on her. "Don't be too quick to thank me just yet, missy." He gestured into the dark in the direction of the basement door. "Off to bed with you, for a few hours, at least. This business isn't going to get any easier if you're asleep on your feet."

Neither Kirisin nor Erisha made any objection as they rose and headed back the way they had come, anxious for the new day to begin.

THEY STOOD CLOSE TOGETHER in the shadows just outside the door through which Kirisin had entered the Belloruus home hours earlier, sheltered by a screen of heavy bushes as they whispered.

"He was a lot more helpful than I thought he would be," Erisha said. "I've known Culph since I was a little girl and I've never known him to volunteer his help. He rarely even speaks to anyone."

"Maybe he feels that this is important," Kirisin answered. He glanced around uneasily, not liking the way they were exposed to anyone getting close enough to hear their voices. "He said he'd made his choice. Maybe that's the difference."

"Well, he's taking a big risk with my father. If he gets found out, my father will exile him. He won't think twice."

"Your father won't find out anything if we don't tell him."

Erisha gave him a sharp look. "He finds out a lot that people don't want him to know. He has ears everywhere. We have to be careful, Kirisin. We can't even tell the other Chosen. None of them. This stays between you and me."

"They wouldn't believe me anyway. They didn't about the Ellcrys."

They were silent a moment, listening to the night sounds, staring off into the dark. Kirisin could hear an owl's mournful hoot somewhere close by. He could hear the sound of a stream trickling over rocks. "Something is bothering me," he said.

The Elven girl looked at him. "What do you mean?"

"I mean that something doesn't feel right. About the way your father is acting. About the way the Ellcrys is telling us what she needs us to do. About *what* she needs us to do. About the lack of anything written down in the histories about either the blue Elfstones or the Loden." He shook his head, frustrated with not being able to better explain. "Doesn't it seem odd that there isn't something written somewhere, given how important the Elfstones are?"

She stared at him without answering, then said, "Maybe there was something written down once, but it's been lost."

"That seems like a huge coincidence to me." Kirisin ran his fingers through his tangled hair and rubbed his eyes. "But I'm too tired to think clearly about it now."

"Maybe we both are," Erisha said, giving his arm a squeeze.

They were silent again, and then Kirisin said, "I want you to know I am proud of you for doing this. It took a lot of courage. You could have just done what your father wanted."

She shook her head, her eyes on the ground. "I knew that I was doing the wrong thing listening to my father. I knew that the Ellcrys needed me and I was abandoning her. I just needed to be reminded." She looked at him. "It took more courage for you to stand up to me and then go to my father when everyone told you not to. You're the brave one."

"I didn't have so much to lose."

"Maybe you did."

He smiled. "I'm glad we're on the same side in this. I'm glad we're friends again."

"We've shared a lot of good times, haven't we?" She grinned. "Remember hiding in my house until everyone thought we were lost in the forests somewhere? We got in a lot of trouble for that, but it was still fun." She shook her head ruefully. "I've missed that. Sometimes I wish I could have just stayed that age forever."

He shrugged. "Well, maybe in your heart, you can. Maybe we both can. And should. It might help us get through the rest of what we have to do for the Ellcrys."

"No," she said somberly, "I think maybe we have to grow up." She leaned into him and kissed him on the cheek. "Good night, cousin. See you in a few hours."

She disappeared back inside the house. Kirisin stood where he was for a few moments longer, thinking about how quickly things could change in life, then slipped back into the shadows and the night and headed home.

SEVEN

WITH THE ENRAGED HOWLS of the demon echoing in her ears and the chill certainty of the pursuit that would follow all too quickly chasing her down the roadway, Angel Perez rode the Mercury 5 north through the night. She drove at breakneck speed, pushing the solar-powered ATV hard, ignoring the dangers of spinning out or colliding with abandoned vehicles and scattered chunks of debris, her one thought to put as much distance as possible between herself and her nemesis.

A single thought repeated itself over and over in her mind, haunting her with its terrible insistence.

She is too powerful for you.

She had never thought such a thing before, but she was thinking it now. She knew with bone-chilling certainty that if they met again and she were forced to do battle, she would die. She didn't know what sort of monster the demon had transformed into, becoming a beast in appearance rather than a woman, but she knew that it was stronger and more dangerous than she was, and she could not defeat it.

"Angel, slow down!" Ailie pleaded from where she sat right behind her on the Mercury, clinging to her shoulders, tiny fingers gripping so tightly that Angel could feel fingernails digging into her shoulders. Her slash wounds from her battle with the demon throbbed and burned where Ailie's fingers gripped, and her body ached from the struggle she had endured. But none of it could penetrate the red haze of her fear.

"Angel!"

She heard Ailie this time and realized that she was out of control, racing toward an almost certain collision, charging toward her own destruction. She throttled back on the ATV, fighting both the machine and her emotions, trying to bring herself under control.

¿Que pasa, Angelita? ¡You are never like this!

Johnny's voice was a sharp, quick warning in her mind, an admonition that she could not mistake. She clenched her teeth, tightened her grip on the handlebars, and resurrected the steely determination that had seen her through so many terrible battles.

Do not be such a coward! Her own voice this time, her own scathing admonition to match Johnny's. She knew better. She had allowed herself to panic over possibilities and not for any good reason. It was a weakness she could barely tolerate in others and not at all in herself.

She rode the Mercury over to the side of the road and parked it with the motor still running, taking deep breaths to steady herself, aware of how hard her heart was beating in her chest. Behind her, she felt Ailie sit back on the seat, her grip loosening. She felt the pain in her body return in a sudden flood that racked her with enough force to cause her to jerk sharply in response.

"I'm sorry," she said to Ailie without looking at her.

She shut off the engine and sat motionless in the ensuing silence, breathing in the night air, feeling the intense heat of her body begin to diminish and the wild churning of her emotions subside. The highway was a black ribbon to her left, stretching north and south as far as the eye could see, empty of everything, including the trash that was so prevalent everywhere else. Mountains hemmed in the highway from both sides, their peaks outlined in stark relief against the sky by ambient light from the stars and a sliver of moon.

"You had reason to be afraid," Ailie said quietly.

Angel tightened her lips and flexed her shoulders against her tenseness. "I had reason to be afraid, but not reason to panic. Panic is a road to destruction, and I know better than to turn down that road." She exhaled sharply. "The demon managed to make me do so back there, but it will not do so again. That much I can promise."

"I believe you," said Ailie.

She climbed down off the seat and walked around in front of the ATV where she could see Angel's face. The tatterdemalion was a wisp of white gauze and pale flesh that shimmered with ghostly translucence. Her luminous eyes fixed on Angel.

"I am afraid all the time," she said.

Angel stared at her. "Why would that be so? What are you afraid of?"

The tatterdemalion's gaze did not waver. "Everything." The dark eyes blinked. "I am afraid of everything, Angel. It is a condition caused by the nature of my existence. I live only a short time, and I know that other creatures live so much longer. If I did not think and were not aware of life spans, if I were an insect perhaps, it would not matter. But I do think and I am aware, and so I can appreciate how precious my time is. It does not help that I know I am in constant danger because of what I am and whom I serve. The demons hate creatures like me. So I am afraid even when I do not want to be or even when I do not need to be."

"That sounds very unpleasant." Angel hugged herself. Tatterdemalions lived a mayfly existence, their lives spanning not much more than thirty days on average. They were there and gone in the blink of an eye. "No one wants to be afraid. Even if it's only now and then, let alone all the time."

Ailie nodded. "I have learned to live with it. I have learned not to be ashamed of or angry with myself. I have learned that some things are simply a condition of our lives, and we cannot help them."

Angel pursed her lips. "You are telling me I should be more like you. I should not be ashamed or angry about my fear. I should accept it."

Ailie's smile was small and winsome on her somber face. "At least you could think about it."

Angel smiled back. "I guess I could, little conscience."

Ailie climbed back up behind Angel. "I think we better go. The Elves have need of us."

Angel nodded. "Elves." She brushed at her thick black hair. "I still can't get used to the idea. But I suppose I better."

She turned the engine on again, engaged the throttle, and steered the Mercury back onto the highway headed north, its engine a dull roar in the night's silence, its metal body sleek and silvery in the pale wash of the stars.

Hunched close together on the padded seat, the Knight of the Word and the tatterdemalion rode north in search of their future.

*   *   *

IN THE DARKNESS behind them, still miles back but coming steadily on, the demon, in its newly acquired form, loped down the center of the highway, an indefatigable machine. That part of her that had been Delloreen was all but wiped away by her physical transformation. Once human in appearance, she was now all animal. Her skin was turned to scales. Her fingers and toes were turned to claws. Her hair was mostly gone; fringes remained only on pointed ears. Her human features were feral and wolfish. She no longer walked upright, but ran on all fours. She had lengthened out from well over six feet to well over ten. She was heavily muscled and sinewy and terrifying to look upon.

She had become something else entirely, and she reveled in it.

She had never been invested in her appearance, never cared for how she looked or what she seemed to be to those she encountered. She knew what she was: she was a demon. That she might become bigger and stronger and more ferocious was all that mattered. That she might become the most dangerous of the Void's creatures was her primary goal.

She had not forgotten about Findo Gask, not entirely, but he no longer mattered to her. His insolence and his attempts to motivate her to do his bidding no longer mattered, either. The old man was her past, a vague memory at best, a reminder of dissatisfaction and frustration, a momentary distraction that had now all but faded from memory. Her goals, her purpose, had narrowed down to a single preoccupation—to find and kill the Knight of the Word who had twice now escaped her. She didn't look beyond that. Hunting down and destroying the Knight was everything. After that, she would decide if anything else mattered. For now, there was only the pursuit and the satisfaction that awaited its conclusion.

Her long tongue lolled from between her fangs as she ran, and the pad of her rough paws and the click of her sharp nails on the blacktop sounded a steady tempo that set her pace. Lost in the workings of her sleek new form, in the steady rush of adrenaline the excitement of the hunt generated, she panted with undisguised eagerness and dreamed of the taste of the Knight's fresh blood.

IT TOOK ANGEL AND AILIE the rest of the night and through the bulk of the morning to find their way north up the highway and then east onto the side roads that would take them to the Cintra. This was foreign country to Angel, who had never been north of Southern California, but Ailie, who by all rights should have known even less, seemed to know exactly where to go. Angel saw a few signs advising travelers who were long since dead and gone in a world equally dead and gone that they were passing into the Willamette National Forest. When Angel asked Ailie about this, the tatterdemalion said she didn't know what it was called by humans, only by Elves. She added that she could already feel their presence.

Angel was in a somewhat better mood by now, her fear subsided, her steely determination regained. The darkness of the previous night with its attendant onslaught of black willies had faded with the rising of the sun and the beginning of the new day. She hadn't conquered it entirely, but she did have it under control. When it surfaced again, she would be ready for it.

The forests through which they passed initially resembled most of the others they had traversed coming north—large sections sickened and wilted, the leaves turned gray, the bark scabbed over by parasites and mold. Many trees were already dead, their skeletal frames suggesting the bones of giant animals standing upright and frozen in time. But as they reached the mountains and climbed into the passes, a change similar to the one that had begun to manifest only yesterday surfaced. Where before the trees had thinned to almost nothing, they now grew close together. Where before the leaves and bark were sickened, they now looked healthy and clean. The colors that had been leached away from the other forests were deep and vibrant here. Angel glanced back at Ailie, but the tatterdemalion just smiled enigmatically and gave her a reassuring hug.

A short time later, Ailie directed her off the main road onto a dirt track that was barely more than a woodland trail. They rode the Mercury down its length for several miles, passing through long stretches of old-growth trees so massive that Angel felt dwarfed in their presence. Streams ran through metal culverts that tunneled under the road, the waters rippling and singing before angling off into the woods. Once, they caught sight of a small waterfall off in the distance. Once, they saw a deer.

Finally, Ailie told her to pull over. Angel drove the ATV off the trail into the trees and parked it. Together they climbed down and stood looking into the cool, shadowed depths of the forest. Angel could hear the rippling of a stream nearby. She could hear birdsong. The air she was breathing was fresh and clean. She could not help thinking that somehow they had driven into a different world entirely.

"What has happened here?" she asked softly. "It looks as if the poisons never touched this forest."

"The Elves have happened, Angel," her companion replied. "The Elves have kept the forest clean and alive with their skills and experience."

Angel shook her head in wonderment, tasting the air, breathing in the scents, wishing she could stay here forever. "Is this where we are supposed to go?"

"This is where we will find the Elves."

"How do we do that?"

"We walk."

They left the Mercury where it was, left the dirt road that had brought them in, and set out. Almost immediately, every sign of where they had been before had vanished, and they were deep in the trees, layered in a mix of sunshine and shadows, making their way through the underbrush and tall grasses that grew among the trunks. It looked to Angel as if no one had passed this way in decades. There was no sign of any disturbance of the forest floor, no indication of anything having come through. Ailie took the lead, picking her way through the trees, choosing a path that for all intents and purposes was invisible to Angel. The tatterdemalion seemed to glide through the grasses and scrub, barely causing movement in the foliage as she passed. Angel, on the other hand, found herself snagged and tripped and scraped at every turn. It didn't help that her wounds from her battle with the demon throbbed relentlessly beneath the tattered remains of her clothing and her entire body ached. In truth, she could barely manage to keep up.

Nevertheless, they moved ahead steadily, the time slipping away, the forest vast and unchanging. Angel knew that if she were left alone at this point, she could never find her way back to the dirt road and probably not out of the forest at all. She experienced a sense of claustrophobia as the trees thickened, the shadows deepened, and the sunlight faded to a pale wash. Angel, a city girl all of her young life, found the woods a creepy place. It had the feel of a warren filled with bolt-holes and hiding places where bad things could spring out at her at any moment.

They pressed on, working their way deeper in, and Angel could not tell in what direction they were moving. It was impossible to see much of the sun, let alone to try to orient it with anything. The mountains had disappeared entirely. The only reassurance Angel could find was in Ailie's steady forward movement, an indication that the tatterdemalion, at least, knew where she was going. Angel followed dutifully and without asking the obvious, fighting against the insidious feeling that she was drowning.

The sun was no longer above them, but moved west and out of view entirely, leaving the forest darker, the shadows longer, and the chill of the air deeper. Then Ailie slowed as they entered a clearing, looked around as if she was testing the air for scent, and stopped altogether.

"We will wait for them here," she advised.

Angel looked around doubtfully. As far as she could tell, they were standing right in the middle of nowhere. The forest looked exactly the same in all directions, and Ailie's choice was indistinguishable from any other they might have made.

"The Elves?" she asked, wanting to be sure she understood.

Ailie nodded. Her face was calm, and her breathing even. She did not look as if the hike in had cost her anything.

Angel shook her head. "How will they know we are here?"

"They will find us. I have put us in their path. They are already coming."

She sat down, so small and insubstantial nestled in the tall grasses that she looked to Angel like a child peeking out from behind a screen of slender blades. Angel chose the remains of a fallen tree, finding a flat open space on its heavy trunk, settling herself wearily. She was thirsty and wished she had something to drink, but she didn't want to go looking for fresh water by herself or disturb Ailie's vigil. She glanced down at her garments and wrinkled her nose. She looked like one of LA's homeless, and she imagined she smelled like one, too. She cradled the black staff of her order against one shoulder and worked idly with a torn strip of her shirt to rub off some of the dirt.

Time passed. Slowly.

The forest stayed quiet, the only sounds those of birdsong and the soft rustle of wind through the leafy branches of the trees. No Elves appeared. Angel wondered how long they were supposed to wait to be discovered. She couldn't decide whether Ailie was justified or not in her confidence about the chances of that happening. The Willamette was a big place. The odds of someone stumbling on them out here seemed extremely remote.

But Angel wasn't going to question her about it. If the tatterdemalion was mistaken, there was nothing else to be done in any case. She was the one who knew how to find the Elves; Angel was just along for the ride.

Or the walk, she corrected herself, thinking suddenly how good it would feel to slip off her boots and give her hot, aching feet some much-needed relief.

"They're here," Ailie said quietly. She didn't look up or change expression. "Don't do anything, Angel. Just wait."

Angel had no intention of doing anything but exactly that. She had come a long way under difficult circumstances to see these creatures, and she was anxious to make it happen. She sat quietly, listening to the forest sounds, gazing in the general direction she was facing without focusing on anything in particular, waiting for movement to reveal an Elven presence.

But she never saw or heard the one who finally appeared, a girl no older than herself, who was nothing of what she had expected Elves to be. The girl was tall and strong looking, not tiny and frail in the manner of tatterdemalions or what she perceived Elves would look like. One moment the forest was empty of life and the next the girl was standing there, just off to one side. Her features were unusual, but not markedly different from those of humans; her face was narrow, her eyebrows slanted, her ears pointed slightly at their tips, and her coloring fair. She wore her long blond hair tied back in a scarf, and her clothing was loose fitting and dyed green and brown like the forest itself. She carried a bow and a quiver of arrows strapped across her back and a pair of long knives belted at her waist. One hand gripped a strange-looking javelin, short and slender, a cord grip wound tightly about its center and razor-sharp metal tips fitted at both ends.

The Elf's blue eyes swept from Angel to Ailie and back again. "A Knight of the Word and a tatterdemalion," she declared with a small smile. "Tell me your names."

"Angel Perez," Angel answered, still coming to terms with the fact that Elves weren't what she had thought they would be. "This is Ailie."

The girl came forward a few steps. "You are the first of your order to come here, and I am guessing that you would not do so without good reason. We never reveal ourselves to humans; you aren't even supposed to know that we exist. The tatterdemalion must have told you otherwise."

Angel nodded. "She did. I didn't believe her at first, but she is very persuasive."

"I had heard there were still tatterdemalions in the world. The old ones have told me what they look like. But until today, I had not seen one." She stared openly at Ailie for a moment, and then turned back to Angel. "You, on the other hand, carry the black staff of your order. No one who has heard of the Knights of the Word could mistake that. I am Simralin Belloruus. How did you find me?"

"We didn't," Angel said. "You found us."

"But you called. You used my name. I heard you."

"That was me," Ailie said, managing to look slightly sheepish without changing expression. "I called you."

Angel stared at her. "I didn't hear you call anyone."

Ailie nodded. "Only Simralin could hear me. And perhaps the Elves who travel with her."

Simralin held up one hand reassuringly as Angel glanced around in alarm. "It's all right. They were told to wait in the trees until I was certain of you. I didn't know at first who you were." She paused, shifting her stance but keeping her eyes on Angel. "Now that I do know, tell me what you are doing here."

Ailie stood up, a small and inconsequential wraith against the huge forest trees. "The Word sent us," she replied.

"The Word?" The Elf girl spoke the name softly, as if even the sound of it was sacred. "Why would the Word send us one of its Knights and a tatterdemalion?"

Ailie looked at Angel, waiting. The tatterdemalion was deferring to her now, giving over the job of explaining what had brought them. Angel sensed that Ailie understood something about the dynamics not only of their own relationship, but also of the relationship they were establishing with the Elves, that would require the Knight of the Word to take charge.

"We were sent to help the Elves find a missing talisman," Angel said. "An Elfstone called a Loden. You must use it to take the Ellcrys from the Cintra and travel to another place. A safer place. The Word believes you are in danger of being destroyed if you stay where you are. The outside world is changing. Things are getting worse. You have a chance of surviving if you leave, and I am instructed to help you."

Simralin Belloruus stared at her as if she were from another planet. Angel held her gaze, waiting for her response. She tried not to look at the girl's pointed ears and slanted brows, at the curve of her facial bones. She was still coming to terms with the idea that there really were Elves in the world.

"You must take us to Arborlon to speak with your King and the Elven High Council," Ailie added quietly.

The girl glanced at her. "Must I?" She paused, and then whistled sharply in the direction of the trees surrounding them.

A handful of figures emerged, slender and possessed of similar features, a couple of them fair like Simralin, a couple of a darker hue. There were four in all, three young men and a second girl. The girl was short and wiry, the young men of varying sizes. All were dressed in the same manner as Simralin and carried similar weapons.

"Ruslan, Que'rue, Tragen, and Praxia," Simralin introduced them, pointing to each in turn, ending with the smaller girl. "We're Elven Hunters, Trackers assigned to the Home Guard, returning home from a long-range reconnaissance of the human settlements east and north. We've been out five weeks, so you'll forgive me for wondering how you knew to call to us just now, when we haven't been in the area for better than a month."

Ailie's smile was childlike and unassuming. "I just did. I am guided by more than my own instincts."

Simralin shook her head. "Apparently." She glanced at the other Elves. "Did you hear what the Knight of the Word said about why they are here? About an Elfstone called a Loden?"

The other four nodded doubtfully, and Praxia said, "The Word sent a human to help Elves?"

"A Knight of the Word," amended Tragen. He was big and broad-shouldered, his Elven features dark and sullen. "She carries a staff of power, rune-carved in the old way of Faerie."

"Perhaps." Praxia did not look convinced. "How do we know any of what she says is true? Are we supposed to take her word for it? Are we to allow a human into our city with nothing more than that? Are we to abandon hundreds of years of secrecy on a whim? I don't like it." She looked at Angel. "Why can't we convey your message to the King ourselves?"

"Your King needs to hear the words come from me," Angel responded, staying calm, not letting herself engage in an argument that she knew she could not win. "There will be questions, and Ailie and I are the only ones who can answer them."

"You must let her speak before the King and the Elven High Council," Ailie repeated. "The Word requires it."

The Elves looked at one another. "They seem awfully certain about this," Simralin ventured. "Perhaps with good reason. A Faerie creature traveling with a Knight of the Word—how could they have found us without divine guidance? She knew how to call to us when no one should even have known we were anywhere near. She knows about Elfstones and Arborlon and the King and the High Council. That isn't information we generally share."

"She knows more than she should," Praxia declared, suspicion mirrored on her young face. She shook her head firmly and faced off against Simralin. "I don't think we can take a chance on this. The risk is too great. I think we need to ask the King if he wishes to meet with them."

She glanced at the other Elves. Ruslan and Que'rue, who had said nothing at all so far, said nothing now, looking first at each other and then at Simralin. "I don't know," said Tragen. He looked doubtful, as if sensing that something was wrong with this suggestion.

It was Simralin who put it into words. "Ailie is a messenger of the Word. Nothing can be hidden from her. If she found us so easily, she could find Arborlon, as well—whether we want her to or not."

"We don't know that," objected Praxia.

"I think maybe we do." Simralin nodded at Ailie. "Am I right, Ailie?"

"I thought it would be best if we came into the city with an escort," the tatterdemalion replied. Her child's features were open and frank. "We are not looking to intrude. We are here as friends, to help the Elves, not to trouble them."

There was an awkward moment of silence as the five Trackers tried to decide how much of a threat the two intruders presented. It was impossible to read the faces of Que'rue or Ruslan. Tragen looked sullen all the time, even though his disposition seemed otherwise, and although Praxia gave no further indication about how she felt, Angel could read it in her angry eyes.

Only Simralin, perhaps because she was their leader, seemed willing to voice an opinion. "No human has entered the city of Arborlon in recorded history. It will break every rule the Elves have so carefully followed if we guide you in now. I don't know how you will be received."

Angel shook her head. "Our reason for coming overshadows any concerns about the reception we might expect. But if you feel strongly about this, why don't you send someone on ahead or even go yourselves, and we will find our own way to the King."

"That would be cowardly on our part," Simralin said. "We would be playing a fool's game and knowing we did so. We can't keep you out, and there isn't much point in pretending that we can. The best thing we can do for all concerned is to make sure you get to where you want to go and say what you want to say."

She glanced at the other Elves, and then looked back at Angel and Ailie. "Perhaps there is a way for all of us to save a little face. If you are willing to make a small concession to protocol?" She reached behind her back and pulled scarves from a ring in her weapons belt. "Blindfolds. I expect they are pointless, but it will help blunt an obvious breach of the rules if it appears they are serving their purpose."

She paused, a faint smile creasing her strong features. "So. Will you agree to wear them?"

She held out the scarves and stood waiting for a response.

EIGHT

KIRISIN DRAGGED his weary body home in the slow fading of the light, evening shadows settling in around him in deepening layers. He meandered down the trails and paths that bypassed the city and led to his home, lost in thought, the growing darkness mirroring his deep disappointment with the day's wasted efforts.

He had been so sure they would find something.

He had met Erisha and old Culph as planned at the entrance to the Ashenell burial grounds at just past midday, excited and anxious to begin their search. But Ashenell was vast and sprawling, a forest of headstones and monuments, mausoleums and simple markers that defied any easy method of sorting out. The terrain itself was daunting, hilly and wooded, the burial sections chopped apart by deep ravines and rocky precipices that made it difficult to determine where anything was. Searching out any single grave without knowing where it was seemed impossible. Nevertheless, they had begun on a hopeful note with the older sections, the ones where members of the Cruer

family were most likely to be interred. They found recognizable markers quickly enough, dozens of graves and simple headstones embedded
in the ground that gave the names and dates of birth and death of
members of the family. Oddly, for a family that had enjoyed such pres-
tige and power, there were no sepulchers or tombs that could be entered. They had finished looking them over in little more than an hour
and had nothing to show for it.

"Sometimes these families sent their dead back into the earth without any sort of marker at all," Culph had observed. "Sometimes they
chose to be buried apart from the family. No way of knowing. We have
to keep looking until we're certain."

So look they did, all the remainder of the afternoon, combing the
burial ground from one end to the other, searching out every grave site,
gaining entry to every sepulcher and tomb, and digging up anything
that might have been a Cruer marker covered over by time and nature.
It was hard, exhausting work, and by the time it had grown too late to
see clearly anymore, all three of them were covered in dirt and debris,
hot and sweaty and sore from their efforts.

"We'll have to leave it for today," Culph announced, grimacing as he
straightened his aching back. "We've covered as much as we can this
day. We can try again day after tomorrow. Best I can do. We'll meet at
midday. Maybe we'll have better luck, but I wouldn't bet on it."

At this point, neither would Kirisin. They hadn't searched everywhere yet; there were still large sections of the Ashenell they had failed
to explore. What worried Kirisin most at this point was that Pancea
Rolt Cruer, Queen of the Elves and the mother of Kings, might have
decided to let the earth reclaim her and leave no mark of her passing,
as Culph had suggested. If that was the case, they would never find either her or the missing blue Elfstones.

He brushed dust from his thighs and the front of his shirt and
wondered how bad he looked to anyone passing by. Pretty bad, he
thought. Like he had rolled in dirt and leaves. Like he had been lost in
the forest.

Well, he was lost, all right. He was so lost that he was having difficulty believing he would ever be found again. The Ellcrys should have
picked someone else to depend upon. All he could manage was to

thrash around in the playground of the dead, wasting the one opportunity he had been given to make a difference. He kicked at the dirt pathway, furious and frustrated and scared all at the same time. Time was slipping away, he told himself. Time he didn't have to waste.

Still muttering under his breath and cursing himself for being so stupid and worthless, aware as he did so that this wasn't helping anything and wasn't, in fact, even true, he passed out of the trees that fronted his home and stopped.

Someone was sitting on the steps of the veranda, leaning back against the roof support, arms resting loosely on drawn-up knees, a glass of ale in one hand. Not his father or mother. They were away for a few nights at his grandparents' home in a small community to the south. This was someone else, someone who looked like . . .

He blinked in disbelief. Simralin! It was Simralin!

She saw him and waved. "Hey, Little K!" she called out, using the nickname she had given him.

"Sim!" he shouted in delight and rushed forward to greet her, bounding up the steps, throwing his arms around her, and hugging her tight. "You're back!"

"Take it easy on me, will you? You're crushing me!"

She laughed as she said it and hugged him back. She was strong and athletic, so it would take a lot before he could do any real damage to her. Kirisin idolized his sister in the way little brothers have idolized older sisters forever: there wasn't anyone like her and never would be. She was six years and a lifetime of experience older than he was. More to the point, he thought her everything he wasn't—tall and smart and beautiful. She was a Tracker of exceptional skills, well liked and respected by everyone, and was to many the kind of friend you always hoped you would find and keep.

"I missed you," he said.

"Good. I'd hate it if you didn't."

She glanced down at his clothes. "Where in the world have you been? Rolling in dirt? You look like a groundhog! You don't smell very good, either." She pushed him away and sat him down on the steps. "Here," she said, handing him her glass of ale. "Drink this and tell me what you've been doing."

He never considered not telling her. She was Simralin, and he always told her everything—even the things he would never tell his parents. He started with the Ellcrys speaking to him and asking for his help, and then related the details of his efforts to secure help from the King, his discovery that he had been lied to, his confrontation with Erisha and her change of heart. He ended with today's futile efforts to find the grave site of the Elven Queen Pancea Rolt Cruer. He explained how he and Erisha had thought to find some mention of the Elfstones in the Elven histories and how old Culph had discovered them, threatened to expose them, and then became their ally. He even threw in his concerns about the King's behavior and how strange it seemed that he would sacrifice the Ellcrys to save his daughter.

When he had finished, Simralin stared at him for a moment, as if making up her mind about something, and then said, "That's a pretty strange story, Little K. Are you sure about all this? You're not dressing it up for me, are you?"

"Of course not! I wouldn't do that!" He was indignant and irritated at her. "Why would you ask me that?"

"Calm down," she soothed, reaching out to grip his shoulder. "I said it because things are a whole lot stranger than you think. Listen to what just happened to me."

She told him then about her encounter with the Knight of the Word, Angel Perez, and the tatterdemalion, Ailie. She explained carefully how it had happened, the strange way she had heard Ailie calling to her, how they had found the two waiting for them, and how they had revealed what had brought them to the Cintra and the Elves.

Then she told him what Angel had said about the Loden and the Elfstones and the end of the world.

"I knew it!" he exclaimed, his voice fierce. "This wasn't just me and Erisha! The Ellcrys really did know that she was in danger and that the Elves were threatened in some way and that she needed us to do something! It wasn't just my imagination!"

"But the King doesn't think so," Simralin pressed.

Kirisin shook his head. "I don't know what he thinks. Neither does Erisha. He knows something we don't, though. He wouldn't be acting this way otherwise. He won't even consider letting Erisha do what the Ellcrys wants her to do, and he's been avoiding me for days. He's been lying to me, come to that!"

"Maybe. Or maybe it just seems that way. You can't be sure what his reasons are for not wanting to act on what you told him." Simralin shook her head. "Our family hasn't been close to Arissen Belloruus for some time, not since his falling-out with our parents. But I know him well enough to question that he would ever do anything that would endanger our people. He is devoted to the Elves. I've seen him demonstrate it time and time again. I think there must be something more."

"Maybe so," Kirisin allowed. "But I don't know what it is or even how to find out. Maybe Erisha can manage it, but she hasn't had much success so far. She says her father seems diffcrent. Even old Culph thinks something's changed in him."

Simralin was sitting again, her knees drawn up to her chest, her face somber. They were both draped in shadows, the night descending rapidly now, what remained of the daylight a pale wash against the horizon west above the wall of the forest.

"Let's have some more of that ale," she suggested.

She went inside and returned with fresh glasses. They sat together in the growing darkness and sipped the smooth, dark amber liquid, not saying anything right away.

"I remember Erisha when she was little," Simralin said finally. She pursed her lips at Kirisin. "She used to follow you around like a newborn puppy. She thought you were so clever." She smiled. "I always thought something might come of that. Especially after both of you became Chosen."

Kirisin grimaced. "Well, at least she's speaking to me again. For a while, she wasn't even doing that much."

"It seems like she's doing a whole lot more than that now. She's going up against her father. Risky, for a King's young daughter."

Kirisin thought about it. It *was* risky. But he wasn't sure he understood exactly what the nature of the risk was. It was more than a threat of punishment for disobedience, he sensed.

"I like her better for taking that risk," he said.

"I expect you do."

He gave her an impish grin. "But I like her best because she looks and smells like me."

"Speaking of which, maybe you ought to go clean up." She loosened her headband and shook out her long blond hair. "I might want to think about that myself. Our guests have been summoned before the High Council to make their presentation, and I have been told to be present. I could do without that, but I was not given a choice."

"Do you think you are in trouble for bringing a human into Arborlon? Even if you did it in the best way and for the right reasons?"

She shrugged. "Probably. Praxia was certainly angry enough about it, and she let it be known to everyone within listening distance. There will be others who are equally unhappy. But it was the right choice."

"The King might not see it that way."

"Probably not. But the matter is decided."

Kirisin grinned. That was Simralin's way of saying it was over and done with, so what was the point of talking about it now? He liked how she could be so matter-of-fact about the way things were. She wasn't much for revisiting the past.

"So here we are," he said.

"So here we are."

They were silent again for a moment, then Kirisin said, "I was thinking. Doesn't it seem odd that the Word's messengers summoned you and the Ellcrys summoned me to do essentially the same thing? To carry a message to the Elves about the danger they are in and how maybe they can avoid it? You and me, a brother and sister, out of all the possible choices? That seems like a rather large coincidence."

"Not large, Little K." Simralin finished off her glass of ale and stretched like a big cat. "Huge."

Kirisin frowned. "You think it was planned, don't you? That the tatterdemalion was told to bring the Knight of the Word to you specifically, maybe *because* we are brother and sister?"

"Like you said, it could have been anyone in the entire Elven nation that Ailie called to her. But it wasn't just anyone; it was me. It feels deliberate."

They stared at each other in silence. Kirisin said, "Can I come with you tonight? It might help if I'm there to advise the High Council that what the Knight and the tatterdemalion are telling them is what the Ellcrys already told Erisha and me."

Simralin shook her head doubtfully. "They are going to want to know why you didn't come forward with this sooner. If you tell them that you did, that you told the King, you are going to be a very unpopular member of the Belloruus royal family."

"I'll be in good company," he said, giving her a pointed look.

She laughed softly. "It's good to be home again, Little K. I've missed having you around. Go take your bath and change your clothes. Then we'll see if we can find out where all this is going."

AN HOUR LATER, they were walking toward the buildings adjacent to the Belloruus home that housed the meeting chambers of the Elven High Council. It was night by now, the daylight faded completely, the sky a mix of scattered clouds and pinpricks of starlight. They walked the back trails skirting the city, avoiding the more heavily traveled roadways. They were already late, and they needed to get to where they were going without being stopped. Neither spoke as they walked, keeping their thoughts to themselves. But each knew what the other was thinking.

Kirisin glanced over at his sister, then down at himself. They were both washed and dressed in a clean set of clothes—the loose-fitting pants, slip-over shirt, and soft boots favored by most Elves. They were presentable, if unimpressive. But making any sort of impression on the members of the High Council and the King was probably out of the question anyway. It wasn't as if everyone didn't already know who they were. It wasn't as if they were strangers.

Even so, Kirisin felt a little bit as if he were.

He adjusted his wide belt. The weapons loops hung slack and empty. Neither carried even so much as a long knife. If they needed weapons this night, they were already beyond help.

Even so, Kirisin found himself wishing that he had brought at least one blade.

He could not account for this sense of misgiving, a nagging uneasiness that lacked a recognizable source but was present nevertheless. He felt foolish for letting it trouble him and roughly pushed it away.

When they arrived at the building that housed the Council chambers, they found Home Guards stationed at the doorway, armed and watchful. The building was a large, circular structure constructed of interconnected logs stretched between huge old-growth spruce and sealed with a packing compound. The roof was high and domed, the foundation raised on plank flooring. Admittance was gained through a pair of wide double doors opening into a hallway that formed the outer rim of the wheel-shaped building and encircled the chambers themselves, which were housed at the hub. The exterior of the building didn't look much different from the forest surrounding it, but the interior, where the chambers were situated, was smooth and sleek and polished, a haven of quiet and soft light.

The Home Guards recognized Simralin at once and waved her through the doors and into the hallway. Kirisin followed, riding her coattails. Inside, they came right up against Tragen. The big Elf's brooding face was even darker this night as he frowned at Simralin in greeting. "We could have used you here a little earlier."

Kirisin glanced past him to where two figures were seated on a bench against the inner wall, almost lost in the shadows of the dark space they occupied between a brace of smokeless torches.

One appeared to be a tiny girl, a creature so insubstantial she looked as if she might disappear on a strong gust of wind. She had long bluish hair, eyes as dark as midnight pools, and skin as pale as chalk. She wore clothing that seemed to drift loosely from her body in the manner of moss from tree limbs, somehow more a part of her than something worn. She glanced at him with an inquisitive look that quickly changed to recognition—which made no sense at all because he had never seen her before.

The second was a young woman, older and stronger, her skin brown, her hair dark, her eyes hard and challenging as she looked at him. She gripped a black staff in both hands, a polished length of wood that had been carved from end to end with symbols he did not recognize. He stared back at her, and she looked away. Her eyes were no longer so dark and angry; instead, they simply looked tired.

"What's wrong?" Simralin was asking Tragen.

The other grunted in disgust. "Praxia hasn't learned yet to leave well enough alone. She tried to take the staff from the Knight. I told her to let it be, but she insisted it was a weapon and shouldn't be carried into the presence of the King. It wasn't her business, but you know Praxia. The Knight knocked her all the way across the hall and into the far wall. She went down hard and didn't get up."

"Praxia," said Simralin in dismay.

"Que'rue and Ruslan carried her out. I stayed because someone had to, but I haven't gone close to those two. Even the Home Guards are keeping back until someone tells them what to do. Got any thoughts?"

Simralin nodded. "Your advice was right. Leave them alone. They're guests, not prisoners. The Knights of the Word consider their black staffs symbols of their office. They never give them up to anyone for any reason. The staffs probably are weapons of some sort, but I don't think the Knight and the tatterdemalion came here to kill anybody. If they wanted to do that, they wouldn't have bothered summoning us. Praxia would have realized that if she had stopped to think it through."

"Let me know the next time she stops to do that about anything," Tragen muttered. He glanced at Kirisin for the first time. "Evening, Little K."

Kirisin blushed. He hadn't realized Simralin's nickname for him was general knowledge. Hearing someone other than his sister use it made him feel like a little boy.

Simralin walked him over to where the Knight of the Word and the tatterdemalion waited and stood before them. "I apologize for what happened," she said to Angel. "Praxia should have known better."

Angel studied Kirisin's sister a moment, and then nodded. "I reacted too strongly. I am the one who should apologize."

Kirisin peeked around Simralin. "My brother, Kirisin," she said. "He seems to know something about why you came looking for the Elves." She moved him in front of her. "Maybe he should explain it."

But before the boy could ask any of the questions that were crying out for answers, the doors to the inner chambers opened and Maurin Ortish, the captain of the Home Guard, emerged and walked toward them.

"Simralin," he greeted. He was a tall, slender man in his middle years, his Elven features pronounced, his voice unexpectedly soft. "You are to come inside now. Please bring your guests with you."

He limped badly from an accident he had suffered several years ago that had left one leg shorter than the other. But he was still a commanding presence, a calming influence wherever he went, and still so identified with his office that there had never been any real consideration given to replacing him, even after his injury had hampered his movement.

He glanced at Kirisin. "What brings you here, young Belloruus. Shouldn't you be sleeping so that you can rise early to tend to your duties as a Chosen?"

"I was hoping I might speak to the Council, as well," Kirisin ventured. "I know something of the reason that the outsiders are here."

"This is true," Simralin affirmed. "His presence would be helpful."

"That may be so," acknowledged Ortish, giving Kirisin a quick smile. "But the High Council has asked that no one be present save you and your guests. That decision is firm."

"But they need to know—" Kirisin started.

The Captain of the Home Guard put up his hand to silence him. "The King himself has given the order. Neither of us is in a position to overrule him. Perhaps after the Council hears what Simralin's guests have to say, they will arrange for you to speak later."

The King himself. Kirisin felt a flush creep up his neck and into his cheeks. The King was making sure he didn't interfere with things, that he kept what he knew to himself. That was how it felt, and that was what he believed.

"Patience, Little K," his sister said softly.

She beckoned to the Knight of the Word and the tatterdemalion, and the three of them followed Maurin Ortish into the Council chambers. As the doors closed behind them, a pair of Home Guards took up watch. Kirisin stood where he was, consumed by frustration, thinking how unfair this was, how wrong. He was tempted just to barge right in and insist that he be allowed to speak. But doing so would remove any chance of persuading the Council members that what he had to say was credible. Simralin was right. He had to be patient.

But for how long?

He was still thinking about it when the outer doors of the building opened and Erisha pushed through.

"There you are!" she snapped, her irritation apparent. She stalked up to him, breathing hard, her face flushed. She had been running. "What are you doing here? I've been waiting for you to come find me!"

He was surprised by her anger, but he faced her down without flinching. "I thought maybe Simralin could get me into the chambers so I could speak before the High Council. She couldn't. Your father made sure I was kept out."

"I could have told you that if you had bothered to include me in your plans! I asked the same thing of him several hours ago when I overheard him talking with Maurin Ortish about shutting the doors to everyone except your sister and the two she brought into the city. He told me to stay out of things that didn't concern me. He dismissed me out of hand, like a child!" She grabbed his arm. "I thought you'd come to the house, not here! Come on!"

He allowed her to drag him toward the door. "Where are we going?"

She gave him a look. "Outside."

Her eyes flicked momentarily to the guards, and he understood that she didn't want to say anything that might be overheard.

When they were through the doors and some distance away from the building, she quit pulling on him and waited for him to fall into step beside her. The night air was cool and sweet and smelled of the jasmine that bloomed at the perimeter of the Council buildings.

"We're not going to sit around waiting on my father, no matter what he thinks!" She knotted her fists and looked at him. "What is going on, Kirisin? Why did Simralin bring a human into the city? Has she lost her mind? My father is furious!"

"Don't blame Simralin," he replied quickly. "She knew what she was doing. The tatterdemalion, Ailie, already knew where the city was and how to find the Elves, so what difference did it make? And the human, Angel Perez, is a Knight of the Word. You can't keep creatures of magic out. If Simralin hadn't brought them in like they asked, they would have come anyway. Then there really would have been trouble."

Erisha stalked on, not speaking for a moment. "I suppose. But what are they doing here? What does this have to do with us?"

Kirisin took a quick look around. "The Knight says that the Elves are in danger from demons. She says the Elves have to leave the Cintra and go to a safer place, that we have to use the Loden to do so. Everything the Ellcrys already told us, she's telling us again!"

He waited for her response, but the silence stretched on between them. "Why is my father resisting this advice?" she asked softly, almost to herself. She brushed absently at her dark hair, her face troubled. "I don't understand."

Kirisin shook his head. "I don't know. I still think he's hiding something. What do you think he will say to the members of the High Council when the Knight and the tatterdemalion tell them why they are here?"

"I don't know," Erisha answered. She took his arm roughly and pulled him ahead. "But we're going to find out."

NINE

ERISHA DRAGGED KIRISIN along at such a rapid pace that he found himself practically running to keep up with her. He had never seen her so determined, and he knew better than to question her until he had some idea of where they were going. They were coming up on the Belloruus family home, which sat back from the High Council buildings at a distance of perhaps a hundred yards. The windows of the home were dark and the grounds empty of everything but shadows. It appeared that this was Erisha's destination.

A member of the Home Guard materialized out of thin air, took note of who they were, nodded to Erisha in polite acknowledgment, and then vanished again.

"What are you doing?" Kirisin demanded. "You let that guard see me! He'll tell your father I was here!"

"I'll tell him myself," she snapped. "Stop worrying, Kirisin. I don't have to answer to my father for everything!"

Kirisin made no response. This was a different Erisha than from even as little as forty-eight hours ago, no longer tentative and afraid, no longer caught up in the ritual of being her father's obedient daughter. Instead she had developed a strength and determination that suggested there wasn't anything she wouldn't do to assert her independence. It was a complete turnaround, and he wasn't sure what to make of it.

She led him to the same side door she had brought him through the night before when they were searching the Elven histories for mention of the Elfstones. Without pausing, she yanked it open and pulled him after her.

"Did you find him?" a voice demanded angrily.

It came from somewhere back in the darkness, and Kirisin jumped and was ready to bolt until he recognized the voice as Culph's.

"He was trying to get into the Council chambers with help from his sister," Erisha answered. She continued pulling Kirisin forward. "Hurry up! We haven't much time."

They picked their way through the house without using lights, Kirisin following his cousin blindly. He could just make out Culph's bent shape as the old man led the way through the gloom, a spectral figure muttering to himself.

"Culph was there when Maurin Ortish came to tell my father of the arrival of the Knight and the tatterdemalion," Erisha whispered. "He overheard everything, including their reason for coming to Arborlon. So he took a chance and tried to persuade my father that it was time to tell the members of the High Council about the Ellcrys. He kept what he knew about you to himself, but made a strong argument about me. My father refused to listen. So Culph found me. He said we wouldn't be allowed into the Council chambers, but there was another way."

"Another way?" Kirisin peered at her through the darkness. "What way is that?"

"An underground tunnel connects the house to the chambers," Culph answered from out of the darkness. "It's been there for centuries. Mostly it was used as a way to allow the Kings and Queens to enter the chambers without being seen." He chuckled drily. "But it gives those of us who know about it a way in, too."

"The tunnel ends at a concealed door that opens into the chambers through a section of the wall," Erisha picked up. "But just before you go through, there is a small viewing area that allows anyone using the tunnel a way to peek into the chambers first to see who is there. It looks out from right behind and to one side of the dais on which the King sits and around which the High Council gathers. If we can get to it without being caught, we can overhear everything that's said."

They continued on through the darkness to the meeting rooms at the back of the house and entered a small chamber off the entry that ended at a windowless alcove. Culph, still leading, stepped into the shelter of blank walls so deeply recessed they were barely visible in a faint wash of torchlight that seeped through a pair of narrow windows from the outside. He fumbled about for a moment, and Kirisin heard a catch release. Then the rear section of the alcove wall swung open, and Culph stepped through into the darkness beyond. He beckoned them to follow, closing the hidden door behind them.

A moment later, the old man had a smokeless torch lit, and they were descending a set of narrow steps into an even deeper gloom. At the bottom of the stairs, they found the tunnel and moved into it, the torch providing sufficient light to guide the way. The passageway wound on through the darkness, a rough-hewn corridor shored up by wooden beams and finished with plank flooring raised off the earth. The walls and ceiling were mostly dirt and roots. The tunnel looked as if it had been there a long time, but someone had kept the roots cut back and the spiderwebs swept away. When Kirisin touched the earthen walls, he found them hard and dry and smooth. The air was close and stale, but breathable. Even so, it reminded him of the crypts at Ashenell, and he was anxious to get clear.

The tunnel ended at a second set of steps leading up. Culph turned and put a finger to his lips in warning. They climbed the stairs silently, and as they neared the top a sliver of light became visible in the distance. Culph extinguished the smokeless torch, and they ascended the last several steps in darkness and crept forward toward the light. The outlines of a door grew faintly visible; to one side, cut horizontally in the wall, was a narrow slit.

When they reached the slit, they could just see through to where the members of the High Council were seated in chairs at the foot of a dais. The King sat atop the dais, the back and right side of his tall frame just visible. Simralin stood at the foot of the dais, facing the King and the Council. Maurin Ortish had positioned himself off to one side, dark face impassive. Angel Perez and Ailie were waiting back near the chamber entry in the company of a pair of Home Guards.

The King was speaking.

"THERE IS NO PRECEDENT for what you have done, Simralin," Arissen Belloruus was saying. "You know that outsiders—and humans, in particular—are not allowed inside our home city. *Never* allowed inside. You know why this is so: our survival depends to a very great extent on being able to maintain the secrecy of our existence. If there are no exceptions, there is no risk."

He paused for effect, and then made an expansive gesture toward Angel and Ailie. "But we have never had a Knight of the Word or a tatterdemalion seek admission. Faerie creatures and others who serve the Word are rumored to share our concerns for the well-being of the land and her creatures. They do not come to us as enemies; they come as friends. Bringing them here, in this instance, must have seemed to you to be the right thing to do. Circumstances sometimes force us to make exceptions to the rules. I am inclined to think that this is the case here. Your decision is judged a reasonable one, Simralin, and your actions appropriate."

He paused, waiting for her response, his gaze steady.

"Thank you, High Lord," she acknowledged.

He nodded. "You are dismissed, Simralin. Wait outside."

Angel, who was watching closely, realized at once from the flicker of surprise that crossed the Tracker's smooth face that this was not what she was expecting. Having been invited in at the beginning of things, she was expecting to be allowed to remain until the end. But this Elven King, this Arissen Belloruus, was used to controlling things, to making sure that those around him were never entirely certain of where they stood. She had seen it in the faces of the Council members when she had entered the room—in their furtive glances and their unmistakable deference. This was a strong king—as he would be quick to remind those who came before him. Dismissing Simralin so abruptly was an obvious example.

The Tracker bowed without a word and went out through the Council chamber doors. She did not look back.

The King turned his attention to Angel and Ailie. "Come," he directed, gesturing for them to rise and approach.

Angel, with Ailie beside her, walked forward. She had bathed and changed into clean clothes, her own so badly soiled and torn that the Elves had simply thrown them away. She found she liked the Elven clothing, which was soft and loose fitting and gave her a freedom of movement that she found reassuring. Her wounds, cleaned and bound with bandages and treated with Elven medicines, did not hurt as much as before. She felt oddly new, standing there; she felt a kind of physical reemergence.

She took a deep breath as she faced the King and the members of the Council. She was still trying hard not to stare—at their Elven ears and brows and narrow-featured faces. She was trying hard to pretend that they were simply humans of a different sort. But she could not ignore what Ailie had told her of their history, a history that could be traced back to a time before humans even existed and in which magic and mythical creatures were real and alive.

Nor could she forget Ailie's warning to her earlier this evening about what she could expect would happen.

Remember that you will appear less strange to them than they do to you, the tatterdemalion had told her while they were still alone. *They have studied you in your world while you have been shut out of theirs. They dislike and mistrust humans. They believe that humans stole their world from them and then ruined it. Your status as a Knight of the Word will not make them forget entirely the nature of your origins. They will use your uncertainty about them against you. They will try to keep you on the defensive. Be aware of their intentions.*

She was, but she was also uncertain about how to deal with them. At least she could understand their language. Ailie had told her that she would be able to do so because of the magic bequeathed to her by the Word through her staff, and so far the tatterdemalion had been right.

"You may present yourselves to the members of the High Council," the King ordered.

She had given their names already to both Simralin and Maurin Ortish, so Arissen Belloruus could have presented them himself. But he was after something more. He wanted them to understand clearly that he expected them to do what they were told. He wanted to make certain that they understood he would not tolerate any form of resistance to his commands.

He was testing them as he tested everyone.

Fair enough, she decided. She would do whatever was needed.

"I am Angel Perez," she replied, straightening slightly, her dark eyes locking on the King's. "I am a Knight of the Word. My companion is a tatterdemalion. She is called Ailie."

The King leaned back comfortably in his chair, not inviting them to sit. "We have allowed you to come into our city despite the rules that forbid it," he declared. "You know this from hearing my comments to Simralin. We have allowed this because of who you are and because we are led to believe that your coming to Arborlon is of great importance. Now is the time for you to reassure us that this is so."

The King was a big, strong man with handsome features and a smooth, commanding voice. He used that voice and size both to intimidate and to reassure. Angel had seen how effective he could be when he had dressed down Simralin. He would attempt to do the same thing with her. But she was a child of the streets and a survivor of far worse than anything the King had encountered. She would be stronger than he was.

"We have been sent to you by the Word," she said, addressing her remarks not to the King, but to the Council. "That is our first and most important reassurance."

"The Word did not speak to us of this," the King declared quickly.

"The Word does not speak to us at all," added another man. He was stooped and hawk-faced, and he did not smile.

"Perhaps not directly and not in the way you would expect," Angel replied. "Nevertheless, the Word watches over you and cares for you. That is why we have been sent as messengers. The Elves are in great danger. The world outside the Cintra is changing. The demons and their followers are winning the war against the human race and seek to destroy it. Worse, they would destroy the world itself. It is necessary for you to protect yourselves if you are to survive. To do this, you must leave the Cintra and go to a safer place, one where the destruction elsewhere will not impact the future of your race."

"Leave the Cintra?" the Council member who had spoken before interjected in disbelief. "On the basis of what you are telling us and nothing more? That is ridiculous!"

"Enough, Basselin!" Arissen Belloruus cut off anything else the man might have wanted to say. He turned back to Angel. "You will understand, lady Knight of the Word, if we are hesitant to believe this. Humans are the ones who have destroyed the world, acting foolishly and recklessly at every opportunity. Demons have prodded such actions, but humans have carried them out. We have stayed safe by staying where we are. Now you tell us we are to leave? Are you going to tell us where it is we are expected to go?"

"We do not know that," Angel answered.

Arissen Belloruus looked at her as he might look at a difficult child. "Very well. You have delivered your message and fulfilled your purpose in coming to us. We will discuss the matter and make our decision. You are free to go."

Angel shook her head. "There is more. In order for you to leave the Cintra, you will need the use of an Elfstone called a Loden. We are sent to help you find that Elfstone."

There was stunned silence. No one seemed willing to say anything, even the King, whose expression suggested that he was deciding if he wanted this discussion to go further. "We have no Loden Elfstone," he said finally. Then, as if realizing he was simply reaffirming what Angel had already said, he added, "No Elfstones of any kind. They have all been lost for centuries. There is no way of knowing what happened to them."

"Perhaps there is," Ailie said suddenly, her small voice surprisingly strong in the large chamber. "Perhaps one among you already knows a way."

She might be guessing or she might know something that she had not told Angel. But the look on the King's face, at once dark and angry and startled, was a clear indication that one or the other was true. He knew more than he was giving away to anyone in this room, and now everyone realized it.

"Historically," said another of the Council members, an older man who spoke not to the King, but to Angel, "the Loden Elfstone was meant to protect the Ellcrys in time of danger. The legend, as recorded in my own family's journals, says the Loden possesses magic that will allow it to encapsulate the tree and keep it safe while it is being moved."

Now everyone was looking at the King. "Old tales of an older time," Arissen Belloruus declared dismissively. "We cannot rely on such tales, Ordanna Frae. You, of all people, should know that."

"What I know," said the other, turning slightly toward him, "is that the tales have more than one source. We should not dismiss out of hand the possibility that they reveal an important truth. Much of our lore comes to us in the form of old stories and legends written down in private letters. These are not necessarily the writer's invention alone."

"Nevertheless, it would be foolish and reckless to act on what these messengers tell us without further proof," interjected Basselin, leaning forward suddenly in his seat. "We have no way of testing the truth of their stories. They may believe what they are saying, but they may also be hiding something from us."

There was a muttering of agreement from a few of the other Council members, and the King pointed suddenly at Angel. "You say you are here to help us find the Loden Elfstone. How do you propose to do that? Do you know something of its location? Does the Word give you insights that we lack?"

Angel hesitated, and it was Ailie who answered. "The insights you require are to be found among your own people, High Lord. They are to be found among the Chosen."

Arissen Belloruus flushed a dark red, and for a moment Angel thought that Ailie had gone too far. Again, this was nothing the tatterdemalion had spoken about to her before, so she wasn't sure why her words were so disturbing to the King, but clearly they were.

"The young boy you sent away," Ailie continued. "Kirisin. He knows."

Now the Council members were all turning toward the King, their muttered questions and exclamations tumbling over one another as they sought to make sense of what they were hearing. It wasn't the tatterdemalion's words that caused this response, Angel realized. The words, while startling, would not of themselves provoke. It was instead something in the way they were spoken, something in Ailie's voice, that had broken through the wall of reticence that held the High Council in thrall to the King and set them free to question him.

"Be silent!" Arissen Belloruus roared suddenly, leaping to his feet. The members of the Council went still, and the King came forward a few steps on the dais toward Angel and Ailie, a menacing look on his strong features. "Kirisin Belloruus, the son of my cousin and his wife, the brother of Simralin, is a well-loved boy, a friend of my daughter, and a Chosen in service to the Ellcrys. He has indeed spoken to me of this, something I chose not to bring before the Council."

He paused for effect. "And for good reason. He *believes* he knows something, but he cannot offer any proof to support his belief. He came to me with a story similar to the one you tell, messengers of the Word. He told me that the Ellcrys had asked him to find the Loden Elfstone and to place the tree within it. An old magic, apparently. Magic long since lost to us. But no one else heard this admonition. More to the point, the Ellcrys does not speak to anyone except in the time of her choosing. Kirisin could not explain why she had done so now. He was certain he had heard correctly, but he had nothing to offer in the way of proof. I did not believe him, nor did any of the other Chosen."

His jaw tightened. "But I am King, and I know my duty. I told him that acting on his word alone, without other proof, was insufficient to persuade the High Council to his cause. I told him I would research the matter. Culph, who has served as our historian for years, was dispatched in an effort to find in the Elven histories the answers to the questions Kirisin posed. He found nothing. There was barely any mention of the Elfstones. All that is magic, all the talismans that were once so vital to our people, belong to the past. We know this. No one who has lived in the last two thousand years has seen an Elfstone. Or if they have, they have kept it to themselves because there is nothing of consequence written about any of it. What we have are private journals of the sort kept by our minister of public works." He nodded toward Ordanna Frae. "Some of those entries are an accurate recording and some are not. Some are simply wishful thinking. What helps us determine which is which is whether or not there is confirmation of these entries anywhere in our official histories."

Again he paused. "In this case, there is none."

"My Lord," Basselin interrupted quickly. "May I speak?"

The King nodded. "You may, First Minister."

"I think we have heard quite enough," said the hawk-faced man. "Enough of speculation and wild imaginings. This business of a danger to the Ellcrys and the Elven nation appears to be based entirely on two sources—a boy barely old enough to know his place in our community and this human and her companion. The boy . . . well, he is just a boy. The young woman and her child companion are unknown to us. There is no hard evidence to confirm what any of them are telling us. We are being asked to change our entire way of life—to move from the Cintra, to uproot the Ellcrys, and to do who knows what else. Mostly on the word of this young woman. On the word of a human. A *human*, my lord. When humans have been the cause of so much misery and destruction, I find it difficult to suddenly decide that perhaps this time they have something valuable to offer. I am skeptical of everything I have heard. I am opposed to acting on it."

He sat back again, his features flushed and angry. "We should all be opposed," he added, his eyes fixed on Angel.

The King nodded. "I am inclined to agree with my first minister," he said quietly.

"So you will do nothing?" Angel pressed.

The King glared at her, and then turned around, walked back to his chair, and sat down. He gestured at her in exasperation. "My first minister makes a cogent point. Am I to accept without evidence of any sort that you speak the truth? That you are not yourselves deceived in some way? That the danger you describe actually exists? I did not accept it when Kirisin told me. Now that you have come to Arborlon, I grant that there is fresh reason to wonder if he might be right. But what are we to do about it? We still have no means of finding the Loden Elfstone."

"Perhaps a further search of your histories is needed," Angel offered. "Perhaps speaking with Kirisin again will help. What cannot be disputed is that the danger confronting the Elven people will not be avoided by ignoring that it exists. Something must be done, High Lord."

"It is not necessary, lady Knight of the Word, that you tell me my duty as King of the Elven people. I know it far better than you do. I will do what is needed, when it is needed."

He stared at her to make certain she understood, then added, "I will arrange for a further, more extensive search of the Elven histories and any other journals or papers that are in my possession. If any members of my Council are in a position to help, perhaps through a search of their own records, they are welcome to do so. We will reconvene in two days to examine what we have uncovered."

"High Lord," Angel said quickly. "I would like to speak with Kirisin myself. If we compare what we know, perhaps between us we will unearth something useful."

The King hesitated, his eyes reflecting his disapproval, and then he shrugged as if it didn't matter. "Very well. I will arrange it."

Some of the arrogance that had been so apparent earlier was gone, and the King seemed both troubled and uncertain. Angel understood something about the need to establish ground rules if you were a leader. She understood what it did to you, how it fostered both arrogance and abrasiveness if you were not careful. She did not condemn him for his attitude; she merely wanted to understand what was driving it, and she believed it was something more than his position as King of the Elves.

"I am grateful, High Lord," she told him, and meant it.

He nodded. "I am granting you a latitude I would normally deny. But I want this matter resolved. If Kirisin can help, then I want you to find out how. Do whatever you feel you must."

He rose and gestured to the members of the High Council. "Enough discussion for tonight. This session is adjourned."

* * *

AS ANGEL AND AILIE followed Maurin Ortish out of the chambers and into the hallway beyond, Angel heard the King ask the members of the Council to stay for a few moments more to review what they had just heard. Angel understood immediately what that meant. The King would wait until they were safely out of earshot, and then declare privately what he felt the Council really needed to do. It rankled her that he would do this when there was so much at stake. But Ailie had warned her that the Elves mistrusted all humans, and no matter her exalted title as a Knight of the Word, she was first and foremost a human. If the Elves believed that she was a detriment to their safety, no matter how much she might argue otherwise, they would probably try to find a way to remove her from the picture.

What she wondered was whether they were capable of doing her harm when she had done nothing to provoke it.

"Did you hear? They intend to work behind our backs," she whispered to Ailie as they stepped outside the Council buildings and into the cool night air. Ortish had gone on ahead, beckoning to Simralin, who stood waiting in the shadows to take them back to their quarters.

"It is much worse than you think," the tatterdemalion whispered back. Her eyes were depthless black pools as she bent closer to Angel, and her voice dropped farther still. "The Elves are already compromised."

Angel stopped where she was. "What do you mean?"

"There was a demon in the Council chambers."

"You saw it? I sensed nothing!"

Ailie shook her head. "I did not see it, but I smelled its stench. It wears an Elven disguise, so I cannot tell which of them it is. Apparently it is talented and clever enough to hide its presence from a Knight of the Word, but it cannot hide from a Faerie creature."

The tatterdemalion shivered suddenly, as if the admission chilled her to the bone. "It was there. It was one of them."

TEN

IRISIN SLIPPED BACK through the underground tunnel steps behind Erisha and Culph, each of them lost in thought. They kept silent for two reasons—to avoid risking discovery, and to give space to ponder what they had just heard. They would talk of it later, when they could do so safely. Kirisin kept thinking that what hadn't been said was almost as important as what had. Erisha's father had been very careful not to disclose that he had both discouraged and delayed Kirisin's efforts to act on what the Ellcrys had asked. He had also been very careful not to reveal anything about his daughter's involvement. None of it felt right to him now, reflecting back. Everything he had heard made him uneasy.

When they reached the Belloruus home, he said good night to the other two, slipped back out the door, and headed home. It was too dangerous for him to remain longer when it was likely the King would be returning. They couldn't afford to do anything that would risk giving away what they were up to. He would see Erisha at sunrise when they rose to fulfill their daily duties as Chosen, and they would talk then.

Even so, Kirisin thought about nothing else as he walked back through the trees toward his house. The coming of the Knight of the Word and the tatterdemalion was all the proof he needed to confirm that the Ellcrys was not mistaken in believing that she and the Elves were in danger. If there was one thing of which Kirisin was now convinced, it was that he needed to act swiftly on her plea for help. Especially pressing was the need to find the missing Elfstones. They had seemed so close to doing so only hours earlier—he and Erisha and old Culph, searching Ashenell—that he could not bring himself to believe it had been wasted effort. A fresh start was needed, a new approach perhaps, but giving up at this point was out of the question.

He pondered again the King's reticence, trying to divine its source. There was something happening with Arissen Belloruus that none of them understood, something that was making him act in a way that was foreign to his character. That he was suspicious of Angel Perez was not surprising; most Elves were suspicious of humans. But his reaction in this instance seemed wildly against reason. That the tatterdemalion had confronted him with the truth about what he knew—about Kirisin, in particular—was the only reason he had revealed anything. All this time, the King had kept everything Kirisin had told him to himself; he had not discussed it with a single member of the High Council. Nor, it appeared, had he acted on it in any way.

The wind gusted sharply across his heated face, causing him to flinch at the contact. There was a chill in the air that didn't belong to the season, one that mirrored the chill in his heart. Despite himself, he glanced around uneasily. This was his home, the only home he had ever known. He had spent his entire life here. He knew all of its roads and trails, most of its families, and many of its secrets. There was nowhere he could go that he would not feel he was in familiar territory.

Yet tonight Arborlon seemed a strange and unwelcoming place; he, an intruder who did not belong and might even be at risk.

He trudged on, hunching his shoulders, glancing left and right into the shadows, searching for things that he knew were not there, but that his instincts warned him might appear anyway.

When he reached his home, lights shone from within and Simralin was back on the porch steps, waiting. She was not alone. Angel Perez and the tatterdemalion, Ailie, were waiting with her.

He brushed his windblown hair from his eyes, gathered himself for what he already knew lay ahead, and marched up to his sister. "Kind of late for visitors, Sim," he said.

"Later than you think," she answered, stony-faced. "But they have something to say that you need to hear. Come up and sit down."

He did as she asked, settling himself in one of the old high-backed wicker chairs facing across the porch to where the Knight and the tatterdemalion sat. He remembered how the latter had looked at him with such intensity several hours earlier, the way she had seemed to recognize him even though they had never met. Now, as Angel repeated everything that had taken place in the Council chambers, he was reminded of it. Ailie had known that the Ellcrys had spoken with him, that he had been asked to provide her help. Otherwise, she could not have used his name before the King as she had.

While Angel spoke, mostly repeating what he already knew from eavesdropping behind the Council chamber walls, he studied her. He had heard of Knights of the Word from Simralin, knew what they did and how important it was. He had formed images of them in his mind, their physical characteristics, the strength of presence they would exude. Yet Angel was not that much older than he was, baby-faced and not very big at all. She was more girl than woman, more child than grown. She held the black staff of her order, carved end-to-end with runes, in a loose, casual fashion, yet he could not mistake the possessiveness of her grip. He found her odd, a human who seemed less so than she ought to, a Knight of the Word who seemed too young to be anything of the sort.

When Angel was finished, she asked Kirisin if he would tell them in turn what he knew. He did so, even though he had doubts about revealing that he had been hiding on the other side of the walls with Erisha and old Culph when they were brought before the King and the High Council. It wasn't that he didn't want the Knight of the Word to know; he was concerned that revealing their presence to anyone might in some way put his two friends in danger. It was an irrational fear, but he couldn't pretend that it wasn't there.

Nevertheless, he told the others everything, including what had transpired when the Ellcrys had spoken to him in the gardens. He told them how he had gone to the King in opposition to the advice of the other Chosen, how the King had lied to him, how he had subsequently confronted Erisha about what she was hiding, and how the two of them had made a pact to join forces. He told them how old Culph had discovered him with Erisha in the archives and decided to help, as well. He gave a brief description of how the three of them had searched the grave sites at Ashenell to find the marker for Pancea Rolt Cruer, where they believed from the entries in her scribe's journal that the blue Elfstones might be hidden.

"We found nothing," he concluded, "even after searching for the better part of an entire afternoon. But we intend to go back for another look the day after tomorrow. Maybe we will have better luck."

"So you cannot leave Arborlon and the Cintra without the Ellcrys?" Angel asked.

"If we leave, we are abandoning her to her fate. She has no defenses against humans or demons and their weapons. She would be destroyed in the conflagration you have come to warn us about."

"In which case, the demons trapped within the Forbidding, the ones from the old world of Faerie, would be set free?"

"If the Forbidding fails, that would happen."

"They would join with those demons already at work destroying what remains of our world?"

He nodded. "We can't leave her. We have to find the Elfstones that can save her."

Angel shook her head. "I don't understand why there is any debate about this. I don't see why your King isn't already out hunting for the Elfstones, doing everything he can to find them. It doesn't matter whether he knows where they can be found; he should be doing something. What possible reason could he have for not wanting to act on what you have told him, let alone what we are asking?"

Kirisin looked down at his feet and scuffed at the porch floorboards. "Erisha and I have asked ourselves that question repeatedly. We still don't have an answer. Not even Culph understands."

"The King is not himself these days," Simralin said quietly. "You said so yourself, Little K. Everyone sees that he has changed, and no one can explain the reason for it."

"Well, we have to find a way to persuade him to do the right thing,"

Kirisin insisted. "It doesn't matter if he's himself or not, he's the King. Personal problems can't be allowed to get in the way of a King's duties. His foremost obligation is to protect his people and his city. He can't do that if he lets anything happen to the Ellcrys."

They were all silent for a moment, pondering the King's behavior. Then Angel said, "There is another problem you need to know about."

"Angel," Ailie said in warning.

Angel nodded. "I know. We take a risk in telling anyone. But we need allies to find out who it is, Ailie."

The tatterdemalion sat back against the side of the house, her presence wraithlike and fluid in the moonlight. She seemed more a child than either Kirisin or Angel, small and delicate and gauzy. "Tell them, then," she said.

"There was a demon in the Council chambers tonight," Angel said. She glanced from brother to sister and back again. "Ailie sensed its presence, even though I could not. The Elves have been compromised."

Simralin leaned forward. "Are you sure, Ailie?"

The tatterdemalion nodded. "I am. Its stench was so strong that it permeated not only the Council chambers, but also the anteroom outside where we waited on the King."

"Who is it?" Kirisin asked.

Ailie shook her head. "I cannot be sure. I would know if I were alone with it, but in a room full of people, I cannot separate it out. The demon wears a disguise. It is a changeling in the true sense, able to take on any appearance. Most demons possess changeling aspects, but only a few can actually transform completely. This is one."

Again, they were silent for a moment. "Could it be the King?" Kirisin asked finally. "I know none of us wants to think it, but is it possible?"

Angel nodded. "It is. And that would be very bad. We need the King to help us if we are to succeed in our efforts to persuade the Elves to leave the Cintra."

"But couldn't it just as easily be Basselin?" Simralin offered. "You said he went out of his way to insist that the other ministers shouldn't listen to anything any of you had to say. He called Kirisin a boy, and he said humans weren't to be trusted. He was insistent about it. And as first minister, he has the King's ear. A demon would be clever enough to persuade the King to do nothing."

Kirisin shook his head stubbornly. "But it's the King who has been acting strangely, who hasn't seemed himself. If he were a demon, that would explain it. He's been the strongest voice against doing anything. He tried to keep Erisha from talking, and then he tried to stop me, as well. He has done everything he can to keep us from getting involved in helping the Ellcrys. A demon would do that."

"Perhaps." Ailie's frail form rippled against the wall, a liquid white ghost. "But above all, a demon would do whatever was necessary to hide its identity and shift suspicion to someone else. The King seems too obvious a choice."

"Only to us," said Kirisin. "Only because we know what we are looking for. No one else knows about a demon presence." He shook his head. "Are you sure about the demon? Is it possible that you were mistaken? A demon living among us just doesn't seem possible. How long would it have been here? Why would it have come in the first place?"

Angel rocked back in her chair. "A demon might not have come here originally for the purpose of destroying the Ellcrys. It might have come just to spy on the Elves. It could have killed whomever it changed itself into and taken that person's place, then waited to see what damage it could do. It could have been living among you for years, maybe even decades. Demons are crafty and insidious. This one might be trying to destroy the Ellcrys, but it might have another, more complex plan, too."

Another plan, Kirisin repeated silently. *What other plan? What could a demon do that would be worse than destroying the Ellcrys and setting free the creatures imprisoned within the Forbidding?* He couldn't come up with anything, the prospect too frightening to bring into clear focus.

"What do we do?" he asked the others.

Simralin shifted forward from where she was sitting, her smooth features coming into the light. "Put Ailie alone with Arissen Belloruus first and then with Basselin to see if either is the demon."

"That would be very dangerous," Angel objected. "Even if I was there, she would be at risk. Demons are very powerful."

"But Simralin is right," Ailie said suddenly. "We have to know."

"What I think we have to do is find those Elfstones," Kirisin declared. "I kept thinking we would find them today. I still don't know why we didn't. I think we are missing something, but I don't know what it is."

No one said anything for a moment, then Simralin asked, "Who is it you are looking for again?"

"Pancea Rolt Cruer. She was Queen after her husband died, centuries ago. There are Cruers in Ashenell, but there is no marker for her." Kirisin hesitated. "What are you thinking, Sim?"

His sister shrugged. "Well, you said she was a Cruer. But that was her married name. Maybe she wasn't buried under her married name. What was her family name before she married?"

Kirisin blinked. "I don't know. It never occurred to me. We could have been looking for her under the wrong name this whole time." He straightened, excited. "I'll tell Erisha tomorrow. She can ask Culph, and he can look for her birth name in the histories. Once we have that, we can search Ashenell again."

"I don't think you should go back there alone," Angel said quickly. "Ailie isn't mistaken about the demon. It's there, among the Elves, and now it knows about you. If it finds out what you are doing, it won't be safe for you or anyone who tries to help you. If you go back, I should go with you."

She stood abruptly, walked over to where he sat, and knelt beside him. "Kirisin. Listen carefully to me. You are in great danger. The demons are ruthless, and they will kill a boy like you without thinking twice. *Madre de Dios.* Tell me. Have the Elves really lost all their magic? Do you have none of it left? Not even you, who are a Chosen of the Ellcrys? You have no way to protect yourself? No magic to call upon?"

"It was all lost centuries ago," Kirisin answered. "The Elves have the ability to hide and not be found. We have healing skills. We have the means to care for the land and the things that live and grow on her, but not much else." He shook his head. "I wish we did."

Simralin rose and touched Angel on the shoulder. "We can't do anything more tonight. I have to take you back before someone finds that you are missing. We don't want to have them thinking you are doing anything but awaiting the King's pleasure."

They clustered together on the porch for a moment in the pale moonlight, and the Elves and the Knight clasped hands.

"I'm glad you've come," Kirisin said impulsively.

Angel's face was dark with misgiving. "Just be careful, Kirisin. Step lightly."

* * *

THE WOLFISH BEAST that had been Delloreen and was now something almost wholly different slouched along the fringes of the Elven city, following the scent of the prey it sought. It no longer cared whom it hunted or even why. It barely remembered its purpose in doing so. All that mattered to it now was satisfying its need. All that mattered was finding and destroying the thing it hunted.

It had tracked her all the way here, a long and arduous hunt during which it had lost the scent any number of times. But it had persevered, searching and searching some more until the scent was recovered and the tracking begun anew. It had eaten and drunk what it could find along the way so as not to lose its strength, but had not slept. Sleep was a luxury for which it had no use. Nothing could be allowed to slow it down.

Now it was arrived at this city, this habitat of creatures it instinctively knew to be prey. It could kill them all at its leisure; they would provide it with days and weeks and even months of enjoyment. But first it must find the one it had hunted for so long, the one it must kill before it could rest easy. There was no reasoning involved in its assessment; it was acting on instinct and hunger. It was acting on a mix of feral and demon needs.

It was closing on its prey, the scent growing fresher, and then suddenly it encountered a new and different scent, one that was both unexpected and immediately recognizable. The scent was of another demon, another of its own kind. That it should surface here, in this place so deep in the wilderness and far removed from the human population, surprised it. Thrilled by its discovery and anxious to learn why another demon would be here, it began to track this new scent. It could not explain its lure, but neither could it resist. Forgotten momentarily was its need to hunt the prey it had tracked with such single-minded diligence. All that mattered now was this new obsession.

It padded through the trees, another of night's shadows, staying off the paths and trails, keeping clear of the creatures that lived there. It must not draw attention to itself, it knew. Secrecy was necessary. Even fighting through the fog of its diminished reasoning, it knew that much. Hunting was mostly reactive; your instincts told you what was needed.

It was approaching a house, one that was set well back into the woods, half buried in the forest earth, when it became aware of the other demon. The newcomer approached unhurriedly, not bothering to hide its presence, its footfalls confident and determined. Delloreen stopped and waited, dark muzzle lifted to catch the other's scent.

"My, my, aren't you a beautiful thing," a voice soothed, a disembodied presence in the darkness.

The demon stepped into the light and gazed with passionate interest into Delloreen's yellow eyes, a smile lighting its face. Its hands clasped in unmistakable joy. "I have seen so few others in my time here," it whispered. "But you—you are beyond my most ardent expectations! Look at you, pretty thing! Such grace and power!" The voice trailed off. "What's this? You have shape-changed recently, haven't you? There are still traces of your human form, bits and pieces showing through the new skin you wear so well. But only traces, and not much of those. Your human self is almost gone, dispatched for the weakness and the burden it is. Yes. Better to be what you are than what I am, trapped in something so loathsome."

Delloreen would have purred had she been able, but settled for a contented growl. This other demon had awakened something in her, a need she had not even known was there, a longing. It was why she had sought it out, she realized. This demon was a missing part of her; finding it made her feel unexplainably complete.

"Sweet thing," it whispered to her and held out its hand.

She surprised herself by nuzzling it. She surprised herself further by finding pleasure in its touch.

"Where have you come from?" The hand withdrew, not presuming to linger, leaving Delloreen unexpectedly bereft. "You track the Knight

of the Word and the tatterdemalion, don't you? What did they do that
would cause you to hunt them so assiduously? You have come a long
way. I can tell. You have chased them. Have you done battle with the
Knight?"

Delloreen whined, a low, rough sound.

"Oh, more than once, it seems. Before you were what you are now,
and not so magnificent. Your change is too recent for it to be more than
a few days old. But now you are so much more powerful than you
were, and when you find the Knight of the Word this time . . ."

The voice trailed off, the intended finish unmistakable. Delloreen
could picture it in her mind, could see the rending of her prey's flesh,
could feel it tearing in her jaws. She could hear the sound of breaking
bones and horrified screams.

"But for now," said the other, breaking into her thoughts, "you must
come with me. If you are seen, they will hunt you down and destroy
you. They could not do so separately, but in force they are too many. I
should know. I have been hiding for years—a recognizable presence
among them, yet so much more than they know—and I have learned to
be careful."

The demon put its hand on the top of her head, a soft and gentle
touch that lingered and was gone too quickly. "We will hide and wait
for the right time. It will not be long, pretty one. The Knight of the
Word and her Faerie companion present a danger that we must eliminate. My plans for the Elves and their precious tree and all the rest that
they think so important are falling into place as I intended they should.
Those who would expose us will be our unwitting accomplices. We
will see the end of them all before another cycle of the moon."

Delloreen growled softly, indicating her pleasure and her wishes.
"Yes, you may kill the Knight. You may kill them all when I am done
with them. The killing belongs to you; it is your province and your
right. Their lives are yours to take. But not now. Not yet. We must let
them fulfill their uses first."

The night breezes blew across Delloreen's scaly hide, and she felt
herself ripple in response. She could be patient for this one. She was a
hunter, and all hunters understood patience. If this one asked for hers,
she would give it.

She could not understand the lure this demon held for her, could not grasp why it made her feel so anxious to do what was asked. There was power here that she could not fathom. It transcended that wielded by the old man she had left behind, the one whose name she no longer remembered and whose face had become an unrecognizable blur. Physical power was hers to employ, but this other power held a strange allure. She longed to be in its presence, to bask in its glow.

"Come now," the other demon whispered. "We will sleep. You have come far, and you are tired. Rest will make you even stronger, even more formidable. I have a place where you will be safe, where we can be together." It touched her again, more boldly this time. "I have much to share with you, pretty thing. I have waited for you a long time."

Delloreen could not understand what it meant, but she was sufficiently seduced that she didn't care. This was one of her own, a demon spawn, a creature of the Void.

She went willingly.

ELEVEN

"I DON'T CARE HOW RISKY you thought it was, you should have come back and gotten me!" Erisha snapped angrily, her face so close to his own that he could feel the heat of her breath on his face. "How many times do I have to say it?"

They were kneeling together in the gardens, working on a border of caerwort, a ground cover of pale green leaves and bright pink flowers that fought back against invasive weeds and was highly resistant to insect pests. Large stretches of it formed a protective perimeter around the Ellcrys, but needed cleaning out and replacing on a regular basis.

Kirisin nodded in resignation. They had been going over this same ground all morning. "I've said I was sorry. I meant it. I just thought it would be better to wait until today. There wasn't anything more to be done last night."

"You were thinking about yourself!"

He gave her a long, searching look. "You know better."

She was quiet for a moment, then sighed heavily. "You're right. I do. I'm snapping at you for no good reason. It was smarter to wait. I just hate being left out of things."

He understood that. He hated being left out as much as she did, and it happened more than he liked to think, mostly because he didn't encourage inclusion by his standoffish attitude. He wished he was better at being a part of things, but it didn't come naturally to him. He had always gone his own way, and by doing so he deliberately set himself apart from other Elves.

"When do you think we will hear something from Culph?" he asked, changing the subject.

She shrugged. "He wasn't sure when he would get a chance to look at the genealogy tables. He has to do it when my father isn't around. My father has him looking for something more on the Elfstones, and he can't afford to be caught doing anything else." She paused, looking at him hopefully. "Maybe my father has changed his mind about things, Kirisin. I mean, if he has Culph searching for information about the Elfstones, maybe he has decided to help us."

Kirisin wasn't convinced, but he nodded anyway. "Maybe."

"Anyway, there isn't anything we can do now but wait until Culph finds what we're looking for."

She had gone to find the old man early this morning, soon after meeting with Kirisin at sunrise and learning the details of what had transpired after she had gone to bed. Leaving with the other Chosen to work in the gardens following the morning greeting, she had disappeared, returning a short time later to whisper that she had spoken with Culph and he would see what he could find out about Pancea Rolt Cruer's maiden name.

Kirisin went back to digging in the caerwort, unearthing the dead vines and scraping off insect bodies and blight from the good ones. He worked smoothly and easily, the effort neither tedious nor difficult for him. He thought momentarily about how gifted he had always been with plants of all sorts, of how natural he found caring and nurturing them. It was an Elven trait, but in his case something more. He seemed to know exactly what was needed and how to do it. It was almost as if he could understand what the plant was feeling, could come so close to communicating without using language.

Was that a remnant of the old magic? Had he inherited just a little of what had been lost to the Elves over the centuries? He liked the idea that he carried inside something of the past that had once been so important and was now little more than myth. He had wondered before if his skills were a residual effect of Faerie. After Angel had pressed him so hard last night about not having even a little of it as one of the Chosen, he was wondering anew if perhaps he might.

The sun was bright this day, the air warm and filled with the smells of flowers and conifers, and all of it felt like it was trying to reassure him of the permanence of his life and home. But he knew it was misleading and unreliable, a trick of the senses that could be swept away in a moment if the course of things was not altered soon.

"What is the tatterdemalion like?" Erisha asked quietly, not looking at him as she worked diligently and seemingly single-mindedly on the caerwort.

Kirisin thought about it. "Ephemeral," he said finally. "It seems that a strong wind could blow her away. You can see right through her much of the time, like she isn't even there. She talks and acts like you and me, but I don't feel there's much of anything about her that is anything like us." He paused. "There is something very sad about her."

"She probably misses her home." Erisha glanced over at him. "What about the Knight? She seems very young."

"But tough," he said at once. "Much stronger than she looks. I wouldn't want to have to fight her. She looks like she's just a girl, but she's a lot more, too. That staff she carries is infused with the magic of the Word. Those runes. I've never seen anything like them."

Erisha nodded. "Culph says the staffs are the symbol of the Knights' order. No one knows where they come from, but all the Knights carry them until the day they die. I asked him how they worked, but he doesn't know. He says a Knight of the Word is very powerful, and almost nothing can stand against it."

"Maybe a demon can." Kirisin looked at her. "Maybe some of the monsters they create."

Erisha nodded solemnly. "Maybe. I hope we don't have to find out."

They resumed work, and little more was said. It was midday and they were eating when Culph appeared, beckoning them away from the others. Kirisin was aware that Biat was watching him closely as he rose and left. Biat watched him all the time now, suspecting from the suddenness of his apparent reconciliation with Erisha that something had happened that the two were keeping to themselves. Kirisin thought more than once to speak with his friend, but couldn't think what he would say and so kept silent.

"I found what you're looking for," the old man told them when they were safely away from the others, hidden back in the screen of the forest trees. He looked tired and out of sorts, his hair and beard matted and his face a sheen of sweat. "Her maiden name was Gotrin. It's an old family, goes back several thousand years in the genealogy tables, but they all died out long ago. At one time, they were more powerful than the Cruers; more of them were Kings and Queens in the time the families overlapped. Pancea left one child, but the tables make no mention of her after her mother's death. That was the only immediate family member to survive her. There's nothing to say what Pancea's relationship was with her husband's family, but she might have considered them beneath her and chosen to be buried with her own people."

He was panting hard as he finished, rubbing at his beard and licking his lips. "Had to run. The King will be back any moment." He screwed up his face. "What are you going to do?"

"Search again," Erisha announced immediately. "Can you help?"

The old man shook his head. "I can't do anything right now except what your father tells me to do. Don't know when I can. Not for a day or two, at best." He paused. "You'll have to do this without me."

Kirisin compressed his lips and breathed in sharply. "All right. We can get my sister to help."

"The Knight of the Word and the tatterdemalion said they would help, too," Erisha added quickly.

Culph looked uneasy. "That's a lot of people. Easier for so many to be seen. If that happens, the Knight and the Faerie creature won't be mistaken for anything but what they are. That will put an end to all your efforts."

"We'll do it at night," she said. "One of us will keep watch while the others work."

The old man shook his head. "If you do it at night, you will need a light to read the engravings on the markers. You might as well set the forest on fire and beat a drum!"

"We won't need a light," Kirisin declared, jumping in. "The moon is nearly full. Unless the sky clouds, we should have light enough. All we need to do is to find the Gotrin section of the burial ground, and then it's just a matter of sorting through the Gotrin markers."

"You make it sound easy, but it won't be. You know that."

Erisha's face tightened. "I don't see that we have much choice if we want to find the Elfstones."

He made a dismissive sound. "Some of the Gotrins were magic wielders, powerful warlocks and witches. This was a long time ago, but it's a fact. The Elven runic symbols next to their names in the tables designate the ones who had the power." He locked eyes with her. "She was one. Pancea was one."

Erisha hesitated, and then shrugged. "As you said, that was a long time ago. She's dead now, and her magic with her."

The sharp old eyes tightened. "Magic, little missy, doesn't age. It doesn't fade. It hides and waits."

There was a long pause as Kirisin and Erisha stared at him. "Are you saying there might be something dangerous in the tombs?" Kirisin asked finally.

"Maybe. It bears thinking on. You need to keep watch, young Belloruus."

Their eyes locked, and for a moment Kirisin had the distinct feeling that Culph was telling him something that had nothing to do with what they were talking about.

Then the old man's eyes shifted away. "I have to leave. Remember what I said. Both of you. Be careful."

"You'd better be careful yourself," Erisha snapped back at him, taking hold of his arm to keep him from going. "Ailie says that there was a demon in the Council chambers last night. One of the Elves!"

Culph stared at her. Then he shook his head quickly. "That isn't possible. A demon? She must be mistaken."

"She says she isn't. She says if she could separate everyone out, she would know which one it is." She fixed her fierce gaze on him, then released his arm and stepped back. "It could be anyone. It could be my father."

It cost her something to say that. Kirisin saw it in her face. Culph looked as if he might respond, his seamed forehead wrinkling. But instead he simply nodded and turned away. "Maybe, maybe not. The world is full of demons of all sorts. Better to worry about the ones you can see and let the others be." He kept walking. "Let me know what you find."

He disappeared back into the trees, leaving Kirisin and Erisha to ponder if what they had decided to do might turn out to be a mistake they would later regret.

MIDNIGHT CREPT out of the darkness like a wraith at haunt, a silent and stealthy creature, and the little company of conspirators followed in its wake. Simralin led the way, using her Tracker's instincts to guide them, her strong figure reassuring to Kirisin as he stayed close. Erisha followed him, and Angel and Ailie brought up the rear. Moonlight, unfiltered by clouds or ground mist, brightened their way, and they were able to pass through Cintra's forest and down Arborlon's trails without need for artificial light, just as Kirisin had hoped.

They had met earlier at his house, the safest choice with his parents still absent. Angel and Ailie had come on their own, able to slip away easily from their quarters and their unseen guards without being detected. Erisha had encountered a few problems from the Home Guards on duty in and around the Belloruus royal grounds, but Culph had shown her another of the secret tunnels, one that exited through a trapdoor just outside an old storage shed at the back of the property. They had waited until just before midnight, when most of the city's population was asleep, determined to reduce the chances of being spotted before they reached Ashenell.

"No talking until we get to where we are going," Simralin had warned the others. And then she had added for his benefit alone, "I hope you know what you're doing, Little K."

He didn't, of course. Not entirely. They would gain entry into Ashenell, locate the Gotrin family burial site, search through the markers for Pancea Rolt Gotrin, and then decide if they should dig up her remains immediately or wait for daylight. How they would determine this, he didn't know. All he knew was that one way or the other, they would find out whether she had taken the Elfstones with her to her grave as the scribe's journal had recorded.

If they couldn't find her marker, he didn't know what they would do.

The night air was cool on his face. A breeze blew down out of the higher elevations of the mountains, gusting at times, chill with what remained of permafrost and scattered snow. There wasn't much of either left now, most of it melted in the change of climate and the destruction of the environment. Once, there had been polar ice caps of enormous size at the top and bottom of the world. But these had been diminished and were shrinking still. The seas had risen, and the lowland countries and coastal areas had flooded years ago. The water had receded with the changes in climate, erosion carving new inlets and water tributaries that had re-formed much of the coastline. But thousands of species had been lost to starvation and an inability to adjust to the radical changes. His sister had said it best, returned from one of her expeditions.

The world is changed, Little K, and I am not sure it will ever change back again.

He hadn't let this bother him before, secure in the haven of the Cintra, safely hidden away from humans and their follies in his own little part of the world. But thinking now of where the Elfstones could take him, once he found them, he wondered at what he might find. If he accepted that both the Ellcrys and Angel Perez spoke the truth and that Simralin's assessment was accurate, then what must the world be like if it was on the verge of being destroyed?

"Stop dawdling!" Erisha hissed in his ear.

He realized that he was lagging behind. Wordlessly, he hurried to close the gap, flushing with the rebuke.

They reached Ashenell without encountering anyone, the moon gone lower in the sky, but not so low that they couldn't see clearly. The burial ground was huge, an area of vast, sprawling forested heights that dipped and rose in a series of gently rolling hills. It was neither gated nor fenced, but the screen of trees and the lift of the terrain provided a natural barrier to those who might wander in by accident. Brush had been left in place, small trees allowed to fill out, and hillocks and humps remained undisturbed. Slender vine-covered alders trained to grow in leafy arches designated entrances from the west and east. Paths leading up to the grounds ended there.

They stood at the west entrance, where the shadows were deepest.

"One of us needs to stay here to keep watch," Simralin said quietly, gathering them close. "Perhaps it should be me. Likely I will know the guards who might find us and can talk our way out of trouble."

Ailie reached out and touched her arm with feathery fingers. "I would be a better choice. I can hide and not be seen by any Elf. If anything threatens, I can give warning more quickly and quietly."

The other four glanced at one another, and then Angel said, "Ailie is right She is the best choice."

They took a last look around, making sure they were still alone, and then, leaving Ailie in the shadowy cover of the trees, moved forward into the dark cathedral of Ashenell. Kirisin glanced back once at Ailie, her child's face a pale shimmer of brightness in the moonlight, then turned away for good.

Erisha took the lead now, winding through the clusters of stone markers, moving deeper into the grounds toward its older plots. Moonlight spilled through the limbs of the trees in narrow bands, piercing the shadows, spearing the dark earth. In places, the light disappeared completely, but for the most part they were able to make their way without difficulty. Night birds gave solitary calls in the near silence, and the shadows of owls passing overhead swept past them like wraiths. Kirisin fought back against the anticipation that was building inside in gathering waves. He wasn't afraid—at least not yet. But his fear lurked just out of sight, a presence that could surface in an instant's time. It kept him on edge, watchful both for himself and the others. They must be very careful, he told himself. There must be no mistakes.

They passed out of the smaller markers into a forest of sepulchers, crypts, and mausoleums, aboveground tombs that hunkered down in the darkness amid the towering old-growth trees. There were bold carvings of runic symbols and strange creatures on stone doors and lintels. These tombs were very old, so old that some of their dates designated times before the advent of the human race. Many were written in ancient Elfish, a few in languages that were unrecognizable. They had the look of stone giants, monsters that slept, waiting to be awakened.

Kirisin glanced at Simralin, but she seemed unbothered by the tombs, her face calm and her movements relaxed as she strode ahead of him. She had always been like that—so under control, so confident in herself—and he had always envied her for it.

Erisha had reached a section of Ashenell that was dominated by a huge stone mausoleum, the crypts and sepulchers surrounding it left diminished in its shadow. The names on all of the mausoleum's lesser children were carved in the same heavy block letters: GOTRIN.

They spread out to cover as much ground as possible, working their way through the maze of markers, reading names and dates, searching for mention of Pancea Rolt Gotrin. It wasn't until they had gone through all the markers once and were working their way back again that Kirisin, drawn to the intricacy of the carvings on the walls of the large mausoleum, noticed a strange symbol carved in an otherwise flat and unmarked surface on one side of the tomb. He stared at it a moment, wondering what it was, started away again when nothing suggested itself, and then stopped and turned back for another look, recognition flooding through him.

The symbol, if you looked carefully, was decipherable. It consisted of three letters in Elfish imposed one on top of the other. The letters were *P, R*, and *G*—the first letters of Pancea Rolt Gotrin's names.

"Erisha!" he hissed.

She turned at the sound of her name and hurried over. He pointed at the symbol, mouthed the three letters, and traced them as he did so. She nodded at once in agreement.

"Why is it here?" she whispered.

He shook his head. "I don't know."

Simralin and Angel Perez had joined them by now, and Kirisin revealed what he had found. Simralin understood and explained the nature of the symbol to Angel. The Knight of the Word brushed at her short-cropped hair and frowned. "Is this her tomb?"

"Doesn't say so," Simralin replied. "It is a family crèche with the remains of dozens and dozens of lesser Gotrins. A Queen would have her own tomb, separate from the others."

They fanned out, rechecking every marker within twenty yards. They found no mention of Pancea. Reassembling next to the symbol, they spoke in low, cautious voices, the night their only witness as they deliberated the puzzle.

"It's a symbol, but maybe it's something else, too," Kirisin suggested.

"What sort of *something else?*" His sister took a closer look. "It seems an ordinary carving."

"Maybe. I don't know." He touched the symbol with his fingers, tracing the letters, then pressed them to see if there was any give and felt around the ridges for anything he might have missed. He shook his head again. "It's something else," he repeated, the words a mumble that ended in a question mark.

"Could it have another meaning besides what the letters suggest?" Erisha asked suddenly. "Could they stand for something besides her name?"

Kirisin was looking all around now—at the other markers, the distant shadows, the leafy boughs of the trees surrounding them, and the ground, strewn with twigs and leaves and woodsy debris. Was he missing something?

Angel Perez stepped forward. "Wait a minute. You said Pancea had command of magic and that she was probably a witch. Maybe she provided for that. Maybe it takes magic to summon magic."

She placed the tip of her staff against the Gotrin Elfish symbol, and her dark features tightened in concentration. The runes carved in her staff began to glow, turning bright with fiery light. Almost immediately the symbol responded; it, too, began to glow.

Then a deep grating sound broke the stillness of the night, the heavy rasp of stone moving across stone, and an entire section of the earth, not a dozen feet from where they stood, began to move. A huge slab, concealed beneath layers of dirt and debris, dropped slowly into the earth and out of sight, leaving a gaping hole.

The four stepped over to its edge and peered down. It was as black as pitch in the hole, but they could see that the slab formed a platform onto the steps of a stairway leading down.

"What do we do?" Simralin asked.

Angel Perez shook her head, the runes of her staff gone dark once more. Erisha started to say something, then stopped herself.

It was Kirisin who spoke the words that the rest of them couldn't.

"We go down," he said.

＊ ＊ ＊

AT THE WEST ENTRANCE to the burial ground, hidden back in the shadow of the trees, Ailie caught a sudden whiff of demon scent. It was borne on the night breeze, coming out of the darkness north along the berm that designated the boundary to Ashenell. A second later, she saw a long, sinewy form leap out of the darkness, clear the earthen rise, and drop soundlessly inside the grounds. Ailie recognized it at once: it was the creature that had tracked them all the way from California, the creature that had twice done battle with Angel and twice been thwarted.

Now it was here.

Ailie wasn't surprised that it had found them. It was a skilled hunter, a feral beast that could track anyone or anything. What surprised her was the timing. How had the creature happened to find them now, in the middle of the night?

Something about it didn't feel right. Ailie watched the beast slouch through the markers, sniffing the ground, its big head turning this way and that, casting about for further scent. She wasn't worried about being discovered. Tatterdemalions left no scent, and she was much faster and more elusive than the demon. She could fly from her hiding place anytime she wished. But she was curious to see what it would do. It would have a purpose in mind, but its wanderings amid the markers seemed so aimless.

She was still watching when she became aware of a second presence, this one much stronger and closer, approaching her from behind. It took her only a moment to remember that there was another demon, the one from the Council chambers, the one disguised as an Elf.

She had time for a single thought.

Flee!

And then there was no time at all.

＊ ＊ ＊

DELLOREEN PADDED over to where the remains of the Faerie creature were already fading, sinking back into the earth from which she had been formed, leaving only the thin white garment she had been wearing. Delloreen licked at the cloth, tasting its dampness, and then glanced over to where the second demon was wiping its hands on the grasses of the burial grounds.

"Remember what I told you," the other said, fastidiously cleaning away what remained of Ailie. "We have a plan, and the plan is not to be changed. Kill only the one. Leave the others for later. Can you remember?"

Delloreen snapped at the air between them, showing all of her considerable teeth. She could remember as much as she needed to.

Head hunched between her shoulders, body stretched out so low that it almost touched the ground, she crept toward the deep shadows and her unsuspecting kill.

TWELVE

As Kirisin and his companions stared down into the black hole left by the opening of the stone slab, two things happened in immediate sequence. First, torches fastened in iron stanchions secured to the rock walls of the stairwell flared to life, allowing them to see that the stairs themselves wound so deep underground that their end was invisible. Second, as they took their first cautious steps down those stairs, leaving Ashenell behind, the stone slab slid back into place with a fresh grating sound that froze them in their tracks. There was no time to turn back, and no chance to escape. The slab filled the gap anew, blotting out the night sky, and they were left shut away in the earth.

"Already, I don't like any of this," Simralin said.

"We are not meant to go back," Angel said. "No mistaking that."

They glanced at one another. Then, reaching an unspoken common consensus, they resumed their descent. Kirisin had started out in the lead, but Simralin quickly passed him by, giving him a look of warning as she did so. If there was to be any sort of trouble, the look said, she was better equipped to deal with it. He found that hard to argue with and dropped back to walk beside Erisha. He was thinking that they had brought almost no weapons at all with which to defend themselves.

"It would be good if we stayed close together," Angel observed from just behind them.

Kirisin glanced back at her. The runes carved in her staff glowed faintly in the dark, pulsing softly. Her face was tight with concentration, and her eyes shifted restlessly as she descended, her footfalls soundless in the near silence. Perhaps in the company of a Knight of the Word, they needed no other protection.

He listened to his own breathing, which seemed to him the loudest sound in the stairwell. He tried to quiet it and failed. The pumping of his heart was a steady throbbing in his ears, and he tried and failed to quiet that, too. The air grew steadily colder with their descent, changing from a dry woodland smell to the scent of damp rock and rain-soaked leaves. Somewhere farther down, he could hear water trickling over rocks. It reminded him of the mountain caves he had explored as a boy and of the graves of the dead on days when burials had to be held in the rain.

The stairs tunneled downward for a long time before ending in a narrow corridor that leveled off into what appeared to be a natural opening. Burning torches continued to mark their way, small flickering dots disappearing into the darkness. They moved ahead cautiously, listening to the silence that surrounded the soft sounds of their breathing and their footfalls, their senses strained and their expectancy heightened. There was something down here, something they were meant to find once they had made the decision to enter. The still-unanswered question, the fuel for their doubts and fears, was whether it was something that would prove dangerous.

Suddenly Simralin held up her hand, bringing them to a stop. "Wait."

They stood silently, listening. After a moment, they could detect a faint sound from somewhere ahead, a soft, sibilant whisper. Kirisin tried and failed to identify it. He felt instinctively and for reasons he could not explain that it was a warning, but he could not tell what it warned against.

Simralin held them in place a moment longer, glanced back to make certain they were alert to the strange sound, and then started them forward once more. The passageway turned sharply left and straightened right again. It began to open up, the ceiling rising and the walls widening. Stalactites began to appear, small at first and then large enough to dwarf the people passing beneath them, huge stone spears from which droplets of water fell, stinging with cold as they struck Kirisin on the face. He glanced up and found himself staring into a forest of tapering stone spirals clustered so thickly that he could no longer see the ceiling at all.

The passageway ended at a cavern dominated by a black water pool that filled a broad depression at its center. The surface of the water was flat and still, as if it comprised not liquid but opaque glass. The chamber itself was so large that its walls receded into blackness, invisible save where tiny pinpricks of torch fire burned bravely in the heavy gloom.

But it wasn't the chamber or the pool that drew everyone's eyes. It was the cluster of stone crypts and sepulchers that sprouted from the cavern floor. Those that were closest had writing that could be read in the flicker of the torchlight. Some had been carved with the letter G. Some bore the name GOTRIN.

Kirisin stared openmouthed. How many of them were there? Dozens and dozens, it seemed. Perhaps more than a hundred.

"They are all buried down here," he said, speaking aloud the words he was thinking, words that had come to him unbidden. "Those from Pancea's time, they are all buried here. The tombs aboveground do not belong to them."

He didn't know how he knew this; he simply did. He was already walking ahead, moving into that stone garden, feeling his way in his mind to the tomb he wanted. He couldn't have said why, but he felt it calling to him, drawing him on as if a voice speaking. He moved in response to that silent voice, conscious of almost nothing else. The others followed, glancing at each other in bewilderment, but letting the boy go where he chose.

He walked down almost to the edge of the pool and stopped before a triangular-shaped block of stone. Carved into its head, on the short, flat side of the triangle, were the letters *P*, *R*, and *G*.

He became aware suddenly that the whispering he had heard earlier was coming from here. But the pitch and tone had changed, and now it was less an unidentifiable sound and more a recognizable voice.

"She is here," he said.

Even as he finished speaking the words, the torches all about them began to flicker and dim and the pool of black water to swirl. There was wind where before there had been only stillness, a sudden rush that whipped down out of the ceiling rock and swept across the cavern floor. It was momentarily fierce, causing the four intruders to drop into a crouch and shield their eyes. Kirisin took refuge behind Pancea's tomb, bracing himself with one hand against the cold stone, head lowered to protect his eyes.

"Kirisin!" he heard Erisha gasp.

—Why are the living come to me—

The voice was low-pitched and gravel-rough, and it echoed through the cavern in the wake of the wind's departure, the silence returned anew, deep and abiding.

He lifted his head and found himself staring at the shade of an old woman.

The shade stood atop the tomb of Pancea, and he knew in an instant that it was her. She was small and wizened, bent at the shoulders as if the bearer of a great weight, her face so wrinkled that it had the look of leather crumpled by time and use. But her eyes were sharp and steady as they regarded him, and her talon-tipped fingers gripped a staff with strength that belied her seeming frailty.

He had never seen a shade. He had heard rumors of them, but they had always seemed to him to be the product of overactive imaginations. He swallowed hard. He would think differently after this.

The light of the torches, steady once more, passed through the old woman's transparent form in a shimmer of refracted light, and her image wavered and settled like mist.

—Why are the living come here. They do not belong—

She spoke again, the question repeated. Her voice scraped and dragged over the words. Her eyes changed color, gone from black to a dangerous green.

"We had no choice," he answered, knowing he must say something.

"We are searching for the blue Elfstones, and a journal we uncovered said they could be found in the tomb of Pancea Rolt Cruer."

She regarded him without speaking, her gaze steady.

He waited a moment, and then asked, "Are you her? Are you Pancea Rolt Cruer?"

–I am *Queen* Pancea Rolt Gotrin. Show me respect–

"I apologize, Your Majesty," he said quickly. He tried to think what to say next. "I am a Chosen. She is another." He pointed to Erisha. "The Ellcrys sent us to find the blue Elfstones. There is a terrible struggle taking place on the surface of the world between demons and their allies and Elves and Men. The demons are winning. The Ellcrys says that she is threatened and must be moved. She says we must use the blue Elfstones to find the Loden and place her inside."

He hesitated, and then gestured at Angel. "This is a Knight of the Word, sent to warn us that our world will be destroyed. The Word says the Elves must leave the Cintra. To do that, we must take the Ellcrys with us. So we've come here, looking for a place to start."

–You would start your journey with the dead? Is that not strange? The dead have nothing to offer the living. The dead are of the past and never of the present. The dead do not pretend to care about what is or will be. The dead seek only to keep what is theirs–

She lifted a hand and pointed at them, one by one. As she did so, Kirisin felt a stab of cold rage spear him, projected from the shade's own dark heart.

–You trespass where you do not belong. You have entered sacred ground and defiled it. Your arrogance is offensive to me–

Her hands lifted and swept the air on both sides, sending strange trailers of light scattering from her fingertips. The light fragmented and settled atop the surrounding tombs, flaring as it touched each crypt.

Then the air itself shimmered, and the shades of the Gotrin dead began to rise out of their resting places, lifting into the near darkness in ghostly white transparencies, the outlines of their bodies and faces a liquid shimmer, the whisper of their awakening a cacophony of hissing that matched that which had first drawn Kirisin and his companions. One by one, they appeared, shades of all sizes and shapes, ghosts come out of the stone that housed their mortal remains.

Kirisin took a step back. He could feel the threat implicit in their presence, as dark and cold as the rage that Pancea had projected from her heart. The dead did not want them here. The dead did not want the living in their private sanctuary, and they were prepared to reveal in no uncertain terms what his intrusion meant.

"We came because we had to!" he repeated desperately. "Would you wish the living as dead as you? Do you think we are wrong to try to save them?"

The shades of the Gotrins began to creep closer, floating on the cold cavern air, tightening their circle. Simralin was standing next to him by now, and he was aware of Angel and Erisha coming up as well. He caught a glimpse of Angel's black staff out of the corner of his eye, its runes glowing with white fire.

"If you do not help us, all the Elves will die!" he insisted.

–The dead care nothing for the living and their problems–

She rose from the lid of her crypt and settled to the ground. She was small, but he could feel her power radiating out from her ethereal form in cold waves.

"Get back from her, Kirisin," his sister ordered. "Get back right now!"

When he failed to move quickly enough, she took him roughly by his shoulder and dragged him away. But the shade of Pancea Rolt Gotrin kept coming, her advance slow and inexorable as she glided across the darkness that separated them.

"What about the magic?" Kirisin demanded, desperate now. "The magic you tried to preserve? If the Elves die, the magic dies, as well!"

–The magic cannot die. The magic lives even beyond death–

"Not if there is no one left to wield it! Without the living, it cannot grow or change! It cannot evolve in new ways. It remains static and dormant! Eventually, it will weaken from lack of use and disappear completely!"

He barely knew what he was saying, acting on instinct, speaking whatever words he thought the shade might respond to. He couldn't tell what they might be; he only knew he had to find a way to reach her.

To his surprise, she stopped moving. Behind her, the other shades stopped, as well. The ripples of ice emanating from their ghostly forms softened ever so slightly. Pancea Rolt Gotrin studied him. One withered hand lifted and pointed.

–What will you do with the Elfstones if I release them to you? To what use will you put them–

"I will use them to find the Loden Elfstone, and use the Loden to save the Ellcrys and her people." He hesitated. "And then I will do whatever I can to persuade the Elves to find the magic they have lost."

–You seek to placate me. The Elves will never find their magic again. They have forgotten its purpose. They have changed their way of life and by doing so have lost the magic forever–

"The old world is ending," Erisha said suddenly. "In the new, they may have need of the magic again. If they are to survive, they will be forced to start over."

"If there are no Elves left, if there are no humans, if there are only demons and demonkind, what is the point of the magic in any case?" asked Kirisin. "The magic needs our people to wield it if it is to serve a purpose. Can we not recover it somehow? It cannot be completely out of reach."

–The magic lies deep within the earth, where it has always been. The magic is elemental, and the Elves had use of it until they gave way before the humans. Why would this change–

She was still not persuaded, but she was listening now, giving consideration to what he was telling her. Kirisin felt a surge of hope. Perhaps there was a way to change her thinking after all.

But just as he was ready to believe that the shades guarding these tombs and their secrets might be willing to share what they kept hidden, Pancea started toward him again, hand outstretched.

–Let me touch you–

He shrank from her. If he was touched by the dead, by a shade, what would it do to him? Was just that touch enough to steal his life? He didn't know, and he didn't care to find out.

He held out his hands. "I don't think you should do that."

"Get away from him!" snapped Simralin, stepping in front of her brother.

The shade turned to her, outstretched arm shifting slightly.

–Foolish girl–

The words hung frozen on the air in the ensuing stillness. Then Pancea's arms swept out and Simralin flew backward, taking Erisha and Angel with her, and leaving them scattered like leaves caught in a strong wind. They lay where they had fallen, unmoving.

Kirisin tried to turn and flee, but found he couldn't move. He panicked, thrashing against his invisible bonds. Nothing helped.

–Let me touch you–

The shade was right on top of him now. It took every ounce of willpower he could muster, but he quieted himself and straightened. If he couldn't avoid this, he must do his best to face it in the right way. "Please don't hurt me," he whispered.

The shade stopped right in front of him. Eyes as blank and empty as white stones stared out of an aged, ruined face.

–If you lie, I will know. If you deceive, I will know. If you lack heart or courage, I will know–

Her hand stretched out to him, touched his chest, and passed inside. He could feel the intrusion, a wash of cold that was deep and aching. He flinched, but held himself steady, watching the hand, then the wrist, and finally the forearm disappear inside his body. The cold radiated out, filling his chest and stomach, ranging farther to his limbs and finally into his head. It was a different kind of cold, one that he had never experienced, one that he could not compare to anything he knew.

He waited to die.

Inside, he could feel a shift in the cold, which seemed to correspond to the slow movement of her arm through his chest.

I am not afraid, he told himself, and wished it were so.

Then she spoke.

–Kirisin Belloruus. You do not lie. You do not deceive. You do not lack heart or courage. You are young, but your word is good. I feel in you a reason to believe again. I sensed it when you touched the letters of my name carved on my family tomb. I sense it now–

Her pale form shimmered and drew closer, until her wrinkled ghost's face was only inches from his own.

–You are indeed Chosen. You are the one. You have the magic inside you, your past and your future. You have the gift–

Slowly, she withdrew her arm from his body. As she did so, the cold dissipated and was gone. Her blank eyes stared at him.

–I will give you what you seek. I will trust you to keep your word. Save the living, if you can. Find the Loden. Take the Elves to safety. But remember your promise. When that is done, you will persuade them to find and make use of their magic once more. You will recover the old ways–

She waited on him, and he nodded. "I promise."

–You must do this alone–

He hesitated. "I have my friends to help me, Erisha and Simralin and Angel Perez, the ones who came with me."

Her mouth opened and closed in what looked to be a soundless scream. Her arms fell away to her sides.

–You must do this alone–

She glided backward toward her tomb, and as she did so the other shades withdrew as well, dozens of ethereal forms retreating into the darkness. One by one they reached their stone resting places and disappeared.

She was the last, hovering momentarily as she whispered to him.

–Brave boy. You must do this alone–

Then she was gone, and the silence that settled like dust from a passing wind was deafening.

HE STOOD where he was for the longest time. It seemed that hours might have elapsed when he thought back on it later, but he knew that it was only seconds. He was thinking about what she had said, about how he must do what she had asked of him. She had been so insistent, so certain. She had dismissed the possibility that his sister or Erisha or Angel Perez would play any part. He couldn't understand it. How could they not be involved in what he was supposed to do?

He felt the cold of the chamber seep into him, a different cold from the touch of the shades, a different burn. He could smell the rock and the water, the scent of minerals and earth, of old stale darkness in a place where the living had not come for centuries.

He could sense how badly he had intruded and how little he belonged.

Then his three companions were surrounding him, gripping him, calling his name, scattering his thoughts into memories.

"Little K." Simralin spoke his name sharply, one strong hand fastening on his shoulder. "Are you all right?"

He nodded, meeting her gaze. She looked decidedly unsettled and distressed in a way he had seldom seen her. He smiled reassuringly. She was worried for him. "What about you, Sim? She threw you a long way."

His sister shook her head. "I don't remember. I blacked out, and when I woke up she was gone—the others with her—and you were standing here alone."

He glanced at Erisha and Angel, and they nodded, as well. "I have never had anyone do that to me," the latter said, a note of bitterness tinging her words. "I don't want it to happen ever again."

"The Elven dead have great power," Simralin said. "Especially when they possessed magic in their former lives. I've heard Father speak of it. Pancea Rolt Gotrin was a sorceress. She took some of that magic with her to the grave."

"Can we leave now?" Erisha asked sharply, hugging herself. Her smooth features were twisted with distaste. "We'll just have to try something else, find some other way to recover the Elfstones. But not tonight. I don't want to be here anymore tonight."

Simralin put an arm around her shoulders. "I don't blame you. I'm still cold from what the shades made me feel." Her grip tightened. "But we came here to find the Elfstones, and if we leave without them—"

"We don't have to leave without them," Kirisin interrupted. His hand rested against the pocket of his tunic, pressing against something inside. He fumbled with the flap for a moment, then drew out a small leather pouch.

He held it out to them. "I just realized it was there. I just felt it. I know what it is. Look!"

He opened the drawstrings and dumped the contents into the palm of his hand. Three perfectly formed blue gemstones twinkled and glimmered in the faint rays of the torches, bright beacons against the darkness.

"The Elfstones!" Simralin whispered.

"She said she would give them to me. It was the bargain she struck in return for my promise to help persuade the Elves to recover their magic. She said she trusted me to do what I promised."

Angel stepped forward quickly and looked down at the gems. "Are you sure of what they are?"

Kirisin shook his head. "No one living has ever seen an Elfstone. But I know. These are Elfstones. Blue, for seeking, just as the books and the Ellcrys promised." He looked down at the stones and then up again at her. "We have what we need to find the Loden."

They were in a much better frame of mind as they started back into the tunnel toward the stairway leading up, their hushed voices excited and eager as they talked about what they would do next. Because they had the Elfstones in hand, Erisha thought they should take them before the High Council and her father and demand that they be allowed to use them to search for the Loden. Angel agreed. It was better if they had the support and approval of the Elven community and better still if they had help with their search. Surely with the blue Elfstones as evidence that what the Ellcrys had asked of Erisha and Kirisin was possible, help could not be denied.

But Kirisin and his sister were not so sure. Both had reason to question how supportive Arissen Belloruus would be. Both worried about the King's reaction to their discovery. What if he chose to lay claim to the Elfstones on behalf of the Elven people? Once they revealed that they had possession, they couldn't very well keep the King from taking them away. Arissen Belloruus was a strong personality and a powerful ruler; if he decided that the Stones should be under the control of the throne, whatever the merits of his reasoning, even the High Council would find it difficult to override him.

But there was an even more troubling problem, one that none of them wanted to consider. What if the King was the demon Ailie had sensed in the High Council chambers? What would their chances of keeping the Elfstones be then?

They were still mulling over the matter as they climbed the stairs toward the exit from the underground. Kirisin gave momentary consideration to how they were going to get out again if the heavy slab was still closed, then decided that if the shade of Pancea had given them the Elfstones, she would surely provide them with a way out. Sure enough, they reached the top of the stairs and found moonlight shining down through the opening, the smells of the forest and the night reaching out to welcome them. Kirisin breathed in deeply as they stepped back out into the Ashenell, the cold of the cavern stone giving way to the softness of the forest breezes.

Behind them, the stone slab slid back into place, closing off the stairs and the underground. Almost immediately, fresh debris blown in on a small gust of wind covered it over; in seconds, no evidence of its existence remained.

Kirisin, in the lead, turned to the others. "We can meet again—"

He stopped in midsentence, his eyes drawn suddenly to Angel Perez. The Knight of the Word had gone into a crouch, her eyes shifting everywhere at once. He realized what was happening an instant before she cried out.

"Demon!"

She wheeled in a circle, black staff sweeping the darkness, and Kirisin saw that she didn't know where the demon was. Erisha and Simralin had just turned back in response to her cry when the monster burst from the shadows in a dark rush. Long and sleek, its body that of a nightmarish four-legged beast, it catapulted into their midst. Simralin, a pair of long knives appearing in her hands as if by magic, lunged at it as it vaulted past. The monster shrieked and twisted its head to one side. Erisha was knocked spinning; she threw up her arms in shock, a gasp issuing from her lips. The beast came on, straight for Kirisin now. He dropped into a protective crouch and fumbled frantically for his dagger.

Then Angel was between them, bringing up her black staff, its magic exploding into the demon. The force of the blow knocked the demon to one side, changing its course of attack just enough that it missed the boy. It tried to renew its assault, but its movements had become erratic, as if chains were dragging at it. It staggered, straightened, and then staggered again.

When it wheeled back again and the moonlight bathed its ferocious countenance, Kirisin saw what was wrong. One of Simralin's knives was buried to the hilt in its eye socket, black blood pouring out over the handle.

The demon shrieked one final time, the sound harsh and chilling, freezing them all in place. Then it was gone into the night.

Angel started after it, face contorted in fury, and stopped. It was useless. The demon was gone, and she wasn't going to catch it.

Simralin's remaining knife caught the moonlight as she whipped it back into its sheath.

"Shades!" she hissed. Her face was pale and tight. "My blade should have killed it. How can it still be alive?"

Then Kirisin saw Erisha. She was sprawled on her back, her throat a red smear against her white skin. Blood pumped from a terrible wound that opened all the way to her neck bones. She tried futilely to speak, her hands groping for her ruined throat. Kirisin rushed to her side, Angel and his sister a step behind. Erisha's eyes found his, a mirror for her desperation and fear, for her realization of what had just happened to her.

Then the blood ceased to pump, her hands fell back against her sides, and her eyes fixed sightlessly in place.

"Erisha," he whispered in horror.

From back toward the gates they had come through, shouting arose. Home Guards, alerted to their presence. Kirisin blinked. How could that be? How could they have appeared so quickly? He had just enough time to realize that it was impossible unless someone had alerted them earlier, and then Simralin was yanking him about.

"We have to go, Little K," she said.

He looked at her in disbelief. "But we can't—"

"They're coming!" she spat at him furiously, practically throwing him ahead of her. "We can't let them find us! Run!"

Angel was already in flight, heading away from the voices. Kirisin took one final look at Erisha, felt everything he had hoped for slip away as he did so, and then began to run.

THIRTEEN

NGEL PEREZ had no idea where she was running to, only what she was running from—Erisha, lying on the ground, bleeding out her life, surrounded by a swarm of Feeders drawn to the smell and taste of her death, dark shadows that her companions could not see. The shouts of the Elven sentries spurred her on, a clear reminder of how horribly wrong things had gone. Still stunned by what had happened amid the tombs of the Gotrins, still wrestling with the inescapable implications of what it meant—implications that perhaps only she yet realized—she was reacting more to her emotions than to reason.

Simralin overtook her, long legs eating up the distance between them. "You don't know where you're going!" she shouted as she surged past. "Follow me!"

Ashenell was huge, and it all looked the same to Angel, clusters of stone markers and tombs, mausoleums and crypts, memorials to the dead amid a scattering of trees and flowering bushes, everything shrouded by cold white moonlight that flooded down out of a deep blue sky. She listened to the sound of her breathing and her footfalls as the cries of their pursuers slowly faded into the distance. She clutched her black staff and agonized in dismal silence over how sometimes even a Knight of the Word could do so little.

"Angel!"

She turned at the sound of her name and saw Kirisin desperately trying to catch up. She slowed and stopped. Ahead of her, Simralin glanced back, saw what was happening, and wheeled around, as well.

Kirisin came to a ragged halt in front of her. "Wait," he panted. "What about Ailie?"

There was blood on his hands and the front of his tunic. Erisha's blood, from his vain attempt to stop her bleeding. His eyes were empty and haunted, staring without really seeing, blinking rapidly, as if trying to adjust. He looked to be on the verge of collapse, chest heaving, face sweat-streaked and dusty, his body all bones and sinew seemingly in danger of flying apart, a ragged scarecrow cut down from its post in the field and set loose in the world, struggling to learn how to move.

"What about her, Angel?" He dropped to one knee, breathing hard. "We can't just leave her!"

Tears filled Angel's eyes, and she shook her head. Little Ailie, her self-appointed conscience, her companion and friend. Thinking of the tatterdemalion made her hurt in a way she thought she would never get past. "She's dead, Kirisin."

Simralin appeared beside her, confusion mirrored on her strong features as she looked from one to the other.

"Dead? How can you say that?" Kirisin was aghast.

Angel tightened her lips. "Because if she weren't dead, she would have warned us. That demon never would have gotten past her."

"But we can't be sure!" Kirisin insisted.

From the way he said it, Angel knew that he needed to believe it. He needed to believe that he was right, that there was still some hope for Ailie. Perhaps it was because there was none at all for Erisha, and losing both would be too much for him to bear. But Angel was a veteran of the streets, and she had lost others she had cared about as much as Ailie. Losing Johnny had nearly finished her, but she had gotten past it. She would get past losing Ailie, too. She had to. The living could not bring back the dead. Memories of the dead were all they could hold on to.

She started to say this to Kirisin, but he was already looking back over his shoulder. "You could be wrong. What if you're wrong?"

She started to say that she wasn't and stopped herself. What if she were? What if, despite what she knew in her heart, Ailie was still alive? It didn't feel to her as if that were possible, but she had been wrong before.

She took a deep breath. "All right. I'll go back and look."

"No," Simralin said at once, stepping in front of her. "You are the last one who should go. They are probably already looking for you. I'll go. Another Elven Hunter won't draw any special attention."

She turned to Kirisin. "Take Angel to the house. Wait inside. Don't light any lamps. Don't do anything to draw attention. If you see anyone coming, get out of there. If we lose each other, we'll meet up at the north crossroads by Tower Rock." She reached out and hugged him to her. "Be careful, Little K."

Then she raced away, heading not directly back in the direction from which they had come but angling off to the right, choosing a roundabout approach that would allow her to slip out of Ashenell and come up on the searchers from the rear. Angel hoped they didn't know exactly who they were looking for, or Simralin would be in trouble.

Then the boy turned to her. "That demon. It knew—"

"*Those* demons," she interrupted quickly. "There were two. But not now. After we reach your house. We can talk then."

They set out once more, Kirisin leading the way. Angel stayed close to him, warding him like a protective shield. He was still in danger, more so perhaps than she was. She was still working through what had happened back there, why the demons had concentrated on killing Erisha, why they hadn't tried instead to kill her. She was the one who presented the greatest danger to them, especially with Ailie gone. If she were really gone. If.

But she knew. She knew it the same way she knew that Johnny was gone when he didn't come back that night so many years ago.

They cleared Ashenell shortly afterward and made their way through a stretch of cottages and gardens along winding paths that

took them close to the surrounding wilderness. There was no indication
of anything out of the ordinary. No lights burned in the houses; no one
walked the paths. Once, a dog barked. Once, an owl flew close. Nothing else. Here, at least, the Elves still slept.

When they reached Kirisin's home, they paused to make certain
that no one was waiting in the shadows, then slipped through the door
and closed and locked it behind them. Kirisin led her into the kitchen,
which was set at the rear of the home, and without asking poured her
a glass of ale. After pouring one for himself, he led her back through the
house to a place near one of the front windows where they could sit
and talk while keeping watch.

Kirisin tried to speak first, struggling to find the words. "Angel, I
don't know . . ."

Angel seized his wrists and squeezed them.

"Let me tell you what I know before you say anything. It isn't
everything, but we can make a start." She leaned forward, keeping her
voice lowered. "There were two demons waiting for us. I detected them
when we came out of the underground, but I was confused because I
wasn't expecting any and then I couldn't figure out why they seemed
to be on both sides of me. The one that attacked us was the one that
tracked Ailie and me north on our journey to find you. The other, the
one that stayed hidden, must have been the demon Ailie sensed in the
chambers of the High Council. Somehow, they found each other and
learned what we were doing."

Kirisin tried to interrupt, but Angel squeezed his wrists anew,
harder this time. "Wait. Let me finish. Just listen." She relaxed her grip
but did not release it. "Those demons were waiting for us. They knew
how to find us and they were waiting. That was a carefully planned attack, Kirisin. They knew exactly what they were doing. They were on
top of us the minute we emerged from underground. Killing Erisha
wasn't an accident. She was their victim all along. She was the one who
was meant to die."

Their eyes locked. "I know this," she said, "because of how quickly
her killer got to her and away again, even with your sister's dagger in its
eye. No hesitation in its choice of victims. No interest in anyone else,
not until it had made certain of Erisha. That demon has tracked me a

thousand miles. It has tried twice to kill me. It was that determination that brought it all the way into the Cintra. But something happened to change its focus. That other demon, the one disguised as an Elf, somehow managed to influence the one tracking me. It has a different plan, a more complicated one, one that doesn't appear to be focused on killing me. What do you think that plan might be?"

She nodded at him, telling him it was all right to speak now. Kirisin hesitated, then said, "To stop us from finding the Loden?"

"Then why not kill you both? Why kill only Erisha? You were the one who stirred things up before Ailie and I got here. You seem the more determined. Why was the attack made on Erisha rather than on you?"

Kirisin stared at her. "I don't know."

"I don't know, either, but I don't like it. Erisha is dead, and you still have the Elfstones. You can still use them to try to find the Loden and do what you set out to do. Attacking us in the graveyard seems almost pointless."

She saw the look reflected in his eyes and grabbed his wrist once more. "But it wasn't. It wasn't pointless. There was a reason for it. We just have to figure out what it was."

Kirisin shook his head in disbelief. "I don't understand any of this. Why kill anyone? Why not just steal the Elfstones so that none of us could use them?"

There was movement in the shadows at the edge of the trees near the front of the house, and Angel held up her hand in warning. Seconds later, Simralin slipped from the darkness and trotted across the lawn, then onto the porch, crouching low in the gloom of the overhang.

Kirisin moved quickly to the door, unlocked it, and let his sister slip inside. "What did you find out?" he whispered as they moved over to where Angel waited.

Angel could already read the answer on Simralin's face. Kirisin's sister glanced out the window, searching the darkness momentarily. Then she leaned close. Even with her face right next to theirs, her words were barely audible. "I might have been followed," she whispered. "We have to get out of here."

Angel's hand tightened on the black staff, and she could feel the magic respond with a surge of sudden warmth. "What happened?"

Simralin continued to search the trees, sharp eyes scanning everything. "Ailie is dead. I found a piece of her gown, torn and soiled, close to where we left her." She paused, registering the change of expression on Angel's face. "I'm sorry. But it's worse than that." Her gaze shifted to her brother. "They know about you. Someone saw you running away."

Kirisin shook his head at once. "That isn't possible. There wasn't anyone else there!" He glanced at Angel. "Did you see anyone?"

Angel shook her head. "Who said they saw us?"

"I couldn't find out. By the time I learned this, I was worried that they knew about me, too. I had to hurry back and warn you. They'll be here any moment."

Kirisin sat back slowly. "I can't believe this."

Simralin looked at Angel. "We have to run. We have to get far away. If they find us, I don't like to think about what might happen."

Angel nodded. "I take your point."

"Well, I don't," Kirisin interjected quickly. "Why can't we just go to them and explain? We haven't done anything wrong!"

Angel shook her head. "Listen to me. If Erisha's father is the demon—wait, let me finish—if he is, he won't bother to take the time to listen to any of us. He will take the Elfstones and have us killed. But even if he isn't the demon, someone close to him is. The King already appears to be under the demon's influence. We know that from his refusal to act on what either you or Erisha have told him. I wish I could tell you that he would act responsibly when he hears what we have to say, but history tells us that he won't."

"I agree," Simralin added. "The demons know who we are and what we are about. They will do what is necessary to stop us. We have to get out of here. I will send someone I can trust to warn our parents to stay away from Arborlon until this business is finished. They will be safe enough. We are the ones in real danger."

Angel shook her head. "I don't know. This feels wrong. It feels like we are being manipulated. Demons find us in Ashenell when no one else even knows we are there. A killing takes place that eliminates the only one among us who could spy them out. A second killing serves no purpose other than to enrage the King. Some unnamed person reports Kirisin at the site, someone none of us saw in return. And now we are

forced to flee. There is something going on here that we don't understand."

"It seems obvious to me." Simralin was looking out the window
again. "The point is to get rid of all of us and steal the Elfstones."

It was hard to argue with her, but Angel was unconvinced. She understood enough of demon machinations and duplicity to question
anything that seemed obvious. Demons never approached anything in
a direct manner. Everything was done with stealth and cunning, with a
reliance on misdirection and false trails. The end result was always
something other than what it appeared. She couldn't help but think
that it was so here.

Her face tightened with frustration. "Who else knew we were going
to be at that graveyard? Who, besides those of us who were there?
Someone had to. Someone gave us away."

Kirisin and his sister exchanged a quick look. "Old Culph knew,"
the boy said quietly. "Erisha and I told him."

"He was also in the Council chambers, hiding behind the walls with
you, when Ailie sensed a demon presence." Angel pointed out.

"Behind the walls, not in the chamber itself!" Kirisin defended. He
rushed ahead. "Besides, he was the one who helped us find Pancea Rolt
Cruer's maiden name so that we could track down her tomb. He was
the one who helped us with the scribe's journal and the Queen's name.
Why do that if he was trying to stop us?"

Angel was not persuaded, already half convinced that they had unearthed their culprit. "Where can we find him?"

"He lives in a small cottage at the rear of the Belloruus home,"
Kirisin answered. "But going there will put us right in the center of
things."

"We'll send someone to ask for him." Simralin pivoted away from
the window. "Someone they won't think to question."

Angel shook her head. "Who can we trust to do that?"

"Let me take care of that." Simralin rose from her crouch. "Right
now we need to concentrate on getting out of here!"

THEY TOOK just long enough to snatch up weapons, rough-weather gear, blankets, and food for two days, and went out the door. In the distance, the forest was filled with the sounds of voices and movement. Arborlon was beginning to come awake, alerted to the fact that something was amiss, lights winking in homes, Elves stepping outside to see what was happening, a low buzz building. They had to assume that Elven Hunters would be searching for them by now, casting a wide net through the city in an effort to discover where they were hiding or in what direction they had chosen to escape. Kirisin knew from listening to his sister that their efforts would not be apparent, that they would rely on stealth and surprise. Some of them would be acquaintances of long standing. Some of them would be his friends. Most wouldn't know yet why they were looking for him, but once they did their efforts would intensify. It wouldn't be personal, but they were soldiers and knew better than to do anything but what they were told. For a soldier, orders took precedence over everything.

He reached down into his pocket and touched the small bulk of the pouch and its Elfstones. He was still finding it hard to believe how badly things had turned out. All their efforts had been directed toward finding and securing the Stones, and he had assumed that once that was achieved the worst of it was over. All that remained was to make use of the talismans and begin the search for the Loden. Halfway there, he had thought.

Now he understood for the first time how difficult the rest would be. It wasn't going to be a simple matter of asking for the support of the King and the High Council in their efforts to continue the search. There wasn't going to be any such support; rather, King and Council were going to do their level best to hunt them down if they ran, which they almost certainly were going to have to do. Running would make them look guilty. But staying behind would put an end to any effort to help the Ellcrys. Whichever way they turned, whatever choice they made, they would be on their own.

And he would not know for a long time to come—if ever—if the risk required was worth the taking.

Simralin, in the lead, glanced over her shoulder at him, perhaps to make certain that he was keeping up. He nodded for her to go on, keeping his thoughts to himself. There was no reason to say anything. She would be thinking the same thing he was. Given her training, she was probably already several steps ahead of him.

They skirted the city along its smaller trails, listening for sounds of pursuit, always moving away from activity that might signal danger. Now and again, Simralin took them off the main pathway into the trees or brush. Once she had them crouch down and wait. Each time, he searched for a reason and found none. But he knew better than to question her. She was far and away the best Tracker among the Cintra Elves, a rare combination of experience and instincts, of quick thinking and steady nerves. Everyone said she was the best. It had always made Kirisin proud. Tonight it made him grateful, as well.

On the trail behind him, Angel Perez was a silent presence. He glanced back at her once or twice, but she barely looked at him, her gaze directed at the surrounding trees. She had a Tracker's look about her, her concentration intense and her focus complete, as if she was able to see and hear much more than he could. Like Simralin. He studied Angel a moment. How much older than he was she? A few years, perhaps, no more. But so much more confident, so much more poised. He found himself wanting to know more about her. She was a Knight of the Word, but what did that mean? What had she endured to achieve that title? How much had she survived?

They reached a small cluster of homes at the northern edge of the city, distant from its teeming center but not so far from the Home Guard and Elven Hunter compounds above the Belloruus home. It seemed dangerously close to exactly where they shouldn't be. But Simralin moved ahead to a tight clump of cedar thick with brush and grasses, and motioned for them to hunker down within its cover.

Then she gave a sharp, quick birdcall, waited a moment, and repeated the call. A few minutes passed; then a door to one of the cottages opened and a dark figure emerged, stepping cautiously through the shadows, searching.

"Wait here," Simralin whispered.

She stepped out of the brush and walked into the pale wash of starlight. The dark figure came toward her at once, big and strong looking, a man. He reached for Simralin in familiar fashion, but she held him away from her, saying something that caused him to look toward the place where Kirisin and Angel were hiding. The light caught his face, revealing his features.

"Who is it?" Angel whispered in Kirisin's ear.

"Tragen," he said.

"There seems to be something between them."

There does indeed, Kirisin thought, and he wondered why he hadn't known. He watched them converse, and then Simralin motioned for them to come out of hiding and join her. They did so, and Tragen, without a word, led them into the seclusion of his darkened cottage and closed the door behind them.

"Little K, you have a knack for getting into trouble," he said gruffly, but there was a smile on his lips, too.

"You know nothing of what's happened?" Simralin asked him, obviously picking up their earlier conversation.

"I've been asleep. I'm not on duty again until day after tomorrow—today now, I guess. Dawn's not far off." The big Elf looked from face to face. "What do you need me to do?"

Simralin told him. He listened without comment, typical of Tragen, who seldom had much to say in any case. "Can you do it?" she finished.

He nodded. "Stay out of sight until I get back. No lights. No movement. Lock up after me."

He went out the door and shut it tightly behind him. Simralin gave him a moment to get clear and then slid the heavy bar latch into place.

They moved over to the shadows behind a shuttered window that let them peer through the slats into the night and crouched down to wait.

After a few moments of silence, Kirisin said, "Are you sure you can trust him?"

His sister nodded without answering.

"You didn't say anything to me about how you felt about him."

He felt her eyes on him as he stared studiously out the window. "I didn't have a chance. This is new." She touched his shoulder so that he was forced to look at her. "Besides, I'm not sure yet how I feel."

"He seems pretty sure." He hesitated a moment, then shrugged. "But never mind. I like Tragen."

Simralin grinned, pretty and flushed. "Well, it's all right, then. But don't get ahead of yourself. He's interesting enough for now, but maybe not for more than that."

Kirisin grinned back. He glanced at Angel to catch her reaction. But the Knight of the Word didn't seem to be paying attention, sitting back and away from them, staring at nothing. He started to speak to her and stopped. What he had mistaken for disinterest was something else. There was pain in her eyes, a ripple of loss and remorse. He could read it clearly, and it surprised him that he could. She might be thinking of Ailie, but she might be thinking of someone else, too. She would have lost more in her short lifetime than the tatterdemalion, he thought. And he wondered again about what she had survived before coming to Arborlon and the Elves.

Tragen was gone for the better part of an hour. When he reappeared, the first glimmer of dawn was beginning to appear through breaks in the forest canopy, and the shadows were starting to recede. He came out of the trees at a swift walk, looking neither left nor right. Simralin opened the door to admit him.

"Culph is dead," the big Tracker announced as soon as the door was closed again. "I found him in his sleeping chamber, torn apart. The damage was bad, but I could tell it was him."

Kirisin squeezed his eyes shut. *We were too slow!* He rounded on Angel. "I told you it wasn't him! I told you!"

"Stop it, Little K," Simralin snapped. "She only said what the rest of us were thinking—that it *might* have been him, not that it was." She shook her head helplessly. "I thought it was him, too. So we're back to the King."

"Or one of his ministers," Angel amended. "Or anyone else standing around when Ailie was in the Council chambers. We can't be sure." She reached over and touched Kirisin on the shoulder. "I'm sorry about your friend."

"We should have warned him," the boy whispered to no one in particular. "We should have done something."

"I don't think there was much you could have done," Tragen said. "He was killed hours ago, long before the King's daughter." He looked at Simralin and shook his head. "I don't know what is going on, but it isn't good. Once they find the old man's body, things will only get worse. They're looking for you. All of you. They're combing the city, house by house. You have to get away while you still can."

Simralin shouldered her pack. "Looks like we don't have any choice. We're leaving." She moved over to him, reached up to touch his cheek, and kissed him on the mouth. Kirisin watched, intrigued. "I have to ask you to do something else. I need you to go to Briar Ruan and warn my parents not to return, to stay where they are until they hear from me. Will you do that?"

Tragen looked at the floor. "I had thought I would go with you."

She shook her head. "Then you would be one of us. I can't allow that. Besides, you will do me a bigger favor by warning my parents. Perhaps I will have need of your help again before this is finished. There has to be someone here I can turn to."

He hesitated a moment, and then nodded. "All right, Sim. But I don't have to like it."

She kissed him again, a deeper kiss, and this time Kirisin looked away. "You don't have to like it," she told Tragen. "You just have to do it."

She opened the cottage door, peered out momentarily, and then led Kirisin and Angel back into the night. They moved swiftly toward the shadow of the surrounding trees, eager to gain their concealment, to blend into the darkness. In the distance, south toward the city, the buzz of activity had grown more pronounced. In the east, the sky was flooded with light from the sunrise.

Kirisin glanced back to where Tragen stood in the doorway watching after them. The big Elf waved halfheartedly, and the boy waved back.

But his thoughts were of Culph and Erisha and Ailie and his nagging certainty that everything he was trying to do—for the Elves, for the Ellcrys, for those with him, even for himself—was going wrong.

FOURTEEN

WITH SIMRALIN IN THE LEAD, the fugitives made their way clear of Arborlon, glancing back over their shoulders at every turn, scanning the trees and pathways of the city they were fleeing, watchful for signs of pursuit. For a time, those signs were everywhere—lights fading in and out of the buildings they slipped through, shouts and cries in the dawn's silent waking, voices in the distance, shadows in the trees, their fears and doubts heightened at every turn. Elves and demons both would be hunting them, and the odds of discovery were huge.

Even as the sounds diminished and the number of cottages dwindled, their fear of being caught trailed after them like their shadows. There was for Kirisin a pervasive sense of futility about their efforts. It was impossible that no one would catch them, that all efforts at finding them would fail. He waited for the movement or sound that would confirm this certainty. He knew his sister and Angel were waiting, too. No one talked; no one even looked at the others. All eyes swept the forest; all ears strained for the smallest sound. The Elven Trackers were too skilled and experienced to be fooled; the demons were too determined and relentless. One or the other would find them.

Yet somehow, neither did. Somehow, they got clear.

Eventually, they were climbing into the mountains, pushing deeper into the Cintra. The high passes were more difficult to navigate, and that was why Simralin was taking them there. She wanted to make it harder for those hunting them to discover their trail by choosing terrain that would hide best any evidence of their passing. Neither Kirisin nor Angel questioned her decision. Both understood that Simralin was the one they must rely on to get them safely away, the one who best knew how. Their primary objectives this day were to put distance between themselves and those who followed, and to hide any traces of their passing.

As their trek wore on, Kirisin found himself feeling marginally better. Although he knew it was coming, no evidence of immediate pursuit revealed itself. Perhaps the Elves and demons were still attempting to discover where they had gone. With luck, neither might have realized they had fled the city. Both might think they were still in hiding, waiting out the storm. Whatever they thought, they did not appear to be tracking them yet.

As well, movement seemed to help lessen the pain of what had happened to them in Ashenell. Even though he could still see Erisha's face in those last moments—confused, scared, and shocked by the knowledge of what was happening to her—the immediacy of her death had diminished and a determination to make it count for something had surfaced in its place. He could not bring his cousin back; he might not even be able to gain justice for her. But he could finish what together they had set out to do. He could find the Loden and use it to help the Ellcrys and the Elven people. Nothing of what had occurred, however dreadful, had done anything to cause him to rethink his commitment or his promise to the tree. He had lost three people he cared about and suffered a strange sense of violation as a result of their deaths, but those losses only increased his resolve.

They climbed into the mountains all morning, ascending until they were through the first of the passes and deep amid the highest peaks. The air was thin, and breathing came hard. It was cold, too, and Kirisin shivered inside his tightly wrapped travel cloak. All around him the sky was a clear, bright blue, and the brilliance of the light caused him to squint sharply as he walked. He felt the solitude of the rock and the earth close about him like a wall, but was not afraid.

He thought of his parents more than once, wishing he had been given a chance to say good-bye to them and to explain what he was doing and why. He thought of how relieved they would have been if he had been able to tell them what had happened. He worried that something bad would befall them because of this failing, that Arissen Belloruus would find a way to make them suffer for what he perceived to be their son's treachery.

Mostly, he thought about the King, who now, almost inescapably in the light of everything that had happened, seemed the demon that had hidden itself among them.

When they stopped at midday to consume a short lunch, he could contain himself no longer. "I just don't see how anyone but Erisha's father can be the one who's responsible for what's happened," he began all at once.

Angel shook her head. "I don't like it that he's so obviously the right choice. Ailie was right. Demons do everything they can to shift suspicion from themselves when they're working in secret. That's been their history since the beginning."

They were eating from a loaf of bread and a hunk of cheese and washing it down with Elven ale, sitting up on the rocks in the lee of an overhang that provided some shelter from the wind. Even so, their words were carried away almost as soon as they were spoken, and they had to lean close to one another to hear. Overhead, sparse clouds spun like great, frothy pinwheels, caught in the air currents generated by the peaks.

Kirisin shaded his eyes from the blinding orb of the sun. "But the King was the one who told Erisha not to pursue the Ellcrys's plea for help. He was the one who told me not to do anything or tell anyone until I heard from him, and then I never heard a word. He was the one who lied to me about what he and Erisha knew. Even when you and Ailie confronted him, he tried to cast doubt on what you claimed. He blocked every attempt to find the Elfstones."

"He also stood to gain from the deaths of Ailie and Erisha," Simralin added. She handed the aleskin to Kirisin, who drank deeply. "Sooner or later, he would have been placed in proximity to Ailie, and she would have exposed him if he was a demon. You said as much yourself, Angel. And killing Erisha gave him a way to blame us for what happened and force us to flee. Now he can hunt us down and kill us, and no one will do anything to stop him."

"Culph was probably killed because he discovered the truth," Kirisin continued. "He was still poking around in the histories, trying to find out something more about Elfstones. He probably got caught where he shouldn't have been."

"Arissen Belloruus hasn't been himself for some time now, but more so of late." Simralin took back the aleskin from her brother and passed it to Angel. "He was always high-strung and temperamental, but in recent weeks he has been especially edgy. Everyone could tell that something was bothering him."

They stopped talking and waited for the Knight of the Word to say something in response. Angel shrugged. She adjusted herself on the rocks, putting aside her food. "Demons live long lives. This one is probably very old and has been in place for a long time. It is a changeling, so it would have assumed various identities over the years, switching off one disguise for another when it became necessary or convenient to do so. It could have been an animal as easily as a human. Changeling demons can take the shape of any living creature. But this is what you should remember. The reason they make their choice of disguise is what matters. This demon was set in place to keep an eye on the Elves, to make certain they don't interfere in the affairs of humans, to keep them in their Cintra enclave until it's time to dispose of them for good."

The Elves stared at her in disbelief. "What do you mean, *dispose of them?*" Kirisin managed.

Angel paused, choosing her words carefully. "The demons and their kind have a very specific goal—to eliminate the human race. They are doing so in a variety of ways, but however they achieve it they want us all dead. When they finish with us, they will go to work on the Elves. They leave you alone for now because you don't present an immediate threat. I didn't even know you existed until Ailie told me. You are only a myth to humans. You work hard to keep it that way, mostly by staying apart, staying hidden. That serves the purposes of the demons exactly. By the time they come for you—which they will—there won't be any humans left to take your part. You will be on your own, and you will be overrun and destroyed. Every last one of you."

Kirisin looked as if he had been struck a physical blow. "They want to kill us all?"

Angel nodded. "The Void's path is one of destruction."

"Is this the destruction the Ellcrys was warning us about?" the boy pressed. He was trying to make sense of what he was hearing, but its implications were so overwhelming that he could not. "The end of the world she says is coming?"

"I don't know." Angel resumed eating, her face maddeningly calm given the pronouncement she had just made. "Destruction comes from any number of sources and in any number of ways, and it is hard to know which form the one that finishes us will take. The Knights of the Word have struggled long and hard just to contain the demons and their armies of once-men. But we lack the ability to see far enough ahead to know what most to fear." She bit off a chunk of bread and chewed. "It takes every ounce of energy we have just to try to keep alive those the demons hunt."

"And now they hunt us," Simralin said quietly.

Angel Perez smiled bleakly. "Now they hunt us." She paused, her expression changing suddenly. She pointed down the slopes of the mountain. "In fact, they hunt us even now."

Kirisin felt himself go cold as he looked to where she was pointing, somewhere off in the heavy forests of the lower slopes. But he saw nothing. Simralin, however, was on her feet. "Movement," she acknowledged. "You have good eyes, Angel. We must go at once."

They set out anew, working their way ahead through the peaks, still traveling east. Their progress was steady, and the long sweep of the western forests soon disappeared from view behind them as they began their descent of the eastern slopes. Ahead lay miles and miles of high desert—the trees sparse, the soil a mix of volcanic emission and dust, and the land arid and barren. If they were forced to travel through it, the going would be difficult. There would be little to eat or drink, and little cover.

They walked until the eastern sky turned dark and twilight began to settle in across the mountains, the shadows lengthening and the air cooling enough that they could see their breath. They were close to the edge of the mountain range, but still high up on the slopes and far from the desert flats. Behind them, nothing moved against the wall of the mountains. Neither Simralin nor Angel had said another word about their pursuers, so finally Kirisin asked.

"It might be that they have turned another way or stopped in the cradle of the peaks for the night," his sister suggested when he asked her of the danger. She smiled. "Don't worry, Little K. I won't let anything happen to you."

He wished she wouldn't make it sound as if he were so needy, as if he were still just a boy and not capable of looking after himself. But he held his tongue. Sim was only trying to reassure him that he wasn't alone in this. She was just being his big sister.

It was almost dark when they finally stopped on her signal. She stood looking back up the slopes of the mountains behind them, searching for movement, for an indicator that there might be pursuit. Kirisin sat down heavily, his legs and back aching, his stamina sapped. He felt drained, both physically and emotionally. For all that he knew he could take care of himself, it had been awhile since he had been forced to do so and longer still since he had made so demanding a trek. A trek, he reminded himself, he was just beginning.

Angel walked over and crouched down so that they were at eye level. "I think we have gone as far as we can without knowing something more about where we need to go." Her dark eyes held his. "Can you make your Elfstones reveal where the Loden is concealed?"

Simralin looked over at them. "She's right. We need to figure out how the Stones work. Do you have any ideas? Did the histories or Culph tell you anything that would help?"

Kirisin shook his head doubtfully. He didn't know anything, of course. All his energy and attention had been directed at finding the blue Elfstones. He had given little thought to what would happen once that goal was achieved.

"I guess I can try," he said.

He reached down into his pocket and extracted the Elfstone pouch, loosened the drawstrings, and spilled the contents into his hand. It was the first time he had looked at the Stones since he had come into possession of them. Three identical gems, cut to the same shape and size, glowing a bright blue, they glimmered softly in the failing light. With the other two peering over his shoulder, Kirisin studied them intently, drawn by their rich color and almost transparent quality.

What to do? He held the stones out in the palm of his hand, where all three companions could admire and consider them. But looking at them did nothing to alleviate his confusion. He glanced at the others, and then closed the stones away in his fist. He tried squeezing them, then rolling them between both palms, and finally jiggling them softly in the cup of his hand. The Elfstones did nothing. He tried casting them on the ground, rolling them as he might a set of dice. Nothing happened. He tossed them and caught them. Nothing. He tried using them one at a time. Still nothing.

"I don't know what else to do," he admitted finally.

"Keep trying," Simralin urged.

"I don't know anything about Elven magic," Angel said quietly, "but with the Word's magic it is first necessary to visualize what it is that you want to happen."

Kirisin looked at her, thinking about how that might work.

"We want them to show you how to find the Loden," Simralin cut in. Her eyes continued to scan the mountainside, which was very nearly dark now with the westward passing of the sun. "Try picturing that."

"But I don't know what the Loden looks like."

"Maybe all you need to do is to imagine the Elfstones showing you the way to where the Loden is hidden," Angel suggested. "Maybe knowing exactly what it looks like isn't important. There must be a great many things that someone using these Stones wouldn't have seen before."

"She's right," Simralin interjected quickly. "They're seeking-Stones. They should be able to find anything you can put a name or a face to. Just try."

"But what am I . . . ?"

"Try." Angel added emphasis to the word. "I don't want to frighten you, Kirisin, but we don't have much time. I just caught another glimpse of whatever follows us coming out of the pass and across the open slopes."

Kirisin glanced westward into the mountains despite himself, a chill running down his spine. He wanted to ask what their pursuer looked like, but knew it could not appear as more than shadowy movement from this distance. *Demon or Elven Hunter?* He glanced down at his fist and brushed at his mop of dark hair in frustration, wishing he understood even a little of the skills necessary to what he was trying to do. But no one had held a set of Elfstones in thousands of years, so there wasn't much point in wishing for help of any sort. Someone had to learn the process anew, and it looked like it was going to be him.

He thought about it a moment more, his brow furrowed, the Elfstones clutched tightly. *Picture what it is you are looking for. Put a name to it.* How difficult could that be?

He held out his hand and closed his eyes. His concentration locked down on what it was he wanted the Elfstones to do. *Show me where the Loden is hidden. Show me how to find it.* He pictured the three of them traveling toward another Elfstone, one that glowed as brightly and deeply as these, one just as perfectly formed. He gave it a color, and then changed it several times. He imagined the forest and the mountains giving way before them. He imagined darkness and mist falling back before sunlight.

His hand tightened further.

Suddenly he felt something change, a shift that he could not put a name to. Then he heard a sharp intake of breath from one of the women.

His eyes snapped open.

His entire fist was bathed in a deep blue glow. He almost dropped the Elfstones in shock, but managed to keep from doing so by reassuring himself that the glow wasn't hurting, that his hand felt all right, that this was what was supposed to happen.

In the next instant, a shaft of blue light exploded from his fist and lanced away into the darkness north, cutting through everything that lay in its path—through trees and mountains and earth, just as he had imagined it would—dissolving away all obstacles to stretch into a distance that he could not begin to measure. From the speed it maintained and the ground it covered, it seemed a long way, a vast reach through the night to a singular peak that rose in snowcapped magnificence against a clouded sky. The light found the peak, held it momentarily, and then moved high up onto its slopes and into caverns that were studded with stalactites dripping with moisture and brightened only faintly by phosphorescence glowing in bright streaks along their walls. The light held this vision for a long moment, flared once as if to punctuate the importance of its revelation, and then went dark.

Kirisin had held his ground through all of this, but now took a step back, nearly falling over in the aftershock of what he had witnessed. Simralin caught his arm, steadying him as she did so.

"That wasn't so hard, was it?" he gasped, swallowing.

"Did you see that mountain, Little K?" his sister whispered.

He nodded. "I saw. A mountain with some caves. A long way off, I think."

She grinned, sharing her pleasure with him. "Not so far. I know that mountain. I know where it is and how to get there."

"Then maybe it would be a good idea if we got started," Angel suggested, nodding toward the darkness of the Cintra and whatever was tracking them.

Without waiting for their response, she shouldered her pack and started away, moving north.

Kirisin dumped the Elfstones back into the pouch and shoved the pouch into his pocket. "You know that mountain?" he asked Simralin, falling into step beside her as she moved after Angel.

His sister glanced over. "You know it, too, even though you've never been there. That's the mountain where Father and Mother wanted to establish the new community of Cintra Elves before Arissen Belloruus rejected the idea." She smiled broadly and reached out to squeeze his shoulder affectionately. "That's Syrring Rise, the mountain our parents called Paradise."

HIGH ON THE SLOPES above them, lost in the darkness of the thinning forest line, the demon put its hand on Delloreen to stop her forward progress. She responded immediately, a shiver running through her. Once, had anyone or anything touched her, she would have responded much differently. But this one knew how to touch her in a way that gave her such pleasure, even in the smallest brushing of clawed fingers, that it made her instantly want more. Already it had taught her more about pleasure than she had imagined it was possible to learn.

"Not too quickly, pretty thing," her demon whispered in that rough, soothing voice. "Let them go on a bit before we follow. Let them be."

She did not want to let them be. She did not want to waste another moment tracking them. She wanted to catch up to them and tear them apart, especially the female Elf who had taken her eye. The knife had blinded her; she would never see again out of her right side. It had been luck, nothing more, but it was done and her sight was gone. Her rage would not be quenched until she had tasted the Elf's warm blood.

"Does it hurt still?" the other asked her softly.

One hand came down to stroke her scaly head, lingering near but not touching the wound. The hand that had extracted the blade and stanched the flow of blood and taken away most of the pain, she thought absently, reveling in its feel. The hand that gave her such pleasure when it touched her.

"You are so eager to kill her, aren't you?" the other said. "But now is not the time. Everything is happening as I intended it should. We have them fleeing the safety of the Cintra. We have them alone and cut off from any help. We have them responding to the incentives we have given them. All we need do is be patient. When it is time, you may kill them all."

Delloreen's growl was a mingled hiss and purr. She showed her teeth and panted softly.

"Lead us down into the trees," it instructed her. "We will make our bed there for the night. We will rest and resume tracking when it is light. Their trail will be easy to follow. Their scent will be unmistakable. But we will stay safely behind them and out of sight."

Delloreen accepted this. She knew that they could not escape her—that once she set her mind to it, nothing ever escaped her. But the urge to kill was strong, and she felt itchy and restless within her scaly body.

She looked up into the eyes of her companion and let it see her need clearly. The other demon nodded.

"Go, then. Do what you must. There will be other prey for you besides our little Elves and the Knight. Take what you need elsewhere, but leave them be for now." It bent down and kissed Delloreen on the muzzle. "Go, but come back soon."

Her blood was hot with expectation and her body taut with the thrill of the hunt as she bounded away into the night.

FIFTEEN

SQUIRREL'S FAMILY buried him at dawn.

They were all awake by then, perhaps because they were no longer safely tucked away in their Pioneer Square home, perhaps because they were already anticipating the uncertainty of the journey that lay ahead. It was barely light, the sunrise still little more than a faint brightening on the eastern horizon, its glow muted by a heavy screen of smoke and ash blown south from the city. Glimmerings of the fires dying out on the docks and in the adjacent buildings could still be seen against the fading darkness. North, a single star was all that remained, a tiny pinprick of light that seemed to have lost its way.

Logan Tom had risen before the rest and was standing by himself on the crest of the hilltop where they had made their camp when Owl rolled up in her wheelchair.

"We have to bury the boy," he told her. "It isn't safe to keep him with us another day."

She knew what he meant. Too many diseases; too many ways to infect the others. There wasn't any choice, no matter how you felt about it. "We can bury him here, beneath this spruce," she said, pointing to a majestic old growth that the wilt and sickness had not yet killed and stripped of life. "He would like sleeping here, I think. Will you help us dig the grave?"

He put down his black staff and retrieved a couple of shovels from the AV while the others were still rising and dressing. Then Bear joined him, big and strong and silent as they worked together to make the hole deep enough to keep the carrion away. Fixit and Chalk wandered over, as well, but there weren't any more shovels, so there wasn't much they could do to help. Chalk sat down with a board and began to scratch something on it. Fixit stood watching with Sparrow.

Panther was staring at the boy inside the Lightning. The boy tried to pretend he didn't care, but Logan could read the uneasiness in the shift of his body as Panther walked from one side to the other, stone-faced.

When the hole was more than four feet deep, Owl called the others over. Bear retrieved Squirrel's body, wrapped it in a blanket, and carried it over. Gently, with help from Sparrow and River, he lowered it into the grave and stepped away. Candle was already crying. Panther kept looking back at the kid in the AV.

"Squirrel was a good little boy," Owl declared, her voice strong as she faced the others from the head of the grave. "He did what he was told and he almost never complained. He was curious about things, and he was always asking questions of us. He never hurt anyone. I think he was maybe ten years old, but none of us knows for sure."

She thought a minute. "He liked books. He liked to be read to."

"Wait a minute," Sparrow said suddenly.

She turned and ran over to the cart that held their belongings, rooted through the jumbled contents for a moment, and then hurried back. When she reached them, Logan could see that she was carrying a storybook. She scrambled down into the grave and laid it on his chest. There were tears on her cheeks when she climbed out again.

"It was his favorite," she said without looking at anyone in particular. "It belongs with him."

There were a few murmured assents. Owl nodded. "He may need something to read on his journey. Even if he can't read all the words, he knows them by heart. We will miss him."

Sparrow turned away and looked off toward the sunrise. The sky east was washed a dull yellow through the haze of smoke and mist, and the world beyond seemed impossibly distant.

"I want him back," Candle said quietly.

"Me, too, sweetie." Owl bit her lip. "But maybe he's happier where he is."

She reached down for a handful of loose earth and tossed it into the grave. Logan took that as a signal to finish, and he began shoveling earth over the small body. Bear stared down into the grave for a long time without moving, but finally he began to shovel, as well. Most of the Ghosts could only stand to watch for a few moments before walking away. Chalk stayed long enough to shove one end of the board he had been scratching on into the loose earth. Squirrel's name was written on it.

Logan was patting the last of the earth into place over the grave when he caught sight of Panther trying to open the door of the AV. The handle would not budge, and he was yanking on it in fury. Logan put down the shovel, picked up his staff, and walked over to stand beside the boy.

"It's locked," he said.

Panther wheeled on him. "What?"

Logan gestured toward the door. "It's locked. You can't open it."

"Then you open it, Mr. Knight of whatever you spose to be! You open it!" The boy's dark face flushed with mingled rage and sorrow, and his hands knotted into fists. "You open it, and then you give me two minutes with that scum inside and see what I can do with *this*!"

He reached into his pocket and brought out a wicked-looking switchblade that opened with an audible *snick* that brought several heads around at once. The blade gleamed in the fresh sunlight, clean and smooth and deadly.

"I'm not going to do that," Logan told him.

"Panther!" Owl shouted, anger etching the sound of the boy's name as she wheeled toward him. "You put that away!"

Panther ignored her, his eyes on Logan. "Don't mess with me. This ain't none of your business, ain't none of your concern. This is about the Ghosts. You open that door!"

Logan shook his head. "Nope."

For just a second, he thought Panther was going to try him. The knife came forward a few inches, the boy's grip tightening. But there were others shouting at him, as well, by now. Bear was almost on top of them, and Owl was right behind him, her features twisted with rage.

Panther stepped back suddenly and shrugged. "Hey, fine. Don't open it. But you can't be watching him all the time. Sooner or later, I'll be doing what you should let me be doing right now!" He closed the blade and slipped the knife back in his pocket. "Hey, what's all this?" he asked, looking around in disbelief, holding out his hands to Owl and Bear, who were bearing down on him. "I was just showin' him, that's all. Just lettin' him see!"

He grinned disarmingly and walked away, whistling. He gave the boy in the Lightning a hard look as he passed, but only Logan saw it clearly.

With Panther's retreat, Bear turned aside, but Owl continued coming until she reached him. "What was that about? What happened?"

Logan inclined his head toward the Lightning. "That boy is going to cause problems if we keep him around."

She looked over at their prisoner. "He isn't a threat to anyone. Look at him. He must be scared."

He stopped her arm as she reached for the door handle. "Don't go in there. Listen to me. We can't keep him with us. Panther hates him. Some of the others probably do, too. You're just inviting trouble."

Her arm dropped away as she swiveled back around so that she was facing him. "He didn't mean to kill Squirrel. I saw what happened. It was an accident. We can't go on blaming everyone for bad things, no matter what sort of . . ." She stopped and shook her head. "We have to learn how to forgive again." She gestured toward the other Ghosts. "*They* have to learn."

"I'm not arguing about what happened or how it should be handled. I'm just telling you we can't bring that boy with us."

She looked away. "I won't put him out until he is well enough to look after himself. Otherwise, it would be just like killing him."

He didn't like the idea, but he knew he couldn't push her any farther. "All right. Another day. No more."

She nodded, saying nothing.

He knelt beside her. "Something else. I had a vision last night, a dream. The Lady came to me. She told me Hawk was safe."

She stared at him in surprise. "Are you sure?"

"She said magic saved him. She said he would come north to find us, but we must travel south to find him. She said he would meet us on the banks of the Columbia. What is that? Is it a river? I haven't heard the name before."

Owl nodded. "It's south of here. I don't know how far. I've never been there. I've only read about it in books." She paused. "It could be more than a hundred miles away."

He thought about it a moment. He looked over at the Lightning and the shopping cart attached to the back of it. Then he looked at the Ghosts, scattered about the campsite, most of them now waiting for someone to tell them what to do.

It could be more than a hundred miles. Not too far if he were traveling alone in the AV. Much too far for a shopping cart and a bunch of kids who would mostly have to walk it.

"We need to find a faster way to travel," he said.

*   *   *

THEY ATE BREAKFAST, Logan dividing up portions from their meager supplies, realizing already that they didn't have enough to last the week. Too many mouths to feed for the distance they needed to travel. They would have to forage somewhere along the way for both food and water.

While the others ate, Owl fed the boy chained inside the AV—Bear keeping close watch—and River trickled a little water down the throat of the semi-conscious Weatherman. Afterward, Logan checked the bindings on the old man and the shackles on the sullen boy, did a quick survey of the loads strapped onto the AV and the shopping cart, informed Owl and Candle that they would be riding with him, and prepared to set out.

"I spose you get to ride the whole way, Mr. Knight?" Panther sneered at him. "We walk, you drive?"

"Panther, stop it!" Owl admonished.

"I'm the only one who knows how to drive her right now," Logan answered him. "If one of you was to learn how it's done, you could help me. Interested?"

Panther hesitated, and then shook his head. "Naw. I'm just asking. I don't want nothin' to do with it."

"I do!" Fixit said at once.

Logan nodded. "Good, Fixit. We'll start your lessons right away. Climb aboard." He winked over his shoulder at Owl. "Let's go."

They set out at midmorning, the day bright and sunny but hazier than usual, a combination of smoke and ash from the dock fires and the general pollution of the air. As they made their way down off the bluff along the service road and onto the freeway, Logan could hear the steady beating of the invasion force drums overlying the sharp *snap* and *pop* of automatic weapons fire. The fighting was still going on in the streets. When it was over, things would quiet down while the demons and once-men began staging the siege of the Safeco Field compound. A few days later, the real madness would begin.

He thought about the doomed people trapped there, but only for a moment. They weren't the first and they wouldn't be the last. He couldn't save them all, no matter how much he might want to try. He would be lucky to save the few he had managed to take with him in his flight. He would be lucky to save himself.

Their progress was slow, though steady. He drove the big machine at a crawl to allow those afoot to keep pace. Fixit rode next to him, watching what he did, asking questions constantly and paying close attention to the answers. At one point the boy said he thought he was ready to try driving the AV, but Logan shook his head. Better if he waited another day, gave himself some time to think about everything. Fixit looked disappointed, but he didn't object. He just settled back in the seat, watched Logan some more, and then began asking about the vehicle's weapons systems. Logan hesitated, debating the matter, and then told him about the cannons and missile launchers, which were locked down anyway, but kept to himself what he knew about the laser trackers and shields.

Behind them, Owl talked to the boy who had shot Squirrel, telling him about the Ghosts, asking him questions about himself, trying to draw him out. It didn't seem to be working. The boy slouched down in the rear seat and looked out the window and never said a word. Now and then he was forced to look at her when Panther dropped back to walk next to the AV, his eyes on the boy, a half smile on his dark face. Logan could see the fear in the boy's eyes; he knew what Panther had planned for him. Owl tried to motion Panther away from the AV, but even when he moved off, it was only for a while and only to return to walk next to the window and the boy, the same look on his face.

They continued on through midday at a slow, almost desultory pace. Logan allowed them to stop for lunch but did not plan to stop again until nightfall. The walkers shared bottled water slung on straps across their shoulders and energy bars he had salvaged from some warehouse in the Chicago area several months back. He had a case of the bars, but with this many sharing them it would be empty in a week. He wished he had been given a better opportunity to stock up on supplies before leaving the city. The Ghosts hadn't brought much, either, concentrating on hard-to-find items like purification tablets and medicines along with their clothes and bedding. They were a ragtag bunch for sure, he thought, and not likely to find themselves better off anytime soon.

Candle rode up front with Logan when they set out again, her intense gaze focused ahead, her blue eyes filled with hidden knowledge. He remembered that she experienced premonitions, that she saw things that foretold the future and warned of danger, things hidden from the others. She was their guide dog through dark places.

He remembered, too, how she had defended him to the others.

Once or twice, he caught her looking at him out of the corner of her eye, but he let her think he didn't notice. She was still taking his measure, deciding how she really felt about him, how far she wanted to trust him. He was a part of the outside world, and for a girl of ten years who had seen so much darkness and experienced so much doubt and fear, there was a great deal of which to be wary.

At one point, she asked, "Do you think we'll see Hawk soon?" She gave him a quick look as she did so.

"I don't know," he answered, cocking one eyebrow. "I would feel better about things if we did."

"Hawk belongs with us."

He maneuvered the Lightning past a downed utility pole. "The Ghosts are a family. Isn't that right?"

She nodded. "Hawk will lead us to the Promised Land." She did not look at him this time. "Owl tells the story better than me." She hesitated. "Do you believe that?"

He smiled despite himself, thinking of Two Bears and the Lady and the destiny of the gypsy morph. "As a matter of fact, I do," he said.

He saw her smile back. That was all she said for a while, gone back inside herself, her gaze directed out the window to the gray landscape of the countryside.

And then, "Were you a street kid like us when you were little?" She was looking at him again, studying him closely this time. "Did you belong to a tribe?"

He shook his head. "I was a compound kid."

"What happened to you? Why did you leave the compound? Did they make you leave?"

"The compound was overrun and my family was killed. I escaped with a band of rebel freemen that managed to save a few of us. Their leader adopted me."

"Do you remember your real parents?" she asked.

"A little. Not very well anymore."

"I don't remember mine at all."

He thought about it. "Maybe that's okay."

Her head cocked slightly. "Why would you say that?"

"Because the dead belong in the past."

She didn't say anything for a long time, watching his face, her blue eyes intense. Then she said softly, "I don't think that's true."

"No? Why not?"

"Because they were our friends and they need to be remembered. Don't you want to be remembered by someone when you're dead?"

It seemed strange to hear this little girl talk like that; it seemed too grown-up for a ten-year-old. In any case, talking about the dead made him uncomfortable.

"Don't you?" she asked again.

He glanced over and shrugged. "I guess maybe I do."

She hunched her thin shoulders. "I know I do. I don't want everyone to forget about me."

It was nearing midafternoon, and they had covered almost twenty miles. They were well below the big airfield that stretched along the highway south of the city when they passed a huge industrial complex closed off by heavy chain-link fencing topped with razor wire. The fence and the wire reminded Logan of the slave camps, but the buildings beyond were of a different sort entirely and there was no sign of life anywhere. A service road branched off the highway and climbed an incline through a grove of withered spruce interspersed with ornamental stone to a pair of gates, which were chained and locked. A sign, faded and weather-stained, hung from the mesh:

ORONYX EXPERIMENTAL
Robotics Systems
Building for the future.

He glanced at it as they passed, his gaze continuing down the line of the fencing as it stretched along the highway and stopping suddenly at an equipment barn. He braked the AV, shut off the engine, and climbed out.

The Ghosts who were on foot wandered over. "What now?" Panther demanded. "You gonna let me drive?"

"You didn't want to earlier." Logan gestured toward the fence. "See those?" He was pointing to a series of metal haulers, flatbed units with oversize tires, trailer bars, and low rails that surrounded the bedding. "We could use one of those."

"We'll have to break in," Fixit declared, glancing back toward the chained, locked gates. "Spring the locks. Or maybe cut the wire."

Logan walked back to the AV, told Owl what he planned to do, and then lifted her out of the vehicle and into her wheelchair, where Candle promptly took up watch. He unlocked the boy chained in the backseat, led him over to the shopping cart, and chained him anew through the wheel spokes. He put Chalk on watch and told him to make sure nothing happened while his back was turned, that he was responsible. Then he went around to the storage compartments at the rear of the vehicle, unlocked the one on the driver's side, reached inside, and brought out a pair of heavy cutting shears and two black-barreled Parkhan Sprays. He carried his load around to the front of the Lightning where the others were standing.

"Whoa, that's some Freak-size firepower," Panther hissed, eyes wide as he caught sight of the Sprays. "You know how to use those without shootin' off your foot?"

Logan shrugged. "The question is, do you? These aren't for me. I need someone to go in with me, cover my back."

"Hey, you and me, like before," Panther declared.

"Take me instead," Sparrow suggested quickly, stepping forward. "I know how to use those better than Panther Puss." She gave him a smirk.

"Hey, me and him already worked together," Panther snapped at her. "He ain't done nothin' with you—don't know nothin' about you. You just a little bird, all feathers and squeak."

Sparrow stomped up to him. "Who saved your worthless baby butt back in Pioneer Square, Panther Pee? You think you got away from those Croaks all by your cat-brained little self? You remember back that far, all the way to last night?"

"Wasn't you saved me, beak breath! Was me saved you! You had an ounce of—"

Logan felt his patience begin to slip. He had no time for this. "I'll take you both," he interrupted, tossing each a Parkhan Spray. He was gratified to see Panther stagger slightly as he caught his. Sparrow snatched hers out of the air smoothly, swung the barrel into position, and released the safety, all without missing a beat. She snapped the safety into place again and grinned at Panther.

Logan gave the cutting shears to Bear. "Make a hole big enough to let us through. When we're inside, widen it so that we can pull one of those haulers back out. It might take you some time, but keep at it."

Bear nodded, saying nothing as he walked over to the fence and went to work. Logan turned to the rest. "Stay here. Stay together. Keep your eyes open. No one wanders off. If there is any kind of danger, get inside the Lightning, all of you. It won't be comfortable, but it will be safe."

He took Fixit over to the driver's side, showed him the security buttons, and told him what they did. By the time he had completed his explanation and had the boy repeat it back to him, Bear had finished cutting open the fence. With Panther and Sparrow in tow, he stepped through the ragged opening and onto the concrete apron beyond.

"Stay behind me and stay close," he told them, glancing over his shoulder. "Don't shoot each other."

He couldn't have said why he was being so careful about an empty storage facility except that he was bothered by the fact that apparently no one had tried to break into the complex and take one of these haulers before. It was the sort of vehicle that almost anyone would have a use for, including the compounds. Yet here a dozen sat, untouched.

He tightened his grip on the black staff of his office and started forward.

SIXTEEN

THE DISTANCE FROM the fence to where the haulers were lined up like obedient pack animals was less than a hundred yards, but it felt much longer as Logan walked it. The buildings behind and to either side were low, squat, windowless structures with metal roofs and siding. Doors on rollers stood closed, but he could not see any locks. The apron was surprisingly empty of debris, a condition that was almost nonexistent anywhere else in the country. Even more troublesome was the clean, polished look of the haulers, which lacked any hint of rust or dirt and had the appearance of newly minted machines. Even though the complex seemed to be deserted, the pristine look of the haulers suggested that someone had been caring for them.

Logan looked around uneasily. "Hello!" he called out. "Anyone here?"

No one appeared. Nothing moved.

He glanced back the way he had come. The Ghosts were out of the Lightning and crowded up against the fence, faces pressed into the mesh. Bear was the only one not watching, his attention given over to widening the opening through which they had come. In the silence of the fading afternoon light, Logan could hear the dull *snip-snip* of the heavy cutters.

He was all the way up to the closest of the haulers when he caught sight of the sensors. Partially embedded in the surface of the apron, they were spaced strategically around the perimeter of the painted oval inside which the machines were parked. No lights flashed on their casings; no beeps sounded from within. He stopped Panther and Sparrow from advancing, pointed to the sensors, walked forward a few steps, and knelt down for a closer look. The sensors lacked any sort of recognizable features—no antennas, no scanners, no identifying protrusions of any sort. They ringed the haulers, but weren't connected visibly to one another or to anything else. There was nothing to suggest they were even working.

Yet he had the unshakable feeling that they were.

What to do?

His choices were limited. He could not deactivate the sensors without knowing something more about them. So he could either test whether or not they were active, knowing that if they were he might not be too happy with the results, or he could turn around and go back the way he had come and forget about going any farther with this. He could not help thinking that if he were alone, none of this would be happening. He was here, taking this chance, only because he had taken in a bunch of street kids who needed hauling.

He pushed the thought away. After all, they hadn't asked for any of this, either.

He took another long look around the complex, searching for something that would tell him what to do, and didn't find it. A quick glance over his shoulder revealed that Bear had finished cutting an opening in the fence, high and wide enough to permit them to pull a hauler through. Haulers were big, but easy enough to move by hand when they were unloaded. With Panther's help, he should be able to pull one of these clear.

All he had to do was walk up to it. Through the sensors, past the alarms, and into whatever waited.

He tightened his grip on his staff of office, feeling the heat of the magic beginning to build. He wasn't afraid, but he was cautious. For himself and for the children with him. Street kids were still kids. The haulers sat in front of him, lined up and ready. Why would there be any serious protection set in place for haulers, anyway? They had no real value, nothing that warranted firepower of the sort that the compounds employed.

Yet no one had touched these.

He made up his mind. He turned around abruptly and motioned for Panther and Sparrow to back away. "I don't like how this feels. We're leaving."

"Leaving?" Panther stared at him with dark, angry eyes. He gestured toward the sensors. "Because of those?"

"You heard!" snapped Sparrow, already walking away.

Panther was shaking his head in disgust and turning after her when something caught his eye—something that Logan had missed entirely or maybe didn't even exist. But it was enough to trigger an immediate response in the boy, who wheeled back and fired a sustained burst from the Parkhan Spray that peppered the haulers and blew several of the sensors that sat closest into scrap.

No! Logan thought, eyes sweeping the concrete apron. Panels concealed in the flat surface were already sliding open, and the remaining sensors were dropping from sight. Huge doors set into the walls of the buildings to either side of the haulers, their weight balanced on huge steel rollers, opened like hungry mouths, and from the darkness within there was a whirring of motors and the soft, ominous *click* of gears engaging.

"Get out!" Logan shouted at his young companions.

But Panther couldn't seem to move, frozen in place, perhaps stunned by his own reaction, perhaps simply caught up in the moment. Sparrow was shouting at him. From somewhere back behind the severed links of the fence, the other Ghosts were crying out in either dismay or support, it was impossible to tell which. But Panther didn't seem to hear any of them, his eyes fixed on the black holes that had opened in the sides of the buildings.

An instant later, a clutch of metal-legged machines skittered into the daylight, heavy and squat. They had the look of monstrous insects, their bodies supported on multiple legs, their heads studded with orbs that pulsed and glowed, weapons jutting like mandibles from their jaws. There were five of them, all of a size that suggested they were meant to repulse anything short of a nuclear strike that might try to invade the complex.

No hauler was worth this, Logan thought. Not that a response like this had anything to do with haulers. This had to do with something of far greater importance, something that Oronyx Experimental had been working on when the end came. The human workers might be gone, but the guard machines they had built to defend their efforts remained in place, programmed to repel any invasion.

He rushed over to Panther, seized his shoulders, and spun him about. "Run!" he shouted in his face, shoving him toward the fence.

Then the heat of the lasers began to scorch the concrete apron, thin red beams slicing past him. He wheeled back in response, hands gripping the black staff, and sent a burst of the Word's white magic into the closest of the attackers. It cut the legs out from under the machine and caused it to stumble into another so that both went down. But they were slowed only for a moment before righting themselves and continuing their advance. Logan backed away hurriedly. The machines were big and looked ponderous, but they moved quickly and smoothly. They were meant to survive enemies stronger than himself.

He glanced over his shoulder and saw Panther and Sparrow turn and fire their weapons at the approaching behemoths. "No!" he screamed at them. "Run!"

They were wasting their time. Their best chance was to get back outside the fence and hope that the machines were not programmed to advance beyond the boundaries of the complex. The Parkhan Spray was a formidable weapon, but not nearly enough to stop these monsters. Even his magic might not be enough.

He used it anyway, hammering at the insect-like machines with sustained bursts aimed at the joints of their crooked legs. He brought one down, its legs sufficiently damaged that it could not rise again. But the others kept coming and were nearly on top of him. He turned and ran hard, dodging the lasers that sought to cripple him. The machines were not concentrating on Panther and Sparrow, whom they had judged less dangerous. They were concentrating on him. His magic shielded him from the worst of the blasts that were scorching everything around him, but he could feel himself weakening from the effort. The chain-link fence was still a long way off, too far to be judged a sure thing.

Then an explosion right in front of him sent chunks of concrete flying into his face, and he went down in a tangle of arms and legs, his staff sliding out of reach.

Outside the fence, there was instant pandemonium. All the Ghosts began shouting at once, gesturing wildly, trying to bring the three trapped inside the fence to safety through a combination of sheer willpower and deafening sound. All of them pressed up against the mesh, gripping the metal links fiercely. Bear even tried to go through the gap until Owl's cry of dismay stopped him in his tracks.

For a few brief moments, all of them lost control.

All except Fixit.

*   *   *

FIXIT IS A BOY *who has always been good at finding ways of making things work. Mostly, such things are mechanical in nature. Machines of all sorts, big and small, whole or in component pieces, useful or pointless, taken apart or put together—it is all the same to him. If there is a possibility that he can make it work, he wants to know how. He can't explain what is so intriguing about machines; he can't even remember what initially triggered his interest in them. He only knows that he can't think of a time when working with machines hasn't been his favorite pastime.*

He is the middle child in a family of five, two older, two younger, both parents still alive and looking after them. They are living on a farm in eastern Washington, a run-down operation out in the middle of nowhere, their closest neighbors at least five miles away, the closest town at least twenty. They seldom see anyone except for the Strayhorns, the family up the road, whom they visit a couple of times a year and who visit them in turn about the same number. That is in the beginning, when he is still only four or five and just starting to take an interest in how things work. Shortly after that, the Strayhorns don't come anymore. His mother says they have moved away. His father begins carrying a shotgun everywhere he goes.

Fixit, as the middle child, has no identifiable place or purpose in the family. The older two work with their father, and the younger two are too young to do anything, twins of fourteen months. They don't live long anyway. They catch something, plague in all likelihood, the two of them sleeping together in a single bed or sharing a fenced-off play area, and they are dead in a week. He can't remember their names after a while; they aren't even real to him. Like so much of what is lost, they seem a fragment of a dream.

After they die, his parents start talking about moving somewhere else, although it is never clear exactly where they think they can go that will be any better. Fixit is seven by now and is immersed in his love of mechanics so thoroughly that he is already disappearing in plain sight. There simply isn't any reason for the others ever to wonder what he is doing; he is always doing the same thing. Because he is now the youngest, he is treated with a deference that his older siblings do not enjoy and is left pretty much alone. He is smart, and already he is reading old repair manuals and books on various types of engines. By the time he is nine, he has gained a reasonable understanding of solar power, and has begun work on a solar energy collector that can power the lone vehicle they possess but hasn't worked since the last of the storage cells gave out. He pays some attention to what is going on around him, but mostly he concentrates on his projects.

It's while he is testing the collector, having taken the casing out into the low hills and away from the house in case anything goes wrong, that one of the renegade militias operating as slavers finds his family, overpowers them, and takes them away. He would never have known that much if he hadn't seen the smoke from the burning buildings and come running in time to see the trucks disappearing into the distance.

For a few days, he doesn't know what he should do. He thinks vaguely of going after his parents and his siblings, but has no idea how to do that or even where to look. He stays out in the hills, working on the collector, the concentration the effort requires giving him an excuse not to think about what has happened to his family and what is likely to happen to him. Focused, intense, he completes his work and falls into a deep sleep. When he wakes, he straps the collector to his back and sets out, intending to reach the coast. He is discovered by a small caravan of families traveling out of the sun- and radiation-blasted heart of the Midwest to look for something better. The caravan could abandon him and go on—not needing another mouth to feed, not particularly interested in acquiring strays—save for the collector. Impressed by his extraordinary skill at only nine years of age, they decide to take Fixit along.

By the time they reach Seattle, he is ready to go his own way and leaves them in the middle of the night, slipping away along the waterfront. He is living in an abandoned machine shed when Bear discovers him several weeks later, dirty and ragged and starving, the collector in front of him like a shrine as he sits poring through sets of old manuals he has scavenged. Bear, uncertain what to do with him, nevertheless takes him to Hawk, who recognizes his value immediately and invites him into the family.

But he is still the middle child, even in his new family. He is appreciated when his skills are needed, but otherwise frequently ignored. It doesn't help that the others have already staked out positions in the pecking order—Hawk the leader, Bear and Panther the soldiers, Owl the voice of wisdom and reason, Candle the seer, Sparrow wild and unpredictable, and River mysterious. He is just an average boy, ordinary looking without much in the way of athletic ability or intelligence. They are strong and beautiful and smart, and he envies them all. Sure, he is the one who can fix things, but it is not an ability that generates much excitement. His propensities for wandering off and frequently forgetting what he is supposed to be doing don't help, either. They make him the butt of too many jokes. His place in the family is important, but he doesn't really feel valued for himself.

That changes with the coming of Chalk, a boy his own age and with his own set of problems, a boy even goofier at times than he is. They become fast friends immediately, and suddenly it doesn't matter so much that the rest frequently despair of them. They value and appreciate each other and occupy the solid middle ground of the family. Fixit with his mechanical skills and Chalk with his artistry are very different on the surface, yet much the same beneath.

But in that private place where even Chalk isn't allowed to go, Fixit still dreams of doing something that will make the others look at him differently. Something like Sparrow did in facing down and killing that mutant insect. Something so exciting and wonderful that they will never stop talking about it.

Something heroic and awe inspiring.
Just once.
At Oronyx Experimental, he gets his chance.

*   *   *

WHILE THE OTHERS scrambled frantically at the barrier of the chain-link fence, Fixit kept his head. He ran to the Lightning S-150 AV and keyed in the security code on the touch pad. He had watched Logan Tom set the code earlier and paid close attention to the sequence of numbers. His memory did not betray him, and the locks released. He slipped inside, flicked on the switches that would power up the engine, engaged the shift, and shot forward. The vibration of the vehicle throbbed through him like a shot of adrenaline, and he was grinning broadly as he wheeled toward the opening in the fence.

He knew what he had to do.

He caught a glimpse of Chalk's pale face, shocked beyond words, as he tore across the flats from the highway toward the fence. The Lightning hit a deep rut and nearly tore the steering wheel out of his hands as he bounced wildly to one side. For just an instant it occurred to him that this was a huge mistake, that he wasn't up to it, and then he was through the gap and rocketing toward the battle. Logan Tom was down, sprawled on the earth, his staff a dozen feet away as the machines closed on him. Sparrow and Panther had turned back and were firing the heavy Parkhan Sprays into their attackers, desperately trying to keep them at bay. But it was a futile effort; the machines were too well protected.

Fixit glanced down at the array of weapons buttons on the dash, just below the loran's bright lock-on screen, sorted through his memories of what they did, and chose two of four with red arrow symbols. He punched them in as he swung out and away from his friends to get clear of them, and a pair of dart missiles launched from the vehicle and into one of the machines, exploding with a blinding light and sending out a shock wave that rocked the AV and knocked Panther and Sparrow sprawling. Two of the machines disappeared. It caused the others to turn toward him, and he punched the second set of buttons. But this time nothing happened. Two were all that were loaded, he guessed, wishing he had asked a few more questions when he'd had the chance.

His grin tightened as the AV rocked and lurched through laser fire. *Oh, well. Too late now.*

He roared toward the machines, their lasers stabbing the concrete all around him and then the Lightning itself. He held the machine steady, his arms aching with the effort, and increased speed. He was on top of them in seconds, sideswiping the closest, crumpling several of its metal legs and crippling it. Then he was past them and tearing toward the hangars from which they had emerged. Not where he wanted to go. Were there more? He wheeled back, the AV skidding, tires shrieking. For just an instant, he thought he was going to lose control completely. Logan Tom was on his feet again, sprinting for his staff. He snatched it up and wheeled back in a single fluid motion. Blue fire exploded from the tip and rocked another of the machines. He was yelling at Panther and Sparrow.

Fixit charged the one that remained, throwing the levers to what he believed to be the heavy BRom charges, shells that could punch through concrete. But torch wire uncoiled instead, ripping free from the containing spools and wrapping the last attacker in yards of corrosive thread that burned the metal skin with white-hot intensity. In seconds the wire had eaten through, and the machine was lurching like a drunken animal.

Fixit reached Logan Tom and skidded to a halt. The Knight of the Word leapt for the passenger's door and threw himself into the machine. "Go!" he snapped, hands flying over the weapons panel. Fixit did as he was told, and the AV screeched toward the fence. Panther and Sparrow had already reached the barrier and were charging through, the other Ghosts crowding around in celebration. Fixit took the Lightning through right after them and jammed on the brakes at the highway's edge. He was breathing so hard that for a moment he just sat there, his hands on the wheel, his body shaking, his eyes staring straight ahead.

"You can let go now," Logan Tom told him, and reached over to help pry his fingers loose. The dark eyes met his own. "That was good work, Fixit."

Fixit nodded, and then grinned. "Thanks."

Logan nodded. "You might want to look in the backseat now."

When he did so, he found himself staring at the prone figure of the Weatherman, still strapped to his stretcher. Fixit took a deep breath. He hadn't even noticed that the old man was there.

The Weatherman's eyes were wide and staring. It didn't look as if he was breathing.

"Get out of the vehicle and join the others," Logan ordered, his voice strangely calm. "Go on, before they come over here. Hurry!"

Fixit did as he was told, his heart in his throat, his mouth dry as he opened the door and staggered away on legs that were unexpectedly weak. He got only a dozen yards before he was surrounded by the other Ghosts, who cheered and clapped and pounded him on the back, celebrating his daring rescue.

"That was so wonderful!" Sparrow declared, her grin huge.

"You got some iron in you, little man," said Panther. "Takes some hard edges to do what you did. Some tough stuff."

Only Owl seemed to realize what was wrong. Logan Tom caught her eye as she lagged behind the others, and she wheeled herself over to join him. Out of the corner of his eye, Fixit could see her peering inside the Lightning. He tried not to look, but he couldn't help himself. Logan Tom was bending over the old man, putting his ear on his chest, then close to his mouth. *Please*, Fixit prayed. *Don't let him die.*

"Hey, man, I'm talkin' to you!" Panther snapped, giving him a playful shove. "Least you can do is pay attention when someone's tellin' you how great you are. You saved us, you know? Frickin' Creepers! That's what they are, Creepers! Would have had us, if not for you."

Fixit gave him an awkward grin, and he shouted to demonstrate his euphoria. But when he looked again at the Lightning, Logan Tom was climbing out to stand beside Owl, and Owl was crying, and Fixit felt the last vestiges of his joy turn to ashes.

SEVENTEEN

FIXIT WAS DEVASTATED. He was in despair. Owl could see it in his face as she wheeled herself over to where he was still being congratulated for his daring rescue. He might want to believe that it wasn't his fault that River's grandfather was dead, but she could tell that he couldn't quite convince himself. She knew what he was thinking. If he hadn't been so quick. If he had just taken a moment to check. If he hadn't driven so wildly. If he had not become distracted.

If.

She wanted to talk to him, to reassure him that it wasn't his fault. But before she could reach him, Logan called out sharply.

"All of you! Get away from the fence! Get back over here by the Lightning! Now!"

Everyone looked at him in surprise, and then to where he was pointing. Dozens of tiny machines had emerged from out of the complex, machines of all shapes and looks. Like ants, they swarmed over the corpses of their fallen brethren, extruding tiny welders and tools.

Without pausing, they went to work on the larger machines, repairing or replacing the broken parts, slowly but surely putting them back together. Another dozen had come straight for the fence and were reattaching the damaged links. The entire concrete surface surrounding the haulers was alive with activity.

Panther snatched up his Parkhan Spray and swung the barrel toward the enclosure, but Logan shouted at him. "Leave it, Panther! We don't want to give them a reason to come out here. Let them do what they were programmed to do. Pack it up, and let's go."

Reluctantly, Panther turned away, muttering something about "Creepers." The Ghosts trotted back over to the AV and the shopping cart, where Logan assigned them their places. He put Candle in the front passenger's seat of the Lightning and River in back with her grandfather. He was heading for Owl when she waved him off. Instead she wheeled herself up to Fixit. "Would you push me for a while?" she asked him. "I need to be out in the open air."

Logan chained the boy with the ruined face to the shopping cart, told him he could walk for a while, put Bear next to him as guard, and ordered Panther to stay away. They set out within minutes, once more heading south, leaving Oronyx Experimental and its machines behind. They did not yet have the hauler they needed, but Logan told them not to worry. They would find something on the way, something not so heavily guarded.

The afternoon was waning, the sky losing its light and the shadows beginning to lengthen. There was an unusual chill to the normally sultry, stagnant air, but Owl didn't want to ask Fixit to bring her a sweater or blanket because she was afraid of losing him. She wanted to keep him close until she had said to him what she thought needed saying. She didn't speak to him right away, however. She let him push her in silence, let the tension drain away. It was late in the day. They would travel just far enough to make camp, and then they would stop for the night.

"Did you read about machines like those in any of your magazines, Fixit?" she said finally. "I didn't know such things existed."

He didn't reply. He just kept pushing her along at a steady, even pace. Perhaps he hadn't even heard her. She glanced ahead to where

Bear and Chalk walked next to the shopping cart and the chained boy. Ahead of them, the Lightning crawled down the highway like a big beetle. Panther was farther out, walking alone.

She glanced to either side without turning her head. Sparrow was walking behind her and to her left, staying just far enough back so as to not intrude, but close enough to come if called. That was Sparrow, she thought.

"I read something about it," Fixit said suddenly. "They were building computers that could think like humans and were programmed to perform one or two specific functions. But I never actually saw one before today."

"I wonder what else was in those buildings," she mused.

There was silence between them again for a time, only the crunch of the wheelchair running over gravel and debris intruding. Owl watched a hawk fly overhead and was reminded of why they were traveling south. She thought back for a moment to how things had been in Pioneer Square for all those years, when they had a home and the outside world hadn't yet intruded. She thought about how much she missed it.

"I wish it hadn't happened," Fixit said suddenly, the words so soft she almost missed hearing them.

"I know." She kept her eyes directed forward. "I wish we could change all the bad things that happen to us."

"I didn't mean for it to happen."

"I know."

"I didn't even think about him being back there." She could hear his voice break. "Why didn't I look? All I had to do was turn around. I would have seen him."

"You were trying to do something brave and dangerous," she said. "You were trying to save your friends. There wasn't time to stop and think about anything else." She looked at him now. "If you hadn't acted so quickly, they would be dead. All of them. The rest of us didn't know what to do. You did. You were the only one."

He glanced down at her, then up again quickly. "I should have looked."

"It is easy to second-guess yourself now," she said. "Now, when everything is quiet and peaceful and safe. But you did the best you could in the heat of the moment. I don't think anyone blames you for what happened to River's grandfather. Not even River."

"You don't know that. She won't even talk to me."

Owl took a deep breath. "Let me tell you something, Fixit. Something true. The Weatherman was very sick. He had the plague. He had a strain I couldn't treat, something I didn't have medicines for. It was a sickness he had suffered from before. River told us. This was just the latest incident. But this is what I haven't told anyone until now. He was going to die. He was getting weaker, and I couldn't do anything about it. He was already almost gone."

There was a long silence from behind her. She waited patiently. "You're just saying that to make me feel better," the boy said.

"Yes, I am saying it to make you feel better," she admitted. "But it's also the truth."

It wasn't the truth, of course. It was a white lie. River's grandfather might have gotten better, might have recovered. No one could be sure. But she didn't think so. She hadn't seen anything to indicate he would. And no one could know for sure whether anything that Fixit had done while driving the AV had contributed to the old man's death. For all they knew, he might have already been dead and no one had noticed. Death in their world was like that: it claimed those around you like a wind gathering fallen leaves, and you didn't even notice right away that they were gone.

"Did he make any sounds while you were driving?" she asked.

"I don't know."

"Did you hear anything?"

Silence. "I guess not."

She let him think about it for a moment, then said, "You saved three lives. Three very important lives. If we had lost those lives, we might ourselves be lost. We probably couldn't complete this journey, our search for Hawk and Tessa, without those three to help us."

She didn't say anything more, nor did he, and they passed down the highway behind the AV and the shopping cart like sheep to a pasture as the sun faded into the west. By twilight, they had reached a wayside park where they could pull off and take cover in the trees, back where there was a shelter and fireplace and a few weathered old benches. As soon as they were stopped, Logan set about digging a grave farther back in the small stretch of forest. Bear and Panther were lending a hand when Fixit walked over to ask if he could help, too. Panther looked at him, and then gave up his shovel wordlessly and walked over to where Owl was unpacking the supplies that would provide them their dinner.

"That old man would have died anyway," he said without preamble.

"You and I know that, but Fixit isn't sure," she replied, looking up from her work. Sparrow, who was helping her unpack, didn't look up at all.

"Don't make sense, him blaming himself for this. He did what needed doing or we'd be dead, right, Sparrow?"

"You tell him that, Panther Puss," she said.

"Fixit ain't got nothin' to be sorry for."

"Tell him that, too."

Owl smiled at the boy. "He needs to hear it from all of us. He needs to hear it enough times that he'll start to believe it."

Half an hour later, they buried the Weatherman, the darkness nearly complete, the soft glow of a cloud-shrouded moon providing their only light. They gathered about his grave in a tight knot, and one by one they spoke about him.

"He was a strange old guy," Bear declared in his slow, meticulous way. He shifted his big frame from foot to foot, uneasy at having to speak. But Owl had asked them all to say something, and Owl was their mother. Bear cleared his throat. "He wasn't always easy to understand. But he was kind and never did anything to us. He was always looking out for us, even when we didn't know it. Hawk said so. We'll miss him."

"The Weatherman always told us when to watch out for things," Sparrow added. "He was good about that, even if we didn't always understand him. If he was a kid, we would have made him a Ghost."

"Say what you want about that old man," Panther declared, after thinking about it a moment. "Say what you want, but then remember that he gave us River, and she's special."

It was so unexpected that for a moment no one else said anything. They just stood there in the shadows, looking at Panther.

"What?" Panther said finally, his face turning darker than usual. "I'm just sayin' what's so!"

"The Weatherman was our friend," said Chalk, and after pausing for a moment couldn't seem to think of anything else. He cleared his throat, glanced around at the others, and shrugged. "He was our friend," he repeated. "Always."

Then it was Fixit's turn. The boy stood there, looking at the ground, his body stiff and tight with emotion. He shook his head. "I don't know what to say," he whispered.

"I do."

River walked over to him and put her arm around him. "My grandfather was a good man, and he lived a good life. It wasn't always easy, but mostly. He liked all of you; he told me so. He got to come with you when you left, even though he didn't think he would be allowed to. That made him happy, even when he was sick. I know it did."

She paused, her arm still around Fixit. "If he was here, Fixit, he would tell you that what happened to him wasn't your fault. You are not to blame yourself for his dying. You were a good friend to him and you are a good friend to all of us, and we don't any of us want to think about it anymore. It's over."

She leaned in and kissed him on the cheek, then put her arms around him and hugged him. Fixit was crying, but Owl, sitting in her wheelchair and watching his face, knew it was going to be all right.

LOGAN TOM wasn't so sure.

He was unsure not only about Fixit, whom he was already viewing as damaged goods, but also about the way all of this was going to turn out. The expectation was that they would travel south toward the Columbia River, finding Hawk and Tessa on the way, and everything would work out. But this assumed a few things. It assumed that they would get there in one piece. It assumed that Hawk would be easily found once they arrived. And it assumed that the journey itself would not do such emotional and psychological damage that they would not be able, over the course of time, to heal themselves.

The first two added up to enough wishful thinking to sink a barge, but the last was the one that bothered him the most. He knew something of the sort of damage that journeys undertaken in this world could inflict on you. He had made more than a few over the past twenty years, and he still carried the scars deep inside. The Ghosts had overcome a lot to get to where they were, and their bonding as a family had helped to shield them. But they were still just children, with only Owl, Panther, and Bear old enough to be viewed as grown-up, and for all their bravado and determination they were likely so much cannon fodder for what lay between them and their destination. For half a dozen years, they had not left their sanctuary in the city of Seattle. They had not traveled more than a few miles from their home. Everything they knew was behind them. They were starting life over, a little family setting out on a strange road for a strange land.

Could they finish such a journey when things like the insect machines and the Freaks waited for them around every twisty bend and in every dark corner?

What were the chances they could survive?

Could they manage without him?

These weren't idle questions. They were considerations he had been worrying over ever since they had set out from the city. He needed to know if they could make their way alone. Because he was thinking that at some point they might have to.

Because, in truth, he was thinking it might be best if he left them behind.

It sounded harsh, but it was the pragmatic choice. His charge from the Lady by way of Two Bears wasn't to save the Ghosts. It was to find and protect the gypsy morph, who just happened to be one of the Ghosts in its current transformation. He was to give the morph a chance to save humanity from the coming conflagration, to give it a chance, he assumed, to repopulate and rebuild the world. That charge did not involve the other Ghosts in any way, shape, or form.

It wasn't that he didn't want to help these kids. He did. But they were slowing him down. He could get to where he needed to go much faster on his own. He could travel more quickly and in greater safety. Every decision he made was affected by their presence. He wasn't used to this kind of responsibility. He had lived alone since Michael's death, and he had developed habits and patterns of behavior that improved his chances of surviving. Of necessity, much of what he had come to rely upon had gone by the wayside since he had taken on the burden of responsibility for the Ghosts.

Leaving them sounded callous and unfeeling. But this was a world where thinking too much about others could get you killed.

He put the matter aside that night after burying the Weatherman and settling in, thinking that he wasn't ready to make the decision to leave, no matter the arguments in favor, no matter the risks of staying. The timing just didn't feel right, and he would let things be for now.

But by the following morning, Fixit and River had both come down with a severe fever and were showing symptoms of the same form of plague that had claimed the Weatherman.

"I don't have enough medicine left to treat them for more than a few days," Owl advised him in confidence, her plain, no-nonsense features lined with worry. "We used most of what we had on River's grandfather."

He had just finished placing both kids on stretchers in the back of the Lightning, taking it upon himself to secure them, using his own store of blankets to help keep them warm. They were flushed and coughing, their throats scratchy and dry. The first telltale signs of purple splotches were starting to show on their necks. River was much worse than Fixit, her breathing harsh and irregular. But then she had been exposed to her grandfather for longer than the boy. Logan was already dreading the ride ahead, shut away in a plague-infested space that even a steady influx of fresh air might not help. He was not afraid of demons and once-men, but ever since the sickness that had almost killed him at sixteen, he was deathly afraid of plague.

He looked off into the distance, past the knot of kids watching, past the bleak landscape with its wintry, dry vistas and empty spaces, past everything he could see to what he could only envision. It would be so easy to leave them. It would be the smart thing to do.

They found an old hay wagon sitting out in a field not long after they set out, and they abandoned the shopping cart and loaded the wagon with all their supplies and themselves, as well. Only Panther preferred to walk, striding out ahead, keeping a steady pace. Owl rode inside the Lightning with Logan so that she could watch over Fixit and River, insisting that she would share the risk, that she had survived contact with plague all her life. Logan was impressed. Not many in her place would have done so.

They made better time that day and the next, covering a much greater distance, traveling all the way south to the next city down. Logan didn't know its name; all the signage had long since been torn down. Owl produced one of her tattered maps and told him it was called Tacoma. By nightfall, they had reached the outskirts and found a field sheltered by a small copse of withered spruce in which to make camp. There were some buildings and a few pieces of rusted machinery, all of which helped hide and protect them against the things that prowled the night. River and Fixit had not improved; if anything, they were worse. Logan had already decided to go looking for the medicine Owl needed to treat them.

"Write it out for me," he asked her. "Describe what I'm looking for, especially the container. I'll take the Lightning and have a look in the city. Maybe I'll get lucky and find some medical supplies."

He didn't think he would, but it didn't serve any purpose to tell her that. Most of what might help had long since been picked over and taken by others. Drugs of any sort were rare, but especially those that protected or cured the various forms of plague.

"It's called Cyclomopensia," she told him, handing him a scrap of paper with the name carefully printed out. "It will come in large white pills with CYL-ONE imprinted on each." She handed him a plastic container. "This is what the ones I have left came in."

He studied the container and the paper a moment, and then shoved them into one of his pockets. He called the Ghosts together. "Listen carefully. I have to leave you for tonight and maybe all of tomorrow, too, if I'm going to find the medicine that River and Fixit need. I'll need the Lightning to get the job done. You have to be careful while I'm gone. No one leaves this place. No one does anything to draw attention. Someone stands guard all the time. If you have to move, carry River and Fixit on the stretchers and walk toward the city. Leave everything else. Look for the Lightning or me. We won't be far from each other."

He gave the Parkhan Sprays to Sparrow and Panther, and then

handed a short-barreled Tyson Flechette, like the one his father had carried the day he had died, to Bear.

"Don't use any of these unless you have to. If you fire them, you will draw a lot of attention. The best thing you can do for yourselves is to be as inconspicuous as you can. Understand?"

They all nodded solemnly. "We know what to do," said Panther. "We ain't stupid."

That remained to be seen, Logan thought, remembering that it was Panther who had caused the incident with the machines at Oronyx Experimental. But there was no help for it. He couldn't leave them out here unarmed. He had to trust that they would use good judgment and common sense where the weapons were concerned.

"Owl," he said, drawing her attention. "I'll put River and Fixit inside that shed over there." He pointed to the building that was in the best shape of the bunch. "No one goes inside except you, and you only go in to give them medicine or liquids or whatever you think might help. But everyone else stays out. If this thing spreads, we could all come down with it."

She nodded wordlessly. He hesitated, trying to think what else he should tell them, worried suddenly that this was a mistake and he was leaving them here to die. They were only children, he told himself for what must have been the hundredth time since they had set out from Seattle. They did not have his survival skills. They did not have his experience or training. But there was no point in worrying over things that couldn't be helped.

He drove the hay wagon over to the buildings and behind the other machinery, then unhitched it. Mostly it looked like everything else, and it would go unnoticed if no one stopped to look or got too close.

"Remember what I said," he told them in parting. "Be careful. I'll be back as soon as I can."

But even as he was driving away, he was thinking again about leaving them for good.

EIGHTEEN

LEAVING THE GHOSTS and their field camp behind, Logan Tom drove down the highway through the deepening twilight toward the darkened buildings of Tacoma. The city hunkered down on a mostly flat plain bordered by water on one side and hills on the other. Its look was a familiar one, residences on the perimeter, downtown in the center, the whole of it a shadowy presence, unlit and seemingly uninhabited.

But there would be people, of course, perhaps living in a compound, perhaps living on the streets. There would be Freaks. There would be the usual strays and homeless. There would be things no one could imagine without first seeing them, creatures formed of the poisons and the plagues, the monsters of this brave new world.

And always, there would be feeders, waiting.

He scanned the shadows as he drove, weaving through the debris, angling for the open spots on the cracked, weed-grown pavement. He searched for movement, for any indication of life, and found little. Feral dogs and street kids. The flicker of solar-powered lamps from the dark recesses of buildings. The faint sounds of life that belied the otherwise deep silence. Now and then, he passed the remains of the dead, some of the bodies so old they had been reduced to little more than bones and bits of clothing. He tried to imagine how it had been before the wars had begun and the way back had been lost, and he could not.

His mind drifted to other times and places. It was like this in so many other cities, the aftermath of destruction, the leavings of madness and despair. So much had been rendered useless. He looked around at the devastation, at the emptiness, and it made him want to cry. But he didn't cry anymore. Not for this. He had seen it too often. It was the legacy of his time, a world depopulated, a civilization destroyed.

Ahead, a huge domed building rose against the skyline, and in the fading light he could make out its massive support arches. It was an entertainment arena, a leftover from the time when there was order in the world. It was black and silent now, an edifice that had lost its place and purpose, a mausoleum for a time of life that was dead and gone.

He drove toward it.

The highway dipped slightly in a long sloping ramp toward the domed building, but huge piles of trash and parts of discarded cars had been hauled over to form a barricade that blocked the exit. He drove a bit closer and abandoned his plan to follow the pavement. Instead he began driving across the open spaces adjacent to the highway and then through the yards of perimeter residences, cutting past other, smaller roads, choosing rougher terrain that offered more accessible passage for the AV. The Lightning was built to crawl over barriers from which other vehicles would have turned back.

When he had gone as far as he could, close now to the dome and in sight of buildings that were clearly storefronts and warehouses, Logan stopped the AV and got out. He stood looking around for a few moments, taking in the feel of his surroundings, watching and listening. Nothing drew his attention. Satisfied, he triggered the Lightning's security locks and protective devices and, picking up his staff, set out on foot.

He walked softly, noiselessly, in the way he had learned from Michael, an almost invisible presence, just another of night's shadows. The houses on either side were squat, dark structures empty of life. Once or twice, cats crossed his path, and once a pair of street kids, furtive and hunched over as they moved across his line of sight. Once, he thought he heard voices, but he could not decipher the words or detect their source.

And once, like a vision, a woman appeared—or maybe a girl—sliding out of the shadows into the light, her hair long and blond and flowing, her form slender. He could only imagine that she was beautiful—her features hidden behind the night's dark mask—yet he felt certain of it, even though she was there for only a moment.

She made him feel something unexpected with her passing, a deep, inexplicable loss coupled with a sadness that left his throat tight and his mouth dry. He could not explain it, could not find a reason for it. He had disdained companionship since Michael and the others had died. He had jealously safeguarded his solitary existence, actively avoiding the company of others. It was his nature as a Knight of the Word. It was one of the dictates of the life he had chosen. The presence of others only complicated his work. Attachments only served to tie him down.

Like the Ghosts threatened to do.

And yet . . .

He took a moment longer to search for the woman, peering into the shadows between the houses as, without thinking, he slowed. The silence deepened around him; the night closed about. There was no sign of her. It seemed to him now that he might have imagined her.

He quickened his pace and moved on.

He was twenty-eight years old, if his calculations were correct. He relied to a great extent on the calendar that Michael had built into the AV. Without it, time would have been lost to him completely. The seasons were unrecognizable, often passing from one into the other with little evidence of change. Clocks and watches had ceased to work years ago, save for a stubborn few that he came across now and then, and most of these only gave the time of day. There was an order to things when you could recite your age, when you could say with some certainty that you knew the day and month and year. There was a sense of being grounded in the world.

Twenty-eight, and he felt disconnected from everything. Except for his work as a Knight of the Word. And now, perhaps, even from that. Now that he had been saddled with these street kids and their problems. He would have to leave them, he knew. He would have to find a way. Once they were no longer sick and safely away from the threat of being overtaken by demons and once-men. Once it felt right to him. He shook his head at the confusion this caused. Because his charge, his mission, was to find and give aid to the imprisoned and abandoned. His life was dedicated to helping those who were not as strong as he was, who required deliverance from evil and could be saved only by his special power.

Were the Ghosts not most of these? Was he not bound to help them, too? Still, they were not of the same sort as those imprisoned in the slave camps or imperiled by the dark things that prowled the countryside. They did not need him in the same way as so many others.

Or at all, really, if you thought about it. If you weighed their need against that of so many others. They did not need him.

Did they?

He was aware suddenly of a cat walking next to him. It had appeared out of nowhere, a burly, grizzled beast, brindle and black in color with a strange white slash across its blunt face—as if it had been slapped with a paintbrush. It had a peculiar gait, the like of which he had never encountered in a cat. Although it mostly ambled, it also hopped. It took no more than a couple of hops at a time, but that was enough to be noticeable. It was while it was trailing along slightly off to his right that he caught sight of the unusual movement out of the corner of his eye and was alerted to its presence.

He stopped and looked down at the cat. The cat stopped and looked up at him.

"Shoo," he whispered.

The cat blinked, then hissed back at him.

He hesitated, thought about chasing it away, and decided it wasn't worth the effort. He started walking again. Right away the cat followed. He picked up his pace, but the cat picked up its pace, too. When he stopped again, the cat stopped with him, staying back and well out of reach of the black staff. Not that he would strike out at it, but the cat couldn't know.

"Go on, get out of here," Logan muttered.

He continued on, trying to ignore the cat, turning his attention to the task at hand. The dome loomed ahead, a dark monolith against the skyline. He was close enough to it by now that storefronts and warehouses had replaced the residences of earlier. He began searching for signs of what he needed, but nothing useful revealed itself. Most of the stores had seen their doors and windows broken out and their fixtures and contents smashed. The warehouses were in similar condition. If there was anything to be found, it was probably only because it was well hidden. Medicines and bandages were the first things people took once the plagues and chemical poisonings began in earnest, after the governments had collapsed and the demons and the once-men had surfaced. It seemed unlikely that anything was left after this long.

The cat made a series of sudden hops until it had drawn even with him, and then it gave a mournful cry that stopped him in his tracks.

"Shhh! Don't do that!" he snapped. He looked around in dismay. Everything within a hundred yards must have heard!

. The cat regarded him intently, and then did it again—a longer, deeper, more poignant cry. It held it for an impossibly long time, as if it might be trying for a record.

Logan started for it, brandishing his staff, and the cat was gone in a blur of black and brindle. In the space of a heartbeat, it had disappeared. and Logan was left alone.

"Just as well," he muttered reproachfully.

He walked on alone, upset by the encounter for reasons he couldn't explain. He guessed it was the strangeness of the cat's behavior, the way it was willing to approach him so boldly when most creatures, even larger ones, would have kept their distance. Maybe he felt a sense of kinship with it, a creature at once both aloof and unafraid. Maybe it was something about the way it had cried out, the sound so disturbing.

Whatever the case, he had just managed to put the cat out of his mind when it was back again, walking a few paces behind, its familiar amble punctuated by the peculiar hopping motion. Logan glanced over his shoulder at it without slowing, smiling to himself at its persistence. It probably thought he had food. In fact, he realized abruptly, he did. He was carrying a piece of a packaged ration he had stuffed in his pocket before leaving. The cat must have smelled it.

"Aren't you the clever one," he said, turning.

He reached into his pocket, extracted the food, broke off a chunk, and tossed it toward the animal. The cat watched the offering hit the ground and roll to a stop. It examined it without moving, and then looked up at Logan as if to say, *What am I supposed to do with this?*

Logan shook his head. Feral cats; they learned early on how to be cautious or they ended up dead. They didn't trust anyone. Besides, this one didn't look particularly hungry. If anything, it looked overfed.

He shrugged. "Fine, don't eat it, then. Not my problem."

"She doesn't ever eat food from strangers," a voice said.

Logan had been surprised enough times in his life to not jump out of his skin at unexpected voices, but he was startled nevertheless. He looked around without seeing anyone. "She doesn't?"

"She likes you, though. If she didn't, she wouldn't bother following you. She is very particular."

A girl not yet a woman, he guessed from the sound of her voice. He kept looking, and then saw her detach herself from the tree against which she had been leaning. Before, she had been part of the trunk, so closely assimilated that he had missed her. Even now, she was barely recognizable. She was cloaked and hooded, and her features were hidden. She stood facing him and made no move to come closer.

"Is this your cat?" he asked her.

"She thinks so. Her name is Rabbit. Mine is Catalya, sometimes Cat for short. What's yours?"

"Logan Tom." He paused. "Your name is Cat and your cat's name is Rabbit. Your cat acts like a rabbit. It makes me wonder."

She regarded him in silence for a moment. "What are you looking for?"

He shook his head. "Supplies."

Rabbit moved over to her and began rubbing up against her legs with her grizzled face as if to scratch an itch. Catalya reached down and tickled the cat's ears. She was still concealed within the shadows of her cloak and hood. "What kind of supplies?"

"Medical. Plague medicine."

She did not flinch or back away. She kept tickling Rabbit's ears as if what he had said was no more significant than a comment about the weather.

"Why are you out here by yourself?" he asked her.

"Who says I am?"

The reply was quick and certain, not sharp or defensive. He resisted the urge to search the surrounding shadows. If he hadn't been able to detect her, he might have missed detecting others who were with her.

"Don't worry, there's no one else," she said. "I can take care of myself."

He nodded and let the matter drop. "Is there a compound inside that dome? I thought I might find something there."

She straightened, taking her fingers away from the cat. Not once when she moved did she reveal even the slightest detail about herself. "You don't want to go there. No one there will help you."

"You seem awfully sure . . ."

"I am. Do you know why? I was born in that compound. My parents and my brothers and sisters still live there. All except my sister Evie; she died when I was four. The rest are still there. They live underground, in the basement rooms. They hide during the night. No lights or movement is allowed aboveground. That way, no one knows they are there."

He stared at her.

"Stupid, isn't it? If you pretend no one can find you, then maybe no one will. That's what it amounts to. Pretending. They pretend a lot. I guess it's what keeps them from falling apart."

"How old are you?" he asked.

"Eighteen. How old are you?"

"Twenty-eight. How long since you lived inside the compound?"

"Six years. I was put out when I was twelve."

He hesitated, wondering how far he should pursue this. "Why were you put out?"

"I got sick."

She didn't offer anything more. He stood watching her, leaning on his staff, studying her posture for some clue about what was wrong with her. The night tightened about them, as if to hide the secret she was obviously keeping. Rabbit stood up, walked over to him, and sat down again, just out of reach but close enough that her eyes reflected the moonlight.

"Why do you need plague medicine?" she asked.

"I have some sick kids with me. They need it. We're traveling south."

"There isn't anything south," she said. "Just more of the same. More plague and poisoned air and water, and bad chemicals. And insects— lots and lots of insects."

He had heard something of this but not yet come across it. Apparently the disruption of the ecosystems and the poisoning of the earth and water had fueled rapid growth in certain species of insect life. The giant centipede the Ghosts had killed was one example. But in other cases, the results were different. Instead of one giant insect, accelerated procreation resulted in thousands and thousands of smaller forms, hordes that were eating their way through every type of plant life that was left, denuding the earth.

"How old are your kids?" she asked suddenly.

"They're not my kids. I'm just helping them. The oldest is maybe twenty. The youngest is ten."

"Are they street kids or compound kids?"

"Some of both, I guess."

"What about you?"

"What do you mean?"

"Were you a street kid or a compound kid?"

"A compound kid, but I was orphaned at eight. Why are you asking all these questions?"

"Do you want my help finding your plague medicine?"

He sighed. "I want any help I can get."

"Then just tell me what I want to know. Where are your kids?"

"I left them outside the city when I came to look for the medicine."

"That's dangerous, coming in alone at night. Aren't you scared?"

"Aren't you?"

"I know my way around."

"So do I. Look, can you help me find what I need?"

She came forward a step. "Maybe. Maybe I'm the only one who can help you. The only one who's willing. No one in the compound will help you. No one in the streets, either. Just me."

He gave her a hard look. "Uh-huh. Only you. Why is that? Because your cat likes me?"

"Because I need something from you."

Rabbit was rubbing up against him, acting as if they had been friends all their lives. He hadn't even noticed her until just now. He glanced down and shifted his leg away by stepping back. The cat looked up at him with saucer eyes.

Logan faced the girl. "What is it you need?"

"I need you to take me with you when you leave."

As if he needed another kid to look after. As if he hadn't just been contemplating finding a way to lose the ones he already had. It struck him as incredibly funny; he found himself wanting to laugh, even though he knew it was no laughing matter to the girl. But it didn't matter how she felt. He wasn't going to take her. He wouldn't.

"Do you know why they put me out of the compound?" she asked suddenly. "My parents and my brothers and sisters and my friends and all the rest? Why they never stopped to think twice about it, even though I was only twelve years old and had been born in the compound and had never been outside, even with adults? Why do you think?"

She started toward him.

"They were afraid of you?" he guessed. He held his ground against her advance, not sure what was going to happen but unwilling to back away.

She stopped when she was less than ten feet away. "That's exactly right. They were afraid of me. Of this."

She pulled back the hood of her cloak and tilted her head into the pale wash of the moonlight. Dark splotches covered large portions of her face and neck. When she stretched out her arms so that the concealing folds of the cloak fell away, he could see the same markings there, as well. She turned herself slightly so that the color and shape of the markings were more clearly revealed by the angle of the light. The skin had turned rough and scaly like the hide of a reptile.

He understood at once. She was turning into a Lizard.

"Are you afraid of Freaks, Logan?" she asked him. She came forward another few steps, bold and challenging, but stayed just out of reach.

"No. But the people in the compounds are."

"Terrified. Even my own family. They thought it was catching. They didn't know, but they didn't want to take the chance. What's one kid's life against so many? Easier to put me out than risk a widespread infection of Lizard skin."

Her voice had turned harsh and bitter, but she faced him squarely and did not try to turn away. There were no tears. He wondered how long it had taken her to learn not to cry when she talked about it.

"It's happening everywhere," he said. "I've seen it over and over. I don't think anyone knows what causes it. Something about being exposed to all the chemicals. Something about the air or water or food. Like everything else that's happened to create mutations, there are too many possibilities to know."

She nodded, said nothing.

"How did you survive? You were put out of the compound more than six years ago."

She smiled. Her smile, beneath the patch of reptilian skin that covered the entire left side of her lower face, was pretty. "A family of Lizards helped me. They took me in, fed me, clothed me, and then raised me. They understood what it was like to change because it had happened to them. They knew others who had been put out in the same way I was, others who had the disease. They were street people, this family. But they understood."

"What happened to them?"

She hesitated, then shrugged. "Nothing. I just decided I wanted to be on my own. Will you take me with you if I help you?"

"You get me my medicine, and I take you back with me. Then what?"

"I go with you and your kids, wherever you are going. It doesn't matter. I just don't want to be here anymore. I want to get away."

"Why?"

"I told you, I just don't want to . . ."

He walked up to her then, reached out and ran two fingers along the rough patch covering her jaw. Uncertainty reflected in her blue eyes. Her hair, he saw, was cinnamon-colored. But even in her scalp, the patches showed.

"I know something of your disease," he said. "I've seen a lot of it, talked to those who had it. It covers the skin and absorbs it. It changes a human into a mutant. It acts quickly. That doesn't seem to have happened to you. You've had this disease six years, you said?"

"It doesn't work the same with everyone." She looked away now, and then reached down quickly to snatch up Rabbit in her arms and backed away. "If you don't want me to go with you, just say so."

"I want you to tell me the truth," he said. "Why are you living out here on your own?"

She started to tell him something—another lie, he guessed—but cut herself off with a tightening of her lips and a muted sigh.

"I quit changing. Something stopped it. I knew that when my new family realized I wasn't going to be like them, they would put me out, too. I decided not to wait around for that to happen."

Logan stepped back, giving her some space. She didn't belong anywhere. She wasn't one thing or the other, and no one wanted you if you weren't like them. Not in this world. The Lizards were no different. They understood what it meant to change, but not what it meant to get halfway there and then stop. Catalya wasn't about to have the same thing happen twice, not when it hurt as much as it must have the first time.

"So," she said. "Will your kids want to put me out, too?"

"Maybe. Some of them. I don't know. I've only been with them a few days now."

"What about you? Now that you know."

He looked off into the darkness, making up his mind. For some reason, he found himself remembering Meike. How much trouble would it have been for him to have taken her with him? Even knowing as little about her as he did. Even knowing he might not have saved her anyway.

Rabbit was looking at him from the cradle of her arms. Waiting.

"I don't put people out," he said.

She waited, too. To hear the words.

"Okay," he agreed. "You have a deal."

* * *

THEY WALKED THROUGH the darkened streets, the girl leading, the cat ambling along beside him, hopping every now and then as if to prove to him how strange things had become. The world was silent around them, the buildings dark and the sky vast and empty.

"Why do you carry that staff?" she asked him.

"I'll tell you sometime. How do you know where to find plague medicine?"

"The Lizards keep stores of it to trade with. They don't have much use for most of it. Their immune systems aren't affected in the same way as humans, so the medicines mostly don't help. What kind is it that you need?"

"Cyclomopensia." He reached in his pocket, took out the empty container Owl had given him, and handed it to her. "Look familiar?"

She examined it carefully and then pocketed it. "I think I've seen it. We can take some of the other kinds, too. In case."

He glanced at her, but she kept looking straight ahead, a step or two in front of him. "What if my kids don't like you?" he asked after a moment. "I probably can't change it if they don't."

"Some of them will like me, I bet."

"Some of them, yes." He thought of Owl. She would be quick enough to take Cat under her wing. Maybe Candle, too. But he wasn't so sure about the others.

"Are you worried about me?"

He thought about it a moment. "I don't know."

She reached down abruptly and scooped up Rabbit, cradling him in her arms. "Don't be. I can take care of myself."

He didn't know about that, either.

NINETEEN

BEAR STOOD IN THE SHADOWS fifty yards from the little shed in which Owl kept watch over River and Fixit. It was nearing midnight—or maybe midnight had already come and gone, he couldn't be sure. He had taken the first watch after dinner and carried the heavy Tyson Flechette out into the darkness, choosing this spot in which to hide, the shadows so thick and deep that no one approaching would see him until they were within a dozen feet. At least, that was what he hoped. If a predator had eyesight good enough to spy him out from any farther away, they were all in a lot of trouble.

But experience had taught him that even the most dangerous predators in this postapocalyptic world lacked good eyesight. Something about the quality of the air or the ingestion of poisons from food and drink had weakened the vision of living things in general. There were exceptions. Hawk was one, Cheney another. But the eyesight of the monsters and the Freaks had not evolved in proportion to their appetites and their cunning and strength. Their hearing was keen, though. It didn't pay to move around a whole lot at night if one of them was hunting. Their sense of smell was pretty good, too, most times. If they were four-legged rather than two-legged predators.

He knew these things because he had made it his business to know. All the way back to before he was a Ghost, before he even knew where Seattle was or that he might one day end up there. He knew it from the time he was six and had to stand guard while the rest of his family toiled in the fields. In those days, it was believed that not all of the land had been poisoned and that some of it, particularly in distant corners of the United States, was still fertile enough to grow crops. That idea lasted about five years, and then it became clear that whether or not everything was contaminated was beside the point. There was no way to harvest what was grown and no sustainable market to purchase it. You could grow crops if you wanted, but you were likely to end up feeding the wrong mouths.

Bear learned it the first time the raiders appeared, took what they wanted of the crop, and burned the rest to the ground. He learned it when they took his two uncles, whom he never saw again. He learned it when they killed his dog.

He tried to tell his family that it was too risky even before the raiders appeared, but they were not much interested in hearing what he had to say. They never had been. Bear was big and slow and gave the impression of being a trifle stupid. He took his time answering questions and seldom spoke unless spoken to first. He ambled when he walked, and he always seemed to be trying to figure out where he should go and what he should do. He was enormously strong, but his strength seemed to bother him. He walked carefully and responded tentatively. He thought everything through. He saw life in slow motion. His brothers liked to joke that he could do anything, but by the time he got around to doing it, everyone would have gone to bed.

Bear didn't like being thought of as stupid. He didn't like being called names and made fun of. Who does? But there wasn't much he could do about it that didn't involve crushing someone's ribs, so he learned to live with the abuse. His parents had too much else on their minds to spend time worrying about him, let alone trying to protect him. So he was pretty much left to deal with things as best he could.

He dealt with them by choosing jobs that kept him apart from the others. Standing watch. Running errands. Engaging in heavy lifting for which only he, of all his siblings and cousins, was suitable. His father worked with him, and his uncles sometimes, and they didn't make fun of him or call him names. Mostly. He wondered about that now and then, thinking back. It might be that they had, and he just didn't want to remember.

Bear was smart, beneath his slow-moving, slow-talking, slow-acting veneer, and he knew how to pay attention. While others got along as best they could in a world they hated and a family that valued work over everything, Bear spent his time absorbing and remembering. He learned, and he didn't forget.

Little things.

Big things.

Everything he could.

That's how he knew how best to keep watch against the predators. That's how he knew how to stay awake and not fall asleep in the slow, heavy hours of early morning when your most pressing need was to close your eyes. That's how he knew that no matter what Panther or Sparrow or the others thought—even Hawk—it was his job to protect them all.

He glanced over to where his family lay sleeping on the ground, Candle and Sparrow in sleeping bags, the boys rolled up in blankets. There was no fire, no warmth to be found other than from their own bodies. But the night air was mild, and there was only a little wind. Behind the sleeping forms, the shed in which Owl tended River and Fixit was still and black. On the dark ribbon of the highway, some hundred yards from where they were settled, nothing moved.

He shifted the weight of the Tyson Flechette from one thigh to the other with a slow, methodical movement. He glanced over to where the boy who had shot Squirrel lay curled up next to the north side of the shed, a small black puddle in the darkness. He didn't like the boy, and if Owl had allowed it, he would have agreed to give him to Panther for disposal. But Owl wanted the boy unharmed and had charged Bear with seeing that he was left alone. Bear took this charge, as he took all charges that either Owl or Hawk gave him, very seriously. He didn't have to like it. He just had to do what he knew was right.

Bear was a soldier; he understood orders and he responded to them. Not because he couldn't think, but because he believed in order. He believed in a place for everyone and everyone in their place. He didn't understand kids like Panther, who often did whatever they felt like. In a family, you survived by knowing your place and behaving in a consistent, orderly fashion.

You did what you were told to do. You did what was right.

When you reached a point where the two didn't agree, it was time to move on.

He had found that out the hard way.

* * *

HE IS ELEVEN *when the stealing begins. It isn't anything important at first—a tool, a small sack of grain, a piece of children's clothing, that sort of thing. One by one, they disappear, not all at once, but gradually. Bear thinks nothing of it, but his father and uncles take it seriously. Theft is an unpardonable offense in the world of his childhood. Too much has already been taken away to allow the taking of anything more. The older members of his family still remember the world as it was before everything was ruined or destroyed. There is bitterness and resentment at that loss, a rage at the inexplicable madness of it. Blame is easy to assess and difficult to fix. But the sense of deprivation is raw and festering, and theft is a reminder of how easily you can be dispossessed.*

His father believes it is one of his children, perhaps going through a phase. He questions them all. Rigorously. His brother, perhaps frightened at the intensity of the accusation, points to Bear. For reasons that Bear will never be able to fathom, his father believes his brother. Bear is convicted without a trial. None of the missing items is found. No one steps forward to say that they have actually seen him stealing. But he is different than they are, aloof and circumspect, his motives not entirely clear, and that is enough. He is not punished, but he is consigned to a back corner of their lives and watched closely.

He accepts this, just as he accepts everything else—stoically, resignedly, with a quiet understanding of how it will always be for him. But he thinks, too, that he should solve this puzzle. He doesn't like being thought of as a thief. Someone else is doing the stealing, and he will find out who it is. Perhaps that will convince the others their behavior toward him has been wrong.

He waits for the theft to happen again. It does, although not right away. This time, it is a weapon, a small automatic handgun. An antique, by all reckoning, a relic in an age in which lasers and flechettes and Sprays are the norm. But it is a theft nevertheless, and his father is quick to act on it. He searches Bear's space in the house first and questions him anew. Bear has been too visible, too much in the family eye, to commit these offenses, yet neither his father nor his siblings seem to notice. Even his mother, who still loves him as mothers will their disappointing children, does not stand up for him. It is as if their perception of his character has been determined and cannot be altered. Stung by this injustice, Bear feels the distance between himself and his family widen.

But three nights later, he catches the thief. He has taken to patrolling the grounds and buildings at night, keeping watch in his slow, patient way, determined to prove to them that he is innocent. The thief is trying to steal a box of old tools when Bear comes on him unexpectedly and throws him to the ground. It is a boy, not much older but much smaller than Bear. The boy is dirty and ragged, a wild thing. He admits that he is the thief and that he stole to help his family, a small group of vagrants who have taken up residence in an old farm not far away. He pleads with Bear not to give him up, but Bear has made his decision.

Bear takes the boy to his father. Here is the real thief, he announces. He waits for his father to apologize. He cares nothing for the boy who stole from them beyond redeeming himself. He has not given any thought to the boy's fate beyond that. It is his belief that the boy will be whipped and released. Bear is neither angry nor vengeful. He does not think that way.

His father does. Thieves are not to be tolerated. The boy begs and cries, but no one listens. Bear's father and his uncles take the boy out into the small stand of woods at one end of their property and do not bring him back. At first, Bear thinks they have released him with a warning. But small comments and looks tell him otherwise. They have killed the boy to provide an object lesson to his family and others of what happens to thieves.

Bear is stunned. He cannot believe his father has done this. The other members of his family support the decision—even his mother. It does not seem to matter to any of them that this was only a boy. When Bear tries to put his thinking into words, he is brushed aside. He does not understand the nature of their existence, he is told. He does not appreciate what is necessary if they are to survive. He finds them all alien and unfamiliar. They are his family, but they are strangers, too. He sees them now through different eyes, and he does not like it. If they can kill a small boy, what else are they capable of? He waits for understanding to come to him, but it does not.

Then, one night, without thinking about it, without knowing it is what he intends until he does it, he leaves. He packs a small sack of food, water, and tools, straps his knife and stun gun to his waist, and sets out. He walks west without knowing where he is going, intending to follow the sun until he reaches the coast. He has no idea what he is going toward, only what he is leaving behind. He has misgivings and doubts and fears, but mostly he feels sadness.

Still, he knows in his heart how things will end if he stays.

He is twelve years old when he crosses the mountains and enters Seattle for the first time.

BEAR CAUGHT SIGHT of movement out of the corner of his eye, a slight shifting in the shadows. It was almost directly behind him, all the way back by the shed in which Owl slept with River and Fixit. If he hadn't looked that way at just the right moment, he would have missed it entirely. He remained motionless, watching the darkness, waiting for the movement to reappear. When it did, it had spread from a single source to several, a clutch of shadows emerging from the darkness and taking on human form. But the movement was rough and jerky, slightly out of sync with that of humans.

Bear felt the hair on the back of his neck prickle.

Croaks.

He shifted the Tyson Flechette so that it was pointing toward the shadows, already thinking ahead to what he would have to do. The Croaks were weaving their way through the darkness, coming from the direction of the city, heading for the outbuildings and the sleeping

Ghosts. He counted heads quickly, at the same time trying to make certain of what he was seeing. But there was no mistake. There were more than a dozen of them, too many to be anything but a hunting party. He had no idea what had drawn them here or if they knew yet that his family was directly in their path. But the end result was inevitable. In seconds, they were going to stumble over the sleeping forms.

He released the safety on the flechette and brought up the short, blunt barrel, leveling it. But his family lay on the ground almost directly between himself and the Croaks. He couldn't fire without risking injury to them. The killing radius of the flechette was too wide and too uncertain. And, he added quickly, the distance was too far for the weapon to be accurate.

For the span of about five seconds, he froze, uncertain of what he should do.

Then he was on his feet and sprinting into the darkness, yelling back at the Croaks, intent on catching their attention and drawing them after him, away from his sleeping family. His ploy was successful. The Croaks stiffened and swung about as they caught sight of him. In seconds, they were after him.

He could not tell if any of the Ghosts had been awakened or were aware of his dilemma. There wasn't time to stop and look; there wasn't time for anything but flight. Besides, it didn't matter. His first obligation was to act as their protector. His own safety was secondary and could not be considered.

For Bear, it had never been any other way.

He ran hard for a short distance, far enough so that he was safely away from his family. He was big and strong, but running for long distances was out of the question. When he stopped and wheeled back, he was already breathing hard and his forehead was coated in sweat. He watched the Croaks lumber toward him, bigger and slower than he was, but a whole lot harder to kill. He blew the first two to pieces at fifty paces, turned and ran some more. A hundred yards farther on, he wheeled back and fired again. He brought down a third, but the second blast missed its intended mark. The sound of the weapon's discharge was earthshaking. One thing was for sure: everyone sleeping would be awake and warned by now.

He fired once more, catching another of the Croaks in the legs. He watched it tumble to the ground, disrupting the pursuit of the rest. There were more of them than he had thought at first, and they were not giving up the chase. He turned and began to run again, but he was tiring quickly now. He gained another fifty yards, coming up on the highway, a dark ribbon stretching away into the dark, its blacktopped surface glistening with a dust-covered slick.

Behind him, he could hear the growls of the Croaks. They were still coming.

He turned and fired again, killing another, and the flechette jammed. He hesitated, then braced himself as the remaining Croaks closed on him. It would end here. Not what he would have wished for, but for a good cause in any case. His blunt features tightened, and the muscles of his big shoulders bunched. Even though the barrel of the weapon was hot, he gripped it with both hands, holding it like a club. The Croaks growled and slobbered, spittle running from their ruined mouths, eyes mad and shifting in response to the disease eating them. They were covered with lesions and jagged scars, and the sounds they made were the sounds of wild animals. Bear had never faced this many alone.

Claws reached for him, blackened and sharp. He swung the flechette as hard as he could, and the closest attackers collapsed like rag dolls into the others. But the claws ripped his clothing and flesh, leaving ragged wounds that burned.

Bear backed away, taking a fresh stance.

And then the night exploded in streaks of red fire, and Panther and Sparrow surged out of the darkness, screaming like banshees and firing their Parkhan Sprays in steady bursts. The Croaks broke and fled before this fresh assault, less than a handful left as they disappeared into the night.

THE MIX OF GROWLS and yells brought Owl awake inside the shed. She was dozing, staying close to River and Fixit so that she could use cold compresses to help keep their fevers down. She was lying on the floor, close beside them, her wheelchair several feet away. At first, she just stared in the direction of the door, waiting to see if something more would happen. Then she heard the booming discharge of Bear's weapon and was hauling herself upright and into her wheelchair when Chalk burst through the door, eyes wide and frightened in his pale round face.

"Croaks!" he shouted in what appeared to be a failed attempt at a whisper. "Bear drew them off, and Panther and Sparrow went after him. What should we do?"

She rolled herself over to the door and peered into the night. The sounds of the battle were evident in the continued discharge of the flechette and the growls and cries that followed. But she couldn't see anything.

"Where's Candle?" She looked over her shoulder at Chalk, who mouthed wordlessly and shook his head. "Take me outside!" she snapped.

The boy did so, pushing her clear of the entry and into the darkness beyond. She stared off in the direction of the battle, and then looked around for the little girl. No sign of her. She felt her stomach tighten with fear. "Go find her! Don't come back without her!"

Chalk disappeared at a run, and Owl wheeled herself over to the discarded blankets and pallets where the others had been sleeping, calling out as she went for Candle. There was no response. She picked up one of the prods that the others had dropped in the excitement, laying it across the arms of her wheelchair.

Then she remembered the boy with the ruined face.

She rolled her wheelchair around to the side of the shed where Logan had left him chained to an iron ring. The chains lay in a heap, still attached to the ring, but the boy was gone. Somehow during the night he had managed to free himself and had fled.

Had he forced Candle to go with him?

Chalk charged back into view, gasping for breath. "I looked everywhere! I can't find her! I can't find any sign of her!"

There was no reason for the boy to take the little girl with him when he fled, nothing to be gained from taking her.

Yet Owl was convinced that he had.

TWENTY

"IT ISN'T MUCH FARTHER," the girl named Cat told Logan Tom as they continued their march through the empty buildings of the city.

Logan hoped not. They had been walking for the better part of an hour, and there was nothing to indicate what it was they were walking toward. He had thought to ask her once or twice, but then decided not to. Cat seemed to know exactly where she was going. He had little choice but to trust her if he didn't want to have to start over on his own—a thought that held little appeal. Time was precious for River and Fixit, and he needed to get the plague medicine to them as quickly as he could manage. Cat still seemed his best bet.

"Are you worried that I don't know where I'm going?" she asked suddenly, as if reading his mind.

Her dappled face turned toward him, the patches of Lizard skin glistening faintly in the moonlight. He was struck anew by the strangeness of her look. "I'm worried about time, that's all," he said.

She nodded. "Otherwise you wouldn't have been so foolish as to come into the city on your own and with no weapons." She continued to study him. "Or maybe you're better prepared than it seems. You look pretty confident. Do you have weapons I can't see?"

He shook his head. "Only my staff."

"Then your staff must be pretty special."

"What about you?"

"What about me?"

"You don't seem to have any weapons, either. What do you do if you have to protect yourself?"

She turned away from him. "I show my face. It terrifies my enemies, and they run and hide."

She tossed it off, quick and light, almost a verbal shrug. But it cost her something to say it, and she had said it before this, perhaps practicing how it would sound. Her transformation was more than skin-deep, and she was still coming to terms with it.

In any case, she was too confident not to have some sort of defense against predators. She wouldn't be out here like this if all she had to rely on was a cat that hopped like a rabbit.

Speaking of which, he hadn't seen the cat in quite some time. He glanced around, but there was no sign of her.

"What happened to your cat?" he asked.

"She's gone ahead."

"Ahead to where?"

"To where we're going. Not far."

He gave it up and just kept walking after that, staying alert for any danger but oddly unworried in her company. The streets down which they passed, while as cluttered with debris and overgrown with weeds and scrub as every other road in America, were otherwise empty. Now and then, he caught sight of feeders working their way through the shadows, their sleek forms quicksilver and ephemeral as they flitted past building walls and around tree trunks on their way to destinations that only they knew. He had seen little of feeders since leaving the city of Seattle, but he was conscious of the fact that they were always there, watching and waiting for an opportunity to feast. Humankind's heritage to the world, the product of their dark emotions, he thought. He wondered if feeders had been there before humans and if they would survive when humans were gone.

Were demons and Faerie creatures fair game, as well?

Were Knights of the Word?

He thought again about the gypsy morph and its purpose—to save the human race, its only chance. And maybe he was the morph's only chance, but how could he be sure? The Lady had said so. O'olish Amaneh had said so. But they were Faerie creatures, and Faerie creatures never revealed to anyone the whole of what they knew. Logan had been told only what he needed to know and nothing more. That was the way it worked. He had learned that from his time attacking the slave camps.

He was still contemplating the nature and extent of his efforts when he caught sight of movement off to one side. The movement was slow and deliberate, the shifting of a large body against a building wall. They were in a section of old warehouses, close by the water where it extended south from Seattle. Logan glanced at the girl, but she seemed preoccupied. He glanced back at where he had seen the movement, but now there was nothing.

He tightened his grip on his staff and summoned the magic.

The runes began to glow a deep blue in response.

"I thought so," the girl said suddenly, looking over at him.

Her words startled him. "What?"

"I thought that your staff was special. What makes it do that?"

"A kind of power." He shrugged dismissively.

"Like a fire?"

"Sort of."

"You can summon it when you want?"

"Yes. Did you see something move a minute ago?"

She grinned through the darkness. "Sure. So did you. That's why you did whatever you did to your staff. I wanted to see or I would have said something. Those are Lizards watching us."

He felt a flush of irritation heat his face. "I don't like games. Why didn't you just say something?"

"These Lizards know me. They guard this place. We're in the Senator's territory now. He's the one who's going to help us."

Logan let the magic settle back into the staff, the blue glow diminishing to darkness, the heat of its power cooling. "I thought you knew where we were going."

She nodded. "I do. But this is in the Senator's territory, so we need to visit him first. He expects it."

"Who is this *Senator?*" he asked.

"You'll see."

She clapped her hands sharply, and a clutch of Lizards slid from the shadows, their big, cumbersome forms materializing as if by magic. Logan did not panic. There was no effort made to seize or restrain him, and the girl began speaking to them almost immediately. She did not use any language with which he was familiar, but a kind of guttural speech that relied heavily on grunts and slurs. The Lizards seemed to understand, answering her back, one or two nodding and gesturing, as well. Cat glanced at him briefly and smiled her reassurance, pointing ahead.

"Our destination," she said.

It was a majestic old stone building with a long rise of broad steps leading to a veranda lined with pillars that supported a massive over-hang, the face of which was carved with strange symbols and figures. From within the building, through windows scarred by time and weather and between cracks in fifteen-foot-high doors closed tightly against the night, light glimmered in a soft, pulsating rhythm. A steady murmur emanated from within, rising and falling like an ocean's tide. Atop the steps stood a dozen more of the Lizards bearing an odd assortment of weapons—prods, flechettes, and antique single-shots—a ragtag arsenal for a ragtag band.

Cat headed directly for the stairs and the Lizards.

"Is this really necessary?" Logan asked, catching up and falling into step beside her.

She gave him a sideways glance. "Like I said, we are in the Senator's territory. We are here at his sufferance. He considers it rude not to pay a courtesy visit. He says it is all part of the political process."

Political process? Logan looked closely at the building ahead. "Was this a church once? A temple of some kind?"

She shrugged. "It belongs to the Senator now. He uses it to conduct debates and pass laws. He uses it as a forum to speak to his constituents."

He gave a mental shake of his head and let the matter drop as they

began to climb the steps toward the huge doors. When they got to
within a dozen feet, one of the Lizards came forward to speak with
Cat. She answered briefly and turned to him.

"You aren't carrying any weapons, are you? The staff is all you
have?"

He nodded.

"Because if you are and they find out, they will kill you on the spot.
There have been several assassination attempts on the Senator already
this year."

"Nothing but the staff," he reaffirmed.

She said something more to the Lizard, and it nodded and stepped
back. A second pair of Lizards, stationed to either side of the entrance,
pulled down on the door handles to open them.

Logan and the girl stepped inside.

And into another world.

Rows of benches faced a dais filled with a strange collection of statues and hangings and artifacts. There were cases stocked with ancient,
leather-bound books, their spines an identical mix of red and gold,
lined up in symmetrical rows. There were pictures and paintings of
people who were dressed in clothes from an earlier time. A huge
wooden cross hung from the wall at the back of the room, its arms
draped with silk streamers. The statues were of iron and marble, some
of men and women posing, some of strange creatures with bodies half
human and half animal. One statue was of a woman blindfolded and
holding forth a set of scales. One wall was covered with old clocks that
no longer worked, but all of their hands pointed straight up.

There were stuffed animals of all sorts. There were flags that Logan
didn't recognize, streamers and banners and pieces of old cloth, all
nailed to the walls or hung from the ceiling. A huge old desk and chair
sat to one side and forward of the motley collection, its scarred surface
covered with papers and more books. Lizards with weapons warded
the stairs that led onto the dais from either side, and these carried stun
guns and dart launchers. The benches were crowded with people—
humans and Freaks alike—their faces uplifted and their eyes directed
toward the dais and the speaker who addressed them, his voice rolling
out over the assemblage, deep and powerful.

"We are the future, and we must embrace our destiny. We are the promise of our forefathers, the bearers of their laws and their vision, come together in this darkest of times, in this deepest of glooms, to bring light to a troubled world. We must never forget our mission. We must stay the course."

The speaker was short and squat, and from the sound of his voice, male, but his species was virtually unidentifiable. He stood upright, but just barely. He had arms and legs, but the arms were truncated and the legs misshapen. His reptilian hide suggested that he was a Lizard, but there were patches of dark skin, as well, and clumps of hair sprouted from his torso and head like saw grass from a barren field. His face was so scrunched up and twisted that it was difficult to identify individual features. He stood center stage, his short arms gesturing dramatically as he spoke, his head tilting and nodding for emphasis. It was the voice alone that seemed most normal to Logan, the voice of a practiced speaker, of an orator of great skill and confidence.

Of a leader, Logan thought suddenly.

He leaned over. "The Senator?" he asked the girl.

She nodded. "Once an elected lawmaker, back when there were such things. He was one of many, but the rest are all gone. He is the last, and he carries on in the tradition, making and passing laws for the benefit of his constituents." She looked at him and shook her head. "I don't pretend to understand. But it seems to work. People come from all over to listen to him."

The truncated arms waved in sharp motions. "We must never despair, my friends. We must never give in to our uncertainties and our fears. We must move forward, following the road that was laid before us by those who have gone ahead. We must act in a decent and reasonable way, and we must keep our goals before us, ever present, ever conscious of their importance to a civilized world. Because we *are* civilized and we *are* a world, though some would have it otherwise. Laws bind and define us. Order gives us purpose. This house of government provides the physical evidence of our societal resurgence, risen from the chaos and the murk.

"Look about you! Look upon the faces of your friends and neighbors and fellow believers. Look upon their faces and see the hope radi-

ated there. We give one another that hope. We give one another the reassurance that our way of life, while changed, is not gone. There may be
dark things seeking to pull us down, to drag us away to places where
there is only pain and suffering. But that will not happen here. We are
too strong for them! We are too powerful! Recite the words! Recite the
Pledge!"

As one, the assemblage began to speak:

I pledge allegiance to the flag
And to the man we call the Senator
And to the Republic for which he stands
One people, under his law
With a brighter day promised for all.

The words rolled out across the chamber floor, strong and certain.
Logan had no idea what they were supposed to accomplish or even
what they meant. There was no Republic, no one rule or people, and
probably no brighter day anytime soon, either. But the people gathered
here obviously believed otherwise. There was no pause in the recitation
of the words, no hint of doubt or confusion.

"My friends," the Senator intoned, his squat, ugly form shambling
back and forth across the dais now, his head bowed. "I will be offering
new laws on the morrow and would ask all and sundry gathered here
to come witness and participate in the political process. A public hearing will begin at noon. All speakers will be heard and their words honored. Our attention will be directed primarily to the equitable
distribution of foodstuffs and water. Our stores are plentiful, but not
inexhaustible."

He wheeled about and spread his arms wide. "Hear ye, hear ye, this
august body is dismissed and this legislative session terminated. Thanks
and praise to all for the work done here; may it be forever recognized.
You are dismissed. Go forth and be well."

There was a long, sustained clapping from the audience, and then
they began to rise and move toward the doors at the back of the room.
Logan and Cat stepped aside to let them pass. Logan was struck by the
fervor he saw in their faces. Even though to him it all seemed another

variation on smoke and mirrors, they had obviously found something here to believe in.

The Senator had moved to his desk and taken a seat. A scattering of people had crowded forward and taken places on the closest benches, obviously waiting to be summoned to speak privately with him. But it was to Cat and Logan that he gestured, beckoning them forward from the back of the room.

"Come here, little kitten!" he boomed out. "Don't hide in the shadows! And bring your big friend with you!"

They walked down the closest aisle to the dais and climbed the stairs to where the Senator sat behind his desk. He rose to embrace Cat, a sort of quick half hug that was over almost before it began. A perfunctory act, Logan decided. A tradition that was not necessarily indicative of any true feelings.

Nevertheless, Cat was smiling. "Your words give hope, as always," she said.

"A poor effort from a poor public servant. But what else do I have to offer?" The mouth was shoved to one side in his lumpy face, twisted and scarred like the rest of his features. But his voice was strong and compelling. His one good eye shifted to Logan. "You've made a new friend?"

"This is Logan," she said. "I found him on his way into the city. He was heading for the compound."

"No, no, no, Logan," the Senator declared grimly. His ruined face twisted into something new. "You don't want to go there. You don't want to have anything to do with those people. They are selfish and greedy. They are evil."

"They are probably scared," Logan said.

The Senator smiled crookedly. "Why are you here?"

"He needs plague medicine for sick children," Cat answered quickly. "I told him I would share what we have."

"Sick children? Where are you taking them?"

Logan hesitated. "That's a difficult question to answer. I'm still not sure. I'm searching for their home."

The Senator's gnarled features tightened. "Why not here? We have space for new arrivals. We have homes that can be opened to those seeking shelter." He paused. "Or are we not a suitable choice?"

"He already has a destination," Cat interjected, giving a dismissive shrug to the suggestion. "Besides, he is not a constituent. He is a traveler passing through."

The Senator stared at her. "You seem to have taken an unusual degree of interest in our friend, little kitten. Is there something you are not telling me?"

She gave him an exasperated-little-girl look. "Please don't treat me like a child. I am doing for Logan what I would do for any visitor requiring help. You have said over and over again that medical care for children is central to your political platform. Why is this suddenly a problem?"

The Senator seemed to consider this, his good eye fixed on her, unmoving and unblinking. Then he nodded. "It isn't a problem, little kitten. As you say, we are here to help all who ask for it. We are not like those in the compound." He pointed at her. "See that he finds what he needs. But remember our bargain."

The girl nodded and said quietly, "You don't need to remind me."

The Senator eyed her sharply, and Logan wondered what they were talking about. He said, "I appreciate your help."

The Senator's gaze fixed on him. "I think you'll need more help than I can give you."

Logan stared at him uncertainly.

"Even here, even though we are Freaks, we have heard of those who carry the black staffs with the strange carvings. We have heard of the power you possess and the fear you inspire in your enemies. We could use a man of your talents should you change your mind and choose to stay."

Logan shook his head. "I am not my own master in this business. I go where I am sent."

Cat was looking at him in surprise, but she kept silent. The Senator's mouth shaped itself into a crooked smile. "Maybe you were sent to *us*."

"It would shorten my journey considerably," Logan answered him, smiling back. "But I'm afraid I have to go on."

"Then you had better get started," the Senator declared, and waved him away dismissively.

Two of the Senator's Lizard bodyguards followed them as they walked from the temple hall and into the darkness once more.

"Don't say anything," the girl told him quietly.

She took the lead, walking them back down the street they had just come up and then off to the west and into a district of collapsed buildings. Mounds of debris and rubble covered what must have been dozens of square blocks. The entire area had the look of a war zone, and for as far as Logan could see in the moonlight there was nothing standing that was even halfway whole.

They were well into the center of the rubble, an unfathomable maze, when the girl turned into an opening between two partially collapsed walls and moved to a door that sagged open and splintered on its broken hinges. She stepped through the entrance into a room partially lit by moonlight that streamed down through a collapsed roof. Logan followed, but the Lizards remained outside. Debris lay in heaps against the walls and in the corner spaces. Without a word, she began pulling away stones and pieces of wood from one such pile. Logan was quick to help her, and within minutes they had uncovered a trapdoor.

Logan started to say something, but the girl quickly put a finger to her lips and pointed at the door. Together they heaved upward on the iron ring, and the door opened on a set of stone steps leading to a cellar.

Cat went down the steps first, with Logan right behind. The Lizards made no move to follow, standing with their backs to the entry, staring out at the night.

"The Lizards are said to be family," she told him once they were all the way into the cellar, speaking softly so that only he could hear. "I don't know if it's true or not, but they are fiercely loyal. Several have died for him during the assassination attempts."

"Who tried to assassinate him?" Logan wanted to know.

The girl shrugged. "People from the compound, mostly. Fanatics who think all Freaks are dangerous and should be eliminated. Some blame the Freaks for what has happened to the world in general." She shook her head. "Some just need to find a way to make someone—anyone—pay for what has happened to them."

She reached into the darkness and switched on a solar-powered torch. "Not that the Senator hasn't brought much of it on himself. He's as dangerous as the things he claims to protect his constituents from. He might even try to kill you."

Logan grabbed her arm. "Kill me? Why?"

"He doesn't like you."

She tried to pull away, but he held on to her. "Wait a minute. What are you talking about?"

She glared at him. "You'd better let me go if you want to get out of this in one piece."

"I'm not the one who got me into this. You are. Tell me what this is all about, Cat. Right now."

She held her ground, shaking her head slowly. "You won't take me with you if I do."

He heard the despair in her voice, and he softened his own. "Just tell me, please."

She was silent for a moment, and then she said, "It's because of me. He owns me."

At first, Logan didn't think he heard her right. "He *owns* you?" he repeated, trying to make sure.

"That was the bargain I made with him when he took me in. He agreed to give me food and shelter, but in return I became his property. He said it was an old tradition dating back to the beginning of politics. He said I would belong to him until I paid my debt." She looked down at her feet and sighed. "I agreed. I was desperate. I was starving, and I knew I was going to die." She paused. "I guess I would have done just about anything."

The way she said it suggested to Logan that maybe she had. He felt a tightening in his throat and a sudden anger. "So he doesn't want to give you up. That was what he was talking about back in the hall when he reminded you of your bargain. He thinks you might try to leave with me."

She nodded, saying nothing.

"And all that business about being saved by a family of Lizards who took you in when you were exiled from the compound was just something you made up?"

She shrugged, not looking at him.

He released her arm and looked around at the room, which was filled with boxes of all shapes and sizes. "Is the Cyclomopensia here? Or did you make that up, too?"

She tightened her lips and walked over to one set of boxes, peeled back the covering, reached in, and pulled out half a dozen packets. She handed them to him. "Enough for a month's treatment. I wasn't lying. I know about medicines. I was put in charge of the medical supplies because I had some experience in the compound. They don't use them much out here. Their immune systems changed when they became Lizards. But there are humans among us, too. Street people. I treat them when they get sick. Sometimes, I trade medicines to the compound for stuff we need. But the Senator doesn't like me doing that, no matter what. He hates the compound people."

Logan glanced around. "Are all these boxes filled with medicines?" She nodded. "Okay. Pack up the ones you think will do the most good. We'll take them, too."

She stared at him. "Are you still taking me with you?"

"Why? Do you think I should leave you behind? I thought we made a bargain."

"They'll try to stop you. They might even try to kill you. I wasn't making that up."

"Just do what I told you."

She began gathering packets from various boxes, stuffing them into pockets sewn inside her cloak. She worked quickly and without talking while he made another quick survey of the room, keeping one eye on the open doorway. If they intended to kill him, they would do so when he emerged, thinking to get to him before he could even think to defend himself. The Senator would have told them who and what he was, would have warned them about his staff, would have told them to act quickly.

He shook his head.

He saw a second door at the back of the room.

"What's behind that door?" he asked her.

She stopped what she was doing and looked to where he was pointing. "Nothing. Another room, but it's empty. Sealed, too. The Senator fused the locks to make sure there was only one entry. If we try to break them, the guards will hear and call for help."

"What if they don't hear?"

He walked over to the door, laid his staff against the hinges, and summoned the magic. In seconds, the fire had burned through the iron clasps and the door was hanging open. Debris blocked the way through from the other side, but gave before him as he pushed past it. The room beyond was cavernous, but mostly empty. It might have been the basement level of a warehouse in an earlier time, but whatever had been stored there was long gone.

On the far side of the room, a broad roll-up door stood open at the top of a ramp.

"Are you finished?" he asked her.

She nodded and walked over to join him. "How did you do that?"

He gave her mottled face a deliberate stare. "My special staff."

They moved past the debris and through the room to the roll-up door. Logan took a moment to be certain the Lizards hadn't guessed what he might do, but he did not sense their presence. Nor did he detect any danger. He stepped through the opening, the girl right behind, and was back outside.

They walked for a long time after that, circling away from the storeroom before heading back to where he had left the AV. The silence was deep and pervasive and the dark of the night a willing accomplice to their flight. They didn't speak at first, keeping silent out of necessity, not wanting to give any indication of where they were. If the Senator decided to come looking for them, they didn't want to give him any help.

"We don't have to hurry," the girl said suddenly, turning her mottled face toward him. "He won't come looking for me right away."

Logan raised a questioning eyebrow. "He won't? Why not? Won't he want his property back?"

"He won't believe you've agreed to take me with you. Not at first. He'll think you've left alone."

"I thought you said he was worried about losing his property."

She looked away. "He is. He knows I will try to go with you; I've tried leaving before. He just doesn't think you will agree to take me."

"He won't? Why is that?"

"Because I'm a Freak, and he doesn't think anyone would want me but him."

They were passing back through the neighborhood where he had first encountered the girl when Rabbit reappeared, falling into step beside them, her strange hopping motion revealing her identity even before they could make out her features.

"Can we take her with us?" the girl asked.

Logan shrugged. "A cat who knows enough to look beneath the skin to judge a person's character is too valuable to leave behind."

Even though her face was turned away, he could have sworn he caught a glimpse of a smile.

TWENTY-ONE

MOONLIGHT BATHED the shadowed landscape, draping the roofs and walls of buildings, staining the flat, empty fields and layering the highway's dark surface. Candle trailed the boy with the ruined face by a few paces, working hard to keep up, not wanting to feel the sharp jerk of the cord he had tied about her neck to prevent her from bolting. She had said almost nothing since they had started out, too frightened to do more than follow his directions. But they had walked a little more than two miles by now, and she was already growing tired.

"How much farther are we going?" she asked.

"As far as I want to."

"How far is that?"

"Far as necessary to get back."

"Back to where?"

His scarred face turned toward her. Irritation reflected in his one good eye. "To where I was when your friends took me away."

"To your family?"

"To my tribe." He cleared his throat and spit. "You're the one with the family, not me."

She walked on a little farther before saying, "I don't want to go."

"I don't care what you want."

"Why are you doing this?"

"Doing what?"

"Taking me with you."

"Because I feel like it. Because I can." He muttered something she couldn't hear, then said, "I'm doing to them what they did to me. I'm taking you away like they took me. Let's see how they like it."

She was silent again for a moment. "What are you going to do with me?"

"I don't know yet. I haven't decided."

"You shouldn't do this." She was on the verge of tears. "You should let me go."

"Shut up."

She did, and they walked on without speaking, following the dark ribbon of the highway as it stretched away into the distance. She found herself thinking of the booming sound of Bear's flechette as it discharged, wondering what it meant. Something had happened, and she hadn't been there to prevent it by warning them.

And it was all because she had tried to do the right thing.

"I set you free," she said defiantly, believing her declaration said everything that needed saying.

"Thanks," he replied.

"So you should let me go."

"Don't try to tell me what to do. You don't know anything."

"I know I helped you, and now you won't help me."

"You helped me because you were afraid of what I might do to you and your friends if I got loose on my own."

"That's not true!"

"Sure it is. I saw the way you looked at me. You were afraid."

"I was afraid of what might happen to you. I was worried about what the others might decide to do when Owl wasn't looking."

He shrugged. "Doesn't matter. You set me free. That's all that counts. It's over and done with. You better learn to live with it."

She tightened her lips against the urge to cry that kept trying to surface. She was ten years old, she told herself. That was too old to cry.

Her thoughts drifted. She had done what she believed was right in setting him free. She had seen the way Panther looked at him. The first chance he got, he would hurt the boy. He might even kill him. One of the others might do it if Panther didn't. She couldn't be sure. Owl couldn't protect him forever, and Candle didn't want to let anything happen to him. Squirrel wouldn't have wanted him hurt, and neither did she.

She had pretended to be asleep, then risen and walked over to the boy and watched him for a long time as he slept. When he had woken, alerted somehow to her presence, she had watched him some more, even after he had turned away from her. Finally, her mind made up, she had gone over to him, unlocked the chains with the key she had taken from Owl, and set him free.

"Run!" she had whispered to him. "Get as far away as you can!"

But instead of running, he had clapped his hand over her mouth, picked her up, and carried her away, taking her behind the shed and then off toward the highway, keeping to the deep shadows where Bear couldn't see them. She would have struggled harder, but he had whispered to her that if she did he would hurt her really bad. Terrified and confused by what was happening, she had kept quiet until it was too late. By then, they had reached the highway, he had found some cord with which to collar her, and she was his prisoner. Even then, she had thought he would get tired of her and let her go or that he would see that what he was doing was wrong. Even then, she had believed he would come to his senses and do the right thing.

Now she didn't know.

"No one tried to hurt you," she said. "Even after you killed Squirrel and couldn't fight back, no one did anything bad."

"I didn't mean to kill that kid," he said defensively, his mouth twisting. "It was an accident. They frightened me. The gun went off on its own." He shook his head, his face troubled. "It was only a stun gun, anyway. It shouldn't have hurt him that much."

"But they could have hurt you back, and they didn't. So why are you being so mean to me?"

He wheeled about and snatched at the front of her shirt, pulling her so close to his face that she could see the particulars of the scars of every wound he had suffered. "If I wanted to be really mean to you, I could. I could hurt you enough that you would look like me. So just shut up!"

He threw her away, knocking her off her feet, and then yanked hard on the cord until she scrambled up again.

His face darkened. "I could kill you if I wanted."

He started walking again, forcing her to follow. She trudged after him, tears in her eyes, her mouth tight. She refused to cry. He was mean and she wouldn't let him see her cry. She tried to think why he was like this. He was angry about what had been done to him, she guessed. About his face, especially. About his lost eye. She wanted to know more because maybe she could say something that would make him feel better, but she was afraid to ask him. He was too angry.

"I might just come back with my tribe and kill your whole family," he said suddenly. "It would be their own fault for taking me away like they did. They should have given me what I wanted. Freaks!"

His bitterness was a slap in the face, and she flinched and looked away from him quickly. She heard him make a sneering, dismissive sound, and then he was yanking on the cord again, dragging her forward at an even quicker pace.

"They had no right," she heard him mutter, and she wasn't sure if he was talking about the Ghosts or about someone else.

The night wore on. After a time, she quit thinking about what she was doing, concentrating on putting one foot ahead of the other, on simply moving forward. The moon shifted in the sky, the shadows lengthened once more, and the world was a silent, empty landscape. Now and then she recognized landmarks from when she had passed this way earlier. Mostly she kept her eyes on the roadway and tried to think what she could do.

Until suddenly the decision was made for her.

You have to get out of here! the voices said urgently, abruptly. *You have to get out of here now!*

"Wait!" she called out to the boy. Her urgency was sufficient that he turned back in surprise. "There's something very bad coming."

He stared at her a moment, and then laughed. "You'll say anything, won't you?"

She shook her head. "I can always tell when there are bad things near. The voices warn me. There really is something. Just ahead."

He looked in the direction she was pointing, hands on hips. "What are you talking about? I don't see anything."

"It doesn't matter if you see it. It's there."

"I'm supposed to believe this?" He paused. "What do you mean, you hear voices?"

She tried to think what to say. "I can sense things. It's a gift. I can always tell. We can't go that way."

"We can't, huh? I suppose we have to go back? Is that it?"

She ran her hands through her mop of red hair and said, as firmly and bravely as she could manage, "We can't go that way."

"Do I look like I'm stupid or something?" he asked abruptly. "What sort of idiot do I look like? *Can't go that way*. What crap! You'll go any way I tell you to go, like it or not. So stop playing games with me."

"I'm not playing games."

He shook his head, glanced at the night sky, and sighed. "You know what? I don't know what you're doing. Making me crazy, mostly."

She took a deep breath. "I'm not going with you any farther."

"You're going wherever I want you to go, you little Freak."

She dropped down on the pavement in a heap. This time she couldn't help it; she began to cry. "Please let me go," she begged.

"Get up!" He stood right over her, his words cutting at her like razors.

She cried harder and shook her head. "I won't!"

He began to drag her by the neck, the cord cutting into her skin, harsh and burning as it choked her. She grasped at the cord in an effort to ease the suffocating pain, fighting for breath. But she refused to get to her feet. The boy with the ruined face turned back and kicked her in the ribs.

She curled into a ball, sobbing. "Stop," she pleaded.

"Get up or I'll kill you!" he screamed at her.

Suddenly there was a piece of broken glass in his hand, a shard retrieved from the roadway, its sharp edge glittering in the moonlight. He thrust it at her, inches from her face. She squeezed her eyes shut and quit breathing.

"Do you know what it feels like to have your face cut?" he hissed.

She shook her head without answering, curling tighter.

"If I cut your throat, you'll bleed to death. How would you like that?"

She shook her head again.

"Get up or I'll do it!"

She shook her head once more. "No. I want to go home!"

"I'm warning you!"

Hurry! You have to get out of here right now!

The fresh premonition of the danger she had sensed earlier returned in a silent scream. The voices were frantic, a palpable presence, and she knew that if they didn't do something quickly, they were going to be killed.

"We have to hide," she whispered.

She was aware of the boy moving away, his attention drawn elsewhere. She risked opening her eyes, and she saw that he was looking off toward some buildings to their left.

"There is something," he said softly, almost to himself. He stared in the direction of the buildings a moment longer. "Something big."

He looked down at her then, and a change came over his face. "You know what? You're too small and puny to bother with. I don't need you."

He reached down and used the shard of glass to cut the cord around her neck. "Go back, if you want," he said, pointing to the way they had come. "Run away, little scaredy-cat."

She stared at him. "You should hide," she said.

He shook his head. His single eye glittered in the moonlight. "I've got better things to do. Get out of here before I change my mind. I've had enough of you."

He started to set off, and then wheeled about. "They won't come for you, you know. Your family. You think they will, but they won't. No one ever comes for you once you're gone."

Without looking back, he moved swiftly down the highway and into the darkness, and then he was just a shadow. Candle watched him

a moment longer before climbing to her feet and scurrying down off
the road and into the drainage ditch that ran parallel, away from the
danger she sensed. She followed the ditch for a short distance, staying
low and quiet as she moved, like Sparrow had taught her. Then she
climbed out again and slipped into a stand of grasses beyond. The
grasses were so tall they were over her head, and she couldn't see anything beyond. She worked her way through them until she was well
back off the highway before hunkering down. The premonition was
still with her, hard and certain. She didn't know what else to do. She
should try to get farther away, but she was exhausted.

She sat all the way down, hugged her knees to her chest, closed her
eyes, and waited.

THE VOICES *hiss at her, harsh and insistent.*

Run away! You are in danger! Run now!

*She is old enough to appreciate that the voices are real and that when
they speak, it is important to listen. The voices are a part of her, a presence
in her mind, as real and substantive as the dark, ruined world around her.
She tells her parents of them, but her parents do not listen. They are worried for her. She does not seem entirely right to them. Perhaps it is the poisons to which she is exposed. Perhaps it is genetic, she a child born of
parents who were also exposed. Perhaps it is a fresh form of madness that
claims her early, a madness that they believe will eventually claim them
all.*

*She knows what they think of her because she overhears them talking
now and then, and their thinking is always the same.*

They refuse to believe what she knows is true.

*But tonight is different, the voices so strong and angry, refusing to be si-
lenced or dismissed. She runs to her parents, waking them from their sleep,
telling them they must listen to her, that they are all in great danger.*

*Yet even now, even in the face of her pleading, they do not listen. They
tell her it is all right, that she must go back to sleep, that they will sit with
her until she does, that nothing bad will happen. Even at six years of age,*

she knows that this is not true. Even wanting to believe it, she knows. A horror is coming, and no amount of pretending will make it go away.

Please, she begs. We have to run away.

Her father rolls over and goes back to sleep. Her mother walks her to her room, comforting her as she cries helplessly. There, there, her mother soothes, stroking her fine red hair, hugging her as they reach her bed. I will hold you.

No, you must run! You must run away now! Run fast and hide!

The voices talk over her mother, drowning out the comforting words, filling her mind with sound and fury, with sharp twinges of terror. She does not know what to do. She cannot think what else to say.

She is terrified. She is helpless.

When her mother leaves her at last, she lies still only a moment, then leaves her bed and climbs through the window of her home. They live in a house at the edge of what is left of the city of Seattle. It has been her house since she was born, and she knows everything about it. She spends hours in her backyard, playing games. One of her favorites is hide-and-seek. She practices hiding, waiting for her mother or her father to come looking for her. Her parents have asked her not to play this game without telling them first, but most of the time she likes to keep her game a secret.

Tonight is one of those times.

She runs to the very back of her yard and hides in her favorite place, a deep hole that runs under the storage shed in back. The opening is narrow enough for her to squeeze through, but too narrow for anyone or anything bigger. It makes her feel safe to be in the hole, in her secret place. She needs to feel safe this night, the voices so loud and demanding. They quiet the moment she is inside, scrunched back in the darkness, deep in the shadows.

When the screaming begins, she pulls her knees up to her chest and hugs herself tightly. She tries not to listen, to pretend that it isn't happening. She hums softly to herself, rocking back and forth. The screaming doesn't last very long, and then she hears footsteps coming her way. The steps are heavy and are accompanied by heavy, guttural breathing. They approach the shed, circle it once, and move away.

She stays where she is until sunrise. When she crawls from her hiding place, she sees her mother's nightgown lying on the dry, wintry grass of the yard. There is blood all over it. She stares at it a moment, and then she

stares at the house, at the back door hanging open, at the walls and win-
dows. She listens to the silence and peers at the shadows that lie just inside
the open door. She waits a moment, and then she turns away.

She does not need to go inside. She knows what she will find. The voices
have told her, and the voices are never wrong.

She leaves her home and walks down into the city, not knowing what
else to do. She will find a new home, she tells herself. She will find a new
family. She is certain of this in the way that small children are.

When she comes upon Owl, her faith is rewarded.

THAT WAS WHEN she was Sarah and before she became Candle, and it was a very long time ago. She sat in the darkness with her knees drawn up to her chest and rocked back and forth and remembered. Time slowed to a crawl, and she listened for the warning voices, but they had gone silent. She was no longer in danger. She was safe.

But the boy who had left her . . .

The screaming began with shocking suddenness, long and sustained, and she cringed from the sound as if struck a physical blow. She clapped her hands to her ears, not wanting to hear, knowing where the screaming came from, knowing its source.

Why wouldn't he listen to her? Why wouldn't her parents? Why wouldn't anyone?

But only the Ghosts had ever listened. Only the Ghosts had known the value of her voices.

She took slow, deep breaths to calm herself, to blot out the fear and the horror, to make the moments pass more quickly. She hugged herself more tightly, feeling cold and abandoned. Then, unable to stand the waiting further, she stilled her breathing and listened.

Silence.

She waited a long time for the silence to break, for the sounds of whatever predator was out there, but she heard nothing. She got to her feet and peered through the grasses toward the roadway. Nothing moved. She hesitated, wanting to know for sure, but at the same time wanting to keep alive some small hope that she was wrong. The latter won out. There was nothing to be gained by looking. She turned away from the highway and continued walking through the grasses to their end, and from there across an empty, barren stretch of earth that had once been a planted field, and from there through a yard past several farm buildings and back toward the highway and the family from which she had been taken.

She was very tired and very sad.

They won't come for you, you know. No one ever comes for you once you're gone.

She could hear the boy with the ruined face speaking those cruel words, and the memory chilled her. But he was wrong. This was her family, and her family would never leave her. Not the Ghosts. Not Owl and Sparrow and Panther and the others. They would come.

She gained the highway and followed it south toward the place where she had left them. They would come, she told herself again and again.

Just before dawn, as the rising sun turned the sky a strange silvery red below a bank of heavy smoke and ash from a fire whose origins she could only guess at, they did.

TWENTY-TWO

FOR NEARLY TWO WEEKS, Simralin led her brother and
Angel Perez north through the high desert east of the Cintra,
following the spine of the mountains they had entered after
fleeing Arborlon. The days were hot, the nights cool, and the air dry
and filled with the taste and smell of iron. They traversed long stretches
of sandy soil studded with scrub brush and wiry trees whose branches
had somehow kept their bristle-ridged leaves and rocky lava fields that
suggested how the world might have looked when it was first being
born. The miles disappeared behind them, but the look of the land
never changed. After a time, Kirisin began to wonder if they were actually getting anywhere or simply going in circles, but he kept his concerns to himself and placed his trust in his sister.

In any case, all his spare energy was tied up in keeping watch for the
demons tracking them. He knew they were back there, following
soundlessly and invisibly, waiting for their chance. Sooner or later they
would appear, intent on killing them all, probably when least expected.
He tried not to let his distress show, to be more like his sister and Angel

Perez, who were always so calm and steady. Nothing seemed to disturb either of them. Of course, they were more used to living like this, to being either the hunter or the hunted. They had learned long ago to co-exist with uncertainty and edginess. He was still trying to figure out how to deal with both, and the effort was draining him. He wasn't sleeping, he wasn't eating, and he was barely able to think of anything else. The repetitive nature of their travel only added to his sense of dread. Each day was a fresh slog through a forest of fears, a mind-numbing trek toward the disaster he knew was waiting. Nothing he did could dispel this certainty and the effect it was having on him. He could barely remember what life had been like before. His time as a Chosen, as a caretaker for the Ellcrys, might have happened a hundred years ago.

But there was an unintended and oddly positive aspect to his dis-tress that he had not anticipated. He had begun this journey filled with pain and grief for the dead he had left behind. He had thought he would never feel good about anything again, haunted by what he had witnessed and how he had failed to prevent it. But day by day he found himself experiencing a gradual erosion of his despair, a wearing-away of the once seemingly unforgettable images of Erisha as she lay dying. He was able to stop trying to picture Ailie and old Culph in their final mo-ments, as well. It didn't happen all at once or even in a way that was immediately recognizable. It wasn't that he was healing, but that his hurt and grief had been crowded out by his fears and dark expecta-tions. There was no room for the former when the latter consumed his every waking minute.

The strength of his conviction that the King was responsible for all three deaths continued to grow. Perhaps it was that certainty and the anger that accompanied it that kept him from collapse. Each night, as they huddled together in whatever shelter they were able to find, they spoke of the killings and the reasons for which they were carried out. There seemed little doubt about any of it, save for the part that had al-lowed Kirisin to survive and escape with the blue Elfstones. Given the fact that they had been caught so completely off guard coming out of the underground tombs of Ashenell, it seemed that killing both Cho-sen should have been a sure thing. Angel thought that perhaps it was

Simralin's quick action that had saved him. Putting out the four-legged demon's eye and leaving the dagger embedded in the socket had worked just enough damage that it was only able to reach Erisha. Simralin, on the other hand, thought that the demon had simply taken on more than it could handle, and that they had all contributed to its failure to succeed.

Kirisin wasn't sure what he thought, save that he was certain the demon in hiding among the Elves was Arissen Belloruus. He wondered what they were going to do to reveal this even if they found the Loden and returned it to Arborlon and the Elves. How were they going to remove the threat before they closed away the city and the Elves as the Ellcrys had asked of them?

"One step at a time, Little K," his sister replied when, after more than a week out, he finally managed to voice his concerns. "We can't solve it all at once and maybe we won't even know *how* to solve it until we get to that point. You don't want to look too far ahead in something like this."

They were seated on a ledge at the beginning of a downslope off the high desert, looking north toward the eastern slopes of the Cintra Mountains and beyond to the silvery thread of a wide river. It was after crossing the river that they would reach Syrring Rise.

"You didn't solve the secret of the hiding place of the Elfstones all at once," Angel pointed out. "You had to solve it piecemeal."

Kirisin screwed up his face. "It's just that I keep thinking we aren't going to have much time to do anything but use the Loden once we find it and get back to Arborlon. Maybe we will have to shut the demon away with our own people just because we can't figure out who it is."

"One demon, thousands of Elves," said his sister. "Pretty decent odds, even if it happens."

"Tell me something more of the history behind this tree we're trying to save," Angel asked suddenly. "What is it that makes it so important?"

Simralin and Kirisin exchanged a quick glance. "You tell her, Little K," his sister said. "You're the one who knows the story best."

Kirisin drew up his knees and hugged them to his chest. He didn't want to tell anybody anything, didn't want to talk at all. "This is what our histories tell us, so I'm just repeating," he said, forcing himself anyway. "But I think it is mostly true. Before there were humans in the world, there were Faeries. The Faeries were the first people. All sorts, all kinds, good and bad. Like humans. Elves were one of the stronger, more dominant species. They believed that all life had value and should be preserved. Others did not. The bad ones. So there was a war. The Faeries fought in the same way humans fight except that many had the use of magic and some of their magic was very powerful. Eventually, the practitioners of dark magic began to gain an advantage. Their intention was to dominate the other species and redesign the world in a way that better suited them. They could do that, given enough time and space.

"The Elves led a coalition of Faerie creatures who opposed the dark magic users and their allies. The war lasted a very long time. Centuries. In the end, the Elves and their allies prevailed. They created a talisman through the use of a combination of elemental and blood magic—the most powerful magic of all—to construct a prison for their enemies. The talisman was the Ellcrys, the only one of her kind, a tree that would live thousands of years and maintain a barrier behind which the Faerie creatures that practiced dark magic and their allies would be shut away. The barrier was called the Forbidding."

"And the Ellcrys is what keeps the Forbidding in place?" Angel interrupted. "Her magic is the catalyst?"

He nodded. "For the Forbidding to endure, the Ellcrys must be kept healthy and strong. The Chosen were formed after her creation to ensure that she stayed so."

"So if the Forbidding fails . . ."

"The demons escape," Kirisin finished. "Back into our world. Faerie demons no one has seen in thousands of years. Monsters of all sorts. Creatures of dark magic. Worse than those the humans have spawned, maybe."

"Perhaps they would kill each other off," Simralin offered with a wry smile.

"Perhaps they would kill all of us off first," Angel replied. She shook her head. "How is it that these things are created? What permits them life? I believe in the Word; I have seen its power and spoken with its servants. The Word created everything. But I keep asking myself. Why did it create things like this? Why does it permit demons to exist?"

Kirisin shrugged. "In the world of Faerie, the demons and their kind were always there. What difference does it make? They exist and they threaten us. Humans have done nothing about it. Humans don't even work to protect the world they live in like the Elves do. They don't seem to know how to stop the demons from claiming everything. That's why we're where we are now."

His anger surfaced and carried him away for a moment, and he remembered too late to whom he was speaking.

"Little K," his sister said softly. "Angel knows."

He stopped talking abruptly as he felt the color of his embarrassment rise from his neck into his cheeks. "Sorry," he said. "I didn't mean it."

"It's nothing." Angel gave him a quick smile. "You meant it, and you were right to mean it. Humans have failed themselves and their world, and they are going to lose everything because of it. That's why we're here. Because all we can do now is pick up enough pieces to begin putting everything back together again."

"Seems that way," he mumbled, still ashamed of his outburst.

"Tell me about the Loden, Kirisin."

He shook his head. "There isn't much to tell. No one knows exactly what it does. Not even old Culph knew. It is a powerful Elfstone, mined and formed in the early days of the Faerie world like the others. It operates alone—unlike most Elfstones, which work in sets. It disappeared a long time ago, and the histories don't say anything about it."

"That's odd, isn't it?" she asked. "That there's no mention of it at all?"

Kirisin had thought that himself more than once. A talisman of magic as powerful and important as the Loden should have had a special place in the Elven histories. Why wasn't there any mention of it?

"I don't know why there isn't anything written," he admitted. He thought about it some more. "The Ellcrys said, when she spoke to me that first time, that I was to use the seeking-Elfstones to find it, then to carry the Loden to her and place her within it."

"Maybe the Loden acts as a sort of barrier in the same way as the

Ellcrys," Angel suggested. "But what are you supposed to do with it once you find out how to put the Ellcrys inside?"

"And what about the Elves?" Simralin finished.

There were no ready answers for any of these questions, and in the end all they could do was speculate. But it helped them pass the time and gave them a chance to examine anew the nature of their undertaking and its importance to the Elven people. Kirisin was already invested in the effort and Simralin, too, if less so. But Angel was a different story. Her commitment was tenuous, at best. She was still trying to come to terms with what she had been given to do. The boy understood her reticence and accepted it. The Elves were not her people and the battle not hers to fight. She had her own struggle against her own enemies. As a Knight of the Word, she was fighting for the human race, not for the Elves. She hadn't even known of the existence of the Elves before Ailie came to her. She had accepted what the tatterdemalion had told her she must do, a charge given directly by the Word. It was in the nature of her service that she must do so. But that didn't mean she had embraced it emotionally. Her charge had been a different one until now. It wasn't as if she could simply walk away from it without looking back, without wondering if she had made a wrong choice, without asking herself if she had jumped from bad to worse.

Kirisin would have wondered the same thing if he had been in her shoes. He would have balked at helping the humans who had done so much to destroy his world and endanger his people. He might easily have refused. He gave her credit for not doing so. She was risking every bit as much as he had in believing that what she had been asked to do was important and necessary.

But her heart was not necessarily as committed as his sister's and his own to their undertaking, and he worried that at some point her reticence would prove a dangerous failing.

He worried, but unlike so much of what troubled him, he kept this particular worry to himself.

ANGEL PEREZ was indeed conflicted. Conflicted enough that she was becoming increasingly disenchanted with her place in the world. It wasn't that she didn't intend to do her best to help Kirisin and his sister in their efforts to find the Loden Elfstone; it was that she wasn't yet convinced that this was what she should be doing. Ailie had said so, but Ailie, her conscience in this strange business, was gone. She had only herself to turn to for reassurance, and she wasn't finding much of what she needed by doing so.

She could chart her discontent like a map. She had gone from the East LA barrio and its residents to the magically enhanced Cintra forest and its Elves in a matter of only days. She had gone with almost no warning or preparation. Everything with which she was familiar had been stripped from her. She had never been anywhere but the neighborhood and city in which she was born until now. She had never believed in even the possibility of the existence of Elves. Since losing Johnny and finding O'olish Amaneh, she had fought a battle that involved helping children.

What battle was she fighting now? A battle to find a magic Stone that would help save a magic tree? Just thinking the words seemed to point out the obvious. She didn't understand them, didn't really know what obeying them was meant to accomplish. She was here because the Lady had sent her but, as Kirisin feared, that didn't mean she was emotionally committed to what she was doing. Commitment for her did not come easily and was not given without strong reason. Helping children from the compounds and on the streets of LA was something she understood. She had been one of those children. But these were Elves she had come to serve—Elves, who were a people of which she knew practically nothing. A people, she added quickly, who in large part did not like or trust humans. They looked and acted like humans, but their thinking was formed by centuries of life and experience that preceded human existence.

She was doing what she had been sent to do, but was she doing the right thing?

Her misgivings haunted her in a dull, repetitive sort of way, always present to remind her of her blind and possibly foolish trust in the words of a dead tatterdemalion.

She could not get past it.

THEY WALKED on into the second week, coming down off the slopes of the northernmost peaks in the Cintra Mountain chain and within clear sight of the river that separated the states of Oregon and Washington. Humans called it the Columbia, Elves the Redonnelin Deep. Ahead, across the river and hidden by haze and distance, Syrring Rise waited.

As they stopped to assess the lay of the land they must travel through, Angel found herself thinking of the children she had left in the care of Helen Rice and the others, the children rescued from the Southern California compounds. Helen would be bringing them north to the Columbia as Angel had asked her to do and would wait there for help. What sort of help and from whom remained a mystery. It should have been her, but Ailie had left that particular issue in doubt. Angel felt consumed by helplessness. Had they gotten this far? Had they even gotten out of the state? Or had the demons and the once-men tracked them down? Those children were her responsibility and her charge to herself, and she had let herself be persuaded to give up on both.

"Not so far now," Simralin said quietly, passing Angel her waterskin.

"Far enough," Angel murmured, thinking of something else entirely.

The Elven girl glanced over. "We've done well, Angel. A lot that could have happened hasn't. We could have been caught and attacked by those demons, but we've managed to stay one step ahead of them."

"You don't think they've given up, do you?" Kirisin asked hopefully.

His face was haggard and worn, and his eyes had a haunted look to them. Angel did not like what she was seeing. The boy's physical condition had deteriorated since they had set out, and there was no way of knowing how he was doing emotionally. He looked worn to the bone.

Simralin was shaking her head. "No, I don't think they've given up. I don't expect them ever to give up. All we can do is make it as hard as we can to find us. Now that we're coming up on Redonnelin Deep, I have a chance to make it almost impossible."

Angel glanced over, her brow knitting. "What do you mean?"

Simralin stopped and pointed ahead to the broad stretch of the river. "I mean that if we can get across before they catch up to us, we can hide from them where we come ashore. It could take them days, maybe weeks to find the right spot. If they can't track us to where we land, they won't know where we are going."

Angel shook her head. "I think they already know."

Simralin and her brother stared. "How could they?" the Tracker asked. "We didn't know ourselves until Kirisin used the Elfstones."

"Just a hunch." Angel handed back the waterskin. "Ever since this business started, they've been one step ahead of us. One of them tracked me all the way north from LA. It shouldn't have been able to do that, but it did. The other seems to have known what Kirisin and Erisha were trying to do almost from the moment they did. I just have a feeling they know this time, too."

Kirisin gave her an exasperated look. "Well, what should we do, Angel?"

She smiled unexpectedly. "We do what we are here to do. When the demons surface, they become my problem. Yours—yours and Simralin's—is to find the Loden and use it in the way it is meant to be used and save your people."

They traveled through the rest of that day and into the next, a long, torturous slog through hot, dry, open country denuded of plant life and filled with the bleached bones of humans and animals alike. It was a graveyard of indeterminate origin, a grim memorial to the presence of the dead and the absence of the living. Finally, when they were within a mile of Redonnelin Deep, Simralin turned them sharply northeast.

"We're going to need help getting across," she announced. "We require a boat."

"Aren't there bridges?" Angel asked. She was hot and tired and still sick at heart about the children she felt she had abandoned. She constantly found herself looking for some sign of them along the river-bank, even when she knew there wouldn't be any, that there hadn't been time for them to get this far. "A river this size, there must be one or two that would take us across on foot."

"More than that, actually. But the bridges are in the hands of militias and some others that are even worse. We don't want to fight that battle if we don't have to." She gestured ahead. "Better to use a boat. I know someone who can help us. An old friend."

"No one who sees us looking like this will want to help," Kirisin declared.

They were dust-covered and dirt-streaked from head to foot. They hadn't bathed in almost two weeks, traversing the high desert and lava fields with only the water they carried for drinking and nothing with which to wash. Angel looked at the other two and could only imagine how bad she must look.

But Simralin simply shrugged. "Don't worry, Little K. This particular friend couldn't care less."

They trudged across the flats approaching the river through the heat of the afternoon and by nightfall's approach had reached it. There were houses along the lower banks, dilapidated and empty, docks to which boats had once been moored and now were crumbling, and weedy paths that meandered in between. There was no sign of life anywhere.

The river itself was swift and wide, the open waters churning with whitecaps and the inlets thick with debris and deadwood collected and jammed together by deep rapids. In the fading light, the waters were gray and silt-clogged, and from its depths emanated a thick and unpleasant odor that suggested secrets hidden below the surface of other creatures' failed attempts at crossing.

"Are you sure about this?" Kirisin asked uneasily. "Maybe a bridge would be safer, after all."

Simralin only grinned and put a reassuring arm around him before setting off anew. Angel wasn't sure, either, but the Tracker had gotten them this far without incident. She thought briefly of the children whom Helen Rice and the other protectors were guiding north and wished she could do the same for them. She glanced up and down the banks, and then looked behind her for what she knew she wouldn't see.

I can't seem to help myself, she thought.

Afraid, as she thought it, that she would never see any of them again.

TWENTY-THREE

DARKNESS CLOSED ABOUT the three weary travelers as they entered a stand of skeletal trees as bare and lifeless as the bones of the dying earth, bleached white and worn smooth. The woods seemed sparse at first, but the trunks stood so close together that two dozen feet in, it became impossible to tell which way led out. Simralin looked unfazed, picking their path without hesitating, taking them deeper in. After a time, they reached an inlet that had cut away into a ring of surrounding cliffs. Piles of jagged rocks broken off by time and upheaval lay all along the shoreline, their sharp-edged outlines suggesting the ridged backs of sleeping dragons. The travelers angled right along the shoreline, skirting the rocks when they could, climbing over them when they couldn't. In the dark it was hot, arduous work, and Angel kept feeling that both time and opportunity were slipping away.

Finally, several hours after they had begun their inlet trek, they caught sight of a pinprick of light ahead, dim and hazy in a thick stand of ruined trees, burning out of the window of a small cottage.

"We're here," Simralin advised, giving them a quick smile.

They climbed over a tangled mound of fallen trees, forded a stream that branched off the inlet, and arrived outside the cottage with its solitary light. The sheltering harbor was so draped with shadows from the cliffs and trees that the gloom was all but impenetrable. Angel, who had excellent eyesight, could barely make out the details of the cottage and the surrounding landscape.

"Larkin?" Simralin called into the darkness. "Are you home?"

"Right behind you, Simralin Belloruus," was the immediate response.

The answering voice was so close that Angel jumped despite herself. She wheeled about to find a solitary figure standing not three feet away. The nature of the speaker was not immediately identifiable. Male and grown, but the rest was a mystery. The face and body both were concealed by a long cloak and hood wrapped tightly about. A hand that was definitely human emerged from one sleeve and gestured.

"Heard you coming half a mile away." The hand withdrew. "You made a lot of noise for a Tracker."

"Hiding our approach wasn't my intention," Simralin declared. "If I didn't want you to know I was coming, you wouldn't."

"Wouldn't I?" A small laugh drifted through the dark. "Well, now that you've arrived, would you and your companions like to come inside and have something to eat?" There was a pause. "Traveled a long way to get here, didn't you. Through the high desert, maybe? Not your usual route, Sim." Another pause. "Um, a bath might be a good idea before you eat. Then straight to sleep. You all seem a bit used up."

The speaker stepped around them carefully, started toward the cottage, and suddenly stopped short. "Oh, here's something I almost missed!" The hand gestured toward Angel. "A human! Making friends with the enemy now, are we, Sim? Or is she something special?"

"This is Angel Perez," Simralin replied, giving Angel a wink. "And she is something special. She is a Knight of the Word."

"Ah, a bearer of the black staff. Pleased to meet you." The hand extended, and Angel took it in her own. It was lean and hard. "And the boy? Is this your brother?"

"The very one. Kirisin."

The hand extended again, and Kirisin gave it a quick shake. "Larkin Quill. Now we all know who we are. Come inside."

He took them through the shadows and gloom and the door of the cottage. The solitary light they had seen earlier burned from a smoke-less lamp set on a table, but there were no other lights in evidence, and the little house was buried in darkness. Angel had to look carefully be-fore moving so as not to bump into things. Kirisin wasn't so fortunate and promptly ran into a chair.

"Put on some lights, Sim," their host ordered. "Not everyone can see in the dark as well as I can."

Simralin moved comfortably about the cottage, obviously familiar with its interior, lighting lamps with only a touch of her hand. Angel could see no power source and smell no fuel burning. She had never seen anything quite like it. She was also surprised by the deep, rich, loamy smell of the cottage, as if it were as much a part of the forest as the trees. She had even caught a strong whiff of that smell on Larkin.

But these were only small surprises compared with what followed. As the light chased back the dark, Larkin removed his hooded cloak and turned to face them. He was a lean Elf of indeterminate age with strong, sharp features and a shock of wild black hair. He looked strong and fit beneath his loose, well-worn clothing, and his slightly crooked smile was warm and welcoming. But his eyes, flat and milky and fixed, caused Angel to take a quick breath.

Larkin Quill was blind.

"I can always tell when someone first notices," he said to her. "There is a kind of momentary hush that is unmistakable. Isn't that how it was with you, Sim?"

"That was how it was," she agreed.

Angel was stunned. How could this man find his way about in the tangle of the forest so easily when he was blind? How had he been able to tell who they were or of what sex without being able to see them? How had he known they were dirty or had traveled far?

Simralin gave her a knowing smile. "Hard to believe, isn't it? He takes great pleasure in showing off his skills. He went blind about five years ago, but his other senses have compensated for it in an extraordi-nary way. He can see much better than you or I over short distances.

Sometimes I wonder about the long distances, as well. He sees things that I don't think sighted people even notice. That's how he manages to live out here all by himself."

"I was a Tracker like Sim," Larkin said. "When I lost my sight, I lost my job. No one thought I could do it anymore. I wasn't too pleased about that because I knew how well I could see. Better than they could, those who thought I had no further use. So I moved out here, away from everyone but the few like Sim who would take the trouble to come see me. It was my way of proving I was still whole, I suppose. Childish, in a way. But it suits me."

He moved over to the tiny kitchen and without pausing or fumbling brought down glasses and poured out the contents of an ale jug until each was full.

"Long-range Trackers like myself know about Larkin," Simralin continued. "We rely on him. He keeps a boat to ferry us across the Redonnelin Deep so we can avoid using the bridges. He takes us across and then comes back to get us when we're done. He reads the currents of the river the same way he reads the faces of the Elves who think he can't see." She smiled. "Don't you, Larkin?"

"If you say so. Who would know better than you?" He took a deep swallow from his glass. "She hasn't told you yet that she was the one who saved me when I lost my sight. We were on patrol together below the Cintra and came across a mantis field."

"The insects," Simralin interjected. "Thousands of them."

"Thousands, devouring everything in their path. But some of these had mutated. They spit out a poison that blinded me before I realized the danger. Poor instincts, that day. Simralin was lucky. They missed her, and she was able to get us both away. The Elves went out later and eradicated the mantis field. Too late for me, though."

"He was my mentor before and after the accident," Simralin said, continuing the story. "He taught me how to be a Tracker, taught me everything I know. He still teaches me. He still knows more than I do."

"That's because I'm older and I've had time to learn more. Now why don't you go bathe, you and Angel Perez? Then we'll wash down our junior member of the family. Meanwhile, Kirisin, you can keep me company and tell me everything I don't know about your sister. Come on, now. Don't be shy. I'm willing to bet that there's lots you can tell me that she doesn't want me to know."

There was a rudimentary shower out in back of the cottage at the base of the cliffs that took its water from a narrow falls. Angel and Simralin stripped off their clothes and began to wash. The water felt icy cold as it splashed over Angel's hot skin.

"I can't believe anyone who is blind could live out here alone like this," she said, scrubbing off the dirt. "In fact, I can't believe that he can tell as much as he can about what's going on around him."

Simralin caught the bar of soap she was tossed. "He sees in ways none of us can. He won't talk about it, but it's there in the way he knows things no blind person should be able to know. Not even with enhanced senses. He's a different breed."

"But the Elves don't know this?"

The Tracker shrugged. "Elves aren't so different from humans. They make up their minds and pass judgment without knowing as much as they should. 'Blind people can't see. Blind people can't do as much as sighted people.' You've heard something like it. No one questions that it could be any different for him. Certainly, they don't want to take a chance on him as a Tracker."

They finished washing, and then sent Kirisin out to do the same. When they were all clean and wearing the one change of clothes they had brought with them as they fled Arborlon, they sat down to eat. Dinner was hot and tasty. Angel never even bothered to ask what it was she was eating; she just ate it and washed it down with ale and felt a little of the aching weariness seep from her body.

Afterward, they sat out on Larkin's tiny porch while Simralin told him what had brought them north from the Cintra and what sort of danger he might be in if he agreed to help.

"We need a crossing," she finished. "We need to get to the far shore without being seen and without anyone knowing you helped."

The blind man said nothing, made no movement.

"In truth, you shouldn't help," she added as they stared at one another in the ensuing silence. "A smart man would tell us to take our troubles somewhere else."

He nodded, and his Elven face wrinkled with amusement. "Good advice, I'm sure."

"Arissen Belloruus will have sent his Elven Hunters looking for us. Those demons will come looking, too."

"I expect so. They might even show up at the same time."

Simralin gazed at him. "You don't sound as if you are taking this seriously enough. You sound like you think this is amusing. But there are three dead people back in Arborlon who would tell you differently if they could still talk."

Larkin brushed off her comments with a wave of his hand. "Do you want my help or not, Simralin? Did you come all this way to talk me out of doing anything or to talk me into it? You can't have it both ways."

"I just want to make certain you understand—"

"Yes, that this is dangerous business." He leaned forward, his milky eyes fixed and unseeing, but his attention all on her. "What have we ever done as Trackers that isn't dangerous? We live in a world that is filled with dangerous creatures, infected with plague and poison, and saturated in madness at every turn. I think I have the picture."

She stared at him, her lips tight. "Sometimes you make me want to scream."

"Please resist the urge. Now then. We should make the crossing at first light, when the tide is out and the world mostly still at rest. In the meantime, it looks to me as if young Kirisin has the right idea."

They glanced over. The boy was asleep in his chair.

Larkin rose without waiting for a response to his suggestion and gestured toward one corner of the room. "We can make a place for all three of you right over there. A little crowded, but if you are as tired as you look, it shouldn't matter. I'll keep watch while you rest."

He paused, his head cocking slightly in the silence that followed, his blank gaze fixing on the space that separated them. "Have I been clear enough for you?"

◼ ◼ ◼

ANGEL SLEPT POORLY that night, plagued by dreams of Johnny. In her dreams, he was still alive, walking the streets of the barrio, keeping watch over the people who lived there in the wake of civilization's collapse. She was a child still, and he was her protector. She would sit in the doorway of their home and wait for him to return, scanning the faces of those who passed, searching for his, afraid until she found it.

And then one day, in her dream as in her life, she searched for him in vain.

The dawn was unexpectedly chill and damp as they set out across Redonnelin Deep, the air thick with moisture off the river and the sky gray with roiling storm clouds. A change in the weather was coming, something no one saw much of anymore. It might even bring serious rain, although Angel was doubtful. No one had seen more than a trace of rain in LA in almost a year. Could it be so different here?

"The higher mountains might even see snow," said Larkin Quill, smiling brightly into the wind and the light as he steered the boat from the shelter of the inlet toward the open water. His face was lifted into the wind, as if he took direction from its feel. "Once, there was snow on the upper slopes year-round. I was told that. Imagine. Snowcaps all year long, brilliant veils of white. Wouldn't that be something to see? Syrring Rise, draped in white?"

The boat that conveyed them northward was a blunt, heavy craft with a metal-reinforced bow, the cleats of her gunwales wrapped with old tires and lashed with protective fenders. She boasted a pilothouse, an open aft deck, a galley, and two berths below through a hatchway. Twin inboard engines thrummed softly and, in the same way as the lamps inside the little cottage, seemed to lack any source of fuel. When Angel asked Larkin how they worked, he just smiled and shrugged.

"Magic," he said.

Not magic of a sort that she was used to, she thought. She had believed until now that the Elves had lost all their magic, but it seemed that a revision of her thinking was in order. She let the matter alone for the moment, but made a promise to herself to follow up on it later. For now, it was enough that they were leaving the land in which the demons prowled and the Elven King hunted and the dream of Johnny still haunted her in her sleep.

Adios, mi amigo, she whispered to the wind, thinking of him once more. *You were the best of us all. Rest in peace forever.*

The chop of the waters quickened, and the waves grew higher. The earlier haze had settled lower on the waters, long trailers fanning out, weaving strange patterns. She looked back at the shoreline and found that it was already fading away.

Vaya con Dios. Tu madre sueña contigo. Your mother dreams of you.

Then, as she lifted her eyes toward the high bluffs that Larkin Quill's little cottage backed up against, she caught sight of something moving. Three figures, indistinct and shadowy, appeared out of the veil of the mist. They stood at the edge of the bluff and looked down at her.

A boy, a girl, and a very large dog.

They were visible for just a few seconds, and then they faded back into the mist. As the boat moved farther out into the channel, she tried repeatedly to find them again, but could not do so.

When she finally turned away, setting her gaze on the shoreline ahead, she was not even certain of what she had seen.

ON THE FAR BANK, two figures crouched behind a screen of heavy brush and peered out at the boat that was crossing toward them. The boat could not put in anywhere close to where they waited, which was atop a sheer cliff wall that dropped straight into the rough waters of the river. Instead the boat would land farther upriver, where an inlet offered shallow waters running up to a small sandbar. After disembarking, the occupants would be forced to ascend a steep, rocky slope to the heights, a climb that would consume the better part of an hour. By then, the watchers would be gone, leading the way to their mutual destination, a place known as well to them as to the three they shadowed.

Shadowed, rather than tracked, thought the one.

"It would trouble them to know that we will be there to greet them," the two-legged demon whispered to the four. "See how they look behind, searching the shoreline for some sign of us? How worried they must be that we will catch them unawares! How helpless they must feel! They have no idea that we passed them by more than a week ago, do they?"

It reached over and stroked the other demon's sleek, scaly form, feeling it press itself against its hand, anxious for its touch.

"They have no idea of anything," the speaker whispered.

They watched the boat sail slowly closer, buffeted by the waves, knocked about by the current, straining mightily to stay on course for the inlet. But the watching quickly grew tedious, and the four-legged demon became restless. The other demon understood. It was time to quit this place, to continue on with their journey.

The two-legged demon edged backward until it could no longer see the river, then rose to a standing position. "We know where they will go next, don't we, pretty thing?" it murmured to its companion. "Oh, yes, we know. We know everything."

The Elves and the Knight of the Word would soon find that out.

TWENTY-FOUR

WHEN HAWK WOKE, it was dawn on a gray and mist-draped morning, the sky and earth of a single hue, the air smelling of damp and old earth. He lay in a sparse woods close by the edge of a bluff that sloped away toward a deep gorge; through this a broad-banked river churned, its surface white-capped and choppy. He could see the far side of the river and the high, cliff-edged bank beyond, but the land after that was shrouded in a deep, impenetrable haze.

He had no idea at all where he was.

He glanced over to find Tessa lying several feet away, still asleep, and beyond her—a dark shaggy lump against the wintry grasses—was Cheney.

For just a moment, his thoughts returned to the gardens of the King of the Silver River. His senses were infused with its colors and its smells, his memories of what the old man had told him fresh and new, and his vision of his destiny as clear as still water. Then the moment was gone and he was staring into the gray, past the sleeping forms of his companions to a future he could only imagine.

Tessa woke. Her eyes opened and she sat up slowly, her eyes fixing on him. "We're alive," she said softly.

He moved to sit close to her and took her hands in his. "Are you all right? Are you hurt in any way?"

She touched herself experimentally. "No. Are you?"

He shook his head.

"How can that be, Hawk? We were thrown from the compound wall and we fell and . . ." She trailed off, brushing nervously at her tousled hair. "And what?" She stared at him in bewilderment. "I can't remember anything after that."

"And we lived happily ever after," he said, smiling. "Just like Owl's stories."

She arched one eyebrow. "That would be nice. Now tell me the truth. What happened to us?"

So he told her, taking his time, remembering things as he went, trying not to leave anything out. Mostly Tessa just listened, but once or twice she couldn't help herself and had to stop him to ask a question. There was incredulity and disbelief mirrored in her eyes, but she did not try to tell him he might be mistaken or had dreamed this story or was a victim of delusion. She sat facing him, and her eyes never left his.

When he was finished and silence had enveloped them, she sat without moving for a moment. Then she leaned forward suddenly and kissed him on the lips, her hand behind his neck so that he would not move away, and she held the kiss for a very long time.

"I love you," she told him when she finally broke away. "I love you so much." She cupped his face in her hands. "I knew there was something special about you. I knew there was nobody else like you. I knew it from the moment we met. The stories Owl told are true. You are the boy who will save his children. You are the one who will find a safe place for all of us."

He took a deep breath. "It's only what I've been told. I don't know how much of it I can believe."

"But you're not like the rest of us, are you? You're something different. I mean, you don't look it, but you are. You're a Faerie creature of some sort. Both Logan Tom and the old man said so. So maybe it's true. Maybe you are." She seemed to consider the idea more carefully. "What does that mean, Hawk?" she asked finally. "How are you different? Can you tell me anything?"

He studied her for a moment. "Does knowing I might be different make you afraid of me?" he asked.

She shook her head quickly. "No, that isn't what I mean. What I mean is . . . I just want to know. I want to understand. Are you put together differently? When you were born, were you . . . ?"

She squeezed her eyes shut, and he saw tears. "Sorry. I don't know what I was thinking. I wish I hadn't asked. It doesn't matter. You are still the boy I fell in love with. You are the one I will always love. It doesn't matter how you are made or what you can do or any of it." She clasped his hands tightly in her own. "Just forget I asked. Please. We won't say anything about it again. Let's talk about something else. Tell me what we are going to do?"

Cheney was waking up now, his big head lifting to look over at them. His gray eyes were calm, and his gaze steady. He did not look to Hawk as if he thought anything strange had happened to him. He looked just the way he always looked—alert and ready.

"I don't know where we are going," he told Tessa, getting to his feet and then helping her stand, as well. "I don't even know where we are. I know there is a river in the gorge below us. That's about all."

"You must have some idea," she insisted. Her dusky face broke into a sudden grin. "How can you save anyone if you don't know how to find them?"

He shrugged. "I'm kind of new at this. I have to learn as I go. Do you have any ideas?"

She looked around. "Let's walk over to the edge of the bluff and see if we can tell anything from that."

They left the shelter of the trees, walked across the bluff to its edge, and peered over. A solitary boat was making a slow, arduous passage from their side of the river to the far bank. There were four passengers. The first of them, cloaked and hooded in black, stood at the steering wheel on the bridge, staring forward into the haze. Two more were seated on the decking benches just below. The last—a woman, Hawk thought—stood at the aft railing looking up at him. For a moment it seemed their eyes met, and it almost felt to him that they knew each other.

Then the mist rolled in again, and the boat disappeared. Hawk stared after it for a long time without speaking.

"We have to cross that river," he said finally.

"Do you know where we are now?" Tessa asked him.

"No, but it doesn't matter. What I know is that we have to cross that river."

"How do you know that?"

He shook his head. "I can't explain it. I just do." He looked over at her. "Something inside tells me."

Cheney moved up beside them, his big head lowering to sniff the ground. A light rain was beginning to fall, and the mist on the water was thickening. The dawn should have brought a steady brightening into day; instead, the light seemed to be failing and the dark growing stronger.

"I wish I could tell you something more," Hawk said softly.

Tessa looked at him for a moment, and then she took his arm and turned him toward her. "You've told me enough. We'd better get started."

HAWK CHOSE THEIR PATH. They could have turned either way along the riverbank, but his instincts sent them right, upriver toward the faint brightness of the sunrise. The rain fell steadily, but not in sheets, only as something slightly damper than a mist. Rain of any sort was unusual, and particularly so for any length of time. But it rained all morning as they traveled, and into the afternoon. The river followed a mostly straight course, and they were able to stay within sight of it as they walked the bluff. They saw no other traffic on the river and no sign of life on the banks. The land stretched away about them—hills and forests, fields and meadows dotted with rocky monoliths, and in the distance huge, barren mountains.

By early afternoon, Hawk was beginning to wonder if he had made a mistake. It bothered him that the King of the Silver River had deposited him back in the world with no clear idea of where he was supposed to go. It was difficult enough coming to terms with the idea that he wasn't entirely human, that he was in part, at least, a creature of Faerie, imbued with wild magic and the promise of performing an impossible feat. How he was supposed to find and lead thousands of people—children, in particular—to safety, to the gardens from which he had been sent, was difficult to imagine, no matter what anyone said. At least he should have been given a better idea of how and where he was supposed to undertake this task.

Instead he was in a foreign place, not even Seattle and Pioneer Square, the only home he had ever known. He was separated from the Ghosts, his only family, and told that his memories of his early life of growing up in Oregon were not real. All he had to sustain him was his dog and the girl he loved.

He glanced covertly at Tessa, at her fine dark features, her dusky skin and curly black hair, at the way she carried herself, at the sway of her body as she walked. Her presence comforted him as nothing else could, and he was grateful for her beyond anything words could express. Tessa. She made him ache inside. She made him feel that everything he had been asked to do was not too much if she was with him. He remembered anew how frightened he had been for her during the tribunal at the compound when the judges had pronounced the death sentence on them both. He remembered how terrible he had felt for her when her mother spit on her and refused to take her side.

His determination hardened.

We are the Ghosts, and we haunt the ruins of the world our parents destroyed.

He repeated the litany silently, testing the strength of the words. The world they had inherited was poisoned, plague-ridden, and decimated. Adults who ought to have known better had left it in tatters. How much would it take for an eighteen-year-old boy to salvage any part of what was left?

More than he had to offer, he thought. Much more. They could say what they wanted about who and what he was, all of them. They could say anything. But deep down inside, down where his heart and his determination were strongest, he knew that he was just a boy and that his limitations were brick walls through which he could not break free. He was expected to save thousands of children. He was expected to help them survive. He was expected to find a safehold that would shelter them all from a fire that would consume everything.

He was expected to perform miracles.

It was too much to ask of anyone.

It was nearing midafternoon when they saw the first roofs of the distant buildings, a cluster of gray surfaces that reflected back the dull slick of rainfall and dust that had collected. The buildings were set down in a flat between two higher bluffs facing out toward the river at a narrows. A bridge spanned the water about a mile farther on where the river narrowed even more. Although the rain clouded his vision sufficiently that he couldn't be sure from this distance, Hawk thought that its steel trusses and cables were intact.

Tessa took his arm suddenly. "Look, Hawk," she said. "Down there."

He shifted his gaze to where she was pointing, away from the river and back toward an open field that extended from a cluster of large warehouses to woods backed up against low hills that disappeared into the haze. The field was filled with tents and vehicles and people—hundreds, perhaps thousands of them. Many were busy doing things, but from where he stood he couldn't tell what those things were. He saw fires and makeshift kitchens through which lines of people passed with their plates empty and reappeared with them full. He was looking at a camp, but he had no idea why there would be a camp of any kind in this place.

Then he realized all at once that most of the people he was seeing were children.

He took a closer look at the perimeter of the camp and found guards, all of them heavily armed and keeping close watch on the approaches. He knew from the extent of their vigilance that he and Tessa had already been spotted. But he stood where he was awhile longer, not wanting to appear furtive or frightened, not wanting to create a wrong impression, studying the busy sprawl below, waiting to see what would happen. These were not Freaks or once-men or anything threatening; they were people like himself, and if he did not pose a threat to them perhaps they would not cause problems for him.

When Cheney growled, low and deep in his throat, he knew he was about to find out if he was right.

"Stay," he told the big dog softly and reached down to touch the grizzled head.

A man emerged from the trees to one side, carrying a flechette. He did not raise it in a threatening manner or even look particularly worried. "Hello," he said.

"Hello," Hawk and Tessa said together.

"Are you looking for someone? Can I help you find them?"

He was a tall, thin man with glasses and a soft look that suggested that serving as guard for this camp was not his usual line of work. But he held the flechette in a familiar manner, and Hawk knew that no man or woman who had survived in this world outside the compounds was doing what he or she had done before.

"I'm looking for whoever is in charge," he said.

The man studied him a moment. "What's the trouble? Are you lost?"

Hawk shook his head. "No. In fact, that's why I'm here. To help you find your way. I came to be your guide."

A flicker of amusement crossed the man's face, but then he simply smiled and shrugged. "Can't wait to hear how you plan to do that. Is your dog okay down there with the kids?"

Hawk nodded. "He does what I tell him."

A white lie at best, a misplaced hope at worst. The man gave him a doubtful look and said, "He better. If he doesn't, I'll shoot him."

He took them down off the rise through the trees and into the camp. They passed other guards on the way, men and women of all ages, a ragtag bunch if ever Hawk had seen one. A few were big and tough looking, hardened veterans with obvious experience, but most were something less. It looked like whoever could still walk and was over the age of eighteen had been pressed into service. Those placed in their care were much younger. They were playing games and reading stories and completing small tasks to occupy their time. Older children supervised the younger. Everyone was behaving. Everything looked well ordered and thoroughly organized.

The guard brought them through the camp and across the field to one of the tents. A small cluster of men and women were gathered around a makeshift table that had maps spread out on it, most of them worn and heavily marked. A small, slight woman with short-cropped blond hair and quick energetic movements was speaking.

". . . patrols along both banks, and let's keep a close watch on that bridge, Allen. Those militia boys may want to play rough, and we want to be ready if they do. We don't want to encourage them by looking unprepared. All right. Now, the woods are ringed with sentries all the way along the tree line and back to . . ."

She stopped and looked up as the guard approached with Hawk, Tessa, and Cheney in tow. She gave the wolfish dog a long, hard look before saying, "What is it, Daniel?"

The guard looked flustered. "I found these three on the bluff. The boy says he came here to guide us. I thought maybe you should speak to him."

The woman studied Hawk a moment, as if trying to make up her mind about him. She straightened up from the table over which she was bent, ran her fingers through her disheveled hair, and put her hands on her hips. Hawk could feel her taking his measure, looking hard at this lean, not particularly interesting, dark-haired boy standing in front of her and trying to decide if he was worth her time.

Then she looked at those gathered around her and said, "Give us a moment to talk, please."

Her companions moved away, some reluctantly. One or two stayed close enough that they could still protect her if it proved necessary. The woman herself did not seem concerned. She was the leader, Hawk decided, even though she didn't look the part. The men were bigger and stronger and might even know more about fighting, but she was the one whose judgment they had learned to trust.

"I'm Helen Rice," she told them, and she held out her hand for each of them to shake.

They did so, giving their names and Cheney's, in turn. But Hawk did not recite the litany of the Ghosts. It would be hard enough getting her to listen to him as things stood.

"Someone sent you to guide us?" Helen Rice asked him.

He nodded. "I think so."

"You think so?" She stared at him. "Was it Angel Perez?"

He looked in her eyes and saw something that told him what to say.

"She didn't give me a name. She said I was to come to you and take the children to a safe place."

"Where is she? What's happened to her?"

He shook his head. "Can you tell me where we are?"

"Hawk!" Tessa whispered in astonishment.

Helen Rice was looking at him now as if he had come from another planet. "Let me understand. You were sent to guide us, but you don't know where you are?"

"I know where we are going, but not where we are."

She started to say something and then stopped. "All right. We are on the south bank of the Columbia River, maybe a hundred miles east of the city of Portland, Oregon."

Hawk looked at Tessa. "South of Seattle," she confirmed. "Look, what's this all about? I have to tell you that I am in no mood for games. I just marched two thousand children and their caregivers all the way up here from southern California. The pace was grueling, and not everyone was up to it. Those who made it are exhausted and short of patience. Please get to the point."

"We have to cross the river." He glanced at the maps, and then looked back toward the town. "I saw a bridge earlier," he said. "We can cross there."

Helen Rice shook her head quickly. "A militia has it fortified and defended against anyone trying to cross without paying a fee."

"What sort of fee?" Tessa asked.

"It doesn't matter. We were told to wait here, not cross to the other side." She shifted her gaze back to Hawk. "We outnumber them, but they are better armed and have less to lose. I can't risk the lives of these children attempting to force our way past. Not without a better reason than you've given me so far.

"Besides." She took a deep breath and exhaled slowly. "I'm not convinced I should do what you tell me. You don't know who sent you. You don't know who we are. You don't know where you are. You don't seem to know much of anything. Your intentions are good, I think. But the road to Hell and all that. It makes me suspicious. I'm having real difficulty believing that you are who we've been waiting for."

Hawk understood. He would have felt the same in her shoes. He was just a boy, nothing special. Why should she believe for one minute that he was someone who could help? Why should she place hundreds of children under his direction without knowing more? He understood all that, and yet he had to find a way to make her do exactly what her instincts and training told her not to do.

"You should believe him," Tessa said suddenly, trying to help. "Hawk is more than what he seems. He is special, different than the rest of us. He was told so by a Knight of the Word."

"Angel Perez is a Knight of the Word," Helen Rice said.

Hawk shook his head, unwilling to lie to her. "No, this wasn't her. This was someone else. A man. His name is Logan Tom."

He looked back toward the river again. He could feel his concern for their safety pushing hard at him to do something. The longer they waited, the more dangerous their situation became. He couldn't explain his certainty about this, only that at this moment it was so strong, he could not ignore it. He couldn't explain, either, why he was compelled to guide these people, the children especially, except that something of what the King of the Silver River had told him in those gardens had resurfaced the moment he saw who was down here. Now, standing in the presence of Helen Rice and in the center of all these children, he found a fresh connection with his gypsy morph self—the part of him that was Faerie, the part that was born of Nest Freemark, the part that combined the magic of both.

That magic surfaced now within her finger bones, which were still tucked away in his pocket. It spit and crackled against his flesh like tiny electrical charges, demanding to be set free.

"There is an army coming," he said, knowing all at once that it was true. "From the south."

"That old man," Helen Rice said at once. Her lips tightened. "How do you know this?"

"The army is too big for you," he said, avoiding a direct answer. "You won't be able to stand against it on this side of the river. If you cross, though, you might be able to hold the bridge."

"Or blow it up." Her fierce gaze was locked on him. "But it's still too dangerous to attempt a crossing with the children. Not without something more than the warning you've given me, Hawk."

"If I can get you across that bridge safely, without a struggle and without putting the children in danger," he asked, "will you go?"

She hesitated, weighing the offer, her doubts fighting her need to believe in this boy, her fear that he deceived warring with her desire for him to be the one.

"Please," Tessa said softly. "Let him try."

Helen Rice gave the girl a quick glance. "All right," she said finally, her gaze shifting back to Hawk. "You have one chance."

TWENTY-FIVE

"YOU HAVE ONE CHANCE," Helen Rice told him, then quickly added, "And we don't move the children anywhere until we have complete control of the bridge and I am convinced it's safe to do so."

None of which surprised him. It was what he would have insisted on if a stranger was proposing to take the Ghosts across a bridge guarded by armed militia. Hawk hadn't thought for one minute that it would be otherwise.

His immediate concerns were much larger. He didn't know yet how he was going to get control of the bridge. He didn't know how he was going to disperse the men guarding it. He only knew that he was meant to try.

"I'll bring enough people to hold the bridge against a counterattack if you can find a way for us to take it over," she continued. "Enough to hold it until the rest are able to break camp and bring the children across."

He nodded his agreement in silence. His commitment to what he was about to attempt was strong, but his fears were huge, as well. He understood the reality of his situation. He was acting on faith and on instinct. It was hard to tell which he was relying on more. If either failed him, he was probably going to die. He didn't give any indication of this as he smiled reassuringly at Tessa, seeing his own fear mirrored tenfold in her eyes. He felt small and inadequate. He felt almost foolish.

But there was a voice inside urging him on, telling him to believe, to accept that this was something he could do. The voice was his own and that of the old man in the gardens and his mother's, as well. It was a single voice that shifted in pitch and tone, but never in strength.

You can do this, it insisted.

Helen Rice called back those she had been talking to when the guard had brought Hawk to her and told them what she intended. There was grumbling and more than a few objections, but she overrode them all. She told one of the men, a big fellow with a shock of red hair whom she called Riff, to gather two dozen of their best to take to the bridge. He nodded without argument and left to do as she asked.

Fifteen minutes later, they were marching down the riverbank toward the bridge. The day had turned darker still, the clouds thickening and the air dampening as the promise of a fresh storm grew stronger. The wind had picked up and was blowing dust and debris everywhere, and it forced the company to walk with their heads bowed and their eyes all but shut. Hawk walked with Tessa and Cheney in the forefront of the company next to Helen Rice. His thoughts were of other times and places, of how he had walked the streets of Pioneer Square with the Ghosts not so long ago, carrying prods and viperpricks, living in the ruins of their elders, street kids trying to stay alive. How fast it had all changed. Everyone from that time save Tessa and Cheney was either dead or lost. He couldn't even be sure he would see the other Ghosts again, although he believed in his heart that he would. But he knew that if he did, he would see them and they him as a different person—as this new creature, this mix of boy and gypsy morph, of flesh and blood and magic, and it would not be the same.

It would not ever be the same.

"What are you going to do?" Tessa whispered to him.

He shook his head. How could he respond when he didn't know the answer? And yet, he almost did. He could feel the tingle of the finger bones against his body where they nestled in his pocket, a clear indication that something was happening. He could sense the transformation even as it happened, a shift from what was familiar to something entirely new and different, something that lacked any recognizable frame of reference. It was an awakening of a force that had lain dormant inside him—for how long, he couldn't say. Perhaps only since his visit to the gardens of the King of the Silver River. Perhaps all his life. But it was there, and it was real, and it was growing by the second.

He tried to identify what it was. At first, he couldn't. Then all at once he understood. It was in the way his senses were responding to his surroundings. He could smell the earth, dark and green and mysterious, a well of living things forming a chain of life that stretched as far as his mind could conceive. The smell was of each of them, and he could sort them through and identify them in a way he had never been able to do before. He could put names to them; he could visualize their shapes and uses.

But that was only the beginning. He could taste the wind. He could savor it as if it were food placed in his mouth. He could taste the elements of the storm as they roiled and surged through the clouds overhead, metallic and rough. Thunder and lightning, distant to the point of being barely discernible, were sharp and raw against his palate. Electricity jumped off his skin in invisible sparks, small jolts that he could feel connecting to the tingling of his mother's finger bones, as if they shared a commonality, an origin. He could hear things, too. Things that no one made of flesh and blood should have been able to hear. The whine of limbs caught in the rush of the wind, straining to keep from breaking. The whisper of grasses complaining of the same. The rattle of bark. None of it close enough to be seen, all of it so distant that the sounds should have been undetectable. Yet he could hear.

More baffling, he could hear the groan of the earth herself from deep inside where none of what was happening on the surface had any bearing. Plates shifted and a molten core bubbled and spit, and the heat rose to mix with the cool, causing expansion and contraction, forming and re-forming, the birth of new life and the death of old. He could almost reach out and touch what he could smell and hear and taste and feel, as if his arms extended to the lines of power that ringed the earth and were joined with them.

He knew all this without having been schooled even in the possibilities. He knew from his own transformation, from the way he recognized how he was different, how he had been remade in his visit to the gardens of the old man.

He reached down and touched Cheney between his big shoulders, and the dog lifted his head in response. The gray eyes shifted to settle on him, and for just an instant Hawk believed that the wolfish dog understood what was happening.

He looked ahead to the bridge itself, a huge ugly span of girders and struts, the paint long since peeled and stripped away, the bare metal beneath rusted and scarred by weather and time. It had the look of something that might rise up from its sleep and attack in the manner of a giant insect. The comparison chilled him, recalling the centipede and the terrible struggle the Ghosts had survived in their Pioneer Square home. He stared at the bridge and willed it not to move.

"Better get ready," Helen Rice said sharply, disrupting his thinking.

They had reached the steps that climbed to the bridgehead. Already the militia guards were forming up across the mouth, taking note of the size of the group approaching. No warning had been given yet, so Helen took her company of men and women up the steps in a line, warning them to stay ready, but to keep their weapons lowered. Hawk walked right behind her as she led the way, his stomach churning, his heart beating fast.

What was he going to do? He didn't have a plan. He didn't even have a weapon. He was woefully unprepared.

As they reached the flat that approached the bridge, Helen's company spread out to either side, stopping where she told them to, still fifty feet from the nearest barricades and soldiers. The men on the bridge had all come forward to the near end, weapons held ready, eyes shifting nervously as they waited to discover what was happening. Atop the bridge spans, more soldiers crouched in metal crow's nests. There was a tank of some sort at the far end, and a pair of spray cannons set to either side of the gates warding the bridge entrance.

Too many weapons and men to do this without serious damage to both sides, thought Hawk. He glanced at Tessa, who gave him a brave smile.

"What are you going to do now?" Helen Rice asked him quietly.

He stood where he was for a moment, letting his emotions settle and his scattered thoughts come together. He waited until he was calm inside, until he could measure his heartbeat and feel the steady pulsing of the finger bones against his thigh. He waited until he could sense their response to his thinking—until he could gauge whether they would slow or quicken. He waited until he could feel something of that pulse seep into him, join with him, and become more than an external presence.

He waited to discover what he should do to fulfill his need. He waited for guidance and understanding, for this strange co-joining with the external world to reveal its purpose.

"Hawk," Tessa whispered, an unmistakable urgency in her voice.

He walked forward alone, not directly toward the militia and the barricades, but toward a ragged clump of scrub, stunted trees, and withered vines growing bravely to one side of the approach. He was responding to the voice, but acting on instinct, as well. His course of action was decided, but its intended result still remained vague and uncertain. He could feel the eyes of both armed camps on him, could almost hear what both were thinking. He wondered at the stupidity of the militia holding the bridge, playing with matches while the rest of the world was already afire. What did they think they were going to gain by trying to collect a fee—whatever its nature—from those seeking to cross the river? What was the point of such an undertaking in a world like this?

He knelt amid the scrub and trees and vines, running his fingers over dried-out grasses and leaves.

The world at his fingertips, waiting to be reborn; the thought came to him unbidden. Life waiting to be quickened.

I know what to do, he realized suddenly.

He took the withered plants in his hands, closing his fingers gently but firmly, taking care not to crush their brittle stalks. He held them as he would a child's fingers, reaching down into their roots by strength of will alone. He could feel them stir, coming awake from the deep dormancy into which they had lapsed. They took their nourishment, fresh and new, from him, from the magic that he fed them, come to him from a source still unknown, one that might have its origins either in his mother's finger bones or in his own life force. But it came from the earth, as well, from the elements that were intrinsic to her soil and rock and metal and molten core.

Come awake, he urged the plants he held in his fingers. *Come awake for me.*

That he might be able to do this was at once astonishing and exhilarating. That he could command magic of any sort was the fulfillment of the promise made to him by Logan Tom in the revealing of his origins and the delivery of his mother's finger bones. He had not dared to think it possible—yet he had known, too, that it must be if he was to do what he had been given.

His whole being was attuned to and connected with the earth upon which he stood and to the plants that rooted within, and in that instant he was changed forever. No longer a boy, a street kid only, he was a creature of magic, too, a gypsy morph come into being, its potential realized.

The result was instantaneous. Vines and brush and grasses erupted from the earth at both ends of the bridgehead, exploding all around the barricades and weapons and the men who staffed them. They shot out of the earth as if starved, as if reaching skyward for the sunlight, for the air, for the rain, for whatever they were lacking in their dormancy. But their emergence was his doing alone, and they were obedient to his command. They fell upon the barricades and the defenders, upon metal and human alike, enfolding them in ropes of green that wrapped about like cables to make them all fast.

The militia never had a chance. They never even managed a single pull on their triggers. The handguns were ripped from their fingers, and the tanks and cannons were throttled in place. The men themselves were bound as if by ropes, the greenery first making them fast and then climbing the entire bridge, wrapping about the metal spans and struts, about everything that formed the body of the structure until nothing remained visible. In the end, there was only the bushy, dripping green of plant life extending end-to-end, the whole of the bridge and its bar-

ricades and its defenders become part of a vast jungle. The entire swallowing took only minutes and left the onlookers standing with Tessa
and Cheney staring in shocked silence.

"Oh, my God!" whispered Helen Rice softly, speaking for them all.

IT TOOK THE CAREGIVERS the remainder of the day to decamp and
move the children across the bridge to a new site that Helen and her
advisers had chosen, one that Hawk instinctively felt was easier to defend. After releasing the entrapped militia, they set them free on the
south side of the bridge and assumed control of the barricades leading
to the new camp.

By nightfall, everyone was pretty much resettled and the move
across the river complete.

"I don't know how you did that," Helen told Hawk later when they
were sitting alone, close to where Tessa had gone to work helping the
children. "But it's proof enough for me that you are who you say." She
shook her head. "No one I've ever heard of could do what you did. Not
even Angel Perez."

Hawk didn't know what to say. He was still coming to terms with it
himself. He could not understand yet how he had managed to generate
such rapid growth from a few withered plant and grass ends, a talent so
new to him that it seemed as if it must belong to someone else. He
could not even decide how he had known what to do.

"The children will be safer on this side," he said. "But you may have
to defend the bridge."

"If we stay here, I know we will," she said. "You were right about the
pursuit. Already an army is coming up the coast. We had hoped Angel
would be back before it reached us. Now I don't know." She looked off
into the twilight, as if she might find her friend there. "How long before
we leave? You sound as if it might not be right away."

He nodded. "It won't. We can't leave until I find my family and
bring them here. They are somewhere north, coming to meet me. I
should be back with them in less than a week."

"You're leaving?" she asked.

"Not for long. But you have to hold the bridge until then. You have to protect the children. If others come this way, take them in, as well." He paused, and then added, "Angel would want that."

He didn't know if she would or wouldn't, didn't know the first thing about Angel Perez besides what he had heard from Helen Rice, but he thought that mention of her would help strengthen the other's resolve.

Helen sat silently for a moment, her slight form hunched, her head bent. "I am so tired," she said.

Then she rose, smiled at him momentarily, and walked away. Hawk watched her go. He was already making his departure plans. He waited until the camp began to go to sleep, then found Tessa and told her he was leaving to find the Ghosts. He watched a mix of fear and uncertainty flood her amber eyes and tighten the smooth skin of her dark face.

"You don't have to come with me," he said. "You can wait for me here, if you want."

Tessa laughed. "I could do lots of things if I wanted to. But none of them are things I want to do without you."

"I'm sorry about everything that's happened—the compound, your mother and father, all of it. I wish it hadn't."

"I'm sorry about what's happened, too. But mostly I'm sorry for you. It must be very scary, all of this . . . though it isn't so out of keeping with who you are."

He smiled. "I wish I could feel that way. It all seems so weird." He hesitated. "You're coming with me?"

"What do you think?"

"I want you to come. Maybe we can talk about what's happened while we walk. I think I need to do that. I think it will help make it more real."

She took his hands in her own. "Then we'd better get started."

They gathered a few supplies in backpacks and with Cheney leading the way set out west, following the river as it wound through a chain of mountains that flanked it on both sides.

By midnight, they were ten miles away.

FINDO GASK stalked the darkness, a gray ghost on a shadowy night, the sky heavily overcast and empty of light, and the woods through which he passed deep-layered with gloom. Behind him, the camp of the once-men slumbered, their grunts and snores mingling with the whimpers and moans of the slaves they had taken on their march north from LA. Their journey had been a fast one, coming overland afoot and by flatbed truck, each travel day spanning sixteen to eighteen hours. There had been little time for delay once the gypsy morph had resurfaced, and less time still now that it had revealed itself a second time. It appeared stronger this time, its magic more potent and sweeping, and it was making no effort to mask what it was doing.

Which was more than the demon could have hoped and dreamed for, and it knew it could not afford to let this chance slip through its fingers.

Still, the source of the magic was a long way north, several hundred miles farther on at least, and this second using had not originated from the same place as the first. That meant that the morph was on the move, which meant that it had decided on a destination or a goal. Findo Gask could not know its purpose, but there was no mistaking the need to reach it before that purpose could be fulfilled. The morph was the demon's most dangerous threat, the one servant of the Word who might undo everything the demon had spent so much time achieving.

It still rankled Findo Gask that he had let the morph get free of him all those years ago when it had been within his grasp. Somehow, Nest Freemark had tricked him. He sensed it instinctively, knew that she had bonded with this Faerie creature and kept it safe from him. His victory over John Ross—or any of the other Knights of the Word he had dispatched over the years—felt hollow and insufficient. Nothing less than the death of the gypsy morph would satisfy him now.

Nothing less would ever give him peace.

It was a goal he expected to achieve. John Ross and Nest Freemark and all the rest of the magic wielders from that time were dead and gone, even that big copper-skinned war vet. Only he remained. The

gypsy morph, whatever its form, was alone and isolated from its own
kind, and was also, perhaps, unwitting of its danger. If he could just
manage to reach it before it was warned . . .

Or, he amended, if another could reach it in his place, one even
more lethal and relentless than he was . . .

He left the thought hanging as he moved into the deepest part of
the forest, the part where sunlight never reached, and stopped at the
edge of a pond. The pond was choked with water grasses and reeds and
coated with a thick layer of scum, its waters fouled in the culmination
of the destruction of the environment years earlier. What had once
been clear and clean was now murky and polluted. Nothing that lived
here was what it had started out as. Everything had evolved. The bite
of the smallest insects would sicken a human. Even the air and water
and plants were poisonous.

But Findo Gask walked with impunity, picking his way without fear
through the things that could kill humans. Nothing came near him—
not the snakes or spiders or biting insects or creatures for which there
were no names. Nothing came near because nothing was as dangerous
or as venom-filled as he was. The denizens of the dark woods recognized one of their own, and they stayed clear.

Except for one.

It rose out of the pond's mire like a leviathan surfacing from the
deep ocean, the waters bubbling and heaving about it as it lifted clear,
the gases escaping in spurts and burst bubbles, their stench filling the
fouled air with fresh odors. Findo Gask knew it was hiding but would
sense his approach and reveal itself because that was its nature. He
stood safely distant and watched it emerge, the scum and dead grasses
clinging to its broad back and hunched shoulders in damp patches. He
watched, and he marveled at the monstrosity of its demon form.

The Klee was like nothing else he had ever encountered. Its head
was a conical plate of bone flattened and dented as if struck repeatedly
by a heavy mallet. Its features were submerged in the leathery tissue
beneath its brow, stunted and difficult to discern save for its small,
wicked green eyes. Its long, heavy arms were fringed with hair and
ridged with muscle, its hands crooked and gnarled, its tree-trunk legs
thick and bowed, all of it encrusted with a mix of scale and hair and de-

bris. When it stood clear of the mud and water, it towered over him, dwarfed him with its mass, and gave him momentary pause despite what he knew about it.

Delloreen hated the Klee, calling it an animal and disdaining it as an unthinking monster that knew nothing but killing. She wasn't wrong, but she missed the point. It was because the Klee was all this that Findo Gask found it useful.

Once, it had been a man, a long time ago before he had encountered it in the ruins of a town amid so many dead that he could scarcely believe a single creature had killed them all. Once, it had been human. What had changed it was anybody's guess. The Klee never talked. It barely listened, and it listened mostly to Findo Gask.

The huge demon slogged out of the quicksand and mud to stand close to him, bent forward expectantly. It knew he had come for a reason, and he knew that the reason involved what it craved most.

"I want you to find somebody for me," Findo Gask said. "A Faerie creature, but it will have another form. I will give you a sense of what it will feel like, and you will be able to unmask it from that."

The Klee shifted from one foot to the other, a slow ponderous movement that signaled its understanding. From somewhere deep within its chest, a strange wheezing sound rumbled.

Findo Gask smiled. That was the Klee's expression of satisfaction.

He reached out and touched the demon boldly on the chest with one finger. "Find this Faerie creature, and when you do, kill it," he said.

TWENTY-SIX

REUNITED FOLLOWING Candle's kidnapping by the boy with the ruined face and Logan Tom's search for plague medicine through the dark streets of Tacoma, the Ghosts continued their slow journey south. Departing their camp outside the city while it was still night and there was a reasonable chance that the Senator hadn't yet discovered the loss of his "property," they rolled south on the AV and attached hay wagon in the manner of their namesakes, shadows sliding through darkness. Catalya showed them the way, taking them off the freeway and through backstreets that bypassed the Senator's stronghold and the places where he was likely to have stationed sentries to warn him of trespassers. By dawn, they were well outside the city and moving steadily away.

Owl, riding inside the Lightning with River and Fixit, gave her charges strong doses of the serum that Cat had brought with her from her secret stash, covered both children with blankets, bathed them with cool cloths, and talked them through their feverish dreams in her soft, reassuring voice. Both began showing improvement almost immediately, their temperatures dropping and their restless discomfort turn-ing to a deep sleep. Within twenty-four hours, their purple splotches began to fade, as well, and it became apparent that both would recover.

Logan could tell himself with some conviction that things were progressing well enough that he no longer needed to consider leaving the Ghosts behind while he continued his search for Hawk. His fears over the possibility that shepherding a bunch of street kids would slow him down and burden him with unnecessary responsibilities had faded after the previous night's events. It seemed to him now, in the light of the new day, that the kids could shoulder responsibility for themselves sufficiently that he needn't feel that he must do so for them, and while that seemingly should have given him further reason to go on alone, it had quite the opposite effect. Given the freedom to leave, he found he no longer wanted to. The idea of abandoning the Ghosts had grown in-creasingly distasteful to him, and he found that he was more comfort-able having things continue on the way they were.

Which wasn't to say he might not change his mind later. Events might one day dictate that he do so; you could never tell. But for now, at least, he could let the matter alone and simply concentrate on the journey ahead.

The only problem was Cat. As he had feared, and she had sus-pected, she was not universally accepted by the other kids. Panther, not surprisingly, was the most vociferous, calling her Freak to her face and making it clear to all that he did not think she belonged with them, no matter what she had done to earn the privilege. Chalk took the same stance and, surprisingly, Sparrow. Perhaps the latter's near-death en-counter with the Croaks while they were fleeing Seattle had helped shape her thinking. Perhaps it was something she wasn't telling them. But while keeping mostly silent on the matter, she nodded often enough while Panther was holding forth that Logan Tom had no doubt about where she stood. She, too, had no use for the girl who was nei-ther one thing nor the other.

The rest were more welcoming. Owl embraced Cat immediately and told her they were happy to have her travel with them, ignoring the groans and looks offered in counterpoint by Panther. Candle took her hand and walked with her during their first day on the road, a small gesture that made Logan proud of her.

And Bear, big and steady and mostly quiet, stepped between Panther and Cat at one point when the former was making an unmistakable attempt at intimidation, forcing his fellow Ghost to back away and finally to turn aside. Panther, who normally wouldn't have allowed anyone to do this to him, seemed genuinely confused.

"She's just a Freak, man," he mumbled over his shoulder at Bear. But after that, he pretty much left the girl alone.

Their destination was already settled, and they were quick to resume their journey. They were at least a week from reaching the Columbia River and their promised meeting with Hawk, so there was good reason to press ahead. Logan was wondering anew how they were supposed to find the boy, but knew that it was the boy who must find them. The gypsy morph that was concealed within the human skin would have surfaced by now, and the wild magic taken hold. This was what must happen, Logan realized, if the boy was to be their savior.

Their travels took them out of the city and into the countryside. Buildings disappeared behind them, lost in a haze of smoke and ash that even the sun could not burn through. The corpses of vehicles that littered the highway dwindled, and the bitter metallic taste of the air took on a woodsy flavor. The land stretched away around them in a sprawl of wintry fields and stands of dying trees, of drainage and fouled ponds, of broken fences and collapsing farms. There was almost no sign of life—a bird here and there, the quick movement of a small animal passing through the weeds, a burrowing rodent sticking its head from its hole momentarily, and a pair of stick-thin figures running from an old house far off in the distance.

The end of everything, Logan thought more than once. *The way it will be everywhere before long.* He tried to imagine it and failed. The world was too vast for such a thing. The prospect of it rendered empty and lifeless was too bleak to consider.

Even though he knew it was coming.

Even though it had been foretold.

They drove south for three days, bypassing a handful of small towns that sat off to the side of the freeway, silent and empty. Once, they passed another city. Logan didn't know their names, nor did Cat or any of the Ghosts. The signs that had once identified them were gone, leaving broken-off metal supports with twisted, jagged ends. The days were

hazy with bad air and weak sunlight, and the landscape had the look of
a mirage. The highway wound through oceans of liquid light that shimmered and contorted. In the junk heaps of ruined vehicles and scattered debris, in the clusters of falling-down walls and roofs, and in the
barren fields and empty horizons, the world was a tomb.

As midafternoon of the third day approached, they came in sight of
a fresh cluster of buildings, their roofs just visible above a grouping of
hills in rough country that was chilly and stark, a graveyard marked by
the bones of dead trees.

Logan was sitting in the front passenger's seat of the Lightning,
looking back over his shoulder while he talked with Owl. River and
Fixit were on either side of her, sufficiently recovered that they could
sit upright, but not yet strong enough to walk any distance. The rest of
the Ghosts were riding on the hay wagon with Rabbit and Cat.

Panther was driving.

It had taken awhile for the boy to come around to the idea, but
when Logan casually mentioned earlier in the day that it might be time
for him to try, Panther had just as casually declared that it couldn't
hurt. He had been driving ever since.

"I don't understand why Cat was out on the streets alone at night
like that," Owl was saying. "That seems so dangerous."

"I thought so, too," he agreed.

"And she didn't have any weapons?"

"None that I could see." He paused. "But I think she might be more
capable than she appears. She seemed at home out there. She made a
point of asking me what I was doing coming into the city by myself. It
felt like she thought she knew better than I did how to take care of herself."

That's 'cause she's a Freak, Panther said to himself, his mood darkening as he thought anew about having to put up with Lizard girl.
Sometimes he wished Hawk were back in charge. Even he knew better
than to try to bring a Freak into the family.

"Hey, what's that?" he broke in, suddenly catching sight of something in the road ahead.

Logan turned to look, seeing what appeared to be a tangle of vehicles blocking their way. "Stop the AV," he told Panther at once.

When the boy had done so, Logan got out of the car and walked forward a few paces, searching the road ahead and then the countryside around. Nothing was moving. But it didn't feel right. He glanced back at the kids and then ahead again. The road was straight and undeviating; there were no crossroads visible beyond the tangle. There was nowhere to go unless they drove off into the fields and hills, and he didn't think the hay wagon could handle the rough terrain.

He walked back and leaned down to Panther. "I'm going to walk ahead. Stay behind me. Keep your eyes open."

The boy's face clouded. "Just looks like some junk," he said. "We could turn around, I guess, find another way."

Logan shook his head. "Not much of anything out here to suggest there is another way. Let's have a closer look."

He moved away. Panther reached down to touch the Parkhan Spray shoved down between the door and the seat, and then eased the Lightning ahead at a crawl, letting a sizable gap open between the Knight of the Word and the AV. Everyone had quit talking and begun looking around, searching the countryside. Logan, walking ahead, didn't see anything, but it bothered him that these vehicles blocking the roadway were so far out in the middle of nowhere. The blockade could have been the result of a long-ago crash; it looked as if it was. But it made him uneasy nevertheless.

He was within yards of the tangle when his nerves suddenly turned sharp-edged and raw, the magic sparked at his fingertips, and he decided this was a mistake. He couldn't have said why, but he had learned to trust his instincts. He stopped where he was, one hand lifting to signal Panther.

"Don't move," said a voice from one side.

Without changing position, Logan turned his head and looked over in the direction of the speaker. A gaunt man with a shock of black hair had stepped out from behind one of the wrecked vehicles. He was unarmed, his hands empty, and his arms hanging loosely at his sides.

Logan turned toward him, the runes of his staff glowing brightly as the magic readied itself.

"If you're thinking about using that staff on me, you might want to think again," the man said calmly. "My friends are all around you and they have their weapons trained on the kids. You might save yourself, but you probably won't save them."

The Knight of the Word glanced about quickly. Dark figures surrounded them, more than a dozen, come seemingly out of nowhere. They must have been hiding in ditches alongside the road. Or maybe they had burrowed in and waited. They were as ragged and thin as the speaker, and they carried weapons of all sorts, all of them pointed toward the AV and the hay wagon.

A wave of helplessness washed through him. "What do you want?"

The speaker smiled. "We want you to come with us to see someone. It shouldn't take long. The kids can wait here until you come back. Then you can all go on your way."

"Come with you where?"

"Just over the hill there." He pointed east, toward the mountains. "We saw you coming, you know. This isn't a chance meeting. It was planned. We know who you are. We know why you carry the staff and what it does. We know all about the Knights of the Word. That's why Krilka Koos wants to meet with you."

"Maybe he should have just asked me instead of sending men with guns to threaten these kids."

"Maybe that was his way of making sure you didn't say no."

Logan understood two things right away. First, the man was lying. He might tell them that no harm would come to them and that they would be allowed to go on their way, but it wasn't necessarily so. Release or safe passage of any sort would be a matter of expediency, not honor. Second, whatever this was, it was something personal.

"Why don't you just let the kids go on without me? I can still come with you and meet with . . . what was his name?"

"Krilka Koos. No, that won't work."

"Why not?"

"If we let the kids go, there's nothing to keep you here. We know we can't hold you if you don't want to be held. We know you won't give up the staff, either. All we have to bargain with is the kids. If they don't mean anything to you, then we're in trouble. I'm betting, though, that they do."

Logan nodded. "They won't be touched?"

The speaker shook his head. "Not one hair on their heads."

"Who is Krilka Koos?"

The speaker smiled. "You'll see. How about it? Are you coming?"

Logan hesitated, and then turned back toward the AV.

"No, no, none of that," the speaker said quickly, freezing him in place. "Hard to tell what you might feel you need to talk about. You might say the wrong thing."

Logan looked at him. "Maybe they need to know what's going to happen."

"Maybe they can figure it out on their own." The man shrugged. "A few of my friends will stay with them to make sure they don't figure it out wrong."

Logan stood staring at him a moment, the weight of the situation pressing down on him. He had stepped right into this mess, letting himself be trapped despite all his experience and knowledge. He hadn't even considered that his enemies might use the children against him, might take advantage of his sense of responsibility toward them to break down his defenses. What a fool he was.

He looked down at his feet and shook his head. He had thought long and hard about leaving the Ghosts. He had wondered how they would handle it if he did. Could they survive without him? Could they continue on?

They were all about to find out.

"All right," he said, and walked reluctantly toward the speaker.

* * *

PANTHER, SITTING IN THE driver's seat of the AV and holding up both hands to show that he meant no harm, waited until the Knight of the Word and his captors were out of sight before taking a quick head count of the guards that had been left behind. Three, at least. Might be a fourth back behind the hay wagon; he couldn't be sure. The two standing in front of the AV were human, but the other one looked bigger and stronger. A Lizard, probably. They were all wrapped in dark clothing that partially concealed their features, so he couldn't be sure.

One of the two in front walked over to him and glanced inside. "Shut down the AV," he said.

Panther reached down and with one hand turned off the AV and with the other released the safety on the Parkhan Spray shoved down between his seat and the door. If they were taking the Knight of the Word away, they weren't bringing him back, no matter what that guy said. Which meant, in turn, that once they had disposed of him, they wouldn't need the Ghosts, either. The choices were crystal clear. They could sit there and wait for the inevitable or they could do something to save themselves.

Panther's dark face tightened with determination. He already knew which choice he was going to make.

The guard who had spoken to him walked away again, looking bored. Kids, he was probably thinking. Waste of time.

"Panther, what are you doing?" Owl asked suddenly from the backseat, as if divining his intentions.

"Nothing," he said quietly. "Yet."

He made another quick survey of the guards, counting heads and weapons, making judgments about their abilities. Hard to tell anything about the latter until you saw what they could do. Panther wouldn't know that until he made his move. He wasn't going to be able to get to the Lizard right away because it was behind him. He was going to have to take out the front two and then hope he could get that one afterward. It would be risky. The other Ghosts would be exposed and in danger while it was happening. If they died, it would be his fault.

But if he didn't do anything and they died, it would be his fault, too.

He felt his blood pumping harder. There was no way to win in this business. No way.

He was fortifying himself for what he needed to do, telling himself to stay calm, stay focused, knowing that he had never done anything like this before, never been in a position where he needed to, when he heard someone call out sharply.

"Rabbit! Come back here!"

He glanced over his shoulder. It was Lizard girl. She was climbing down off the hay wagon and running after her stupid cat, which was bounding toward the AV. The guards had turned at once, alerted by her cries. The cat ran and then hopped, looking like it was spastic or some-thing. Panther groaned inwardly. This was messing up everything.

"Look," the guard who had spoken to him earlier called over to the other one. "Target practice."

The cat got all the way to the front of the AV before the girl reached it, snatching it up just as the guards were leveling their weapons. Her hood slipped off her head, revealing her mottled face. The guards saw what she was and recoiled instinctively.

She cradled the cat closer. "The ones in the AV have got plague," she told them. "Want to see?"

"Get back on that wagon!" the speaker snapped angrily, gesturing with his weapon.

She glared at him, and then turned and walked back toward the wagon. As she was passing the AV, she said quietly to Panther, "If you fire that Spray you'll bring them all down on us. Let me handle this."

She was past him before he could reply. What was she talking about, *Let me handle this*? Like she was some sort of special. He glanced over his shoulder at her, wanting to say something about it, but she was almost back at the wagon.

Then her stupid cat got free again and came bounding back toward the AV. She rushed after it, got to it right at the AV door, and scooped it up just as the guards were coming toward her.

"Get out of the AV," she said to Panther without looking at him. "Drop down on all fours and pretend you're sick." She handed the cat to him through the window. When he hesitated, holding the cat like it was made of glass, staring at her in disbelief, she hissed, "Do you want to get out of this alive or not! Do what I say!"

He almost didn't. He almost told her what she could do with her-self. But there was something in her eyes that told him not to. Instead he surprised himself by dropping the cat on the floor, opening the door, and staggering out of the AV like he was suddenly ill, dropping down on all fours and making retching sounds. There were shouts and cries from the other Ghosts, both in the AV and back on the hay wagon. The two guards in front of the AV came running, a mix of sus-picion and surprise mirrored on their faces, not sure yet what was happening.

Panther spit into the dirt and looked up at them as if he were too sick to do anything else, at the same time hoping that this wasn't a mistake, that the girl had something more than words to offer.

He needn't have worried. As the two guards at the front of the AV got to within a few yards of him, she whipped about, cloak flying out in a swirl of fabric. Panther caught a glimpse of bright metal objects spinning through the air, bits of glitter caught by the weak light. An instant later he heard the guards grunt sharply and collapse where they were. Even before they were down, she was moving the other way, waiting for the Lizard to come around the corner of the vehicle. As he did so, her arm whipped out a third time, another flash of metal snapping from her hand. The Lizard gasped and dropped to its knees, its weapon falling from its hands. It swayed like a big tree caught in a wind and went down.

It was over so fast that Panther barely had time to register what had happened. He got to his feet and went over to the guards lying in front of the AV. Pieces of bright metal protruded from their chests.

The girl came up beside him, reached down, pulled the metal bits free, and held them up for Panther to inspect. "Iron Stars," she informed him. "A throwing weapon. Coated with a powerful drug that leaves the victim paralyzed for up to three hours after it enters the body. Works instantaneously."

He stared at her. "Where'd you learn about that?" he asked.

"From other Freaks," she replied, slipping the stars back into the pockets of her cloak. She gave him a look. "Freaks like me."

She walked back toward the last guard, leaving him to stare after her. He didn't know what to think. *She might be more capable than she appears*, he heard Logan Tom saying. He shook his head. She was a Freak, but a scary one. "Cat, huh?" he called after her. "You got some serious claws, Miss Kitty."

She waved back at him without looking, her fingers curled into claws. "Weird," he whispered.

WHILE CAT STOOD off to one side holding Rabbit and ignoring the rest of them, the Ghosts bound and gagged the paralyzed guards, making sure their restraints were tight enough that they couldn't free themselves without help. When that was done, Panther and Bear examined the blockade of derelict vehicles and quickly found that a section of pieces had been fused and attached to wheels that allowed it to be rolled out of the way once certain catches were released. Fixit came up to lend his expertise, and within minutes they had the barricade open and the way forward cleared.

Clustered together, the Ghosts stood looking at the roadway where it stretched into the distance, the twilight beginning to settle in with the close of the day. No one said a word, all eyes on the concrete ribbon and the hazy horizon that lay south

"Well, what are we waiting for?" Fixit demanded.

Panther stared at him, and then shook his head. "We don't stand a chance against a whole camp full of armed men."

"We can do something! We've got his AV and weapons. We can't just give up on him! He went with them to protect us!" Fixit was incensed. "Owl? What should we do?"

Owl sat in her wheelchair, staring straight ahead. "I don't know," she admitted. "I don't really know what he would expect us to do."

Panther looked at the others, his dark face mirroring the gloom he was feeling inside. Bear stood to one side, eyes downcast. Candle looked to be on the verge of tears. River and Sparrow were talking together quietly, their voices too soft to hear. No one wanted to say what every single one was thinking. No one even wanted to admit to it. They all knew what they should do, but they all knew, as well, that doing it was suicide. His gloom deepened. That Knight of whatever he was, he wasn't their problem. Not really. Not when you thought about it. He wasn't one of them.

"Let's go," he said. "Let's get out of here."

He was walking back toward the AV when he caught sight of Catalya, standing there staring at him, petting her stupid cat.

"What are you doing?" he asked irritably.

"Waiting for you to leave."

"Waiting for . . ." He trailed off. "You're not coming?"

She shrugged. "I'm going after Logan Tom."

"Alone?"

She fixed him with her dark eyes. "Looks that way."

Panther stared at her in disbelief. If she had any brains, she'd get back in the AV or climb up on the hay wagon like the rest of the Ghosts and get out of there. She'd go right now and not give Logan Tom another thought. It was one thing to stand up to three stump-head guards. It was something else to go charging into a camp filled with men with weapons—a girl, no less, kitty-cat claws or not. It was beyond foolish; it was suicide.

Shouldn't give him a second's pause, making this decision. He should just go. "Frickin' hell," he muttered.

He walked over to the driver's side of the AV, reached in, and pulled out the Parkhan Spray. Then he walked back to the others. "Fixit, you drive," he told the boy. "Take the rest down the road about a mile and wait for us until you're sure we're not coming. Then drive on. Everyone stays with you. Look out for each other."

"Panther!" Owl hissed in disbelief. "You can't do this."

"Looks like I can," he answered, avoiding her eyes.

"I'm going, too, Panther," Sparrow declared at once.

"No, crazy little bird, you're not. Just me and her." He pointed toward Catalya. "Just us. We're going. You stay here, you and Bear, and watch out for the others."

"What are you talking about?" Sparrow demanded. "You and her? Just two of you?"

He nodded. "If two aren't enough, then four or six or eight probably aren't, either. I don't know. I do know that no one's going but me and her."

"This isn't something you have to do, Panther," Owl said quickly. "This is probably too much for anyone, let alone a boy and a girl. What is it you think you can do? How do you think you can help him?"

"Don't know. Have to try, though." Panther glanced over at Catalya. "Hey! Miss Kitty!" he called out. "You serious about getting your big brother back from those stump heads? You think you got the claws for it?"

She stared at him a moment before walking over. She stood there, sizing him up. "You think you can help me?"

Panther grinned despite himself. "Guess we have to find that out, don't we?"

Catalya handed Rabbit to Owl. "Take care of her for me until I get back." She looked at Panther. "Ready if you are."

Despite the sharply worded pleas that trailed after them, they walked off in the direction in which the men had taken Logan Tom.

Neither one spoke to the other.

Neither one looked back.

TWENTY-SEVEN

LOGAN TOM was marched off the freeway toward the roofs of the buildings cradled by the low hills, his captors fanned out on all sides to keep him securely in their midst. He forced himself not to look back at the AV and the hay wagon and the Ghosts, trying hard not to get ahead of himself, to concentrate on the moment and wait for his chance. He could escape anytime he chose. But escaping meant putting the kids at immediate risk, and he was convinced that he must find a way to avoid that. There was still the possibility that Krilka Koos, whoever he was, only wanted to talk, only sought his help with something.

He needed to give that possibility a chance.

Still, the urge to strike back, to lash out with all the power that was his to command through possession of the black staff, was almost more than he could resist. He could scatter these men like bits of dust, burn them to ash, and flee back to free his helpless charges. He could turn this thing around in an instant's time.

Maybe. But all it would take was one shout, one shot fired, one hint that something was wrong.

The men around him kept their distance, walking in loose, easy fashion, following the lead of the man who had done all the talking earlier. But their casual attitude was only a pretense that was betrayed by the constant surreptitious glances they directed Logan's way when they thought he wasn't looking. He detected wariness in those glances, but something else as well—an excitement, an eagerness for something these men understood and he did not.

It was this secret knowledge that bothered Logan most. He had seen such looks before on the faces of other men like these, and it always signaled a fresh form of bloodletting. But he had committed himself; he had his staff to protect him, and his training as a Knight of the Word to reassure him. Whatever waited, it would find him ready.

They passed down through the hills, winding between the gentle slopes toward the buildings, leaving the freeway and Ghosts behind. No one talked. Logan thought once or twice to ask questions, and then decided against it. He was better off keeping his uncertainties to himself.

"Just ahead, now," the man who had done all the speaking advised.

"You knew I was coming," Logan said, changing his mind about staying quiet. "You were waiting for me."

The speaker glanced at him. "We did and we were. We keep watch on the roads to see who passes. Those who suit our needs, we bring back. Most, we ignore. Not you, of course. We knew you for a Knight of the Word ten miles back. That staff. There's no mistaking it."

"So you only stop Knights of the Word?"

The speaker smiled. "Krilka Koos will explain."

Krilka Koos. Even the name was loathsome by now. Logan kept the rage from his face, his expression purposely blank. Krilka Koos was going to have a lot to answer for. Maybe more than he was expecting.

They rounded a berm, and Logan found himself moving toward a warehouse-size building that had the look of an implement sales and storage facility. There were faded images of tractors and machinery for which he did not know the names painted on the sides of the corrugated sheet metal, and a tractor-shaped weather vane on a squat steeple. Huge doors were rolled open on the long side of the building facing him, clusters of men standing watchfully at their edges. The interior was lit faintly by daylight that spilled through the doors and seeped through cracks and breathing holes in the ceiling and walls. The stale smells of dirt and manure and hay hung mingled in the air, trapped in the low spaces between the hills.

Beyond the larger building were other, small buildings—houses and sheds and livestock shelters. Beyond that was what remained of a small village, its structures falling apart, long since abandoned and neglected. He studied the ruins for a moment, then glanced back at the larger building. The earth surrounding it was muddied and worn, as if trod on repeatedly by many men. Logan did not see those men and wondered why.

They reached the rolled-back doors and entry into the warehouse building, and the man leading him gestured for him to stop. "Wait here," he said.

He left Logan standing in the midst of his other captors and walked into the warehouse. Logan glanced at the men surrounding him. All of them were pointing their weapons at him, uneasiness reflected in more faces than not. Logan decided not to give them further reason to worry. He sat down where he was, his legs crossed, his staff resting in his lap.

A few minutes later, the man in charge returned. "Go on in. Krilka Koos is waiting for you."

Logan got to his feet, smiling. "All by himself?"

The man laughed. "Of course. He's no different from you." He winked. "You'll see."

Logan resisted the urge to turn that wink into something else and passed through the entry into the mix of shadows and suffused sunlight. His eyes worked hard to adjust to the change of brightness as they swept the vast interior. At first he could see almost nothing, but slowly he began to make out a vast open area ringed by bleachers that were set back against the walls. A space had been left between the bleachers at the building entry, and he could see that the flooring below the bleachers had been torn up. The exposed earth had been carefully, almost lovingly raked, the dirt made soft and loose.

An arena, he thought.

He passed between the stands and stepped out into the center of the open space. A man was sitting on the seats to his right. The man lifted one hand in greeting. "You're here!" he called out, sounding decidedly cheerful about it. "The road-weary traveler has found his way!"

He stood up and walked over, whistling tunelessly. He was big, much bigger than Logan, and his dark, seamed features suggested that he was older, too. His black hair was long and uncut, and a heavy beard shaded his jaw. But even the hair and the beard failed to hide the scars that criss-crossed his face like spiderwebbing. One set lasered up from his mouth to what was left of his right ear in vivid red streaks. Another slashed diagonally across his mouth. His eyebrows appeared to have been burned away.

"I've been looking forward to this," he added, breaking into a grin. "Quite anxious for it, really. I can't deny it."

He was dressed in loose-fitting gray and black clothing that was tattered and frayed, but the loosening of the seams and the rips in the cloth seemed to suit him. He carried no weapons, but then perhaps he had no need of them: in his right hand he held a black, rune-carved staff identical to Logan's.

"I'm Krilka Koos," the big man announced. He glanced at his staff, his smile twisting crookedly. "Are you surprised to find that I'm one of your own?"

Logan nodded. "If you mean that you're a Knight of the Word, I guess I am."

"You should be. How could you even suspect? Achille would never tell you. He never tells my guests anything."

Achille. That would be the leader of the men who had brought him here. "He didn't this time, either."

"What's your name?"

"Logan Tom."

Krilka Koos held out his hand, but Logan ignored it. "I was not brought here by polite invitation, so let's get to it. What is this all about?"

The big man laughed, reaching out boldly to clap Logan on his shoulder. "This? This is about—everything!" He extended his arms wide, his laugh deepening. "Everything that matters in this godforsaken world, this hellish killing ground populated by demons and once-men and things that are abominations too terrible to name. It is about being cast out of our lives like rats from a sinking ship. It is about being forced to rebuild those lives in the image of our enemy. It is about who will die and who will survive in the days ahead."

He paused. The scars on his face were livid. "It is about you and me, Logan. Because when you come right down to it, we're all that counts."

Logan stared at him. Krilka Koos might have been mistaken for something approaching normal if not for his eyes. They were eyes that Logan recognized immediately, because he had seen them once before, ten years earlier, staring back at him from Michael's face on the day he had killed him.

He shook his head. "I have no idea what you're talking about."

Krilka Koos nodded, as if Logan were merely stating what he already knew. "Give it time. Now then, let me see if I can guess which one you are. Which of the Knights who remain alive. There are only a few of us left, you know. Only a handful, and that was yesterday's news. Let me guess. You travel with children. I like that. A man who has children fights for someone other than himself. And you drive that modified Lightning S-One-fifty AV. Shows you have talent, skills that other men lack. You'd be the one who's laid waste to the slave camps all through the middle of the country, freeing the prisoners so that they can run off to find a new set of captors and be made slaves once more. Am I right?"

"Probably. How do you know of me?"

"Word gets out this way, if you know how to listen for it. Word travels through one means and another. I came here five years back to make my stand. Fought all the way out from the East Coast while the oceans rose and the seaboard flooded and its cities sank. Fought all the way past the inland cities after that and watched them fall, one by one, to the demon-led armies. Took out my share of demons and once-men while it was happening, and I liked doing it. But there were always more, always others. I grew tired, Logan." He paused. "Isn't that what's happened to you? Haven't you grown tired?"

"Long since," Logan agreed. A dark suspicion was beginning to form. "So you came west to escape all that. Over the mountains?"

"Through the passes."

"North, traveling through what used to be Montana?"

The big man smiled. "You know who I am, don't you? You found those pathetic creatures that worship the mountain spirits, and they told you about me."

Logan nodded, his suspicions confirmed. This was the rogue Knight of the Word whom the Spiders had told him about when he crossed the mountains on his way west weeks earlier. This was the man who'd killed thirty of them for challenging his right to pass.

"I heard they had made the mistake of angering you, so you killed several dozen in retaliation."

"Not in retaliation," Krilka Koos advised with a thoughtful look. "As a lesson. My reputation is not something I can afford to let anyone tarnish—certainly not a bunch of Spiders. If word of that got around, I would be finished. They had no right to challenge me. So I made an example of them. By the time I was settled in this place, ready to make my preparations, word had gotten around. Those who came to join me already knew that there would be no tolerance for disobedience. It saved me a lot of time. You would have done the same in my place. Don't pretend otherwise."

There were many responses Logan could have made, but the bright gleam in the other man's eyes suggested he wasn't open to hearing them. So he shrugged his seeming indifference. He didn't need an argument. He simply needed to get out of there. "What is it you want of me?" he asked.

"What is it I want of you?" The big man laughed anew. "Why, Logan! I want you to join me! I want you to stand with me when it comes time to face them down!"

"Face who down?"

"Our enemies! The demons and once-men! The armies that are coming here to destroy us! Wake up and smell the roses, Logan! They tear down the compounds one by one. They enslave or kill the inhabitants. They eradicate everything. Eventually, they'll come here to try to do the same. But they won't find it so easy when they do."

He leaned forward conspiratorially. "I have been preparing for them for almost three years now. I have been training every day, working at making myself invincible. Testing myself. We exist in a crucible where our metal is toughened by the raw heat of combat. We pass through the fire and emerge purer and stronger. More resilient. When they come, the demons and once-men and anything else that seeks to destroy me, I will be ready for them." He paused. "I am ready now."

"Why can't you do this alone?" Logan asked quietly. "You seem to have been managing all right until now."

Krilka Koos gave him a hard look. "You don't understand."

Logan nodded. "Maybe not. Maybe you should explain it."

"One is good, but two are better. Two would share the burden of the struggle, make it easier, make it more bearable." His voice lowered, and his eyes strayed off into the distance. "What good are you doing anyone, Logan? You travel here and there, you attack slave camp after slave camp, you do battle with one set of once-men or another, you face down a demon or two, and what does it get you? How much better off are you now than you were ten years ago? How much better off is anyone you've tried to help? It won't last, you know. Your luck. Your determination. Sooner or later, it will give out."

"I took an oath to serve the Word," Logan said. "I am doing what I can where I can. It doesn't do any good to sit around waiting for the enemy to find you. You have to get out and find them. You have to destroy them before they have a chance to destroy you." He hesitated. "What about the oath you took as a Knight of the Word? Have you forgotten it?"

The big man made a dismissive gesture. "It was a false oath made to a false god. It was a promise given without adequate consideration for the consequences. What help does the Word offer us? What hope are we given? The Lady and the Indian, where are they when it comes time to fight our enemies? Where are any of them? No, Logan, we owe nothing of allegiance to anyone but ourselves."

The gleam in his eye had grown brighter, and there was an almost rapturous look on his scarred face. Krilka Koos, whatever else he was, had turned his back on his life as a Knight of the Word and embraced something Logan could not yet define. He might carry the staff and wield the power of the Word, but he no longer served the cause he had once committed to.

Logan shook his head. "I don't think it would work out, you and me. Your fight and mine, they're not the same. You decided to go one way, but it's not my way. I have my own path to follow."

"Once you join me, you will be second in command of my army." Krilka Koos seemed not to have heard him. "I have been training my

followers. They are invincible. They will stand and fight against anything that threatens. They will survive because they have no fear of
dying, because they have been tested, over and over. I will not let them
die. There are thousands, and more come to join every day. If you join,
as well, you will have a chance to do something that matters, a chance
to make a difference. No more wasting time and effort on those who
don't merit it. Slave camps were built for sheep. You and I, we're
wolves! We stand and fight! We do what Knights of the Word should
have done years ago: we leave the sheep to their fate and conduct ourselves as warriors."

Again Logan shook his head. "We were given the staffs we carry to
help those sheep. We owe it to them to do so."

"We owe no one!" the other screamed suddenly, the words echoing
off the metal walls of the building. "No one! We have tried that way,
and we have failed! We have been all but broken trying to save those
sheep, those pitiful creatures that won't fight for themselves! We've
wasted enough time on them!"

Logan knew where this was going, and there was nothing he could
do to change its direction. "I can't join you," he said simply.

Krilka Koos, flushed with his passion, stared at him for a long moment. "You might want to rethink that answer. Come with me."

He took Logan to one corner of the building, back behind the
bleachers where the shadows were deep and layered. There was a sort
of alcove there, a recessed portion of the wall perhaps fifteen feet high
and another thirty long. Logan could just make out what appeared to
be a series of implements fastened to the sheet metal by means of ties
and bolts, all carefully arranged.

Krilka Koos walked over to the adjoining wall and threw open a
pair of metal shutters to let in the light.

Logan stared. The alcove wall was decorated with weapons, everything from Parkhan Sprays and Tyson Flechettes to knives and spears
and swords, Iron Stars and viper-pricks and hundreds of others. At the
very center of the collection were three black staffs carved with runes,
their once polished surfaces turned dull and lifeless, their symbols of
power as gray and cold as ashes.

Logan looked quickly at Krilka Koos. "You're not mistaken," the big man answered his unspoken question. "They belonged to other Knights of the Word, men and women who stood where you are standing now, men and women who gave way to the darkness in their hearts. They were asked to join me; they refused. The price of refusal is sometimes much steeper than what we imagine it will be."

"You killed them?" Logan asked in disbelief. "Other Knights of the Word? You killed them?"

Krilka Koos shook his head. "Not in the way you think. I wouldn't do that. That isn't who I am. They killed themselves."

He stepped around so that he was facing Logan squarely. "I asked them to join me, just as I am asking you. For one reason or another, they said no. They were foolish. In this world, you must make your stand. You cannot walk away. You cannot refuse."

He pointed at Logan. "If you are not with me, then inevitably you are against me. Perhaps not today, not right now, but sometime. The potential for it is there; there is no point in pretending otherwise. Those who are not our friends are our enemies in waiting. We cannot afford to let our enemies escape us. We would be foolish to do so."

Logan got the gist of it, but still had trouble coming to terms with what he was hearing. "You said they killed themselves?"

"In a manner of speaking. I used them to measure my own strength and skill. I gave them the choice of joining me or testing themselves in combat against me."

Logan almost laughed. If Michael had been insane at the end, Krilka Koos was beyond even that. "You made them fight you?"

The big man nodded, no longer smiling. "If you choose not to join me, you are choosing to set yourself against me. The matter is settled through a test of strengths, yours against mine. Trial by combat. Have you made the right decision by refusing to join me or have I by insisting you must? A battle to the death will decide. It is nothing new. It has been an approved method of judging right and wrong for thousands of years."

He gestured at the wall. "These three—and all those others whose weapons hang here, those who were not Knights of the Word but who chose trial by combat nevertheless—fought and died in this arena. I was the stronger, the better trained, the more prepared. I was the one who prevailed." He paused. "I was in the right. They were not."

He folded his arms across his chest. "Now you must decide, just as they did. Do you wish to test me?"

Logan shook his head, a great feeling of hopelessness welling up in his heart. He should have tried to make his escape earlier; he should have taken his chances. "I wish to go back to where you found me, take my kids, and go on my way. Let me do so."

The big man shook his head. "Choose. Join me or fight me. Those are your options."

"This doesn't make any sense. What purpose does it serve for Knights of the Word to fight one another? We share a common enemy. Let me go. Let me carry the fight in the way I feel is best. I leave you to do the same. Why can't we do that?"

Krilka Koos gave him a rueful smile. "Because combat is how we settle everything, Logan. Because the world is ending and the battle to save her is lost. What we have left, in the time we have left, is a chance to take the measure of ourselves. Do we stand around waiting to die like the sheep you are so anxious to save? Or do we die fighting like the men we are? You know the answer. In your heart, you know. We are the last and the best. How good are we? Set against one another, we can discover the truth."

Logan shook his head. "I won't fight you. I won't do it."

"I think you will. I think you don't know yourself as well as you imagine." He unfolded his arms and blew into a whistle hung on a chain about his neck. "Trial by combat, to the death. You have one hour to prepare yourself. Achille will keep you company until then. Do not attempt to escape. If you do, you already know what will happen to your children. It will be on your head. If you defeat me, you will be allowed to take them and go. It is the code I have established, and my men will follow it."

He shook his head. "I should have preferred it, of course, if you joined me. But killing you will be exciting, too. One hour."

He started to walk away, beckoning to Achille and the guards who were already responding to the sound of the whistle. "What does not kill us makes us stronger, Logan Tom," he called back over his shoulder. "It's an old saying. Try thinking on it."

Logan watched him disappear into the shadows, lost to everything. It was Michael at the end. It was madness.

"IS IT SETTLED?" Achille asked quietly, coming up to stand beside him. "You will face him in battle?"

Logan looked at him in disgust. "He seems to think I will." He shook his head. "I don't understand. Why do you follow him?"

Achille's face was cadaverous beneath the shock of wild black hair. "Isn't it obvious? Because he is invincible." He gestured toward the wall of weapons. "Because he prevails in combat against all who stand against him. No one has been able to defeat him. No one ever will. Not demons or once-men. Not even other Knights of the Word. He is too much for any of them."

He gave Logan a long look. "You'll see. He will be too much for you, too."

Achille's smile was rueful as he looked away. "You don't know him as we do, we who follow him. He has given us hope, when there is no hope to be found. He is the one who will save us all."

TWENTY-EIGHT

PANTHER PEERED THROUGH the bushes that screened him from the men gathered in front of the warehouse, searching for any clue that would tell him what had become of Logan Tom.

"How long has he been in there, anyway?" he whispered to Catalya.

She shook her head, a barely perceptible movement, her body flattened against the ground next to his.

"Well, what do you think is happening?"

She shook her head again.

"So what do we do?"

She shifted her gaze sideways. "Don't you have a plan?" she whispered back.

"No! I thought you did!" Irritated with her, he scowled in rebuke. "Why would I have a plan? This was your idea!"

"Not my idea to bring you along, it wasn't."

"Your idea to come in the first place!"

She made no response, and he went back to watching the entry to the warehouse, searching the darkness for movement.

Nothing. For all he knew, Logan Tom might have been dropped into a black pit and covered over.

They were hidden on a rise off to one side of the building entrance, safely back and above the outbuildings and the ghost town beyond. Knowing that they must have been seen coming down the freeway initially from some distance off, they had chosen to come directly after the men who had taken Logan Tom, reasoning that while the freeway might be watched, the compound that housed the men might not. So far, they had been proven right. They had seen no one and not been stopped as they moved through the ravines and hollows that snaked between the hills, at last finding themselves in the wooded area they presently occupied.

But now that they had found the perfect hiding spot, a place where they could see what was happening below and not be seen, they were stymied as to what to do next.

Or at least Panther was. He glanced sideways at Catalya. Hard to tell about her.

He studied her mottled face. Strange, at first glance, but once you got past the Lizard patches, rather nice. She was different in the same way as Tessa—unusual, unique. Black hair like Tessa, but she had pale skin like Chalk. He couldn't explain the attraction. Of course, part of it was the way she could fight. Any girl who could take out three men as fast as she did was something special. Even Sparrow couldn't do that. He studied her some more. Couldn't turn away. Didn't want to. He wondered why she worked so hard at trying to make everyone think she was ugly.

She looked over at him suddenly, her mouth twisting into a wicked grin. "Can't take your eyes off me, can you?"

He turned away, burning with embarrassment. *Stupid Freak*, he thought, then squelched the words at once. It was wrong to call her that, even without actually saying the words, wrong to think of her that way, double wrong to suggest that she was bad somehow just because of her condition.

He hated that he thought and said things before thinking them through. Hated that he did it so often. Like when Logan Tom had brought the girl into camp. First thing he did, he called her a Freak, his mouth quicker than his brain, like there was no connection between the two. Sparrow called him on it regularly. River, too, now and then. It was all right. He deserved it. He had it coming.

"I'm sorry I said those things about you earlier," he whispered impulsively, not able to make himself look at her as he said it. "I shouldn't have called you names. You don't deserve that. I didn't mean it. Not really. I was just being stupid."

"Give me your Spray," she said in response, almost as if she hadn't heard him.

He hesitated, surprised by the request, but then handed over his weapon. Cat took it and slipped it quickly beneath her cloak, doing something he couldn't quite see to secure it once it was tucked safely inside.

"Hey!" he objected. "What are you doing?"

She glanced over, giving him a wink. "Saving you from yourself. You'll get it back when you need it."

Below, the open space in front of the warehouse was beginning to fill with men and women, all rather ragged and haggard, all carrying weapons. They seemed to appear all at once and out of nowhere, but in truth they had come from the outbuildings and the hills beyond. They were all talking and seemed excited as they moved toward the open doors of the warehouse and poured inside.

"What's going on?" Panther asked.

Cat looked over at him, her smile gone. "We're about to find out. Don't panic. We've been seen. They're right behind us."

He stared at her, thinking she was joking, that this was another of her games played at his expense. He started to say something in response, and she quickly put a finger to her lips.

"Stay where you are," a voice ordered.

Panther felt his heart sink.

"What do you two think you're doing?" a second voice asked.

"Just looking for something to eat," Catalya answered at once, her voice pitifully frightened and desperate. "We didn't mean any harm. Please, mister, we haven't eaten in days."

"Street kids," said another voice. "That one's a Freak. Look at her face. Don't touch her."

Panther started to turn. "I told you not to move," the first voice said, closer now, and the cold muzzle of a weapon pressed up against his cheek.

"Just let us go, mister," Catalya begged, starting to cry.

"I don't think so," the first voice said. "Not till I find out something more about you. I think you'd better come with us. Get up. Slowly."

Panther was furious. *I knew I shouldn't have given her the Spray!*

"Hurry it up," the second urged. "We'll miss the show."

The muzzle of the gun left Panther's face.

As the boy and the girl climbed to their feet, Catalya gave Panther a sideways glance and a wink and mouthed, *Trust me.* Then she said over her shoulder to their captors, her voice shaking, "What sort of show, mister?"

I hope you know what you're doing, Panther thought sourly.

                              ▪ ▪ ▪

WHEN THE HOUR allotted to Logan was almost up, Achille brought him a suit of worn, scarred body armor that had obviously seen extensive use. Pieces were dented, and a few were cracked halfway across. Logan told Achille he didn't want body armor, didn't even want this fight, but the other man insisted he put it on. Krilka Koos would be wearing body armor and wouldn't allow any disparity in protection or weapons that would lend one combatant or the other an advantage. Each would be identically dressed and armed.

Logan allowed the body armor to be fitted—chest and back plates, upper arm and elbow guards, and upper thigh and knee guards with overlapping plates at the juncture of shoulders and arms and hips and thighs. The armor was lightweight and strong, an alloy perfected in the waning days of the struggle that had seen the end of organized government and its armies. Michael had owned a set. Logan had not.

He found himself standing alone afterward, the body armor cinched tightly about him, his staff held in both hands as he faced the weapons display wall, thinking that this shouldn't be happening, that it made no sense. It was what he had thought from the moment he had learned what Krilka Koos intended, and even now, when it was clearly time to do so, he couldn't make himself face the reality of his situation. It felt surreal to him, a dream that he would wake from at any moment. Even when he heard the sounds of voices outside the building, gathering in volume and intensity, and then inside, changing to shouts and cries of expectation; even when he heard the sounds of boots climbing into the bleachers and hands clapping with rhythmic encouragement; and even when the cacophony was so intense that it blotted out every other sound and left him blanketed in waves of wildness and frenzy, he could not find steady ground on which to stand. He was at sea, cast adrift, and everything around him seemed to be getting farther away.

How was he supposed to prepare for a battle he had no interest in fighting? The question rolled and spun with the bright insistence of sunspots flashing through dark clouds. He wondered suddenly if this was where everything would end for him—his service to the Word, his efforts to find and protect the boy Hawk, his care for the Ghosts, all the unfinished business in his life. Knights of the Word did not have long lives, but somehow he had always believed he would have more time than this.

"They're ready," Achille said suddenly, coming up to him.

Logan looked at the man, at the faint smile on his face, and he knew that no one thought for one minute that this was something he was going to walk away from.

"What do I do?" he asked.

"Walk out into the arena. Krilka will be waiting. The rest is up to the two of you." Achille stepped back. "Good luck."

What he was saying, Logan knew, was *Good-bye.*

He took a last look at the weapons display, imagining for a moment the men—and possibly women—who had carried them into battle. He looked once more at the three rune-carved staffs that had belonged to other Knights of the Word, dull and lifeless in their straps, the power gone with their bearers' lives. They couldn't have wanted this any more than he did. It was obscene that they should have come to this end. Krilka Koos killed to reassure himself of his prowess. He killed so that his followers would believe he was invincible. Everything he had sworn to do as a Knight of the Word had been subverted. Logan felt a slow burn of anger build inside. It would never stop unless someone made it stop.

Unless he made it stop.

He tightened his hands about his staff, took a deep breath, and walked out into the arena.

The roar that greeted his appearance nearly knocked him backward. Shouts of frenzied expectation rose out of the throats of hundreds of men and women. Boots stomped and banged against bleacher aisles, and hands clapped and pounded on metal seats. The faithful were gathered in force, there to witness his destruction at the hands of their leader, savior, and manufactured hero. Logan felt sick to his stomach, fear washing through him. He wasn't immune to the latter, and while he had braved death a hundred times in his raids on the slave camps, he had never faced it down in circumstances like these. His throat tightened and his stomach lurched as the roar washed over him like an ocean wave that would drag him under and drown him.

But it was the massing of feeders all through the bleachers, around and under them, their dark shapes hunched and squirming in eager anticipation of what was to come, that chilled him to the bone. He had not seen this many since the boy Hawk, the gypsy morph, had been thrown from the walls of the compound in Seattle. Hundreds of them, waiting for the bloodletting. Waiting for their chance to drink in the pain and anguish, the dark emotions that would spill from the combatants. This was a battle between two Knights of the Word, and the chance to feed would never be more satisfying. No one could see them but Krilka Koos and himself. No one else would even know they were there.

Logan Tom felt his stomach constrict at the thought.

Krilka Koos stood waiting at the other end of the arena. He was dressed all in black and gray, clothing and body armor of a piece, and he carried his black staff cradled comfortably in his arms. Already its runes were glowing a dull blue. He had the look of a man who was neither afraid nor anxious. He waited with no sign of impatience or expectation. This would be just another battle for him, another killing. It would be a little more special than most because Logan was a Knight of the Word, but nothing more than that. The outcome was predetermined; his certainty of it was mirrored on his face.

He waited until Logan was fully emerged from behind the bleachers, standing open and exposed within the arena, and then he spread his arms wide in open invitation. "Come fight me, Logan Tom!" he roared. "Come test yourself against me!"

The crowd roared, the sound reverberating off the rafters and shaking the sheet-metal walls. The feeders climbed over one another in an effort to get closer. Logan glanced at the open doorway through which he had come earlier, still thinking of the possibility of escape. The men who served Krilka Koos were mostly crammed into this warehouse to watch the spectacle, and there was little chance that they could prevent him from reaching the Ghosts if he could get through the door. But to do that, he would have to fight his way past rows of men and women at least ten-deep and turn his back on Krilka Koos in the bargain. What chance would he have of making it through?

He gave it up and looked over at his adversary. The scarred face was bright with anticipation, the black staff pointing toward him now, leveled and ready for use. Logan shook his head and started to say, "Why can't we take a different—"

He got that much out before the Word's fire, wielded by its failed servant, slammed into him with pile-driver force and sent him tumbling backward, head-over-heels. The force of the attack was shocking. Pain ratcheted through his body, and his breath exploded out of him in a hard, quick gasp. He almost lost his grip on his staff; only instinct and desperation kept him from releasing it.

But the attack had another effect, as well. It knocked aside all hesitation and doubt, banishing in an instant every consideration but one. In his mind, the words screamed at him, harsh and commanding.

Stay alive!

His training and instincts took over, and he rolled back to his feet in a single fluid movement. He didn't bother trying to defend himself against what he knew was coming. Instead, he attacked. He summoned the magic and sent it flying across the arena into Krilka Koos with every ounce of strength he could muster. He watched it strike the big man, shatter against him, and stagger him with its force.

But it did little else. It did not flatten him as Logan had intended that it should. It did not break apart his defenses and give him reason to question his self-confidence. If anything, it reaffirmed it. He shook off the blow, steadied himself, and raised his arms in triumph, almost as if he believed he had already won the battle.

The crowd roared its approval, and the foot stomping and hand-clapping reached new heights. Scattered invisibly through their midst, the feeders lunged and withdrew like wild dogs.

Logan was back on his feet, his staff held protectively before him, his defenses in place. Krilka Koos grinned broadly, beckoning him closer, taunting him. The two men circled each other, feinting without attacking, each looking to find a weakness in the other's approach. Logan, having abandoned his reluctance along with any hope that his adversary could be made to listen to reason, was determined to end this quickly.

But it was Krilka Koos who struck first, again without warning, again without seeming to do anything but shift his stance slightly. He struck at Logan's feet, a searing bolt that erupted from the lowered end of his staff, skimmed the dirt floor, and encircled Logan's ankles, burning through his boots and knocking him to his knees. Instantly the big man followed up with a second strike, this one aimed at Logan's head. Logan deflected the blow at the last moment, fighting back from his knees, unable to rise, his lower legs and feet numb. He threw up the Word's fire from his staff in a shield that broke apart the blow intended to remove his head, and rocked back on his nerveless heels.

"Come, Logan Tom!" Krilka Koos shouted at him. "Surely you can do better than this!"

Taunts issued from the crowd in response, whistles and hoots and jeers of all sorts. Logan barely heard them, scrambling to gather up his scattered thoughts, struggling back to his feet. He was losing this fight. He had to turn the attack back against Krilka Koos. What had Michael taught him that he could use? What, that would keep him alive?

The big man attacked again, the fire of his staff slamming Logan backward once more, this time all the way into the first row of the bleachers. Rough hands shoved him away, fists pummeling and boots kicking at his back and shoulders. He was barely clear when the fire engulfed him once more. His defenses feeble and unfocused, his concentration shattered by the pain and the shock of what was happening to him, he went down on his knees, gasping for breath, fighting waves of nausea. He felt the first of the feeders climbing over him, their touch like cold wet leaves against his hot skin.

Do something! he screamed at himself.

But he couldn't imagine what that something would be.

* * *

"PLEASE, MISTER, what's happening in there?" Cat asked in her frightened-little-girl voice. She reached up and put her hands over her ears. "It's so loud."

Panther wanted to roll his eyes, but kept them firmly fixed on the entry to the warehouse they were passing on their way to whatever lockup their captors were planning to put them in. The metal sides of the building were shaking with the sounds of raucous shouts and stamping feet. Smoke drifted from the air vents and through seams in the sheet metal, and brilliant white light flashed through the building's deep gloom. Bodies were packed tightly against the entrance, blocking any view of whatever everyone had gathered to see.

Didn't matter if he could see or not, Panther thought. He could still make a pretty good guess as to who was involved.

"You don't need to know about that," one of the men snapped at the girl, while the other gave Panther a shove for good measure. "Just keep moving. Hurry it up!"

"We're missing it!" his companion muttered angrily. "The whole thing!"

They passed the building entrance, moved around to one side, and started toward a series of sheds clustered near the back. Panther had a knife tucked into his boot, but he couldn't think how to reach it or even what to do with it if he did. He needed the Spray, but that was safely tucked away inside Cat's cloak. Which their captors hadn't even bothered to look under, he added bitterly. They were so scared of her disease, whatever they imagined it to be, that they had checked only him. Frickin' stump heads, he thought.

They reached the sheds. "Okay, this is as far as you go," one man said, moving toward the nearest door and loosening a chain looped through a metal hasp.

"Are you going to lock us in there?" Cat asked in horror.

"That's right, Lizard face," he said, giving her a knowing grin. "Shouldn't bother you all that—"

She flung out her arm, and an Iron Star embedded itself in his chest. He went down in a heap. The second man stared in disbelief, then tried to bring up his weapon. But by then the second Star was already buried in his neck. He gasped once, clutched at his throat, and collapsed.

Neither Panther nor Cat said a word as they dragged the men into the nearest shed, closed the door, and locked them in by knotting the length of chain through the hasps.

Then the boy turned to her. "You knew we were gonna be captured by these stump heads, and you let it happen?"

"How else were we going to get this close?" She gave him a look. "What? You thought we could sneak in without being seen, maybe? Don't you know anything? How have you managed to stay alive?"

"Stayed alive just fine before you showed up!" he snapped at her.

She reached under her cloak, fumbled with the ties that secured it, brought out the Parkhan Spray and handed it to him. "Here. Maybe you can manage to stay alive this time, too, if you pay attention to me."

"Oh, so *now* you have a plan?"

She pulled up the hood of her cloak so that her face was concealed. "Sure. Go in, find him, and get him out. How's that sound?"

He stared at her. "Sounds brain-dead."

"It isn't. We have the advantage of surprise."

He stared at her some more, then sighed. "Don't know why I should expect anything out of you. Okay, let's do it."

She led the way at a trot across the empty grounds.

LOGAN TOM was back on his feet, the Word's magic summoned from his staff once more, its ragged defenses warding him as best they could. The feeders that had attempted to devour him had been thrust aside, driven back into the bleachers. Not that any of this meant he would be alive five minutes from now. Across from him, Krilka Koos was already celebrating, taunting him anew, stalking him as a predator stalks a wounded animal. Logan knew that he needed a plan, a way to catch the big man off guard, a way to negate his strength and power. He needed to call to mind all of the lessons that Michael had taught him about hand-to-hand combat. But wounded and in pain, fighting to keep himself from falling apart, he was finding it difficult to recall anything.

"Logan Tom! Are you still alive over there?" Krilka Koos laughed, feinted playfully, and stepped aside from an imaginary retaliation. "I don't think you've got much left in you! Do you want this to be over with quickly? Or do you wish to keep dragging it out?"

Overconfident of his victory, he revealed something he hadn't intended. Logan watched him feint and withdraw, feint and withdraw, and he saw a pattern to his movements. If he could take advantage of it, he might still have a chance.

Without giving anything away as to his state of mind or intentions, he started advancing on the other man. Koos could not be uncertain what he was doing; the advance did not seem to signal an attack. If anything, it must seem more a submission, an acceptance of his fate.

"Are you finished, then?" he shouted. It was what he was anticipating, what he believed Logan wanted. "Throw down your staff, and I promise to make it quick!"

Still playing with his captive, he started to feint and withdraw once again.

Only this time Logan was waiting. The moment Krilka Koos began his feint, Logan summoned the magic in a rush and sent it hurtling into the space into which the other's now predictable withdrawal would take him. The big man stepped right into it. He tried to change directions at the last instant, aware of what was happening, but he was already moving and it was too late. The Word's bright fire slammed into him, catching him full-on, knocking him completely off his feet and sprawling into the dirt.

Logan rushed him instantly, charging across the space that separated them, using his own magic not to attack, as the other would expect, but to shield himself. As he had anticipated, Koos struck out at him from where he lay, trying to stop him in midstride. But his defenses held, buoyed by the adrenaline pumping through him and by his determination. He heard the roar of the crowd all around him, the sound heartening this time because it betrayed their dismay at the unexpected turn of events.

Then he was on top of Koos, using his staff like a cudgel, hammering it downward on the other's arms and body in sharp, rapid blows, striving to break past the other's efforts to block him. He was successful enough that he heard Krilka Koos grunt with pain, still sprawled on his back, unable to get back to his feet. Logan would not let him up. Could not, if he wanted to live. He could feel the feeders all around him, climbing over them both, pressing down, sucking in the leavings of their dark struggle. He pressed his attack, doubling his efforts, Word fire spurting from both ends of his staff in response to his rage. Fire burst from the ends of Krilka Koos's staff as well, but he could not bring it to bear.

Then, perhaps in desperation, the big man rolled into Logan, one arm reaching out to grapple with his legs, to try to bring him down. He dropped any semblance of an attack using his staff, tucking it against his body with his free arm, relying instead on his enormous strength. He ducked his head between his hunched shoulders, shielding it as best he could, and tore at the smaller man. Logan was already losing his balance, unable to kick free.

When he went down, Krilka Koos was on top of him at once, pounding into him with staff and fists. Blows exploded against Logan's head, and for a moment he thought he would lose consciousness. He survived mostly on instinct and training, burying his head in the big man's shoulder while his fingers found a set of vulnerable nerves in the other's thick neck. Krilka Koos gasped and cried out, thrashing to break free. His attack on Logan stalled as they rolled across the dirt arena in a tangle of arms and legs, the cries of the men and women on the bleachers rising to a fresh crescendo. Koos was bigger and stronger, but Logan, lacking size and strength, knew more about self-defense. Keeping his fingers locked on his enemy's neck, he lifted his head out of its protective hunch and head-butted the big man in the face, breaking his nose. Koos howled in dismay, and blood spurted all over both of them.

More important, half blind and in desperate pain, he released his grip on Logan.

Logan broke free at once, scrambling to his feet before Koos could stop him. Fire lanced down the entire length of his staff, a blinding blue-white brilliance that brought a collective gasp from those watching. With every ounce of muscle he could bring to bear, Logan slammed the fiery staff against the side of the other man's head. The head snapped back, and Krilka Koos shuddered. Fighting his way past the clutch of feeders that had suddenly shifted their attention, Logan brought the length of his staff down hard on the other's knuckles, first on one hand and then the other, breaking several fingers. Koos cried out once more, dropped his staff from his shattered hands, and curled into a ball.

Feeders swamped him in a frenzied rush, a black, snarling mass of shadows.

The roar of the men and women gathered died to a soft buzz of disbelief. Logan ignored them, standing over his enemy—the enemy he had not wanted in the first place but accepted as one now. Krilka Koos was still gasping, trying to speak words that pain and shock were blocking.

Logan bent close. "Kill me," the other whispered, teeth gritted, fierce eyes fixed on him. He thrust aside the feeders threatening to engulf him, his dark face twisting in fear and disgust. "Do it quickly, before they eat me alive!"

Logan hesitated. It was what the other man would have done to him if their positions had been reversed. It was the smart thing to do. He glanced at the crowd, looked into their faces, and saw that they were expecting it. He felt suddenly sick to his stomach, the magic roiling through him in steady, violent waves. Kill him. It would be so easy.

Instead he straightened, reached down for the staff Krilka Koos had dropped, and tossed it aside. "You won't be needing this again," he replied, bending down so the other could hear him clearly. He kicked at the feeders, scattering them back toward the bleachers. "You won't be pretending at being something you're not after this."

"I'll hunt you down!" the other seethed. The dark, scarred visage twisted with fury. "I'll find you and kill you, no matter where you go. I'll kill all your children first. All of them! I'll do it right in front of you!"

Logan bent close. "You'd better hope you never see me again."

Krilka Koos grinned at him, a death's-mask grimace, and then spit in his face. A moment later Logan felt something sharp pierce his calf, burning into him. He looked down just as the other man was withdrawing his hand, seeing the tiny dart sticking out of his leg.

Viper-prick.

Instantly the feeders were back, swarming this time over Logan.

He lost control then, slamming the hardened length of his staff against the other's right knee, shattering it. Krilka Koos sobbed audibly. Logan hesitated a moment, and then he broke the left knee, as well.

"Find me if you can!" he spit. The feeders had become a dark mass at the edges of his vision. His head was buzzing with the magic and the world was all on fire around him, a bright red haze. "Hunt me if you want! But you'll have to crawl to do it!"

Unaware of what had happened, the crowd was celebrating his victory, cheering and calling out his name. In their minds, he had already taken Krilka Koos's place. He had become their new invincible. He stood without moving amid the cacophony, staring down at their old leader, the fire of his staff running up and down its length like a live thing. The feeders seemed to be everywhere. He felt light-headed and disoriented, and everything around him began to lose shape and form.

He turned toward the crowd. "Get out!" he screamed.

When they hesitated, waiting to see what he would do, he turned the staff on them, sending sheets of fire hurtling into the bleachers, setting everything that would burn aflame. Those who had hesitated a moment earlier went flying down off their seats, fleeing for the entry and the safety of the world outside the building. Logan chased them with his fire, half mad with rage and frustration.

His thoughts were dark and destructive. A kind of battle madness enveloped him, stealing away his reason entirely.

They're animals! Nothing but animals!

His mind reeled and his body swayed. The poison was already working its way through his system. He retreated deep inside to protect himself, shutting and bolting doors, throwing locks and bringing down bars.

Animals!

Burn them all to ash!

PANTHER AND CATALYA, hiding beneath the section of the bleachers they had crawled under after wriggling through an opening in the sheet metal near the back of the building, had watched the last of the battle between Logan Tom and Krilka Koos through gaps in the legs of the audience. When the Knight of the Word turned the fire of his staff on the crowd, they threw themselves backward and lay flat against the flooring as the wooden parts of the bleachers caught fire and people began fighting to get clear. Heat and flames washed over them, and the building took on the red glare of a furnace. In moments it had emptied of almost everyone. Through the smoky haze, they could see Krilka Koos lying prostrate at the center of the arena and Logan Tom standing alone, leaning on his staff, swaying uncertainly.

Catalya jabbed Panther's shoulder to get his attention, then scrambled to her feet. Together they worked their way out from under the bleachers, avoiding the flames and heat, hurrying to reach the Knight of the Word. No one tried to stop them. No one remained to try.

Panther glanced at the display of weapons mounted on the wall behind them as they passed it. Most were scorched or melted, flames licking off the wooden stocks and handle grips, the wall itself seared an uneven gray. Only the three rune-carved staffs seemed unaffected, their smooth lengths a dull, flat black that the flames had failed to damage.

They slipped from behind the bleachers and ran across the floor to the Knight of the Word. He didn't seem to see them coming, was barely cognizant of their presence once they reached him, his gaze distant and empty as he fought to stay upright.

"Logan," the girl called to him.

She got to him before Panther, and without hesitating reached down and pulled free the viper-prick. "Hold him up, Panther!" she ordered.

She tore away the pant leg and exposed the wound, an ugly purplish bruise already swollen to a knot. Panther, both arms wrapped about the Knight of the Word, shook his head. Viper-pricks were always fatal. There was no cure. But he didn't say that, didn't say anything. He just watched as Cat tied off the leg above the wound, and then fumbled in the pockets of her cloak for a small tube of ointment that she smeared on the knot, covering it over with a compress and binding it in place with tape.

"That will help draw the poison out," she said by way of explanation. "Let's get him out of here."

Shouldering him from either side, the boy and the girl began to walk him across the arena toward the entry. Panther held the Parkhan Spray cradled in one arm, ready to use. But the few men and women who lingered outside fled quickly at their approach.

Behind them, they could hear Krilka Koos moaning and calling out Logan Tom's name. Panther wanted to go back and cut out his tongue.

Once outside, they began the slow journey toward the freeway. The afternoon was waning, the light fading. East, the sky was already dark. Panther staggered under Logan Tom's weight, trying to glance over his shoulder, worried that one of those militia stump heads would shoot them in the back.

"Weighs a ton," he muttered, fighting to keep Logan upright.

Across from him, Cat nodded, her mottled face flushed.

"He might not make it, you know." Panther glanced at her. "Most men wouldn't."

Her lips tightened. "He's not like most men."

Couldn't argue with that. Panther tightened his grip about the Knight of the Word, his mind flooding with images of the battle they had just witnessed.

No, Logan Tom definitely wasn't like most men.

TWENTY-NINE

LEAVING LARKIN QUILL to cross back over Redonnelin Deep to his home, there to await their signal that they required a return, Angel and her Elven companions set out once more for Syrring Rise. It was midmorning when they began their trek north, but the journey turned out to be anything but what Angel had expected.

"How far do we have to go?" she asked Simralin after enough time had passed that it had become a concern.

"Just a few more miles," the Elven girl answered, glancing over her shoulder from her lead position, unable to conceal her grin.

Angel peered ahead. There were mountains, but they were some distance off and none of them was particularly distinctive. She guessed she just wasn't seeing what she was supposed to see, that Syrring Rise was lost in the larger mass or in the dirty haze that hung like a pall over most of what lay ahead, a reminder of how bad the air had been polluted.

They trekked on without saying much, making what progress they could through country that was choked with wintry stands of weeds and scrub amid rocky flats and rises. Angel's thoughts drifted to her old life and Johnny, and then to little Ailie, her doomed conscience. The tatterdemalion hadn't had much chance to exercise that conscience, even though she had stated on their first meeting that this was her self-appointed goal. A creature who lived an average of thirty days, and she had offered herself as a voice of reason to a Knight of the Word—a Faerie creature trying to help a human. It seemed incongruous and somehow sad. She wished for what must have been the hundredth time that she could have found a way to save her tiny friend.

They were in the middle of wilderness by now, in country empty of buildings and roads and anything living. There wasn't so much as a rodent poking its head from its burrow or a bird circling the sky. Heavy, dead trees clustered together in skeletal bundles, as if they had sought comfort from one another at the end. Grasses were spiky and gray with sickness and death. Dust lay thick on the ground everywhere, rising in small explosions from their footfalls. In the distance, the mountains loomed dark and bare, no closer now than they had been an hour ago.

"Exactly how far is it to Syrring Rise?" Angel asked impatiently.

Simralin stopped a moment, unslung her waterskin, and took a deep drink. "On foot, about two weeks. As the crow flies, about a hundred miles." She nodded toward the mountain range. "On the other side of that."

Angel stared. "Two weeks! We don't have two weeks!"

Simralin nodded. "Don't worry. We'll be there before dark." She shouldered the waterskin anew. "You'll see, Angel. Trackers know how to get where they want to in ways that others don't."

An enigmatic comment that Angel felt inclined to challenge, but she decided not to. She glanced at Kirisin, who shrugged his lack of understanding but at the same time seemed confident that his sister could do what was needed. Angel wished she could have that kind of confidence in someone, but she didn't even have it in herself.

They continued on for a short time, not much more than another half an hour, arriving at a broad, thick stand of huge old conifers, their once green needles turned silvery by nature and the elements. It was a strange sight, the trees stretching away for miles in all directions, seemingly all the way to the lower slopes of the mountains west. Without hesitating, Simralin took them directly into their center, striding ahead confidently, her blond hair a silken shimmer in the hazy light. Angel and Kirisin followed, neither saying anything. The woods were deep and gray and silent, and the emptiness was its own presence. Such places bothered Angel, who preferred the stones and bricks and concrete of the city. In the city, you could find your way. Here, there was nothing to tell you even so much as the direction in which you were going. The trees blocked the mountains. The haze diffused the sunlight. Everything looked the same.

Then abruptly the terrain changed from dust and scrub to an uneven hardpan that the wind had swept clear of everything loose. There were strange, twisted trees with spiky leaves and peeling bark set in among the conifers. There were tall stands of scrub, some of them more than six feet high. In minutes, they were deep into this new stand of foliage, and Angel was hopelessly lost. Her hands tightened on her staff, reassuring herself that she was not entirely powerless. But the woods seemed to press in against her anyway, threatening to suffocate her, to steal away her power.

"I hate this," she muttered.

Kirisin looked over and nodded, but said nothing.

Angel was just beginning to wonder if this was leading to anything when the trees opened before them and they found themselves at the edge of a broad, shallow ravine surrounding a rocky flat on which two piles of brush covered a pair of square-shaped objects; what might once have been a third pile lay scattered about on the rocks nearby.

For the first time, Simralin hesitated, her forehead furrowing with concern. "There should be three," she said, mostly to herself, but loud enough that her companions could hear her. "What happened to the third?"

Angel moved a few steps closer, right to the edge of the ravine, and peered at the two that were still covered. "Are those baskets of some sort?" she asked in surprise.

Simralin nodded. "They are. But there should be another. Wait here."

She crossed the ravine, walking down into it and climbing out the

other side, then moving over to the discarded pile of brush, peering intently at the ground. When she had seen enough, she cast about at the
surrounding woods, and then looked back at them. "I can't be sure. The
ground is too rocky for a clear read. One man, I think. But it could be
more. I don't understand it. We don't have any Trackers out this way
just now."

She knelt, studying the footprints a second time. "Nothing special
about the few scuffs I can make out." She shook her head. "If it was the
demons, I could read the marks from that cat thing. But if it was just
the other . . ." She trailed off. "All right. Come on over."

Angel crossed with Kirisin and stood looking down at ground so
hard and rocky it told her absolutely nothing. She could not understand how Simralin had determined as much as she had. "What's going
on?" she asked. "What are we doing here?"

"Uncover one of those baskets," she said by way of response. "Kirisin
can help. Remove everything you find packed in the bottom, separate
it, and spread it out on the ground. Don't try to attach any of it. Leave
that to me. I'll be back in a moment."

She walked back down into the ravine, out the other side, and off
into the trees until she could no longer be seen. Angel looked at Kirisin,
and together they moved over to the closest basket, pulled off the dead
limbs and brush concealing it—Angel thinking as they did so that this
sort of concealment would only work against someone looking down
from above, not someone who somehow happened upon it—and
peered down into the basket interior. The basket was divided into four
compartments, interlocking partitions that sectioned the interior and
served as bracing for the sides. A tightly folded piece of material was
shoved into the bottom along with various ropes, metal locking clasps,
and hoses.

"What is this?" Angel asked the boy.

Kirisin shook his head. "I don't know. I've never seen anything like it."

Together they emptied the contents of the basket on the ground,
laying out all the pieces separately as Simralin had told them to do. The
material turned out to be a lightweight fabric that Angel could not
identify, thin but strong, a mottled gray and white in color. Once it was
unfolded and spread out, it took on a recognizable shape.

"This looks like a balloon," Angel said.

"A hot-air balloon," Simralin amended, striding out of the ravine once more. "Which is what will get us where we're going."

She was carrying several solar cells and what looked to be some sort of small motor. She put the solar cells into the basket and the motor on the ground next to the mouth of the balloon.

"This is a burner," she advised, gesturing at the motor. She hooked up one end of the hose to a nozzle and shoved the other into the mouth of the balloon. "It heats the air and feeds it into the bag, which inflates. When the bag is full, it lifts the basket and its occupants off the ground."

She flipped a switch, and the burner roared to life, breaking the silence. Slowly, the balloon began to fill. "Elven Trackers use these balloons for long-distance travel. We keep them hidden away in a handful of places on both sides of the mountains. Humans invented them, but we saw a use for them, too. Our Trackers began appropriating them a generation ago. We were using them even before your government collapsed, but after the wars started we began using them more frequently. We found it impossible to move about as we once had. Much of the open country was flooded with militia and mutated creatures. Much of it was dangerously poisoned. And travel time became a more important factor in many instances. The balloons helped us solve those problems."

"Elves using human technology," Angel murmured, shaking her head.

"Once in a while." Simralin grinned. "We know enough to take advantage of a good thing. I'll show you another example when we get to Syrring Rise."

She gave the pile of brush to one side a quick glance. "We had three, but someone has taken one. Took some cells and a burner, too. All that equipment was hidden back in the rocks. Only long-range Trackers know where all that is; stumbling over it by accident is highly unlikely."

She shook her head, turning to the ropes and clasps. "Here. Help me attach these to the balloon and the basket," she said.

Under her direction, they made the balloon ready, watching the bag fill and begin to lift slowly off the ground. By that time, they had it firmly attached and had placed the burner and their gear inside the basket. Ropes tied to old logs and dead trees held the basket grounded as it strained to rise skyward. When Simralin was satisfied that it was ready, she ordered the other two into the basket, climbed in after them, released the restraining ropes, and they were off.

Madre de Dios, Angel thought.

It was like nothing she had ever experienced. The earth dropped away as they ascended into the midday sky, trees and rocks and rivers and lakes growing slowly smaller, the landscape spreading away in miniature. Save for when Simralin used the compressor to feed more hot air into the bag, they were enveloped by a silence so deep and intense that it felt to Angel almost as if she had left everything terrible in her life behind. The basket bobbed softly on the wind currents, but mostly it just hung there, steady and smooth as Simralin steered it toward the mountains north and west.

"How do you like it?" the Tracker asked her at one point.

Angel grinned and nodded. "Any danger of the bag collapsing?"

Simralin shook her head. "The fabric is one we developed. Very strong, very tough. Rain doesn't bother it. Even resists blades. A lightning strike is the biggest concern, but our weather is good." She smiled. "Much better than walking. We'll be there by sunset."

They flew at a steady pace toward a gap in the mountain chain, the winds favoring a northwest flight. But Angel could tell that Simralin had considerable flying experience, working smoothly to keep the balloon on a course that carried it in the general direction required, maneuvering flaps that opened and closed in the bag, releasing small bursts of air to gain momentum or adjust height. She had learned to read and measure the movement of air currents and, after attaching the extra hoses to side ports in the basket, was able to change direction. It wasn't a perfect science, even when all of it was cobbled together. At times, they drifted off course, but the Elven Tracker always seemed to find a way to bring them back around, tacking first one way and then another.

The hours crawled by, a passage that felt desperately at odds with the urgency of their undertaking. Angel scanned the ground they passed over, searching for something more than changes in the terrain.

Signs of life. Signs of pursuit. Something of the dangers she knew she couldn't see, but were there, nevertheless. It felt safe flying hundreds of feet in the air. But she knew the feeling was false.

They gained the far side of the peaks and caught prevailing southerly winds along the west face of the chain that carried them north. The winds waxed and waned with the passing of the afternoon, gusting at times, dying away completely at others. They flew over miles of blighted forests and foothills, keeping clear of the chain's taller peaks, avoiding the canyons and defiles where the winds were treacherous and might blow them into the cliffs. Although Kirisin was full of questions, his natural curiosity demanding explanations that his sister was hard-pressed to provide, Angel was content just to observe, preferring the luxury of the silence that this wondrous flight afforded them. Silence was not easily found in the city. Until you were dead, of course, like Johnny, and then it was forever.

It was nearing sunset when they reached Syrring Rise. The winds had picked up a bit, and they were encountering gusts that knocked them about, requiring that Simralin abandon her efforts at answering Kirisin's unending questions in favor of keeping them stable. Angel found herself gripping the sides of the basket tightly. They caught sight of the snowcapped peak all at once, a huge block of rock and snow and ice rising up against the horizon as they came out from behind a group of smaller mountains, its mass rising far above where they flew, towering over lesser mountains, over broad stretches of land, over everything for as far as the eye could see. It was the biggest monolith Angel had ever seen, but it was also the most beautiful. Here, unlike everywhere else she had been on her travels, save in parts of the Cintra, the air was clean and clear, and the details of the mountain and its surroundings jumped out at her in sharp relief. She stared in disbelief at how pure everything surrounding this volcanic giant seemed, as if Mother Nature's hand had swept away from this one majestic setting the whole of the world's pollution and sickness.

When she asked about this, wanting to know how it was possible, Simralin said that it was mostly due to the work of Elves who lived on the slopes of Paradise, the name given to this side of the mountain. Her parents had wanted the Elves to form a settlement here, but the most they could accomplish in the face of opposition from Arissen Belloruus was to found a small community of caretakers. These few worked with what small Elven magic they were able to command to blend elements of earth, air, and water to keep at bay the rot and poisoning that had set in so deeply elsewhere. The Elves still had skills enough for this, although it was becoming increasingly clear that it was a losing battle. Their efforts in the Cintra were already failing.

She maneuvered the balloon toward the meadows that blanketed the lower slopes, vast patches of green dotted with wildflowers that Angel hadn't thought existed anywhere. She tried to remember when she had last seen flowers in such profusion. Never, she decided. Even within the Cintra, they had been confined to small areas. Here they stretched away in sweeping blankets that formed a colorful border between the forests lower down and the bare rock and ice farther up. She searched the mountainside for signs of life, thinking she would see some of the Elven caretakers that Simralin had mentioned. But there was no sign of anyone.

When she asked where they were, Simralin shook her head. There were only a handful, and these were scattered all across the lower slopes of the mountain. They were unlikely to find any of them without making a concerted effort. The caretakers were used to the occasional presence of Trackers and, for the most part, left them to their work unless summoned. There was no reason to disturb them here.

The sun had gone far west by now, shadows lengthening across the mountain in great, dark stains. The color was fading from the world, and the air was turning cold. Angel glanced toward the snowcapped peak; the failing light glistened in sharp bursts off the ice field.

"We'll need to take shelter before dark," Simralin advised. "Or freeze to death."

She brought the balloon down at the edge of one of the meadows, shutting down the burner and using the vent flaps in the bag. The basket tipped on its side as it landed, and the balloon dragged it for a short distance before enough air seeped out to collapse it. The three travelers scrambled from the basket and hauled in the fabric, folding it over as Simralin showed them, gathering up all the stays and ties. When they had everything collected and disconnected, she had them stow it in the basket.

"No one will disturb it," she said. "We'll use it on our return, once we're finished here. Let's take shelter and make something to eat."

After gathering up their gear, she led them toward a stand of conifers at the far right end of the meadow, whistling softly in the deep mountain silence.

* * *

THEY SPENT THE NIGHT in a line shack used by the caretakers during their treks across the slopes of the mountain, a tiny shelter set back in the trees that was all but invisible until you were right on top of it. If Simralin hadn't known it was there, they would never have found it. The shelter contained pallets rolled up and stored on shelves and some small supplies. The visitors used the pallets to sleep on, but left the supplies alone. Food and drink were hard to come by, and they carried sufficient of their own not to have to impose.

Sunrise broke gray and misty, a change from the previous day and a type of weather that came all too infrequently. Looking out at the roiling clouds, it seemed to Kirisin that it might even rain. They ate their breakfast, and then Simralin had them stash most of their gear in a wooden bin. They would need warm clothing to protect them at the higher altitudes and food and water for three days. The climb up would take them one, the climb down another. That left the third to find and retrieve the Loden.

"Time enough," Simralin declared.

"If that's where it is," Kirisin interjected quickly.

His sister shrugged. "Why don't we find out? Use the Elfstones. We're close enough now that we won't give anything away by doing so."

They walked outside, passed back through the woods, and stepped out into the meadow that carpeted the land upward to where the bare rock began and the last of the scattered trees ended. The air was thinner here, and Kirisin was already noticing that it was harder to breathe. But it also tasted fresh and clean and smelled of the conifers and the cold, so he didn't mind. The air in the Cintra was good, too, but not as vibrant and alive as it was up here.

When they were far enough out in the open that he could see the peak clearly—a visual aid he didn't necessarily need but would use since it was there—Kirisin brought out the pouch with the Elfstones, dumped the contents into his hand, and began the process of bringing the magic to life. He had a better feel for what was needed this time, having found what worked when he used them back in the Cintra. He held the Stones in a loose and easy grip, his arm stretched out toward Syrring Rise, and took his thoughts away from everything but an attempt to visualize the ice caves the magic had shown him previously. Standing in the shadow of the mountain and beneath the sweep of the skies above it, he let himself sink into the quiet and the solitude.

Closing his eyes and disappearing inside himself.

Picturing the caves in his mind.

Feeling their cold hard surfaces and smelling the metal veins that laced their rock.

Seeing the rainbow shimmer of the sunlight that seeped through cracks and crevices, refracted and diffused, laced with bright splashes of color that seemed of another world.

Hearing their whisper, calling to him.

This last almost took him out of himself, very nearly disrupting his efforts to use the Elfstones. There was something eerie about that whisper, a feeling that the voice calling was real, not imagined—that someone or something was actually summoning him.

Then the Elfstones began to brighten, their blue light flaring to life within his closed hand, slender rays breaking free through the cracks in his fingers, the warmth of the magic spreading into his body and infusing him with a sudden rush of adrenaline. He kept himself as steady as he could, his thoughts focused, not letting the sudden exhilaration he felt overwhelm him. But it was hard. He wanted to cry out with excitement, to give voice to what he was feeling. The magic was intoxicating; he wanted it to go on forever.

A second later, the gathering light lanced outward from his fist, hurtling toward the summit of Syrring Rise, traversing the meadow and the wildflowers, the bare rock beyond, the stunted conifers that Simralin had told him were thousands of years old, reaching for the higher elevations. At a point beyond the snow line, but only just above the edge of the glacier and its ice fields, it burrowed into the white landscape, encapsulating in a flood of azure light the caves they were seeking. He saw them again, more clearly defined this time, walls sculpted by time and the elements, ceiling vast and shadowed beyond the reach of the light, snowmelt churning in a river cored through the center, waterfalls frozen in place where they had tumbled from the higher elevations.

There was something else, too—something he couldn't quite make out. It hunkered down in the very rear of the largest chamber, a thing crouched and waiting, all iced over and brilliant with silvery light. It was massive, and it was terrible; he could sense it more than feel it. It did not move, but only waited. Yet he had a feeling it was alive.

"What was that?" Angel asked softly when the light from the Elfstones died away, and they were standing in the gray haze of dawn once more.

Kirisin shook his head. "I'm not sure. It looked like some sort of statue. A statue carved of ice." He looked at Simralin. "Have you ever seen it before?"

She shook her head. "I haven't been in those caves. Didn't even know they were there."

They looked at one another a moment longer, then Sim said, "The explanation's not here. Let's get going."

THEY BEGAN THE TREK shortly after, taking time out first to eat and then to wait for Simralin to gather together climbing gear that was stowed in one of the line shack's wooden bins. She brought out everything she thought they would need, laid it all out on the ground, and explained the reasons for her choices.

"The ropes are in case climbing proves necessary. The ice screws and clamps are to secure the ropes. The ice ax allows digging and hammering on the ice. The wicked-looking metal objects with the teeth are crampons. You attach them to your boots to gain traction on ice and frozen snow. The fastenings are spring-locked; the releases are down here by the heels." She pointed to the last item. "Be careful of these. These are needle gloves. Something new. See the palms." She pointed again. "Their surfaces are like the back of a hedgehog. Rub it the wrong way, downward like this," she made a downward-rubbing motion with her hand, "and dozens of tiny needles embed themselves in whatever surface they've rubbed up against. Their grip will keep you from slipping or falling. Very strong. They only release if you rub upward again. The gloves tighten with straps at the wrists so that they won't come off by accident."

"Where did you get all this?" Angel asked.

"Borrowed it from here and there." Simralin grinned. "I told you we knew when to take advantage of something good, no matter who invented it." She pointed to a bundle of smooth sticks. "Flares. Break them in the middle, you have light for an hour." She pointed to three lamps. "Solar torches, good for at least twenty-four hours of continual use. Also, the boots and gloves have reflectors that glow in the dark, just in case."

She pointed to their packs. "Food and water for three days—maybe a little more, if it comes to it. Blow-up mattresses and blankets, all made of Elyon, an Elven fabric, extremely light and warm. That's our sleeping gear. Ice visors to cut the glare. All-weather cloaks. Weapons. Knives for all of us. My bow and arrows, short sword, and adzl." For the last, she indicated the peculiar javelin with barbs at both ends and a cord-wound grip at the center. "Angel's staff. And, of course, if all else fails, Kirisin's quick wit."

She grinned at him. "Knife-edge-sharp, I'm told."

Kirisin nodded. "Very funny. You think that the Elfstones could be used as a weapon?"

They pondered it a moment. "Hard to say," Simralin answered finally.

"Be good if we didn't need any weapons," Angel said. "But Kirisin isn't the one who should be doing the fighting in any case."

Simralin nodded in agreement. "You stay out of any fighting if it comes to that, Little K."

They took a moment to study everything one final time, a few additional questions were asked and answered, and they were ready. They repacked their gear, shouldered their loads, and set out.

They climbed through the morning hours, traversing the meadows and passing through the forests until they reached the upper edge of the tree line shortly after midday. They stopped then to eat, winded and hungry. Kirisin was sore all through his thigh and back muscles. He guessed from the look on Angel's face that she was suffering, too. Only Simralin seemed completely at home, smiling as if this climb were nothing more than a morning stroll. She talked and laughed as they ate, describing adventures and experiences from other times and places involving the mountains and Syrring Rise, in particular.

Once, she told them, she had come on a small expedition that included Tragen. The big Elf, still learning about mountains, climbed the paths to the glacier too fast, overexerted himself, lost body heat, dehydrated, and passed out. She said the other Trackers had never let him forget about it; every time a climb was involved, they suggested maybe he might want to give it a pass.

She grinned, tossing back her blond hair. "Tragen doesn't think it so funny, but he lacks a good sense of humor. If he didn't make up for it in other ways, I expect I would have to rethink our relationship."

Kirisin gave his sister a pointed look. "Tragen's all right," he said, repeating her words back to her. "For now."

They resumed their climb shortly after, leaving behind the last of the trees and proceeding onto bare rock and gravel. The trail disappeared altogether, and the slope steepened. Kirisin was finding it increasingly hard to breathe, but he knew the air was thin and that after a time his lungs would get used to it. At least, that was what Sim had told him. In any case, he soldiered on, working his way behind her as they wound through the mountain's rocky debris, advancing toward the snowpack.

When they reached the edge, Simralin walked them forward farther still until they were atop the glacier, high on the mountain now, the wind blowing harder, dry and biting cold. Amid a shelter of massive boulders, she had them lock on the crampons, pull on the gloves, slip the visors over their eyes, and unsling the ice axes. Moving more slowly now, but still climbing, they passed out of the boulders and onto the ice. All around them, the glacier glimmered dully in the pale sunlight. The gray of earlier had dissipated at these heights, the clouds below them now, a roiling dark mass encircling the rock. But the day was passing, the light failing as the sun gave way to an advancing darkness. The western horizon, refracting the change in the light's intensity, was already starting to color.

"Not much farther!" Simralin called by way of encouragement. She had stopped a dozen yards ahead and was looking back at them.

Kirisin slowed, Angel coming up beside him. He hoped she was right. He was getting cold, even through his all-weather gear, and a tiredness he could barely fight off was settling in. He shifted his pack to a new position and began moving ahead again, then realized that Angel wasn't following. He glanced around. The Knight of the Word was standing where he had left her, staring back down the mountain.

He stopped again. "Angel?"

She looked at him, her gaze vague and distant, focused on something beyond what he was seeing. It was almost as if she were in another place entirely. "Go on ahead, Kirisin," she said. "I'll be along in a moment. I want to check on something. Don't worry. I can find my way."

"I'll wait with you," he offered quickly. "We both will."

She held up her hand at once as he started toward her. "No, Kirisin. I have to do this alone. Do as I say. You and your sister go on without me. Do what you came to do."

He started to object, but saw something in her eyes that stopped him. There was a hard determination reflected that told him she was decided on this. Whatever she intended, she didn't want anyone to interfere. He hesitated, still uncertain, his fears deepening. "Don't be too long. It's starting to get dark."

She nodded and turned back down the mountainside toward the clump of boulders they had left earlier. "*Adios, mi amigo*," she called to him. "*Lo siento.*"

He had no idea what she was saying. By the way she said it—almost to herself, rather than to him—he wasn't even sure she was aware of what language she was using. It was as if by speaking the words, she had dismissed him from her mind. He watched her walk away and won-

dered if he ought to go after her. He didn't like the idea of them split-
ting up like this, not staying together when they were so close to finding what they had come all this way to discover.

But mostly he didn't like what he had heard in her voice.

It sounded as if she was leaving.

It felt as if she was saying good-bye.

THIRTY

ANGEL PEREZ WAS AT PEACE. A deep, pervasive calm had settled inside, an infusion of a sort that she hadn't experienced in years. She couldn't explain it. Nothing justified it. If anything, she should have been riddled with fear, terrified of what waited in the rocks below. Her nerves should have been all sharp-edged and raw.

After all, she was probably going to die.

She walked toward the cluster of huge boulders, the mass of dark stone like the jaws of the earth amid the whiteness of the snow, waiting to devour her. The runes carved in the gleaming surface of her black staff glowed brightly. She knew what was hiding in the rocks. The demons. The spiky-haired female that had transformed into a four-legged horror and tracked her north from her home, and the companion it had found in the Cintra. Somehow the pair had discovered their destination and caught up to them. It shouldn't have come as a surprise, and in truth it didn't. She had suspected all along that the demons were one step ahead of them, ever since Ailie and Erisha had been killed in Ashenell. She had known it for sure when they had reached the hiding place for the hot-air balloons and found one of them missing. She had known right away who had taken it. There was no way of determining the truth of it, yet she had known.

She had been waiting ever since for them to surface, knowing that they would in the same way she had known that the struggle between them would end here. Standing on the hillside as Simralin assured them they were almost to their goal, she had felt the demon presence and known it was time. She had been anticipating it ever since she had escaped the last attack, deep in the ruined forests of California, where only Ailie's warning had saved her. She had said nothing to her companions, but she had been waiting for it. Now it was here. The confrontation she had always believed to be inevitable had arrived.

Still, she was at peace.

She did not want Kirisin or Simralin to know what was happening. If they found out, they would want to stand with her. They could not help. She would worry for them, seek to protect them, and thereby lessen her own chances of surviving. Those chances were small enough as it was. If she faced only one of the two, she might be able to kill or disable it. If both were waiting for her, the best she could hope for was a quick death. She had no illusions. In all likelihood, she was not coming out of this.

She thought it very odd that she wasn't frightened. She had been terrified after her last encounter with the female demon, so afraid that she could barely think clearly when she and Ailie fled its attack on the Mercury 5 for the Oregon border. She had known then—*had known*—that the next time she was forced into a confrontation with this particular demon, she was going to die. Twice she had escaped it, but only barely. The third time would be the end of her. She was tough and skilled, but this creature was more than she could handle. She had been extremely lucky before. She could not expect to be so lucky again.

It almost made her smile. Perhaps the inevitability of what waited had leached all the fear out of her. Perhaps by knowing that she must stand and fight, she had become resigned to what that meant. She was not afraid of dying or even of what dying meant. She was not afraid to face this monster, even though she might suffer in ways she had never imagined possible. If this was the death that had stalked her since birth—as some form of death stalked everyone—if this was where it was meant to end for her, she could accept it. She could not explain this willingness to embrace her fate, but she found comfort in it. She had found grace.

She reached the cluster of rocks and stopped. At least one of them waited within, just out of sight. The wolfish one, the one that served the old man. It had made no effort to disguise its coming. It had revealed itself openly, knowing she would respond as she had. Or perhaps it had hoped she would try to flee so that it could give pursuit and take her down from behind, a rabbit caught by a predator. Whatever the case, it wanted her to know before she died that it had found her and she could not escape. It took pleasure in forcing her to anticipate her own death, to know there was no escape.

She wished suddenly that Johnny were there to stand beside her. It would make this so much easier, knowing he was there. But then, she thought, perhaps he was, in spirit if not in flesh. Perhaps he was there still, her guardian angel.

She remembered a time not long after he had first found her—she might have been nine or ten—when he had told her he was going out for longer than usual and that she must wait alone until his return. She was instantly terrified, certain that he would not be coming back, that he was leaving her. She threw herself against him, sobbing wildly, begging him not to go, not to abandon her. Carefully, gently he soothed her, stroking her long black hair, telling her it was all right, that he would be back, that no matter what happened he would never leave her.

When she had quieted enough that she was coherent again, he had said, "*Yo no abandono a mi niña.* I would never leave my girl, little one. Wherever you are, I will always be close by. You might not see me, but I will be there. You will feel me in your heart."

She supposed that it was true: that he had never really left her and had always been there in her heart. She could feel his presence when she was lonely or frightened if she searched hard enough. She could reassure herself by remembering that his word had always been good. Even when he was gone from her life and from the world of the living, some essential part of him was still there.

It would be so this time, too. He would be there for her.

She walked to the edge of the boulders and stopped, searching the air for the demon's smell. She found it almost immediately, rank and poisonous, the stench of something that had cast aside any semblance of humanity. The air was thick with it, the sweet clean scent of the mountainside smothered under its heavy layers. It crouched within the rocks, still hidden, waiting on her. She could feel its rage and hatred and its need to sate both with her blood.

How should she handle this?

She stared into the black shadows of the boulders, searching the twisting passages that wound between. She did not believe it would be smart to go in there. Better to wait out here, to make it come to her.

Then she saw the first of the feeders as they slid like oil from out of the rocks, their shadows splotches of liquid darkness. They seemed in no hurry, their appearance almost casual. But where only a handful surfaced at the outset, there were soon a dozen and then a dozen more.

She glanced back up the mountainside to where she had left Kirisin and his sister. They were no longer in view. With luck, they were no longer in hearing, either.

It was time to get this over with.

"Demon!" she shouted into the rocks.

Then she waited.

*   *   *

KIRISIN CAUGHT UP to his sister, who glanced around as he reached her and said, "Where's Angel?"

He shook his head. "She said she had something she needed to do."

"Did she tell you what it was?"

"She just said we should go on without her. I told her we could wait until she was done with whatever she had to do. But she wouldn't allow it. She was pretty insistent." He shook his head. "I don't know, Sim. It doesn't feel right."

"No, it doesn't." His sister looked back down the mountain slope to where they could just make out the Knight of the Word as she stood before the cluster of massive boulders they had come past earlier.

"What do you think she is doing?" he asked her.

She hesitated a moment, and then said, "I think she's protecting us. I think that's the way she wants it. We'd better do what she says. Come on. The caves are just ahead."

They climbed the gradually steepening slope, relying on the crampons and ice axes for purchase. It was a slow and arduous trek, but they pushed ahead steadily, working their way across the ice field. Kirisin watched how his sister used the ax, driving it into the ice and then pulling herself forward, and he did the same. Once or twice, he glanced back to look for Angel, and each time he found her right where he had seen her last, poised and waiting at the edge of the boulders. Once, he thought he heard her shout something, but the wind blowing down from the higher elevations masked her words.

Again, he almost turned back, the need to do so suddenly compelling. But he kept moving anyway, putting one foot in front of the other, hammering his ax into the ice and pulling himself ahead.

Then he topped a rise that led onto a rocky flat, and he couldn't see her anymore.

"Kirisin!" his sister called back to him, shouting to be heard above the wind. She pointed ahead.

The entrance to the caves was a black hole almost buried within a cluster of snow-shrouded boulders, shards of ice hanging off the opening like a frozen curtain. From where they stood, it looked small and almost insignificant against the broad sweep of the mountain, as if it might be no more than the burrow of some animal. As they drew closer, it became steadily larger, taking on more definition. When they reached it, they stopped for a more careful look. It was hard to determine much from the outside. The entrance sloped downward into the mountain, narrow and low enough that they could tell they would have to stoop to get through. Farther back, it seemed to widen, but the shadows made it hard to be sure. Beyond that, it was too dark to see anything.

Simralin looked at him. "Ready, Little K?"

He nodded, not at all sure that he was, but determined to finish this no matter what.

His sister took out her solar torch from her pack and switched it on.

With a final glance at Kirisin, she started ahead, stooping to clear the entrance, shining the broad beam of the torch into the blackness ahead. Kirisin followed wordlessly, his own torch in hand. In moments they were inside, swallowed by the shadows and the rock, the snowy slopes of the mountainside left behind.

To Kirisin's surprise, the way forward was bright enough that their torches were unnecessary. Light seeped through cracks in the tunnel rock, diffused by ice windows that had frozen permanently beneath the outer layers of snow. Ice coated the walls and ceiling of the cave, sculpted as in the visions shown him twice now by the Elfstones, symmetrically formed scallops running back along the walls and ceiling for as far as the eye could see. The light reflected off the scallops in strange patterns that lay all across the surface of the cave. Here and there, rainbow colors flashed, formed of unexpected and random refractions, small wonders amid the gloom.

Fifty yards back, a frozen pillar of ridged ice rose from the cavern floor to a gap in the ceiling. A waterfall had tumbled through a hole in the cavern ceiling in another, warmer time, freezing in place as the cold set in, creating this strange column. Sunlight channeled downward by the ice created the impression that the column was lit from within. Kirisin stepped close and peered into the ice. Within its cloudy depths, tiny creatures hung suspended in time.

The caves grew darker after that, the sources of light fading one by one, the gloom enveloping everything. The solar torches became necessary, and the way forward could only be glimpsed in patches as the beams crossed from one place to another. The cold grew deeper and more pervasive, matched by an intense silence. If not for the crunch of their crampons digging into the ice-coated cave floor and the huff of their rough breathing, there would have been no sound at all.

Ahead, the walls of the cavern began to broaden and the ceiling to lift. Stalactites dripped and became ice-coated spears, some as thick as a man's leg, some longer than Simralin was tall. The shadows rippled in the glow of the solar torches, and the sheen of ice that coated everything glimmered with colors that danced like flames. From deeper in, still beyond the reach of the torchlight, water rushed and cascaded over rocks.

Simralin stopped. "I think you should use the Stones, Little K." She flashed the beam of her torch right and left. "Do you see? Tunnels branch off in several directions from here. We need to know which way to go."

Kirisin nodded, but looked around doubtfully. He didn't care much for the idea of trying to summon the magic of the Elfstones in this confined space. Who knew what it might do underground? But he dutifully fished out the Stones, dumped them into his palm, held out his fist, closed his eyes, and formed a mental picture of the Loden. The response was so instantaneous that it made him jump in surprise. The Elfstones flared sharply, and the blue light shot from his hand and down the corridor directly ahead to illuminate something crouched in the middle of a massive cavern chamber, something that was more nightmare than vision.

The light from the Elfstones dimmed and vanished. Kirisin stood in shocked silence with his sister, staring down the black hole of the cave tunnel.

"Did you see?" he whispered, shaken.

"I saw something," she replied. "But I don't think it was real."

"It looked real to me."

"No, it was just a carving. Out of ice and rock."

"It was a dragon, Sim."

She shook her head. "There aren't any dragons. You know that."

Well, he did, but that didn't make him feel any better about what he had seen. He tucked the Elfstones back in his pocket beneath his all-weather cloak, suddenly wishing he were wearing something more protective.

"Let's go have a look," she said, and started ahead once more.

They passed down the corridor, moving from one chamber to another, winding their way deeper and deeper into the mountain. The beams of their torches cut through the darkness, giving them some reassurance that they were not about to be set upon. Time slipped away, and still the tunnels and caves continued and there was no sign of the chamber and its dragon. Kirisin began to wonder if he really had seen a dragon. He began to wonder if the altitude had affected him and he was starting to see things that weren't there.

And then suddenly they passed out of a broad tunnel into a huge cavern, and there it was.

They stopped the moment they saw it, tiny figures in its presence. The dragon was huge, fully thirty feet tall if it was an inch, crouched down on four legs at the chamber's very center, its body covered with scales and horns, leathery wings folded back against its body, claws extended at the ends of its crooked toes, spiked tail curled back around its hindquarters like a giant whip.

But it was its mouth—or more accurately, its jaws—that drew their immediate attention. The great head was lowered so that the lower jaw and long, forked tongue rested on the cavern floor. The upper jaw was stretched open to the breaking point, so wide that a man eight feet tall could have walked upright to the back of its throat. Teeth ridged the jaws in double rows, top and bottom, front to back, like bars across a gate leading into a dark fortress.

Kirisin stared at the monster, transfixed. Simralin had been right: a layer of ice covered over what appeared to be chiseled stone, everything frozen in place. It was not alive; it was only a sculpture.

But what was it doing here?

He looked suddenly at its eyes, cloudy orbs within its fierce face. A shiver ran down the back of his neck, and he took an involuntary step back.

–Kirisin Belloruus–

The voice whispered to him, hushed and disembodied, the voice he had heard earlier that same morning when he had used the Elfstones to find the cave entrance. Calling to him. Summoning him.

He took a quick breath. "Sim," he whispered. "Did you hear . . . ?"

"Use the Elfstones," she interrupted, not listening to him. "This has to be where it is."

Kirisin already knew that. He already knew a whole lot more than he wanted to. He couldn't have explained it, not in a rational way. He just knew in the way you sometimes knew things. By how being close to them made you feel. By how logic took a backseat to instinct. He wished it weren't so, but there it was. He just *knew*.

He didn't have to use the Elfstones to find out where the Loden was. It was inside the dragon.

This was more of Pancea Rolt Gotrin's work. Magic of a kind that no longer existed had been used to create this dragon and to place the Loden within. The dragon was the Elfstone's protector. It was its keeper and its warden. If you wanted to take possession of the Loden, you had to brave the dragon's maw. You had to accept on faith or whatever reasonable argument you could make to yourself that it would let you pass.

But how would it know who to admit? There had to be a way, a trigger for determining whom it should be.

"The Loden is inside the dragon," he said to his sister. "I have to go in after it."

She shook her head at once. "Oh, no. That's entirely too dangerous. We have to be certain about this first."

She walked forward to stand right in front of the dragon's mouth, shining the beam of her solar torch through the rows of teeth and into the throat. The beam shone to the front of the throat and stopped as if it had encountered a wall.

"There's nothing back there," she announced, leaning forward to peer inside.

Kirisin knew that this wasn't so. But Sim would have to be convinced. He reached into his pocket and took out the Elfstones. Then he walked forward to stand next to her. He let her see what he was holding, then closed his hand about the Stones, squeezed his eyes shut, and went inside himself once more, searching for an image of the Loden. He had his vision in place quickly, and his response from the Elfstones more quickly still. The magic flared within his fist, and its blue light exploded down the dragon's throat, past where Simralin's torchlight had stopped and then down farther still, traveling a distance too far to determine, coming to rest finally on a pedestal that cradled a white gemstone blazing as brightly as a small sun.

The light from Kirisin's Elfstones died away, and he looked over at his sister questioningly.

"Okay," she said. "But I'm going with you."

He shook his head. "I don't think you can. I don't think it's allowed. This dragon is some kind of watchdog. Pancea Rolt Gotrin and her family probably constructed it with magic. They put the Loden Elfstone inside to protect it. It keeps out everyone who isn't permitted to enter. A moment ago, I was wondering how the dragon would know who to let in. I think the blue Elfstones are the key. I think that's one reason Pancea's shade gave them to me. Whoever holds the Stones is allowed inside. Everyone else gets . . ."

He trailed off, shrugging. "Eaten or something."

"You think this, but you don't know it," she pointed out.

He shook his head. "I think it, but I also feel it." He tapped his chest. "In here."

His sister gave him a long, hard look. "I don't like it. What if you're wrong?"

"Then you can come get me out. That's what big sisters are for. Meanwhile, you can wait here for Angel. She should be along any moment now. She needs to know what we're doing."

He could see Simralin struggling to find something more to say, still unhappy with what he was proposing. But they both knew there wasn't any other choice if they were to have a chance of gaining possession of the Loden. And after all, that was what they had come this far to do. In the final analysis, that was what they must do.

She gave a deep sigh and nodded. "Be careful. If there's magic at work, you won't have much protection."

"About as much as I had in the tombs of Ashenell," he replied, smiling. "Keep the faith, Sim."

She smiled back. "You keep it for me, Little K."

He turned back to the dragon. Its jaws yawned before him, an invitation to enter the blackest of maws. He gave a quick glance at its rows of teeth and then at the strange glassy eyes, wondering again if he had seen them move.

Then he started forward, the blue Elfstones held out before him like a talisman.

THIRTY-ONE

WHAT HAPPENED NEXT caught Kirisin Belloruus completely by surprise. As he stepped onto the dragon's tongue, across the front row of teeth and into the mouth itself, everything behind him disappeared. Simralin, the cavern chamber with its stalactites and layers of ice, and even the smallest hint of light vanished as if they had never been.

The boy stopped where he was, barely across the threshold of the great mouth, and looked back in disbelief. He swung his solar torch in a wide arc, seeking to penetrate the darkness, but he might as well have been pointing it at a blank wall. The powerful beam failed to reveal anything beyond the inside of the mouth. He shone it ahead, into the dragon's throat, and was surprised all over again. Unlike before, when Simralin had tried unsuccessfully with hers, his solar torch shone down a darkened corridor, deep into the interior of the dragon. The corridor was ridged and cored out like an animal's throat, but he could not determine where it led.

Presumably, into the beast's stomach, he thought. Where he might end up as dinner.

But he preferred to think that this was where he would find the Loden. He considered briefly stepping back across the dragon's teeth, but the idea of going back at this point seemed wrong. What if he couldn't get back inside again? Now that he was here, he should continue on and see what would happen.

He started ahead, walking carefully, making sure he was on solid footing. He need not have worried. The tunnel or throat was as solid as the rock of the caves outside. But he noticed that it wasn't as cold in here, as if the dragon was alive and kept warm by its body heat. That prospect was too troublesome for him to consider for long, and so he pushed ahead into the blackness.

He walked for a long time—much longer than should have been possible. The corridor twisted and turned, and that didn't seem possible, either. Now and again he could hear a rumbling sound, the sort that a big animal makes. He tried not to think about it. He tried not to think about anything but what he was trying to do, putting one foot in front of the other, keeping an eye out for what might be waiting ahead.

He also tried not to think about the fact that he didn't seem to be getting anywhere. Despite all his walking, everything around him looked exactly the same.

Then abruptly, his torch went out, and he was left standing in complete blackness.

For a moment, he just stood there, not quite believing what had happened. He worked the power switch back and forth a few times and slapped the light's casing with the palm of his hand. Nothing. He experienced a moment of sheer panic, but quickly fought it down. He hung the solar torch back on his belt and was starting to reach for one of his flares when he suddenly had an idea. Impulsively, he held out the blue Elfstones; using what he had learned from the other times he had done so, he called up their magic.

Blue light flared in his fist and filled the corridor ahead. To his surprise, it didn't seek out the Loden as he had thought it would. Instead, it simply brightened the corridor enough for him to continue on. He did so, following its steadily advancing wash into the ice dragon's throat.

The minutes clicked by, too many to count, time an intangible he could not measure.

Then without warning the tunnel ended and he was standing in a chamber that might have been a cave or the dragon's stomach or another world entirely. It didn't look quite like anything he had ever seen or even imagined. The moment he stepped into it, light exploded all around him, coming from the floor, the ceiling, and the walls, enveloping everything in its white luminescence. It felt as if he were standing at the very center of the light; he could see nothing of anything else.

Except for the stone pedestal that appeared suddenly right in front of him and the Loden Elfstone resting upon it.

It wasn't difficult to know what he was looking at. He had already seen it in the visions shown him by the blue Elfstones. But even beyond that, he would have known. It was so distinctive that it couldn't have been anything else. It rested in the cradle of a tripod formed entirely of white fire, its facets gleaming. The fire snaked about the Stone in rippling bands, licking at it with flames that shone as bright as bursts of sunlight, their look smooth and unblemished, clear evidence of the magic that generated them.

Kirisin walked forward tentatively, got to within a few feet of the pedestal, and stopped. He had come to take the Loden back with him. But what would happen when he tried to do that? The Gotrin witches had placed the Stone within the dragon to keep it safe. Would the magic that they had created to ward it permit him to interfere? The blue Elfstones had allowed him to find the Loden, but he could not be certain they were meant to give him possession, as well. It might be that something more was required, some other demonstration of his right to claim it.

He had no idea what that something might be.

He stood there for a long time, trying to decide what to do, aware of time slipping away. He watched the white fire twist about the Stone protectively, and he didn't think it would be a good idea to put his hand in that fire. He didn't think anyone was meant to do that. He needed to find a way to block the fire, to make it go away long enough for him to snatch up the Stone. He wondered suddenly if the blue Elfstones were the key to this as they had been the key to finding his way here. He took a steadying breath, held the Elfstones out in front of him, toward the pedestal, and envisioned the flames guarding the Loden fading away.

Nothing happened. Not only did the flames not disappear, but the magic of the Elfstones failed to respond to his summons.

Disappointed, he lowered his arm again, thinking it over. Maybe he was approaching this in the wrong way. The blue Stones were seeking-Stones. They were meant to find what was hidden. What if he used them to seek out a way to make the flames disappear? Would the magic respond to him then?

It was worth a try. He stepped back, clearing some space between himself and the pedestal. The light from the chamber surfaces glimmered brightly all around him, a shimmering cushion. He tried to ignore the feeling of displacement it created, the sense that he was disconnected. Instead he fixed his gaze on the flames surrounding the Loden and imagined them vanishing, snuffed out completely so that the Elfstone sat atop the pedestal unprotected.

This time the magic flared to life, a bright blue ball of light about his fist, chasing back the glow of the room. The light brightened, steadied, and then shot forward to a place midway down the pedestal on the side he was facing. In the raw glare of the magic's light, he caught a glimpse of markings that were little more than faint smudges. As the light faded, he rushed forward, not wanting to chance losing sight of what he had been shown. Shoving the Elfstones into his pocket, he knelt down, his fingers searching the stone surface of the pedestal, trying to ignore the nagging feeling that at any moment he might sink through the room's strange glow to whatever lay beneath.

He found what he was looking for right away. A small indentation, not large enough for more than the tip of a single finger. Then he found another, and another, until he had located a place for all five fingertips of one hand. Carefully, he filled all the indentations and pressed.

Instantly the bands of fire atop the pedestal disappeared. When he climbed to his feet, the Loden lay on its side, unprotected. Cautiously, he reached out, hesitated, and then scooped up the Elfstone and lifted it clear. No fire appeared to stop him; no magic surfaced to punish his intrusion.

His grin was bright and fierce as he tightened his fingers about the Stone. He couldn't know for sure, but he reasoned that somehow the magic had identified him through the touch of his fingertips, either as a bearer of the blue Elfstones or as a bearer of the blessing of the shade of Pancea Rolt Gotrin. Either way, he had been recognized and accepted, and the Loden Elfstone was his.

He took a moment to loosen his grip enough that he could study the Stone more closely. It was a perfectly clear gemstone, smooth and exquisitely faceted, all bright mirrors that both reflected and refracted the chamber light. Within its depths, small traces of color swirled and vanished like tiny fish in deep water.

"What is it you can do?" he whispered to the Stone.

Then, tightening his grip anew, he turned back the way he had come, retracing his steps toward the wall of light. He wasn't sure what would happen if he attempted to walk into it, but he knew his only choice was to try leaving and see what happened.

At least the worst of it was over, he thought.

When he reached the light, he hesitated once more, and then, having no other sensible recourse, reached out and touched it.

Instantly, the light disappeared along with the chamber, the pedestal, and everything else he had seen since leaving the dragon's maw and descending into its throat. He blinked against the sudden blackness, waiting for his eyes to adjust. When they did, he found himself standing once more within the dragon's open jaws, peering out through the double rows of its serrated teeth toward the glow of Simralin's torch.

In the shadows beyond the maw of the dragon, he saw her move toward him in the gloom.

"There you are!" a familiar voice that clearly wasn't hers declared. "Come here, boy. Don't just stand there gaping."

Kirisin's mouth was indeed hanging open in disbelief.

* * *

"DEMON!" Angel Perez called out a second time when there was no response to the first. "Are you afraid of me?"

Still nothing. She waited some more. It didn't matter how long this took. The longer the better, in fact. She was buying time for the Elves, and the more she could give them, the better their chances of gaining possession of what they had come to find.

She was suddenly uneasy, standing out in the open like this, exposed to everything, and she began moving to her left, changing not only her position but also her view of the rocks. The feeders, which now numbered more than a hundred, moved with her. Already she had summoned the magic to her staff, filling it with white fire, the runes glowing like embers in a working forge. She felt its warmth flood through her, circulating like her blood, the measure of her life. She would not give up that life easily, she told herself. She would not help the ones who had come to kill her by panicking or trying to flee or acting in haste or desperation. She would show them what real strength meant.

The hissing sound came a moment later, slow and taunting, a wicked whisper from within the rocks.

She held her breath, waiting.

Then the wolf thing appeared, a shadow sliding out of other shadows, long and lean and hungry. Its tongue lolled and its teeth gleamed. It was fully ten feet in length, and its sleek body rippled with muscle. Only now it looked less like a wolf and more like a giant cat, its features become decidedly feline, the scaly body having undergone yet another metamorphosis. The change caught her by surprise. But a demon was still a demon, she told herself, whatever shape it took.

She glanced past it into the cluster of boulders. There was no sign of its companion. Was it hiding back there, waiting for its chance to catch her off guard while she was preoccupied with this one? What had become of it?

But almost before her questions were asked she knew the answers. The second demon was farther up the mountain, tracking Kirisin and his sister. It had gotten around behind her, and while this one distracted her it would take care of her unprotected charges.

She felt her heart sink with the realization. Simralin was tough and Kirisin brave, but they were no match for a demon. A rush of urgency flooded through her. She had to end things here quickly if she was to be of any help to her friends.

"*Acude a mi, demonio,*" she taunted the demon, and then hissed at it cat-like. "Here kitty, kitty. Come play with me."

The demon spit as if scalded, hunching its shoulders. Slowly, deliberately, it slouched toward her. The feeders were leaping all about them, anxious and hungry, anticipating their battle. Angel braced herself in the snow and ice, aware suddenly that she had failed to remove her crampons. The iron teeth were sunk into the snow, pinning her in place. She would not be able to move quickly.

But there was no time to change things now. She would have to do the best she could.

She took a defensive stance as the cat demon stalked her, remembering anew how close it had come to killing her at both of their previous meetings. She had fought it with every ounce of strength and every shred of skill she could muster, and still she would have died both times if not for an intervening fate. She could not count on that here. She did not think she could defeat this creature, did not think she could kill it and not be killed herself. Yet that was what she must find a way to do. She must forget the odds, ignore the past, and change the outcome she was certain awaited her.

Suddenly she noticed something she had both missed and forgotten. The demon had only one eye. Simralin had put out the other with one of her knives when it had attacked them in Ashenell days earlier. A black hole was all that remained. She felt a sudden surge of hope. If it could only see from one side, perhaps she had a better chance than she believed.

And if she could manage to put out the other eye . . .

"*Madre de Dios*," she whispered.

The demon came at her in a sudden rush, hurtling across the short distance that separated them, claws digging into the ice, tearing up white tufts that sprayed the hazy air. Angel swung the tip of her black staff into position and sent the Word's magic hammering into her attacker. The demon was knocked sideways, sprawling across the snow, spinning to a stop.

Without any sign that it was damaged in the least by what she had done to it, the demon came back to its feet and began advancing anew.

Three times it charged Angel, and three times it was sent flying backward. It hadn't gotten within six feet of her when it rose to come at her a fourth time, but she could see now what was happening. The demon was forcing her to use up her strength on attacks that were meaningless. It was breaking her down a little at a time, draining her so that eventually she would not be able to defend herself. Angel could tell that the strategy was working. The demon was much stronger than she was and could absorb more punishment. Nothing she was doing was having the remotest effect on it; she, on the other hand, was already tiring.

The feeders could sense her weakness and were slowly tightening the circle about her.

She had to do something to turn things around. She thought of Johnny. What would he tell her to do?

Use the tools you have at hand.

The demon came at her again. She reacted, but not quickly enough. The demon was on top of her before she could bring the magic to bear. She caught it on the broad length of her staff as it leapt for her, falling backward as she did so, letting the demon's weight carry it right over her. The maneuver worked. The demon tumbled away into the snow, legs thrashing. But searing pain lanced down her right side as claws tore through her clothing and into her flesh.

She ignored the pain, coming back to her feet swiftly, turning to face it anew. Feeders were clinging to her, trying to devour her, but she flung them away.

Use the tools you have at hand.

It rushed her again almost instantly, attacking in the same fashion. But this time she was ready for it. Johnny's words had triggered an idea, and she knew all at once what she must do. She did not try to slow it with her magic; she let it come. Again it hurtled into her, bearing her to the ground, trying to pin her in place so that it could tear her apart. Again she caught it on her staff. But this time she tucked her legs against her body as it knocked her backward, boots pulling free of the ice, the wicked metal teeth of her crampons levering toward the demon's belly. As it landed on top of her she kicked out, jamming the crampons against the beast's exposed underside and ripping downward with all the strength she possessed.

The demon screamed. She had never heard a scream like this, a terrible wrenching cry that echoed all across the mountain slopes and the valleys beyond. She felt flesh and muscle give way beneath her boots, saw blood spurt everywhere. The beast clamped its jaws on one arm and her staff as well, but she used the magic to keep those jaws from closing all the way and the teeth from tearing off her arm.

An instant later it broke away, rolling across the snow in a tangle of blood and scales and ragged flesh, feeders clinging to it in black patches.

It should have been either dead or wounded badly enough that it could not continue the fight. Any other creature would have been finished. But not this one. It was already back on its feet and stalking toward her, ignoring the feeders, its underside a mass of blood and torn flesh it barely seemed to notice. Angel felt her courage fail. She braced herself for the rush she knew was coming, summoning what magic she had left to wield.

It wasn't enough. The demon came at her so quickly that she barely had time to react. Fire lanced from her staff, burning into the creature, breaking through skin and scales and flesh and perhaps even bone. But it didn't stop it. Ignoring her efforts to keep it at bay, it slammed into Angel, knocking her backward across the ice, knocking the wind from her lungs. Claws ripped and tore. Heavy limbs pounded. She felt streaks of fiery pain race up and down her body. She felt ribs snap. She felt her right arm go numb and her left leg collapse. She felt her joints loosen and her head spin. For a second, she thought she was going to break apart.

But she held on. She might have been finished then and there, but the demon had come at her so hard that its momentum carried it past her once again, across the frozen surface of the snow and into the rocks out of which it had come. It screamed and hissed as it flew past, claws digging at the ice, fighting to gain purchase, failing to do so. Angel saw it for only seconds, a dark shadowy nightmare, and she whipped her staff at its head and chased after it with her magic's fire. Slowly, she staggered back to her feet, leaning heavily on the staff. The entire right side of her body was a mass of blood. She could barely keep herself upright. She pulled the all-weather cloak from her back and wrapped it around her injured arm, trying to cushion it against further damage. She couldn't tell, but the bones of her forearm might already be broken. She grimaced. If so, they were not the only ones.

She watched the demon emerge from the rocks once more, slouching out of the shadows. It looked worse than she did, but it was still coming. She shook her head, despairing. She did not know what it would take to stop it, but she did not think it was anything she possessed.

The feeders, she thought darkly, massing all about them, were anticipating that they would feast on both.

The demon charged her again, not so quickly this time, its stamina sapped and its strength depleted. Even so, she could not get out of its way. She used the fire on its face, and as it slammed into her she shoved her bad arm, still wrapped in her cloak, and the length of her staff between its jaws to try to block away its teeth. Then, as fresh pain ratcheted through her, she did the one thing she had always known she must never do. She let go of her staff and with her hands freed, she ripped at the demon's face with the serrated palms of her needle gloves.

A second time, she got lucky. One of the gloves caught the demon just above its good eye and tore downward across its face.

The cat thing shrieked in pain and rage, the entire half of its face turned into a red smear. As she struggled to break free of it, claws tore at her, opening fresh wounds. Angel ignored them, regaining her grip on her staff, calling up its magic the moment her fingers closed about its length. She thrust the demon away, watching it thrash in a blind frenzy as it slid backward. Still collapsed on her belly, she used her pain and rage to fuel the Word's magic and sent it tearing into her adversary.

She screamed at it as she did so, in that instant little more than an animal herself.

The magic struck the demon with a fury that transcended anything of which Angel had thought herself capable. It exploded against the demon's mangled head, bore into it and shattered it like glass. The head flew apart, gone in an instant. The body thrashed for long moments after, as if not yet aware that it was no longer whole, that it had nothing to guide it. Feeders descended on it, burying it in a mass of writhing shadows. It collapsed beneath them, shuddered once, and lay still.

Angel dropped to her knees, her staff gripped tightly in both hands, the fading magic of the Word's fire licking at the smooth black ends like cat's tongues. She stared at the demon's corpse, not quite comprehending that it was lifeless. She waited for it to move. She waited for it to rise and come for her.

But the demon lay where it was, headless and lifeless. When the feeders began to drift away, Angel realized finally that it would not ever move again. She tried to lever herself up so that she could go to her friends. She had to find them and protect them. The other demon could have reached them by now and it would finish the job that this one started and the Loden would be lost and the Elves compromised and . . .

She struggled to rise but found that her legs would not work; her muscles were too weak. She could only get to her knees.

Then she could not even manage that, and she collapsed into blackness.

THIRTY-TWO

KIRISIN STARED AT THE APPARITION standing before him, trying to make himself accept that what he was seeing was real. "I thought you were dead!" he exclaimed in disbelief.

Old Culph chuckled. "Well, now, what led you to believe that, Kirisin?"

"Tragen found your body!"

"Is that what he told you?" Even in the near darkness, Kirisin could see his eyes twinkle. "Were you sad for me? Did you think the demons had found me out? Did you think they had caught and killed me?"

"We all did!" Kirisin declared, relief flooding through him. "After Ailie and Erisha were killed, we thought the demons had gotten you, too! We didn't have time to do more than make a quick check; we had to flee Arborlon right away."

The old man ambled forward a few steps, dropping the beam of his solar torch and nodding his understanding. "You were right to do so. No point in taking unnecessary chances. I certainly didn't. I waited until it was safe to do so, and then I followed you. I tracked you all the way here, to these caves." He looked around. "Impressive, aren't they? An Elven safehold." He looked back quickly. "Did you find it? Did you find the Loden Elfstone? Do you have it?"

Kirisin held out his hand, revealing the Stone cupped within his curled fingers. "Inside the dragon's maw. Guarded by the magic of Pancea Rolt Gotrin, just as you thought it might be. You were right about everything. We couldn't have done this without you." He shook his head. "I still can't believe you're alive. How did you manage to get here on your own?"

Culph shrugged. "Well, I had help. And I know a few things about getting places. Flying hot-air balloons is a skill I mastered some time back, for example. Come out of there, and I'll tell you everything. We can take as much time as we need."

Kirisin walked toward him, treading lightly on the dragon's icy tongue, stepping carefully over its rows of teeth and out into the cavern chamber once more. He had his solar torch back on—it was working again—but he kept the light lowered so as not to blind the old man. Culph, for his part, had set down his own torch, letting its beam flood the space that separated them in a wide arc.

"I still can't believe you made it all this way," Kirisin said. "Or even that you managed to find us."

"As I said, I had help." The old man smiled. Then abruptly, as the boy stepped into the circle of his torchlight, he held up his hand. "That's close enough. Why don't you just stand where you are while we talk?"

Kirisin stopped short, surprised at the change in the other's tone of voice. Then he caught sight of something just behind Culph, a figure slumped on the ground. Simralin. He recognized her clothing and blond hair. She lay motionless, blood on her face.

"Stay where you are, Kirisin," Culph ordered quietly, and now he didn't sound anything at all like Culph. "Don't give your sister another thought. She's fine where she is."

Kirisin stared at Simralin's still form and then at the old man. "What's going on? What happened to her?"

"She took a blow to the head. A rather hard blow, I'm afraid. She's a strong young woman."

Kirisin stood frozen in place, trying to make sense of what he was hearing. "Did you do this?"

Culph shrugged, and then nodded. "I had to. She was a distraction."

"A distraction? What are you talking about?" Kirisin blinked. Then a cold realization swept through him. "You," he said quietly. "You're the . . ." He couldn't bring himself to say the word *demon*. "All this time."

The old man nodded "All this time."

Kirisin's heart sank. He gestured toward his sister. "Did you kill her?"

"Kill her? No, that would serve no useful purpose. I just made sure she wouldn't interfere with us. I need her alive so that you don't do anything foolish while we talk. You won't, will you? Do anything foolish? You won't make me really hurt her, will you?"

Kirisin glared at him. "You killed Erisha. And Ailie. And you tried to kill me. Why didn't you? If you wanted to stop us from finding the Loden, why didn't you just finish the job and kill me, too?"

The old man cocked his head quizzically. "What makes you think I wanted to stop you from finding the Loden? From finding any of the Elfstones, for that matter? Finding them is what I wanted you to do, right from the first time you told me the Ellcrys spoke to you."

He rocked back on his heels. "It's not so complicated, really. You and Erisha were searching for the Elfstones. If you found them, you would use them to save the Ellcrys. I thought it an excellent idea. So I researched the matter. I found the information I needed right away—not all of it, but most. I found some of it in the histories and some of it in the private notes and journals of the old families. As keeper of those records, I had access to all of it. I just didn't tell anyone what I had found. I made certain no one else found any of it, either."

"But you were helping us!"

"Just enough so that you would do what was needed, Kirisin. Never more. I gave you those bits and pieces to keep you looking. I didn't know what had become of the seeking-Stones after Pancea Rolt Gotrin's death. I knew they were buried with her, but not where she was buried. Some things were kept secret even from me. But you and your friends figured it out, and you got possession of them. I couldn't have done that, not as a demon and not even as old Culph, keeper of the Elven histories. It needed the right person, a Chosen committed to saving the most precious of the Elven talismans."

"But that could just as easily have been Erisha!" Kirisin was incensed. "Why did you kill her?"

The demon shrugged. "Killing her was a way to make you run, you and your sister and the Knight of the Word. I needed you to leave the Cintra and go off on your own where you could be dealt with more easily. And of course, I needed you to go looking for the Loden. In any case, Erisha was never the one who was meant to wield the Elfstones. Any fool could tell that she was too weak-minded to do what was needed. It was always you. You were the strong one. You were the one who was determined. Killing her was the perfect way to fuel that determination."

He smiled, and that smile stung like salt on an open wound. "I have lived among the Elves as old Culph for a long time. Years. Before that, I was someone else. Before that, someone else again. But my disguise as Culph was the most useful of them all because it gave me access to everything crucial to understanding the history of the Elves. I could research their lore and discover their weaknesses. It was clear to all of us who serve the Void that at some point they would have to be dealt with. The question was when. And how it was to be done. They were a sizable nation, albeit less populous than humans. But still, a force with which to be reckoned. What was to be done with them when it was time to act? I watched and waited over the years, knowing the time was coming and the answers must be found. Old Culph, hardly more than a part of the King's furniture, was never suspected."

Having survived the first few minutes of the old man's admission of who and what he was, Kirisin was beginning to look for a way out of this mess. He had no plan other than to keep Culph talking—keep the *demon* talking, he corrected himself bitterly, for *demon* was what the thing that masqueraded as Culph was. As long as he kept it talking, he had a chance to find a way to escape. It didn't seem to be armed, didn't seem to have any weapon at all. But it had managed to overcome Simralin, perhaps even to kill her. Kirisin hated himself for thinking it, but he didn't know if he believed that his sister was still alive.

Bitterness welled up, so strong it made him want to throw caution aside and attack the thing standing in front of him. But he held himself in check—talking, talking, and all the while searching for a solution to his dilemma.

He had a sudden burst of inspired hope. He had forgotten about Angel! She was still out there and coming his way. Maybe she would reach him in time to help!

But then he remembered that the demon wouldn't have come alone; it would have brought that thing with it. "Where is your . . . the other demon, the one that tracked Angel?"

The demon smiled. "Both are outside. Renewing an old rivalry, I believe. If it ends the way I expect it will, we won't see either of them again." It folded its bony arms across its chest. "As I told you before, I had help in this business. But I think any need for that sort of help is at an end."

Kirisin's mouth tightened. "Maybe things won't work out the way you think. Maybe you'll be sorry you ever used us like this."

"Oh, I don't think so." The demon made a dismissive gesture. "In any case, it won't affect us. I made sure we wouldn't be disturbed. This time belongs just to you and me, Kirisin. So let's make the best use of it. You are owed an explanation, and you shall have it." It paused. "Do you want to know about the King? Do you want to know why he was so determined to stop you?"

"I would guess it had something to do with you," the boy answered. He was gripping the Loden so tightly that the sharp edges were cutting into his palm. He relaxed his grip and slipped the Elfstone into his pocket. "Did you tell the King something that frightened him?" he asked, still trying to gain time.

"Very good. I did exactly that. I told him that I had found evidence that the Loden was created to shield the Ellcrys—which, of course, is true. I also told him that the wielder of the Stone was at considerable risk from the magic if it was invoked. I told him the lore revealed that the user of the Loden was bound to the magic, and the binding was almost always fatal. The Stone sapped the user's lifeblood. Once summoned, the magic claimed the user's life as its own. I convinced him that his daughter would die as a result. He was desperate for an alternative, but I told him there wasn't any. The Ellcrys had made her choice, and the first summoned was the Chosen who must respond. His only option, I explained, was to let her complete her term as Chosen and force the tree to choose another. A Chosen no longer in service would not be acceptable. I convinced him that the tree was in no immediate danger and he could afford to wait. He was eager to believe this. He would have done almost anything to save his daughter."

"But you killed her anyway."

The demon shrugged. "Expediency. It was more important that you be forced to flee than to let the King have his wish. I wanted everyone turned against you so that you had no choice but to do what I wanted—to find the Loden in the hope that somehow this would give you a means of helping the Ellcrys and convincing the King of your innocence. Admit it—that was what you were hoping would happen, isn't it?"

Kirisin nodded. "I still don't understand why you did all this. Why you didn't just kill me, too. Why you didn't just let the Elfstones be. If you waited, the tree would have died and the Forbidding would have come down. You would have gotten what you wanted, you and the rest of the demons. What point was there in having me find the Loden? Were you just worried that someone else might find it if I didn't?"

The demon gave him a wry smile and a shrug. "No, that isn't it at all. It's much more complicated. You have to understand. The demons are winning the war against the humans. Within a matter of months, the humans will be wiped out or imprisoned in our camps. Then we will have to deal with the Elves."

It reached in its pocket and produced a silver cord strung through two shiny silver rings. Idly, it began to play with the implements, letting the rings run up and down the cord. It seemed completely absorbed in the activity, working the cord into different positions to allow for changes of movement in the rings. Once or twice, it jerked on the cord sharply so that the rings disappeared into its hand for an instant before dropping free again.

Kirisin watched the rings as they slid back and forth, glimmering in the light. Then he looked back at the demon. "You haven't answered my question."

The demon smiled. "Not yet, I haven't. Patience, Kirisin." It was moving the cord and its rings in circles now, its hands inscribing broad arcs on the cavern air. "We have all the time we need."

Suddenly, right behind him, Simralin's right leg moved. Kirisin caught his breath.

"The problem with the Elves is one of logistics," the demon continued, still playing with the cord and the rings. Its eyes followed the movement of the rings, completely absorbed. "To subjugate and eventually eliminate humans, we have been forced to spend years breaking down their system of order, secretly encouraging and fostering them to participate in their own destruction. The wars among their governments, the plagues that have decimated their populations, the poisoning of their world, and the erosion of their sense of security and strength of determination have all required a great deal of time and effort. We are not anxious to have to do it all over again with the Elves. Their population is not as numerous, but there are enough of them that they could prove troublesome. Nor do we have any guarantee that they might not find a way to recapture their lost magic and use it against us."

The demon spun the rings like shining wheels about the cord. "Look at what's happened with you, Kirisin—just in the last few weeks! You've rediscovered several forms of magic, several talismans that had been lost for centuries. Elfstones that can be used as weapons—weapons that even demons must respect. What if there are others and you are able to find them, as well? You are a better-ordered civilization than the humans, and you might just find a way to stop us, given enough time and incentive."

Kirisin kept waiting for his sister to move again, but she didn't. Almost of their own volition his eyes drifted back to the demon with its cord and its rings and its madness. He watched the rings spin about the cord. What was the point of this long explanation? Whatever it was, the demon had just made a big mistake. It had revealed that the Elfstones were a weapon that could be used against it. Kirisin didn't know how, but he would find a way. He would make it pay for that mistake.

His hand drifted into his pocket. His fingers closed about the pouch that held the Elfstones and began to work the drawstrings free.

"How much more convenient, Kirisin," the demon resumed. Its

hands wove and the rings spun. "Are you watching?" it asked softly. Kirisin was. Suddenly he couldn't look away. "How much more convenient if we could gather them all in one place and keep them there until we were ready to deal with them. How much better if we could prevent any chance escape. It would save so much time and effort if we could do that. Are you watching?" The rings spun on the cord, flashing in brilliant bursts. "You are, aren't you? Watching them spin and spin and spin. So beautiful. You like them, don't you, little boy? You like to watch their colors."

Kirisin nodded, suddenly unable to think of anything else, completely absorbed in the movement of the hands and the cord and the rings. He had never seen anything so intriguing. He could not seem to look away. He didn't want to.

"So, if we were able to gather the Elves together in one place—say, inside the Loden Elfstone—why, think how much easier it would be to keep them under control! No worrying about any of them wandering off in search of dangerous talismans, no concerns for how long it might take to determine the best way to dispose of them. All it would require was that we find someone who could wield the Loden's magic. It would require that we find an Elf who had both the right and the power. Someone like you, Kirisin. Someone who was willing to do what was needed." The demon paused. "Someone under our control."

Kirisin tried to speak and found that he couldn't. He couldn't do anything but stand there and watch the rings on the cord, the sparkle of their metal as it caught the light. He was vaguely aware that something was wrong, that he shouldn't be letting this happen, but at the same time he was enormously happy that it was.

"Demons have a little magic, too," the old man standing in front of him said softly, coming a step closer. "Now you belong to me, boy. You are my willing servant, and you will do what I tell you to do. So much easier than threats and beatings and the like. A simple spell and I control your mind. It's all I ever wanted from you. I don't need you to do much. Just to come back with me to the Cintra and use the Loden as the Ellcrys has asked of you. Just to put the city and its people inside, nice and safe. Just to keep them there until it is time to take them out. My friends will be waiting to greet us, a good many of them, an entire army, in fact. I summoned them just before I left to come after you. Demons and once-men. There to be certain that no one leaves until we arrive."

The old-man features twisted into something ugly and mean. "It was so easy to deceive you. You are such a foolish boy. So willing to think that I was your friend. I am sick of you, sick of your kind. I am sick of playing at being one of you, sick of pretending that I am in any way like you. I want you all dead. I want you obliterated from the earth."

The hands wove, and the rings glistened.

"Just a moment longer, boy, and it will all be over. The spell will be in place and nothing will undo it. Just keep watching."

Kirisin couldn't do anything else. He heard the other's voice, but could make little sense of the words. They sounded reassuring and pleasant, but he couldn't seem to grasp their meaning. He stood statue-like within the cradle of the cave's deep gloom, a lone figure in the small light of the solar torch, eyes glazed and fixed on the rings. Some small part of him screamed at him to do something, but he blocked the warning away because it disturbed his concentration on the rings.

The rings were everything.

"Just a little longer, foolish boy," the demon whispered. "You wanted to keep me talking, didn't you? You wanted to gain enough time to find a way to escape me, didn't you? Well, go ahead! Run away! Flee back the way you came and be free of me! What's wrong, Kirisin? Can't manage it? Are you really so happy that you would not try to escape? Can that be? I think maybe—"

Then it gasped sharply, and its head jerked back in rigid shock. The cord and its rings went flying into the darkness. The demon screamed, a frightening wail of disbelief and rage. Kirisin was jerked out of his trance instantly, his concentration on the cord and rings vanishing in the blink of an eye. He was back in the cavern, standing before the old man who was a demon, before old Culph who was groping at the air as if gone mad.

Simralin, levered up on her elbows, had plunged her long knife all the way through one gnarled leg.

"Witch!" the demon cried, turning and kicking out at her.

But she caught its leg, wrapped her arms about its ankles, and pulled it toward her. Her face was rigid with concentration beneath the mask of blood that coated it, her strong muscles knotting with the effort of holding the demon fast. But the demon, for all that it looked to be a frail old man, was more powerful than she, and it tore itself away. It kicked at her again, and this time it did not miss, catching her in the face, snapping her head back. Kirisin heard her grunt with pain as she rolled away and lay still.

Hobbling, the demon went after her.

"Culph!" Kirisin cried out.

The demon turned, wild-eyed with rage. As it did so, Kirisin snatched the blue Elfstones from his pocket and held them out. He had just enough presence of mind to remember what they could do. *A weapon even demons must respect*, his enemy had told him. He gripped the Stones in his fist and pointed them toward the demon, envisioning what it was he wanted. The demon's reaction was instantaneous. It shrank from him, wheeling away with arms raised to ward him off. Kirisin felt a rush of fierce satisfaction flood through him.

"Stupid boy!" the demon shrieked, hands making quick, sharp movements in the gloom.

Too late. The blue fire lanced out, enfolding the demon in a bright shroud of flame. The demon screamed, trying to fight off the flames and failing. It began to burn, clothes and flesh first and then whatever lay beneath. It thrashed in vain as the fire consumed it. Kirisin did not relent; he kept the fire trained on it, kept the power of the Elfstones strong and steady and focused. Old Culph disappeared. Anything vaguely Elven disappeared. What remained was skeletal and as black as night, a child's drawing of a monster.

Then even that was gone, consumed and rendered to a fine ash, a sediment that floated on the air in the haze of the torchlight, drifting in tiny flakes until finally settling on the ice and snow of the cavern floor, tiny leavings of a virulent plague finally overcome.

Kirisin lowered his arm. "That was for Erisha," he whispered. "That was for Ailie. That was for Sim and Angel and everyone you ever touched with your black lying words!"

He was shaking with rage and near collapse. He thought he could feel his heart breaking with the memories his words conjured. There were tears in his eyes and bitterness in his mouth that he thought he would taste forever.

In the chill silence of the ice caves, he hugged himself to keep from falling apart.

THIRTY-THREE

TWILIGHT ON THE ROAD.

Panther walked point with Sparrow, his dark eyes following the descent of the sun as it dropped below the rim of the horizon south. The moon was already up, a three-quarter-full white orb against the gray, hazy sky. Rolling hills turned brown and barren from drought and poisons flanked them in their passage, stark and empty save for small clusters of buildings that surfaced here and there like burrowing animals come up for a cautious look around. Farther away, beyond the hills, mountain peaks loomed black and jagged.

Panther glanced behind him. Catalya walked a few yards back, her mottled face shadowed within the hood of her cloak, her eyes lowered to the freeway they traveled. Rabbit bounced along in front of her, circling back when she got too far ahead. Behind them and much farther back, Fixit drove the Lightning ATV. Owl and River were inside the cab with him, keeping watch over the comatose Knight of the Word. The rest of the Ghosts rode the hay wagon, bundled in among their dwindling stores of food and meager possessions, keeping watch as the shadows lengthened.

The end of the day was silent save for the low hum of the ATV's solar-powered engine, the soft hiss of rubber tires on concrete, and the whisper of a light wind.

Panther found himself thinking of Logan Tom for what must have been the hundredth time in the past hour. Saving him from Krilka Koos and his stump-head followers was one thing. Saving him from himself was another. He hadn't seemed that bad when they brought him back to the others, hadn't seemed as if he were that damaged. Then, all at once, he wasn't there anymore.

He kicked at the surface of the roadway. "Can't nobody do nothing to bring him out of this?" he asked Sparrow suddenly.

She glanced over, shaking her blond head. She looked tired. "He has to wake up on his own, when he's ready."

"But he hasn't moved in two days! He doesn't eat or drink. Man can't live long like that, you know?"

"I know. But that's the way it is with these things. He's hurt pretty bad, so he's gone somewhere inside himself to try to heal. He just isn't done with that yet." She shrugged. "Besides, Owl is doing what she can for him. The wounds are all healing pretty well. There doesn't even seem to be any infection from the viper-prick, and that should have killed him. Whatever's wrong, it's in his head somewhere."

Panther thought that was a bunch of crap, but he kept it to himself. "Man's gonna die," he said instead.

"Don't say that," Catalya snapped at him from behind his back.

He grimaced. "Okay, okay. I'm just making a . . . a observation, that's all." *Girl's got ears like a hawk*, he thought irritably.

Hawk. There was another mystery that didn't seem close to getting solved. Bird-Man disappears off a wall, goes into the light—*isn't that what happens when you die?*—and now they were supposed to find him somewhere just by heading south. Like that was going to happen. A vision said it would, but Panther had never had a whole lot of faith in visions. Not even the ones Hawk used to have, the ones that Owl turned into stories about the boy and his children. He liked those stories, liked the way Owl told them. But he didn't actually believe them. Believing

stories like that was what got you killed in this man's world. You
wanted to believe in something, you were better off believing in a
Parkhan Spray or a Tyson Flechette. Something you could put in your
hands and use to kill your enemies.

Cat believed like that, too, he thought. Practical girl, no nonsense.
She might be half Freak, but she was more like him than any of the
others. He still couldn't believe how she had taken out those militia
clowns. She was frickin' dangerous, was what she was.

She probably thought the same thing he did about this hunting
around for Hawk, too. Waste of time.

Sometimes it made him wonder about things. They did stuff that
seemed to have a purpose, but how much of it really mattered? Right
now, right this moment, he felt like a drowning man treading water in
the middle of the ocean.

"You know, we ain't going to find him," he said to Sparrow. "The
Bird-Man, I mean. We can look until every last one of us is underground with Squirrel, and we ain't ever going to see him again."

She didn't look at him. She was looking straight ahead, into the distance. "We might," she said quietly.

He stared at her in confusion, the way she said it sounding odd, and
then he shifted his gaze ahead to where she was looking. Three figures
were just coming into view from out of the fold of the hills, stepping
onto the freeway surface and turning toward them.

A boy, a girl, and a burly, butt-ugly dog.

Panther's jaw dropped. "Damn!" he whispered.

A bright smile broke out on Sparrow's face, and her somber features
were transformed. The weariness fell away. Fresh life blossomed. Without a word, she sprinted toward the approaching figures, calling out to
them by name, the sound of her voice a beacon that drew the others.

"Damn!" Panther repeated, and then he was running, too.

■   ■   ■

TWILIGHT IN THE MOUNTAINS.

Angel Perez woke to near darkness and freezing cold. She was lying where she had collapsed after her battle with the demon, sprawled facedown on the ice and snow, her all-weather cloak wrapped about her damaged arm, her black staff cradled against her body. There was blood everywhere, and large patches of the mountain's white expanse were burned and still smoking from the Word's fire. The remains of the demon lay to one side, all but unrecognizable save for the lower parts. Angel looked away quickly. Even in death, it was monstrous.

She was aware that she had to get up and find shelter, that she would freeze to death if she didn't. The light was almost gone from the sky, and the temperature dropping quickly. It might be that winter had virtually disappeared from almost everywhere else in the United States of America, but it was present here. She tried moving and found that her body didn't like it. She ached everywhere, but she imagined that the cold was helping to numb the pain and slow the bleeding. She knew she had damaged her ribs and maybe her arm, as well. She knew she was losing blood from a dozen deep slashes. She couldn't be sure of anything else.

She felt momentarily for internal damage and then quickly stopped. "*No toques,*" she whispered. "Don't touch. You don't want to know. You don't want to think about it."

She took a moment to collect herself, taking slow, deep breaths, tightening her resolve. Then she clasped her staff tightly and levered herself to her feet. She almost didn't make it, swaying and stumbling forward a few steps, pain lancing through her like a hot knife through butter. She fought to stay upright, knowing that if she went down it was likely she would not rise again.

She unraveled the all-weather cloak and pulled it on. It took a long time, and when she was finished she looked like a vagrant. Rips and tatters everywhere. Blood smeared in dark stains. Barely any protection at all against the cold.

But some, at least. It was the best she could do. She would take what she could find.

Her pack was gone, and she didn't feel like looking for it. What she needed to do was to take cover. Right away. Gasping for air, leaning on the staff, she looked ahead toward the ice caves, searching for the entrance.

She couldn't see it.

Doesn't matter, she thought. *I know it's there. I know I can find it. I know I must find it.*

"Hold on Kirisin, Simralin," she whispered to the wind and the night and the cold. "I'm coming."

Slowly, she began to stagger up the side of the mountain.

The Elves of Cintra ends here.
The story concludes with the
publication of the next volume.

ACKNOWLEDGMENTS

The publication of this book marks the thirtieth year of my career as a professional writer, which began with the release of *The Sword of Shannara* in 1977. It is a time so distant I can barely remember what it felt like to be a first-time author. What I can never forget is the people who were there to help me every step of the way. I owe them more than I can possibly tell you, but I feel obligated to try.

I have been with Del Rey Books for my entire publishing life. Not many writers can say as much. Our long and immensely successful partnership is due to a number of fortunate and serendipitous factors, starting with my relationship with the founders of the company, Lester and Judy-Lynn del Rey. I will not see their like again in my lifetime: intense, driven, brilliant, and by turns strange and kind beyond imagining.

Lester was my first editor, my mentor, critic, taskmaster, and friend. Most of what I know about being a professional writer, I learned from him. I have heard it said repeatedly from those who worked with him that he was uncanny at finding the weaknesses in a manuscript. You won't get any argument from me. He was a teacher in all the best ways:

he let me make my mistakes, and then find a way to correct them. He was famous for promising that if you could persuade him he was wrong and you were right, he would defer to you. I was successful in my efforts about one out of every twenty times. More often than not he left me frustrated and chagrined in the face of his knowledge and my ignorance. At the same time, he made me a better writer. I could never thank him enough in his lifetime; I don't expect to be successful in doing so now.

Owen Lock, Judy-Lynn's assistant and protégé, succeeded Lester. It was a thankless job if ever there was one, but he made it work. Owen and I grew up in Del Rey together. We were friends from the beginning, and we remain friends to this day. He was there for me more times and in more ways than I can count. I will always be grateful that he was.

My current editor is Betsy Mitchell. I knew her before she came to the company, but knew little of her skills. I am pleased to say now from experience that they are considerable. She keeps me honest and focused, which is not always easy. She is not afraid to tell me when I am cutting corners or attempting to slide by with something less than my best effort. She is funny and smart. It has been a privilege to work with her.

I cannot begin to give you the names of all those who have helped me at Del Rey Books, Ballantine Books, and Random House over the years. If I try to name names, I will leave someone out. I do not exaggerate when I say there are hundreds. In editorial, publicity, art, marketing, and sales, from top to bottom, they have made my books and my life better. They have worked hard on my behalf, over and over again, and I will never forget them.

My friends and family have been enormously supportive, giving me the space and time to be as strange and disconnected from reality as I need to be. The various members of my blended family, in particular, have been patient and understanding to an extent I do not pretend I could ever approach. I am constantly astonished that they do not have me committed. My daughters Lisa, Jill and Amanda, my son Alex, and my grandson Hunter are the bedrock of my sometimes questionable sanity, bringing me down to earth when it is needed, keeping me securely grounded in the real world. My sister Laurie never doubts me, always believes in me, and forever supports me. She has forgotten all the times I chased her with a knife when we were children. Bless her for that. Bless them all for who they are.

Then there is Judine. What can I say that will begin to explain what she means to me? She has been there for me from the first day we met, some twenty years ago. Without her, I would have been lost. She has taught me most of what I know about the retail side of the book business. She has been my first reader, has edited and proofed my manuscripts, and has traveled with me to the far-flung corners of the land on countless book tours. She tells me when I am wrong and reassures me when I am right. She is my conscience and my heart. I love her deeply and without reservation.

Everyone should be as lucky as I am. Everyone should have the kinds of friends and family I do. If there was a way to make that happen, I would. Thank you, all.

TERRY BROOKS
August 2007

ABOUT THE AUTHOR

TERRY BROOKS is the *New York Times* bestselling author of more than twenty-five books, including the Genesis of Shannara novel *Armageddon's Children; The Sword of Shannara;* the Voyage of the Jerle Shannara trilogy: *Ilse Witch, Antrax,* and *Morgawr;* the High Druid of Shannara trilogy: *Jarka Ruus, Tanequil,* and *Straken;* the nonfiction book *Sometimes the Magic Works: Lessons from a Writing Life;* and the novel based upon the screenplay and story by George Lucas, *Star Wars:*® Episode I *The Phantom Menace.*™ His novels *Running with the Demon* and *A Knight of the Word* were selected by the *Rocky Mountain News* as two of the best science fiction/fantasy novels of the twentieth century. The author was a practicing attorney for many years but now writes full-time. He lives with his wife, Judine, in the Pacific Northwest and Hawaii. Visit the world of Shannara online at www.shannara.com and at Terrybrooks.net.

About the Type

This book was set in Berling. Designed in 1951 by Karl Erik Forsberg for the Typefoundry Berlingska Stilgjuteri AB in Lund, Sweden, it was released the same year in foundry type by H. Berthold AG. A classic old-face design, its generous proportions and inclined serifs make it highly legible.